LAND OF THE LEYLINES

LAND OF THE LEYLINES

FRIENDLY NEIGHBORHOOD WIZARD BOOK 3

SmilingSatyr

Podium

Podium

LAND OF THE LEYLINES

CHAPTER 1

On Top of the World

Nothing compared to the feeling of flight. It didn't matter whether it was on a flying carpet or a sky ship. Standing on the deck of the *Flying Calamity* as it sailed through the air over the mountains filled Wil with a sense of awe that took his breath away. Standing at the railing, knowing one clumsy move could send him hurtling over the side made Wilbur McKenzie feel small and helpless.

In truth, he was neither. Out of the hundred plus people on board, he was the most dangerous. If one didn't count his pet.

"Master McKenzie," Captain Nesbitt barked, shaking him from his thoughts. "Please regain control of your animal."

Wil sighed and turned around. Captain Nesbitt pointed straight up. Although the ship had no use of sails, three large masts with enchantments carved into the wood jutted into the sky. Two of the three nests had people watching the horizon. On the mainmast, the wampus cat Isom crouched, peeking at the sailors at work.

The fae predator's tail flicked behind him like he was stalking birds and in seconds would pounce. Isom looked to be having the time of his life, until Wil whistled sharply and ruined his fun.

"Get down here, Isom. I told you to stop scaring the crew. C'mon, we talked about this!" Wil snapped his fingers and pointed to the deck.

Isom let out a grumble Wil could hear over the ever-present woosh of the wind. He let himself drop from the mainmast, disappearing and then reappearing back on solid wood at Wil's feet. He cocked his head to the side, favoring the wizard with his one eye.

"What else am I supposed to do, then?" Isom demanded. "There's nothing to hunt. No one I'm allowed to chase or scare. You're not scared, and I'm not allowed to bother the prince. It's *boring*."

Wil took a deep breath. He wasn't mad, or even annoyed. It took a lot to push Wil into a bad mood, and his new pet wasn't likely to do it. In truth, he was amused. "It's been two days, Isom. Are you really going stir-crazy from two days of not being allowed to maul something?"

The poor wildcat nodded. "And you're not even letting me poke around and have fun."

"Yes, that would be a breach of privacy and would be a bad thing to do to our friends and allies," said Wil, reaching down to scratch behind the wampus cat's ears. Isom pretended not to enjoy it.

But they'd never know, Isom's voice whispered in Wil's mind. *I can listen in for the juicy gossip. C'mon, if I can't gnaw on anything, at least let me have this.*

Wampus cats gained a quality of anything they ate, and Isom's most recent meal had given him the ability to sense and read thoughts.

"I said no," Wil said with a bit more force. "If you can control yourself and behave, we'll grab you a snack. Gods, you eat more than Bram and me combined when you're bored."

As soon as the word *snack* left Wil's lips, Isom threw himself against Wil's leg affectionately and then padded his way over to the door. Together they went through and down the stairs until they got to the floor with the dim galley. Between Isom and Sylano, they spent a lot of time there.

Syl was waiting for them at the center table, surrounded by a few scattered crew members, listening to him tell a story. He had a mug in his hand, already half empty and getting emptier with each second as he gesticulated.

". . . so then my father takes umbrage to that, right? These guests got me hurt and spit in his face. So he calls on satyr magic to—"

"What can satyr magic do?" one sailor blurted out.

Syl pointed in his direction. "A lot! In this case, he lured them in for drinks, making each one more potent than the last. A satyr has a strong connection with the mind, and with all kinds of indulgence."

"And what about fauns?" Wil asked. "What's the difference? I've been meaning to ask."

Syl grinned at Wil. His mostly human, goatlike face was still bruised and puffy from the beating he'd taken a week before, but he looked worlds better.

"Another excellent question! The short answer is time. Fauns become satyrs, who become silenii with age. Not unlike how a nymph will go from maiden to mother to crone. My father is stronger magically than I am, and he has the wisdom of the ages. All at the cost of being slower and more tired, unable to keep up with . . . the endurance of youth." He waggled his eyebrows at the nearest sailor. She didn't seem to mind the attention.

"So what happened next?" the blushing sailor asked, taking a swig of her own drink.

"One drink turned into ten, and before too long they were *out.* Slept so long and hard they overstayed their stated welcome, which let us drag their unconscious forms out into the pasture. The lucky ones were woken up by a cow licking them."

"And the unlucky ones?" Wil asked.

"The cow's other end." Syl made a theatrical surprised face as the crew laughed.

He continued, "If you ever find yourself in Faerie, *never* spit in the face of hospitality. Be a respectful guest and know when's the proper time to leave. We fae will rarely make the first move, but we're more than happy to bide our time and punish the cocky and brash.

"But if you *do* go to Faerie, you go as friends of the prince, and that should count for something. Just don't mess it up." Syl winked, one golden eye with rectangular pupils twinkling with mirth while his long tongue lolled out.

"Boring," Isom grumbled, pushing past Wil and going up to the counter where the cooks worked night and day to provide meals for the large crew. "Feed me!"

The cook backed up against the stove, fear and annoyance plain on his droopy face. "Master McKenzie, *please*."

Wil whistled again and pointed to the table next to Syl. Isom slunk away from the counter, letting his tail run across it until he sat at the end, curling up. He kept his one eye staring balefully at the man.

"I'm sorry, you won't have to put up with him after today, I promise," said Wil. "But until then, do you have some beef I can give him? I swear, every time he eats beef he gets a little kinder."

The chef chewed on his lip. "At this rate, we're running low. Sure, we'll be arriving today, but it's still coming out of our supplies, and—"

"Bill me for it," said Wil. "Anything we need that isn't covered by being a normal passenger or honored guest, you can charge it against me, and we'll square up when we're in town."

The chef capitulated. "Cooked or raw?"

Wil looked at Isom.

"Cooked," said the cat, licking his chops. "And with some of that tangy sauce you put on it. That was delicious."

Finally, the chef relaxed. "And for you?"

"Water." He got his drink and joined Isom and Syl at the table. "Do you mind making a bit of space, fellas? We're coming up to port soon, and we need to talk about a few things."

"Oh, I love when he gets serious," Syl said, finishing his drink and getting off the table. "That's when you know we're in trouble or he's about to do something stupid."

Wil waited for the faun's laughter to die down and for the table to clear. It took a minute of grumbling and moving food and drink to the other tables, but then they were as alone as they'd get. He had their attention, but no telling for how long.

"The ride to Manifee City has been shorter than I expected. I was a little lost in my head yesterday and didn't think to give you guys some warnings and pointers for while we're here. I need you both to listen to me and don't fight me on this. Am I understood?"

The two fae stayed silent, a sign Wil took to be favorable. He opened his mouth to speak, but then the chef came out with beef ribs on a platter. They were slathered with a smoky sauce the wampus cat had become addicted to. Wil waited for the cat to start gnawing on a large bone before he continued.

"Where we're going, there are a *lot* of wizards. Manifee City in particular is the magical capital of Calipan. And as we've seen from Hugo, it's not uncommon for us to have massive chips on our shoulders. When we're there, you need to be careful not to be insulting or invite anyone to show off or want to lash out against you. Wizards are . . . We have a lot of leeway in our behavior if we're valuable."

Syl nodded with understanding. "People with power don't tolerate much from people they see below them, or as a threat. And humans view my people as a threat. When they're not insistent that they can destroy us without trying." The faun didn't try to hide his lingering bitterness.

"If anyone tries anything," said Isom with a mouthful of meat. The sauce all over his face looked like old blood. He swallowed and continued, "I'll eat them too. No one's going to hurt you, Wil."

"No, they won't," said Wil patiently, "because we're not going to give them a reason to. We're going to go along, keep our heads down, and answer questions about what happened. Each of us has a key perspective on what Hugo did when he cracked. Two of us can corroborate that Twist and Grimnar aren't in power anymore.

"We need to keep our stories straight and make us look like a group of reasonable people who are willing to talk things out. Well, two reasonable people and one homicidal house pet." He nudged Isom with his foot.

The wampus cat bared his teeth. "I'm a fierce predator," he said before turning back to his food.

Syl drummed his long, spindly fingers on the table. "What are we to do *when* someone tries to pick a fight with us? You going to talk at them and hope they'll cooperate?"

"I'll shut it down," said Wil. "Anyone who tries anything will find themselves taking a nap or forgetting how to see for a little while. The important thing is, no permanent damage. We'll stick by witnesses and get through this and be back in Harper Valley as quick as possible. But we *must not* give them any reason to detain us for longer than necessary."

Silence descended as Isom ate and Syl thought through Wil's words. He eventually grumbled his acknowledgment, then turned serious. "How worried are you that they'll punish you? We both know you did nothing wrong."

Wil burst out laughing. "That's not even close to true. I ran off to Faerie to try to fix things so they wouldn't find out about what happened with the leyline. And now I'm going to have to answer for that as well as everything Hugo did, and then force the peace treaty through. And now I have to hope they won't arrest me and charge me with something."

Isom looked up again. "I thought you said that wizards have a lot of leeway from your chiefs."

"That's true," said Wil, "as long as that wizard is producing more value than problems. From their perspective, I could be on the trouble end of the spectrum. Before all of this, I was a decent student but a bit of a disappointment for washing out of Mage rank. Literally no one else wanted Harper Valley.

"To them I was a nobody. Just a townie who came back to his farm to help the family. And now I'm going to face a lot of scrutiny. So please, please, *please,* behave and let me handle things. I'm begging you." Wil smiled, but he didn't try to hide his nervousness or desperation.

He wanted nothing more than to stay home and remain that small-town wizard. To help out the little people and enjoy the seasons go by, spending the years making his loved ones' lives better. That ship had sailed.

A loud, piercing whistle made Isom bolt, disappearing from view after.

"What's that sound?" Syl asked.

"Port," said Wil, stomach dropping. "We've made it to Manifee City. So get some water, sober up, and be ready to represent Faerie and Harper Valley with me."

CHAPTER 2

City of Enchantment

Seeing Manifee City again took Wil's breath away. A sprawling port town on the west coast of Calipan, it was the largest city for five hundred miles in any direction. It had started as a settlement to claim the westernmost borders of the continent, and then as a naval base in their hundred-year war with Ilianto. The port and a fleet of ships, military and civilian, stretched out on the horizon.

Despite its start as a military headquarters, the city didn't look like it was built for war. Tall apartment buildings lined the beaches, where everyone shared in year round beautiful weather and a mild climate. Little markets formed between patches of housing and public parks. The buildings were newer than in Harper Valley, and they were made to be enchanted.

Saint Balthazar's Academy of Magic was barely visible as they closed in, the highest tower poking up over the nearest buildings. While connected to the city, it was miles away, set at the foot of the mountains. Wil's heart ached at seeing the academy for real and not as a twisted copy in a mad mage's mind.

"He was a worthy meal," said Isom, reading his master's thoughts. Wil hadn't realized he'd been broadcasting them so loudly.

"I'm glad you think so," said Wil, eyes locked on the growing city. "That meal of yours might cost me my career or life, depending on how things go."

"It could even endanger the peace between our nations," Syl added helpfully. "Rendering everything we've done as useless. That's a lot of impact for one dead mage."

Wil didn't think he could be any more tense, but Syl was talented. "Either way, stay out of my head, Isom. Remember what I said, best behavior. There's a lot of wizards here, and you can't eat any of them."

Isom grumbled, but otherwise didn't protest.

As the *Flying Calamity* met the edge of the city, other ships drifted by off in the distance. People as small as ants looked up at them, some waving. Wil was tempted to send out a harmless illusion to say hello, but the skies above the city were off-limits and the authorities didn't play games.

"This place looks like fun," said Syl, leaning over the railing far enough that Wil dreaded him taking a tumble. "Any places you want to show me while we're here?"

"No time." Wil finally looked away. "We're to meet with our security escort and then they'll take us through town, through the military base, and then on to Cloverton. I doubt we'll be spending much time here. Otherwise, I'd love to share my old haunts. Baxleby's Bookstore is damned near the size of Harper Valley's city hall, and the Slutty Siren was one of my favorite places to do homework. No, it's not that kind of place," he added, seeing Syl light up.

Memory after memory came flooding back. A full quarter of Wil's life had taken place at the academy or wandering the city with the few close friends he'd made. Almost two thousand nights spent studying and playing and honing his craft. It was the first place Wil had ever felt like himself, at home with his gift.

"The best part about Manifee City is that it's got the only school of its level, and even privately taught wizards come here to learn and earn their licenses. There are hundreds of wizards who live here and travel for work whenever they get a decent contract."

Captain Nesbitt walked up to them, looking as severe as ever. "We'll be landing and disembarking within the half hour. Our instructions are to handle your possessions with care, and they'll be waiting for you in Cloverton on the morrow."

"Tomorrow?" Wil grimaced. "And what about tonight?"

"I was not told," said Nesbitt with an apologetic dip of his head. "You will be met with an escort, who will take over your protection and guide you to your hearing. I can't say I am happy about our time together, Master McKenzie, but I am glad to have met you."

Wil bowed his head. "The same goes for you, Captain. I'm sorry circumstances brought us here, but I'm glad to know there are honorable men leading our military. If you find yourself in Harper Valley again, call on me anytime." He reached down and scratched Isom's head.

Captain Nesbit gave a brief salute and returned to the helm, shouting orders at a sailor slacking off nearby. They watched him go, then Syl turned to him.

"How much do you think we're going to need an escort?" he asked. "Do they know I'm royalty and should be treated like an esteemed guest?"

Wil shook his head. "They know, but I wouldn't expect too terribly much at first. You're not exactly the kind of diplomat who carries himself with pomp and gravity. I can hardly take you seriously, and that's after seeing you in action. The copy of the peace treaty and the logs of our meetings should help, but you're going to be stuck in Cloverton longer than I am."

Even with the reassurances that his possessions would be handled, Wil went to his quarters and packed a change of clothes, some money, and a battered old novel. Then it was time to hurry up and wait, with each passing minute slower than the one before.

When the ship lurched to a shuddering halt, Wil all but ran to the deck, where he had to wait another few minutes for the ship to be secured and the gangway lowered. Although many ships sailed in the air, only two others were docked in the marina. Wil waved once more to Captain Nesbitt and walked on down to the busy port.

The only path led through hundreds of people loading and unloading cargo and repairing their ships. It wasn't hard to pass through with Syl and Isom at his side. Everyone stared at the fae, and most kept their distance. It wouldn't be a problem until they got into the city proper, but Wil kept an eye out and put on a friendly smile.

At the customs house, their escort met them. He was a short, dark-skinned, black-haired man with thick spectacles and heavy-lidded eyes that looked like he could nod off at any moment. He wore a suit of actual armor covered in runes, and he had a curved sword at his side.

"Chinis!" Wil cried.

The mage gave him The Nod, face cracking into a crooked smile. "McKenzie. I know you must've missed us, but you didn't have to cause an international incident as an excuse to visit." He spoke in a lazy, lingering drawl.

"Maybe, but it was more fun this way," said Wil, slapping his hand against his friend's. "Actually, that's a lie. It was incredibly stressful, and some days I still have trouble believing it all happened."

Chinis looked over Wil's shoulder, up to Syl. "Hey. You look like a goat. I like your eyes."

Syl bowed theatrically. "Prince Sylano of the Woodlands Association at your service."

"Oh man, royalty." Chinis bowed right back, sweeping his arm out. "Pleasure, Your Majesty. And who's the cat?"

Isom stood at Wil's side, sniffing the mage. "I am wizardbane, hungry and terrible."

"This is Isom," said Wil. "He's my pet wampus cat. Despite how he sounds, he won't hurt anyone. I gotta ask, do you know how mad they are?"

Chinis shrugged. "They don't tell me a damned thing, man. All I know is I am supposed to take you to a safe house. Oh, and guard you, I guess. Not like anyone's going to pick a fight with a knight. Or a big, ugly-ass cat. C'mon, we got a stop to make first."

He turned and left. Wil motioned for Syl to follow and set off after him, Isom padding behind. Rather than take the main exit, Chinis led them through a side passage back outside behind a fence. He led them to a parking lot, where a line of cars waited. His was a deep blue and had seating for four.

"What's this thing?" Syl asked, cocking his head to the side.

Wil couldn't blame him. As far as he knew, only the major cities had widespread access to cars, and even then it was usually only the rich or powerful. As a mid-level mage, Chinis more or less counted as both.

"This is my car," said Chinis with an amused smile. "It takes us places."

"Where's the horse?" Syl looked around.

"Sorry, man, I guess I put the cart before the horse and never looked back. Get in."

Wil took the front passenger seat, while the fae climbed in the back. Syl had to sit with his head at a weird angle to prevent his horns brushing against the leathery roof interior. The car seat was soft, velvety, and had a radical red color Wil loved. Chinis got in and put his hands on the steering wheel.

Sigils on the wheel and the front lit up as the mage powered it with his own magic. Objects like this were the simplest form of enchantments, dormant spells that came to life when given enough power. For someone like Chinis or Wil, it was a slight drain to activate and maintain them, nothing they would miss.

The car rolled forward, magic turning the wheels as one and picking up speed. Two guards at the gate opened it up for them as they approached. Chinis took them out onto the road where a few other cars rolled by, joining the horse-pulled carts and carriages still prevalent.

Manifee City was an explosion of colors and simple magic, used everywhere. Across the side of one building, illusions flickered in and out, advertising new boats or beauty creams. Right before they passed it, the image changed to a picture of Saint Balthazar's from in front, along with a message underneath that read "Think you have what it takes? Get tested for magical ability now!"

Street stalls sold little toys that moved on their own, orbs that heated or chilled the air around them, and even potions. Life there seemed twenty to thirty years ahead of Harper Valley, and it made Wil excited to bring a taste of this back home. Modern conveniences without being choked by factories and machinery.

"So where's that stop going to be?" Wil asked after a few minutes of quiet driving. He'd been surprised that Syl wasn't talking a mile a minute, but the faun's face was plastered to the window, watching this new world go by.

"Someplace you're gonna be real happy to see. You all hungry?"

"Always," purred Isom.

"I could eat," said Syl, still looking out the window.

"Wait," said Wil, "does that mean what I think it means?"

Sure enough, they turned a corner onto a well-loved street. The sign could be read even a quarter mile away. Tall, bold letters proclaimed the establishment to be the Magical Madhouse. Carefully burned into the wood was the image of a bearded, cloaked wizard casting a spell. The spell itself cycled through fire, wind, water, and lightning, changing about once every thirty seconds.

Chinis turned a crooked grin his way. "It sure does. Hope you're ready to put on a show, McKenzie. You didn't think I'd drag your ass to Cloverton without giving you one last meal, did you?"

CHAPTER 3

The Magical Madhouse

It was as Wil remembered it. The second they stepped through the doors, all the hours spent studying, drinking, and messing around with friends hit him like a runaway train. Of all the places they had spent their after-school hours, no place was as fun or prestigious as the Magical Madhouse.

The inside was a chaotic mess of colors, each corner of the ground floor a different aesthetic. One for each of the four corners of Calipan, with the southwest corner representing Manifee City. It was, of course, the most prestigious corner, reserved for graduate students and visiting alumni. The corner was painted to look like a relaxed beach party, complete with an illusory sun overhead.

On the opposite corner, made intentionally grimy and depressing with a rain cloud overhead, was Cloverton. Although the two cities were thousands of miles apart, a portal connected them. The rivalry between major powers, so close and so far, grew by the year. The other two corners represented Tellengren to the northwest and Manta Bay to the southeast. They had their own rivalry.

Chinis signaled the bartender at the island counter in the center of the room. He flipped a switch, and all sound in the room ceased. All the patrons, most of them fellow wizards, turned to look at the newcomers.

"Attention, everybody!" Chinis called out, putting some strength into it. "We got a special guest today. Master Wilbur McKenzie, one of the greatest illusionists the academy has ever produced! He's here to show his love and generosity."

Wil groaned, heat flooding his cheeks. "You bastard."

The bar erupted with cheers and thrown hats. The nearest wizards stood and gave him a hearty round of applause. Isom dropped into a crouch, ears flattened against his skull at the sudden sound. Syl, on the other hand, looked around in excitement.

"What? What did he do?" the faun asked, naked glee in his voice.

"He just told everyone the next round is on me," said Wil with a long-suffering sigh. "What, it's not bad enough I have to face a tribunal, you gotta kick me while I'm down?"

"Absolutely," said Chinis, clapping his shoulder. "Tradition is tradition, McKenzie. But don't worry, I'll cover lunch." He gave Wil a playful shove, throwing him into the throngs of students coming up to meet him.

Wil was assaulted with handshakes and pats on the back, from faces both new and old. Tybalt Granger, banned from every casino and betting house in the city for probability manipulation, slipped him a coin he promised was lucky. George Bjorn, nature wizard, introduced his newest girlfriend, Talia, to Wil. She talked at length about her own illusions, but Wil had no time to do much more than smile and shake hands before the next person came up to him.

Once upon a time, he'd been one of the students clamoring to congratulate and worship a former classmate who had gone on to do bigger and better things. That was the dream, after all. Learn how to harness world-altering powers and then do just that: change the world. Now that he was in the position, he didn't feel worthy. All he'd done was blunder his way into a new world.

A dozen people crowded him, each giving a snippet of a conversation he couldn't keep up with. Wil resigned himself to saying "Great to see you" and "That's fantastic" whenever he couldn't quite make out what was being said. Soon enough, each person who stopped by abandoned him for the free drink at the bar.

Want me to keep them away? Isom asked, sensing Wil's growing distress. The wampus cat threw himself against Wil's leg and bared his teeth, not yet growling.

Not necessary, Wil returned, reaching down to scratch behind his ears. At this time of day, between the lunch and dinner crowds, it didn't take too long for everyone to take their piece of him. But after they had their drinks (including Syl, who had one in each hand), they looked expectantly at him.

"Speech," Chinis stage-whispered.

All around them, their fellow wizards joined in until it became a chant. "Speech! Speech! Speech!"

Wil cleared his throat and looked around. He had no clue what to say, so he shot from the hip.

"Hey, everyone. My time at Saint Balthazar's was one of the happiest of my life, but now I'm out and doing bigger things, I guess. And coming back to Manifee City after spending a while back on the farm . . . Well, it's great to see what direction we're all going, and how proud I am that we're all making Calipan's future. When you graduate, try to remember that you have a special gift, and we have a responsibility to use it for the betterment of us all. A rising tide lifts all ships."

He got a bit of polite applause, but it wasn't a common sentiment at the academy. Chinis shook his head, mumbling about idealists, before a former classmate Wil knew by sight but not by name raised his hand.

"Um. Yes?" Wil pointed at him.

"Is it true you graduated top of your class with a focus on illusions?" The wizard was a meek-looking young man wearing clothes too big for him. "How did you manage that?"

"Well, partly because I also focused on earth magic," said Wil, chuckling. "Illusions on their own can be potent, but they're subtle and are more about manipulation than direct effect. That goes for more than the spells, I mean the mind-set behind them too. You have to be willing to work sideways and not apply direct force."

"Did you beat Chinis?" Tybalt called out, looking pointedly at the mage.

Chinis adjusted his spectacles. "He did. Test scores don't mean much, though. I could take him in a fight any day."

A low ooh ran through the crowd of wizards.

"Do you think so?" Wil asked, understanding the real reason his friend brought him. "Then I challenge you, Chinis, to the Zaz."

Chinis grinned, showing even, white teeth. "You're on, McKenzie."

The Magical Madhouse wasn't just a silly name for a bar. The main floor was for drinks and food, but the basement was where the action happened. Chinis led the way down the stairs, and most of the occupants came after them. A short descent into darkness later and they came out into an impossibly large room.

A square had been carved into the ground about four feet deep. Glowing orbs of light hung from the ceiling, casting the basement in a dim, flickering glow. All around the arena was bleacher seating, and the crowd took their places, chattering excitedly about the coming display.

Syl followed Wil up to the edge before asking, "So, what's the Zaz and what do I do?"

"You don't have to do anything, Prince," said Chinis, hopping down. "All you gotta do is enjoy watching me embarrass McKenzie."

"The Zaz is . . .well, it's silly," said Wil. "It's short for pizzaz. It's kind of like a fight, but not really. We're not looking to hurt each other or anything, just look more impressive. It's a bunch of ridiculous peacocking. You're going to love it. And *you*"—he turned to Isom—"must understand that he's going to attack me without hurting me, so you can't hurt him."

"Phooey," said the wampus cat. He trotted off a short distance and flopped down. His tail flicked behind him.

"Sounds good to me. Put on a fantastic show, Wil. If you could destroy Grimnar for real, you can pretend to beat your friend, right?" Syl patted him and sat down next to Isom.

Hopping down into the arena, Wil took a few steadying breaths and thought about what he knew Chinis could do and how to counter it. It was more difficult than fighting an ogre, to be honest. It was about subtlety and panache more than raw power.

Chinis stared him down from thirty feet away, hand on the hilt of his sword. Wil immediately wished he had brought his staff out with him but he had assumed his superiors would want him separated from it. Neither of them moved for several seconds, until the mage drew his sword.

Frost gathered around the blade as runes came to life in the metal. Chinis swung from low to high and the air flash froze, sending a wave of snowy powder at Wil. Wil spun and used the harmless attack's momentum to throw it back at him. The snowflakes exploded innocuously into brilliant blue butterflies. They fluttered above the fight as the crowd cheered.

Chinis nodded and channeled power through his sword. Wind buffeted Wil, making him take a step back, then another. Wil pushed forward with all his might before clapping his hands together. He raised the ground itself to shield him from the unbalancing gusts. Wil lobbed a glittering ball of energy up over the makeshift wall.

His opponent slashed with his sword and cut through it, detonating the illusion. It flashed bright white, and Wil poured more power in, holding on to that second of dazzling brilliance. The basement remained in negative, the crowd a bunch of black voids in white light. Then it faded back to normal.

Chinis blinked violently, one hand coming up to rub his eyes. "That one hurt," he called out.

"Then close your eyes!" Wil hurled another ball, and another. This time, Chinis didn't try to cut them. The Zaz wasn't only a contest, it was a dance, a show to put on for your friends and peers. When the balls landed, they exploded into light, but Chinis had planted his sword in the ground.

Ice traveled from the blade, spreading across the floor and growing into massive crystalline diamonds. With another slash, they spun on their bases, reflecting the light flashing from Wil's illusions. Faster and faster Wil threw the balls of light and darkness, until the basement strobed and no one could see for more than a split second before plunging into darkness once more.

Chinis changed it up, taking a deep breath and gathering enough power that Wil felt it surge from across the room. The space in between them warped, stretching in places and compressing in others. Wil met the new play with one of his own, changing each ball of light into a new color to be pulled around by the spatial distortion.

The crowd went wild, cheering and screaming at the light show. Syl stuck two fingers in his mouth and blew out a shrill whistle while Isom cowered at the onslaught of sensory input. Wil felt the strain of holding so many illusions while making more and more, but it was nothing compared to the raw power Chinis channeled for the sake of a killer show.

All that remained was to end it before either of them faltered and ruined the illusion.

Wil breathed in, feeling the arena around him, the earth beneath it, the way the stone felt. Although he could not transmute the stone into anything softer, his connection with the earth was different. The earth wasn't one solid mass, it was a collective, and all he had to do was reach for the individual parts and mold them.

He breathed out, and the arena dipped and rose in a repeating wave. The space in the middle distorted even farther as their spells met and turned the center of the room into a chaotic mess of flashing, swirling colors, creating an almost liquid earth.

For ten long, agonizing, beautiful seconds they kept it up. When Wil had thrown his will and power against Skalet's storm, it had felt like this. Power flowing through him and changing the world until it sapped at him and threatened to suck him dry. Chinis faltered first, and space returned to normal. Wil released the colors and the earth roiled once more before settling, more or less, where it had been.

Panting, Wil dropped to his knee. The edges of his vision went dark, and for one panicked second he wondered if he'd pushed too hard and would drop dead. As his heart hammered and he sucked down breath after greedy breath, he determined he would survive. Across the room, Chinis looked to be in about the same shape.

"Call it a draw then, McKenzie?" Chinis called out.

"Sounds good to me." Wil grinned, and the crowd of wizards went wild.

CHAPTER 4

Burden of Power

That was incredible!" Syl cried as he threw his arms around the two wizards. "I've seen bigger, more impressive magic being thrown around in my time, but not often. What would it have been like if you *were* trying to hurt each other?"

Wil panted, grateful to lean against Syl for support. He flashed Chinis a weary grin and said, "I would've been utterly destroyed. He's tricky. He's a master of curse breaking, and he is specialized for anti-wizard fighting."

"What can I say? I like being competitive, and the only people I gotta worry about are other wizards," said Chinis, fatigue slowing his drawl. "It's more fun that way."

Isom perked up. "I also hunt wizards for fun!" he said. "I wonder what I would gain if I ate you."

"The worst stomachache of your life, kitty."

The crowd met them at the stairs, and then it was all backslaps and praise. As much as Wil did enjoy recognition for his work, the show had left him tired enough to want some peace and quiet. Climbing up the stairs left him in need of some food and then maybe a nap.

Because he was the star guest of the hour and paying for a round, Chinis pointed them over to the Manifee City corner while he talked with the bartender. Wil collapsed in the back, glad that his heart had stopped pounding and there wasn't the headache that had come from pushing too hard. Syl sat on his right, and Isom leaped up to the nook in the wall behind the seat, lying underneath a painted beach umbrella.

"Fae magic is so different," said Syl, looking at all the wizards crowding the center island to receive their free drink. "Not better or worse, but more subtle. You people are very direct and aggressive, but there's beauty here too. It's loud, garish, and obnoxious. It's something we would never make, and it's so . . . human."

Wil shook his head with a smile. "As always, Syl, you know how to compliment a race. You're right, though. Human magic is different, and it wasn't always this strong. We're developing at a rapid pace, and there are more wizards coming into their gifts every year. There have been so many discoveries over the last century alone, borrowing what we've known from your people and . . . others."

"Others? What others?"

"Well." Wil wet his lips, trying to think of the least awful way to phrase it. "Aside from learning some things from your people, we've also made contact with devils and demons and the like. It's how we've developed our runic and ritual magics, though we're still starting out."

Syl made a face. "Demons and devils. Bah. Everything they touch turns to rot. Have you ever made contact with one?"

"Absolutely not!" Wil was sick at the idea.

"Absolutely not what?" Chinis asked as he came up with three drinks pressed up against his armor. He set them down on the table and passed them around before joining on Wil's other side.

"I've absolutely not trafficked with demons or devils," said Wil. "I've never needed to for my magic."

Chinis shrugged. "Your loss. You could gain a lot from a contract or some in-depth instruction. But even past that, you're stronger than you used to be. There's no way the Wil I knew could've made the ground do that while spinning a dozen illusions. What happened?"

"I had a growth spurt," Wil deadpanned.

"You sure you didn't do a ritual to boost your strength? Maybe in exchange for your firstborn?" The mage took a sip of his beer. "Naw. What would that do you, back on the farm?"

"I've been meaning to ask," Syl interjected, looking between them. "Wil takes care of Harper Valley, and you're a fighter of some kind, here to guard us, right?"

"Ehhh." Chinis wiggled his hand indecisively. "Guard you and keep an eye on you. I'm your babysitter, to make sure the two of you make it to Cloverton and don't, you know, try to run. But if you're asking what I do in general, I'm a bodyguard and rogue wizard hunter for this city."

"Those are two very different things," Syl said. "The other representatives and I have been wondering what all you wizards are called to do. Is everyone assigned to a city or town to serve? If not every human can do magic, what do the ones who can, do?"

"Okay, so." Wil clapped his hands together. "There are different levels of wizards, based on their education and testing level, right? Adept is the first level, those who have learned to control their magic and not be a danger to themselves or others. They take whatever work they can, but they aren't going to be doing anything impressive.

"Next come apprentices, those who have received a basic, if not thorough education. It's assumed that they'll continue learning and gain more opportunities from there, but they . . . well, they're often apprentices to other working wizards, especially when it comes to crafting. They're learning how they can apply their gifts to make a living and contribute to society."

Wil paused to take a drink of beer. Chinis looked half asleep, but Syl was riveted while Isom pretended to be asleep. Here in the Madhouse, he'd had the big conversations again and again about what to do after he and his friends graduated. It was so weird to be on the other side of things. He'd made it.

"Wizard is considered educated and licensed to work almost anywhere. From here you can do government work or be hired by some of the bigger businesses. They'll do things like provide security, ward and enchant buildings, spy on each other, things like that. Chinis and I knew one guy who got deep into water science and pipes and went back east. Now he's probably the greatest plumber in the world."

"Oh yeah." Chinis came to life, laughing. "Bob! Or David, I guess, but there were too many Davids, so we called him Bob. That guy *loves* infrastructure. Bet he's making bank right now."

"What about masters like you, Wil?" Syl pressed. "You came to Harper Valley, and at this point I'm pretty glad you did, but what else could you have done?"

Too many things. The disappointed looks of Wil's professors still haunted him. No one had liked or supported his decision to go back home, but after the embarrassment of washing out of the mage program, his name was synonymous with wasted talent. Maybe things would be better, now that he had accomplished so much. If they didn't rake him over the coals for it.

"Well, master wizards are prime candidates to be assigned to the overall welfare and health of a community," said Wil, forcing a smile. "That's what I chose. While I handled a lot of silly and petty requests, my job is technically to oversee the growth and prosperity of Harper Valley. Cloverton's highly concerned with making sure there are enough resources and healthy candidates to protect the country from Ilianto and Albetosia."

"War," said Syl, wrinkling his nose. He pointed at Chinis. "That's what you're for too, right? Mages are war wizards."

"Yep," Chinis confirmed, taking a long drink. "I haven't been to the front, but I might sign up for a tour or two. It's good money, and I got family I could visit."

The faun laughed bitterly. "Is there any part of your civilization that *isn't* dedicated to being better at war?"

Wil held up his hands in surrender. "I hear you. That's why I'm doing what I'm doing. I just want to help people. And I didn't want to do it by hurting others or making war machines like a lot of my classmates did and still do. I want to build things and uplift people."

Chinis shrugged. "And you're gonna be making a fraction of what everyone else does."

It always came back to money. Wil was uncomfortable with how much he made compared to the average person in Harper Valley. It was still peanuts compared to the opportunities he could've had.

"I don't care," Wil said, shrugging. "Too many of us focus on money and power."

"Yeah," said Chinis, "because with money and power, you get freedom." Gone was his sleepy, half-dazed demeanor. His eyes were open and focused on Wil. This wasn't the first time they'd had a conversation like this. "You obtain some money and power, and you can help people all you want."

"He's right," Isom growled. "It's the way of the world. The strong do what they want, and the weak stay out of their way."

"Great," Wil laughed, "you have a vicious predator agreeing with you. Just in case you're wondering where your stance leaves you." He thought of the mayor and his friends when he had turned them into toads. He'd given orders and threatened them, but that wasn't usually how he did things. It had been necessary, right?

"That's fine by me," said Chinis, downing the rest of his drink. "Better a predator than prey. C'mon McKenzie, you're a good guy, but you can be pushed around by anyone with a stronger will than you. You'd be a force to be reckoned with if you weren't too damned scared to embrace your power."

Neither of them said anything at first, instead giving the other their best stink eye while Syl watched in interest. The worst part to Wil was the knowledge that his friend wasn't even that ambitious. He didn't go out of his way to gain power or wealth. He worked hard, but Chinis enjoyed his privilege and comfort. He didn't care about *why*.

The bartender came up to the table with three massive plates. On each were hunks of steak on a bed of fries covered in cheese, beans, and scallions. "Here we are," he said. "The Manifee City treat, steak fries!"

"Where's mine?" Isom demanded. The bartender froze.

"Ignore him, he can have some of mine." Wil waved the man off. He grabbed a meaty, cheesy fry and took a bite. His eyes fluttered closed, and he moaned. "Gods, I missed this."

Chinis chuckled and dug into his own. "They're like half the reason I didn't leave." And like that, the tension faded into the background, even when Chinis continued. "Look, I don't mean anything bad. Just that you're kinda odd and don't understand how the world works."

Wil chuckled, shaking his head. He tossed a hunk of steak at Isom, who snapped it out of the air with a loud chomp. "Yeah, as you've been saying for years."

"Maybe it doesn't have to be mutually exclusive," said Syl when silence threatened to ruin their sunny, cheery ambiance once more. "I'm a prince, and I've got power. I use that power well. Chasing power for power's sake is bad, but if it's in service to a worthy goal, and you're not hurting people . . . Is that so bad?"

A half dozen arguments came to mind, and it bothered Wil. He was out with an old friend who went out of his way to bring him here instead of going straight to the safe house. He had amazing food, passable beer, and great company. But no matter how hard he tried, Wil couldn't ignore the itch.

"I've seen what power does to people," said Wil. "Think of Hugo and how it destroyed him. There was never enough for him to be satisfied. That's the problem with power and wealth. You get used to being above people, and that gets comfortable. That's what I don't want, even if I know it's not possible. I don't want to be above anyone else."

Wil understood how useful power was. It had been the only way to get things done at the end of his last crisis, but now he had time enough to regret it and question himself.

Chinis chewed his steak fries thoughtfully. "Then maybe you shouldn't have become a master wizard, McKenzie. Power is part of who you are. You can't run from yourself forever. Gotta make peace with that eventually."

That, more than the food, gave Wil something to chew on.

CHAPTER 5

City of Industry

After lunch, Chinis took them to the safe house. It was a nondescript house near the military base on the north side of the city, with regular patrols of military police down clean, well-lit streets. Once inside, it was Chinis's duty to keep them under surveillance until they left. The trip to the Madhouse had been unauthorized, and Wil saw no reason to tell anyone.

The rest of the day passed uneventfully, although being confined to one building made both Syl and Isom chafe. The hours crept by with little to do but chat or read. The two wizards spent the time chatting about classmates and dreams of the future, until one of the neighborhood's minders was sent out for food. They ate and went to bed, and in the morning were up bright and early to go through the continent's biggest portal.

"Is it always like this?" Syl asked as Chinis drove them through the base's open gates. Soldiers had looked over them, rifles in hand, before the mage produced identification and they were let through.

"Always," said Chinis. "This portal isn't for commercial purposes. Only troops and the most important people come through here. And their pets, I guess." He met Isom's eye in the window's reflection with a smirk.

Luckily for them, the base wasn't too crowded at this time of day. They drove by soldiers jogging in formation while gunshots from the firing range echoed from afar. There were a few other larger cars, but they were far away. The portal itself wasn't hard to find. It stood thirty feet high and sixty feet wide, looking like a sideways egg, chaotic partial images swirling on the other side.

"Are you going to scream this time, Wil?" Syl teased.

"Oh, shut up."

Chinis parked in a marked spot and let them all out. "This is normally a multiple-person job, escorting, but you're a low-risk subject. We'll send a runner to announce us, and security will be higher on the other side. Stick together and try to look harmless."

Several soldiers stared as the motley crew walked up to the portal. Their escort held up a hand and spoke with a powerfully built young woman, who nodded and stepped through the portal. Chinis waited a minute or so before motioning them to join him.

Wil approached the portal with caution. He could already feel it pulling on him, stretching him three thousand miles. He shuddered but got into position. As one, the four of them reached forward and touched it.

It was nothing like the portal in Faerie. Rather than being yanked through the space, Wil plummeted sideways through a near freezing void. He didn't spin or flail, but it felt like he should have. When he came out the other side, Wil found his feet moving of their own accord. Chinis caught him before he made it too far.

Isom, on the other hand, came forward, rolling on the ground. He scampered to his feet, looking as embarrassed as Wil was. Syl calmly stepped through and lit up. "That was incredible! I would love to see how they did it."

"You got a better chance of McKenzie coming to his senses than them telling you anything," said the mage. "C'mon, keep close."

The first part of Cloverton that stood out to Wil was the smell. It stank. Black clouds billowed above the base and across the city, dimming the morning sun. While Manifee City was loud, it was the sounds of the sea and people living their lives. In the Cloverton base at least, a cacophony of people barked orders, and the sounds of machines clanking in the distance proved to be overwhelming. Not just for Wil.

"This is your capital?" Syl looked horrified. "This is depressing."

"This is only the military base," said Wil, privately agreeing with the faun's distaste. The place was crowded and colorless, the same whites and grays used for every building, with only the yellow signs on the ground providing anything to break up the monotony. "The rest of the city is bound to be better."

They found the rest of the city was not better. The streets were wider and busier, with at least double the cars on the road. These ones belched smoke and chugged along at a volume high enough to make it difficult to think. It was a relief when they got into the new car and the closed windows kept the sounds at bay.

"How do you live like this?" Syl asked. He looked no more comfortable in this car than he had the last. "Seriously. It smells terrible and the air burns the lungs. And there's so much iron. Everywhere." Outside their window, they passed dozens of metal lampposts.

"No argument here, Prince," said Chinis. "Cloverton's ugly and a pain in the ass to drive in." He demonstrated his point by honking at a sleek black car with an open roof that cut him off and wove around the other cars. "I wouldn't come here by choice. Thank Cuddles over here for that," he said, nodding in Wil's direction.

"Thanks, Chinis," Wil sighed. "We'll get out of here at the first opportunity."

"You will," said Syl. "Not me. You only have to answer for what we did. I have to represent my people, and who knows how long that'll take?"

It is loud here, Isom whispered in Wil's head. *There are many, many people, all thinking. It's too much.*

Wil turned around in his seat. The wampus cat's head darted around at every new sight and thought he could listen in on. His tail was thick, and he scrunched up to be as small as possible.

"Chinis?" Wil nudged him to get his attention. "We have a place to stay here tonight, right?"

"We sure do," said the mage, braking fast so a mother and her children could walk across the street. "We're staying at Marlowe Manor while we're here. You may have messed up royally, but they're treating you as someone to contend with."

"Marlowe Manor," Wil said breathily. While Manifee City was more magically inclined, Cloverton had one of the original places of study, converted into a workspace for visiting wizards. Archmages and grandmasters stayed there, with only the occasional master or mage allowed. "Well, I need you to do me a favor."

"Sure, if I can."

"When we get to wherever we're going, could you drop off Isom? I don't think they're going to let us in with him, and he can get a feel for the place for me."

"Sure."

I do not need your pity! But I appreciate the chance to escape . . . this. Isom settled down.

Wil knew they were getting close when they passed through wards. A sensation of a heavy blanket settled over him, closing in until it was smothering. It was like being bundled up too tightly in winter and being unable to move, unable to breathe as freely.

"What the hell was that?" Wil demanded, panting.

"Magic suppression field," Chinis grunted. "Sorry, forgot about that. It's all part of the security in the leadership district. You *can* do magic, but it's harder. And not recommended unless you're a fan of splitting headaches."

It made sense, but Wil didn't like it. Syl and Isom didn't look any worse for wear, so chances were it only restricted human magic. That's when it hit him that he had no power here, and he was at the mercy of people who might not be on his side.

As they pulled up to a large, ominous, ancient-looking building, Wil realized how badly he wanted to run away or beg for more time. Instead, he steadied his breathing and said, "I guess this is it, then? C'mon Syl. Isom, behave, and scout out Marlowe Manor for me."

"Fine. Don't take too long, or else I might come find you," said Isom. Wil wasn't sure if it was meant to reassure or threaten.

Chinis motioned with his head to the front doors. "Gotta see you head in before I leave. Good luck, McKenzie and Prince Goat."

Syl saluted him, his discomfort forgotten in favor of friendliness. "Your excellent guard work and transportation is appreciated, and I'll see you again tonight!"

They were let inside without incident, no doubt helped by Syl's presence. Wil could've been any random wizard for all they knew, but only one fae diplomat was expected. They were led through a mostly empty waiting room and down labyrinthine halls of closed doors and low chatter in the background.

They walked all the way to a corner office, where a placard outside the door declared the inhabitant to be I. S. Pierce. Their escort knocked on the door and left them. A voice bid them to enter. Syl looked as nervous as Wil, but they nodded and stepped inside.

"Ah, there you two are," a small, older man with an impressive gray beard and spectacles said, standing up. He wasn't much taller standing up. "Been expecting you for a few days, and I'm sure you've got tons of questions and concerns. Investigative Specialist Pierce, at your service."

Will took his proffered hand and shook it. "Wilbur McKenzie and Prince Sylano. How much trouble are we in?"

Pierce laughed. "A fair bit if things go poorly. But I'm here for *you*, Master McKenzie. Prince Sylano, I believe my partner next door will handle your case."

"Next door? Alone?" Syl made a face. He was no coward, but after the beating from Hugo and his men and the way Harper Valley's most paranoid citizens turned on him? Wil didn't blame him for being reluctant.

"Not alone, Harry's in there. We need to separate you to get your statements on these past few months of incidents." The investigator sat back down and motioned for Wil to join him.

Wil remained standing. "My friend here's had a rough time because of the most recent incident. I don't think he feels safe alone among humans, even with his diplomatic status. Which I am curious about. Shouldn't a foreign prince have an honor guard and red carpet?"

"Yeah!" said Syl. "Where's my honor guard? Does anyone even know I'm here?" He crossed his arms over his chest and glowered at the man.

Pierce shrugged and said, "Discretion is important while we figure out exactly what happened in Harper Valley. Now, I know how scary this must be, but you must understand I'm on your side. I'm not just here to figure things out but to make sure you're protected and things go well for you.

"I'm your legal counsel, son. The more you tell me, the easier job I have of making sure you don't get thrown to the wolves and torn apart as an example." Pierce's smile remained, but he was all business now. "Help me help you out here. Cooperate, tell the truth, and we'll figure out a future where you go back home a hero. But first, we need your statements. Separately."

Syl blew out a frustrated breath. "And then when all is said and done, I get my honor guard and red carpet?"

Pierce shrugged. "As far as I know, sure."

"If you don't hear from me again," said Syl to Wil, "avenge me." He clapped the wizard on the shoulder and retreated through the door, closing it behind him.

Wil sat down in the chair, taking a deep breath. His danger sense was silent, but old-fashioned anxiety ate away at him. Pierce made it worse a second later.

"Now, that's interesting," he said as he eyed the door . "Why would the prince of a foreign nation expect you to avenge him against your own government? What happened out there?"

Wil steadied himself the best he could and started his story.

CHAPTER 6

Questions of Accountability

Although Wil found that he enjoyed presentations and performances, speaking at length about himself was a nightmare. Pierce rarely asked specific questions, instead directing Wil to go back and elaborate on points he'd been vague about. It made the wizard feel like he'd done something wrong, and that was before he even entered Faerie.

Wil found himself at a loss when it came to recounting the past few months. Things that had seemed necessary at the time now came off as silly and panicked. Every time Wil explained the reasoning behind his actions, he felt more and more like a dumb kid.

Pierce did nothing to make it worse. The older man sounded sympathetic, like a kindly old librarian helping out a student. However, his empathy never quite reached his eyes, which were sharp and penetrating. No matter how peaceful or unworried he sounded, Wil couldn't shake the impression of being weighed, measured, and found wanting.

"So Mage Jefferson entered my mind," said Wil, looking up at the clock. He'd been at it for over an hour now, going through everything. "I drove him out and followed him. That's when I . . . when I destroyed his connection with his thralls."

The entire time Wil spoke, Pierce's pen moved along, taking notes. A few times they'd stopped so he could refill the ink, and then it was back to notes. In addition, a magical recording device logged his every word. That had bugged Wil greatly, noting each "um" and "uh" as he fought to find the right way to not sound guilty.

"And that's when you killed Mage Jefferson," Pierce said, peering over his spectacles at him.

Wil flinched. "That's when his thralls killed him. On my orders. So yes, I suppose, that's when I killed Mage Jefferson."

Pierce said nothing else, merely logged his answer. When he was finished, he stroked his long beard thoughtfully. "What happened next?"

The wizard took a breath. It was almost over. "I led a coalition of humans and fae into Faerie along with the completed trade treaty. I went up to the council chambers and interrupted their vote. I persuaded them to hear reason and vote for signing the peace treaty to avoid war with Calipan."

The entire time, Wil faced a problem that gnawed relentlessly at him. How much should he tell? He hadn't told a single lie, but as the interview went on, he left more and more unnecessary details out. Did Cloverton really need to know how close it had been and that Wil had strong-armed Grimnar into doing what he said?

"We signed, with the few stipulations that I have described in my initial messages to Cloverton. Wizards are allowed by invitation only, and the offending Faerie leaders have stepped down and will be jailed." If being confined to one city for a hundred years counted as jailed. For Timothy Twist, it would.

Pierce jotted all of that down, humming tunelessly to himself. When he was done, he peered over his spectacles at him. "And then?"

Wil blew out a breath. "And then I spent the next week cleaning up Jefferson's mess. I managed to free Captain Nesbitt from his mental prison, turned the toads back into humans with the help of the fae, and kept Harper Valley from falling into chaos. And then," he added quickly, "I found Jefferson's journal, contacted Cloverton, and came here a few days later. I don't think there's anything else."

Another few seconds of silence, save for the scratch of Pierce's pen on paper. That quiet left Wil with a lot of room to tear himself apart. Each tick of the clock on the wall was like a stone gently placed on him. The first few weren't bad, but after a full minute had passed with neither of them speaking, the pressure got to Wil.

"How much trouble do you think I'm in?" Wil asked. "As my legal counsel."

"Mmm." Pierce took his spectacles off and cleaned them with a soft-looking cloth he produced from his shirt pocket. "If nothing else, I think I can keep you from being put in front of a firing squad."

"Oh," said Wil. "That's . . . that's good, then."

The older man chuckled. "I won't lie to you, Master McKenzie. You're not out of the fire by a long shot. But with a bit of preparation, we can ensure you come out with the bare minimum of burns. You may even only get singed."

Wil swallowed hard. A million panicked thoughts trampled over him, screaming the entire time. Pierce noticed and said, not unkindly, "You might consider going out to the little waiting room outside and getting yourself some water. Perhaps a small snack. Then we'll pick back up."

The wizard nodded and numbly left the room. Was Pierce joking? Would they consider killing him for stopping Hugo? The idea of prison time or a severe reprimand or fine had crossed his mind, but now Wil worried more.

Throat suddenly dry, he went for the break nook right off the office. He grabbed a mug he assumed was clean and after briefly considering coffee filled it with water and drained it. Two mugs later and Wil almost felt better. The panic couldn't be held off entirely, only kept at bay.

Muffled voices came from the other side of the dim, claustrophobic office, trampling on his trembling nerves. Maybe one of them was worse off than him. The thought didn't help.

Wil leaned against the wall and focused on his breathing. The idea of playing with an illusion came to him, until he tried to feel for the magic around him. He came up against a metaphysical brick wall between him and the land. The reminder his magic was restricted made him squirm. Darlene would laugh if she saw him fretting needlessly.

Darlene. She was waiting for him to come back. Bram too, and his family, and everyone else counting on him. It wasn't only his life at stake. Harper Valley itself would pay for what he'd done. It had been so easy to make the decision in the moment, when he felt like he had no good choices. And now?

"Master McKenzie?" Pierce's head poked out of the door. "When you're ready, come back in. I've got some questions for you."

Wil nodded and set the mug in the sink before returning to the office. He closed the door and sat down. Pierce didn't make him wait long.

"When you fended off the storm dragon and ripped the leyline, why didn't you tell anyone?"

"I didn't know it had happened until a couple months later," said Wil. "I only found out when the gnome Declan and I spoke."

"And why not after then?" Pierce stared him down, his face a neutral mask. "You had critical information on something that could change the country's understanding of magic, and you sat on it. Why?"

Wil flinched. "I . . . At first, I needed to know more about what I did and how it would affect things. I went into Faerie because I thought I'd be able to learn more about leylines."

"And did you?"

"Not as such," he said, shrinking. "Things got busy, and the fae didn't have more information on it than I did."

Pierce made a note and continued. "And when you came home again: why not then? Or when Mage Jefferson arrived and took over the situation. He reported the damaged leyline, but you did not."

The problem with trying to think of an acceptable answer was he didn't have one. Not one in particular. He couldn't bring himself to lie, so Wil sighed and let it all come tumbling out.

"I wanted . . . needed to be sure of what I discovered before I bothered people here. Too many young wizards want to make names for themselves, and they come up with half-baked ideas and try to reinvent the wheel." It was true enough, even if it wasn't his primary reason. "I didn't want to come with a problem and no ideas for a solution."

Pierce made a sound and continued writing. "Let's move on for now. You then went off on an expedition into another world without informing us of what you were doing. Instead, your mayor filled us in and asked for help and instructions. What made you decide to handle it yourself?"

The nearby clock hanging from the wall ticked ominously as the seconds passed. The answer didn't come easily. "My best friend was one of the people taken to Faerie. I wasn't willing to wait to save him. I won't apologize for going to save Bram."

"And I'm not asking you to." Pierce set his pen down. "I need you to understand, I am on your side. You may get different counsel if you wish, but it is my job to make sure that I can sell a specific version of a story to the tribunal, who will be picking you apart from every angle. They will be far less kind than I am, Master McKenzie.

"Right now, the story I have is that an overzealous young man, strong but reckless, did things on his own because he thought he knew better than his government. Someone who might even be compromised and a liability."

"How the hell would I be compromised?" Wil demanded, grateful for the anger. "Everything I've done has been in service to Harper Valley and Calipan by extension."

"Even when your choices reflect a clear bias toward a foreign country?" Pierce sat back and stroked his beard. His eyes bore twin holes into Wil. "On multiple occasions you've made calls that favored our enemy."

"But they're not our enemy," said Wil. "Not anymore. Not with the peace treaty now signed. With the conditions in our favor, my decisions averted war with favorable terms for Calipan. I'll admit I was reckless, but I delivered, didn't I?"

"That's the problem, Master McKenzie. You did a bunch of foolish things and then succeeded at them. You are politically inconvenient." Pierce chuckled. "It would be equally difficult to punish or reward you, and after all of this, Cloverton will need to do one of those things. So we have two possible stories.

"A reckless young man does something thought magically impossible, runs off to another world, and comes back helping out his country's former enemies. This wizard kills the Cloverton representative who may or may not have gone rogue. At a certain point, it doesn't matter. Mage Jefferson is still dead at his command. Regardless of the story, that much is true.

"In one version, the fae got to you after you ran headlong into their world. They either preyed upon your obvious inexperience and got you to turn, or else they used their magic to ensnare you."

"Not likely," said Wil. "I'm a natural mind mage, remember? It would take a lot to break past my defenses."

Pierce smiled mirthlessly. "So you possibly turn on your country and work against us, until Jefferson arrives and throws off your plans. So the fae attack, you defend them, kill Jefferson, and then come up with a story about how you had to do it."

"You can ask anyone who knows me," said Wil, "and they would laugh at that idea."

"I'm sure they would," said Pierce. "And they will likely be questioned in the future as the investigation proceeds. But that is one way you will be presented. The other is . . . mildly kinder."

"And what's that?" Wil asked.

"A well-meaning boy with more power than sense bungled his way into and out of trouble. Moving from one disaster to the next and trying to plug leaky holes in a ship. Leaks you caused and then hid so that you wouldn't be punished. One is the work of a traitor, the other of a fool. Fools can be forgiven. Traitors can't."

Wil's blood ran cold. "So when you say you can keep me from the firing squad . . ."

Pierce sighed. "No, I wasn't joking about that. But I believe I can sell this as the blunders of a country kid who got in over his head and tried to hide things while he fixed them. This will not be fun or comfortable, I'm afraid, but I will not have a blemish on my record. And with that, you are free to go. I have what I need to prepare you for the hearing."

"Thank you," said Wil, though it was hard to put any feeling behind it. "I appreciate any help you can give me. For what it's worth, I *am* just a dumb kid who blundered from problem to problem. I was doing my best."

The investigator stood, and Wil did the same. He offered the wizard his hand. "For what it's worth, I believe you, and my notes will reflect that. Do as I tell you, and you may get to go home."

CHAPTER 7

Marlowe Manor

Wil stumbled out of the office on rubbery legs. It was done. At least, it was done for the day. With any luck he and Syl could unwind over a couple of drinks and swap stories. In a strange way, he envied the faun. Things would be harder for him in some ways, but he didn't have family or a permanent presence in Calipan yet. Chances were, they wouldn't lock up the prince.

The office next to Pierce's was open and empty when Wil peeked his head in. No lights, no life, no faun. It was startling at first, until he realized Syl got finished first. He was probably waiting for Wil at that very moment in the lobby.

All the voices and signs of life didn't seem so bad now that he was leaving. Wil walked past the offices, trying his best to remember the way out. After a couple of wrong turns, he bumped into someone his own age, who directed him to the front. He thanked her and went to the lobby.

Syl wasn't there either, and neither was he outside when Wil opened the door. He turned to the receptionist. "Um, have you seen my friend?"

"You mean the seven-foot-tall goatman?" the middle aged woman said with a wry smile. "Hard to miss. He left about half an hour ago with an escort."

"What?!"

"If it helps," she said in a soothing tone, "he didn't look upset. On the contrary. He had a wide smile on his face and was talkin' the men's ears off."

"That's Syl," said Wil. "Damn. Okay, thank you."

Chinis waited for him in the parking lot, leaning against their temporary car. "You look like hell, McKenzie. I take it they weren't gentle?"

"According to the man I spoke to, they were." Wil joined him and slumped against the car with a groan. "That was rough. And then I come out and Syl's gone."

"Yeah, he got taken to the Ambrose Estate as a guest of the president," said Chinis with a shrug. "I guess Bullworth's curious."

Wil jolted to alertness. "Seriously? Syl is hanging out with the Big Bull?"

President Barry Bullworth was a contentious figure. Wil couldn't say he was particularly fond of him or his policies, but as a master wizard and employee of Calipan, being vocal about politics was frowned upon. Most wizards cared more for which possible candidate was sympathetic to them and their causes. They had more prestige and power at the cost of less freedom and uneasiness from society.

Calipan wasn't a magocracy like old Ramenia had been before it fell, and some people worried about returning to the old ways. Bullworth and his cabinet hadn't overtly increased the power or rights of those with magic, but he surrounded himself with grandmasters and archmages as his closest company. It was enough to make Wil nervous, but also hopeful.

"Seems that way," Chinis said. "He'll be okay. You ready to see your new home for the next year?"

"Don't joke like that," Wil said, making a face. "It's not going to take that long. But yes, I would love to see Marlowe Manor."

Syl was most likely okay, and in any event, Wil had no power to change anything. He got in the car. Chinis followed, powering it up and driving them away from the office. After a few minutes, the constant, claustrophobic pressure eased, and the two wizards breathed sighs of relief.

A minute later, Wil extended his senses to the city around him. It felt sickly and tired, depleted. It was still better than the awkward nothingness of the anti-magic field. It got better as Chinis took them beyond the city proper and out into the frozen wetlands nearby. The feeling of life returned, and Wil breathed it in.

He'd managed to finally relax, when the dirt road spat them out into a massive clearing amid the trees and bogs. Although winter had left a layer of snow on the grounds, it was kept neat and tidy by a team of workers. Even now they kept the walkways clear. The house itself was about half the size of Saint Balthazar's and had room for dozens of high-ranking wizards to stay.

"Beautiful, isn't it?" Chinis asked upon seeing Wil's expression. "You're gonna be stuck here awhile, but at least you'll have a library full of journals written by grandmasters. And the workshop. I'd come here for the workshop alone if they'd have me."

They passed the workshop, its own large building with open doors and windows. The sound of hammers on metal broke through, as did a persistent whine Wil realized came from a magical device, possibly even an artisan's prototype. The land around them felt better, more loved and lived in. And by the time they approached the main house, Wil felt Isom's mental presence brush against his.

The wampus cat came running through the snow at the car, running past it and forcing Chinis to slam on the breaks and swear under his breath. "Stupid cat."

"I think he's excited," said Wil. "This place must seem like a buffet to him, even more than the Madhouse."

"Keep a short leash on him," said Chinis. "For his own safety."

The grounds here are lush, even in winter. There is prey to be found in the woods. Isom's thoughts crashed into Wil seconds before he could get out of the car.

"I'm glad," said Wil as he exited the car and looked around. "Have you been behaving yourself? If you don't cause any trouble, we can see about letting you hunt."

The wampus cat's tail lashed out behind him with interest. He fell in behind

Wil and Chinis as they approached the house. Chinis answered the question Isom avoided.

"I told them he was yours and that he's bound to do no harm, so I guess it's working out well. But if he gets in the way of someone bigger and badder than you . . ."

"I understand," said Wil. As worried as he was, the excitement at being there overrode all other thoughts. Even the day's interrogations were far away now that he could feel the magic in the air, not quite as thick as in Faerie but clearly amplified by the presence of wizards.

"Your things are already here, and someone will show you to your room," said Chinis. "Keep your head down and consider making use of the facilities while you're here."

They stopped in front of twin doors twice as tall as Will, framed by two columns on each side in the old style of Tragopolis temples. "Are you not coming with me?" Wil asked.

Chinis shook his head. "I'll be back tomorrow to check on you, but as far as my bosses are concerned, my job is basically over. I have to report in and discuss my next posting. I'll try to keep it here, so I can see what they do to you."

"Thanks for the vote of confidence," said Wil.

Chinis flashed him a lopsided grin. "No problem. Take care, McKenzie." He saluted Wil with two fingers and walked back to the car. Then it was him and Isom.

"Alright, then. Do you think we ring or knock or just go in?"

Isom tilted his head curiously. "Ring?"

"I don't know why I asked you." Wil chuckled, shaking his head. He rang the bell and waited. Not two seconds later, the door opened and an impeccably dressed maid with a blond bun beamed at him.

"You must be our new guest!" she squeaked in a voice sharp enough to make Isom's ears flatten against his skull. "And with a handsome pet."

"Wil McKenzie," Wil introduced himself. "And Isom the wampus cat. I was told my room is ready?"

"It sure is! I'm Madeline, but you can call me Maddy!" Her enthusiasm was equal parts infectious and off-putting. "Come on in." Maddy opened the door wide and ushered them in.

The inside was even better. The tiles on the floor formed an outward spiral from the center of the room, all different colors of the rainbow. Each arm broke off down a hallway from the foyer. A crystal chandelier hung above them, a pulsing light casting dancing shadows over the walls. Little flying ships containing letters sailed through the air, carefully moving to avoid maids cleaning one stretch of the floor. Paintings on the walls moved in slow, jerky moments, acting out a gesture or expression for all eternity.

"Wow," Wil said breathily. "How enchanted is this place?"

"Enough to need an entire team of enchanters working around the clock to provide enough power and stability to keep everything running," replied Maddy. She gestured to the hallway down to the left. "If you'll follow me, I'll show you to your room."

We are being watched.

Wil shook his head. *Of course we are. This is one of the most prestigious, carefully cared for magical resources in Calipan, and we're under major scrutiny.*

He got the impression of Isom growling, as if he were being stupid, then silence. They followed Maddy down one corridor, which quickly became a windy, uneven tunnel, dark except for flickering balls of light in the air. Wil couldn't help but say, "Wow, Marlowe really was a bit mad, wasn't he?"

"We like to think of him as a genius with understanding of things beyond us!" Maddy recited for what must have been the umpteenth time. "Morgan Marlowe chose the location and built it according to magical geometry only one or two people today understand. No matter how strange things may seem, you may be assured that Master Marlowe knew what he was doing."

They passed by a hall of tall windows, each one showing a different landscape. Wil wasn't sure how he felt about the story Maddy gave, but if the magic was based on geometry, perhaps leylines had something to do with it. He closed his eyes and probed for the nearest one. He found it almost immediately, and that alone gave him a start.

The leylines, multiple, were not close. Each one was miles away, but he could feel them, and almost touch the power waiting. He didn't dare try. Marlowe Manor itself had no leylines running through its edifice, and instead it sat in the middle of many of them. It didn't make sense to Wil, but there had to be something to the stories about the mad Master Marlowe's brilliance.

Maddy directed them to a round, open room in one of the corners of the manor. Doors lined the wall, each separated only by a couple feet, all facing to the recessed center of the room where cushions were laid down. Two middle-aged men and one older woman sat in the pit. One of the men had a book open, while the other two talked in hushed voices. They stopped upon seeing Wil and stared. Did they know what he had done?

"Here we are, number eighteen." Maddy opened the door for him. Isom ran ahead, making the maid flinch.

Wil flashed her an apologetic smile and entered his room. It was about the size of the first floor of his home. There was a sitting area, a desk next to a line of bookshelves, a king-size bed, and a separate bathroom and small kitchenette. It took him several seconds of gaping before the obvious hit him: it was bigger on the inside.

The amount of constant magical power to keep all the enchantments going and the rune work preserved made Wil lightheaded. This was what the true masters of the craft were capable of. The ones capable of sensitive, intricate work. Wil could only dream of reaching that level.

"It's acceptable," Isom declared, jumping up on the bed and making himself comfortable.

"Sure, *acceptable* is a word for it." Wil walked over to the closet where his meager luggage had been opened and his clothes hung up. Not only that, but there were formal, expensive-looking clothes he'd wager would fit him perfectly.

"Well," said Wil, breathless. "If I had to be stuck somewhere . . ."

CHAPTER 8

Reputation

After a few days of being confined to the property, Wil didn't want to be stuck there anymore. He had enjoyed it at first. It was hard not to enjoy free access to multiple libraries, food on demand, beautiful grounds he was allowed to traverse with Isom, and the magical manor itself. Exploring the artwork and the secret crevices for hours on end thrilled Wil, but at what cost?

He hadn't seen Chinis in four days. No one official had sent any messages to him or asked after him as far as Wil could tell. He'd asked Maddy a few times, but that hadn't gone anywhere.

"You'll be summoned when they want you," said the maid with a shrug. "I can't help you beyond that."

"Isn't there someone who runs this place I can talk to?" Wil asked, growing worried about his predicament. "Or at least make a trip into town and explore the capital for a day or two?"

"I'm afraid not." Maddy shook her head, clicking her tongue sympathetically. "Most people who come here do so with an invitation to study or rest while conducting business. You, however, are something of a special case. I am told that if you were to try to leave or cause a fuss, you might be moved to . . . less pleasant surroundings."

Wil had understood the message loud and clear. He was a prisoner until further notice, but they were extending some trust to him. If he abused that trust . . . well. There were far worse places to be held captive. He had a lot more sympathy for Bram and the others after their stay in Faerie.

Of course, they had each other to spend the time with. Wil only had Isom, but the wampus cat proved to be a poor conversationalist, focused on his own sensory indulgences and a constant urge to hunt, stalk, and bother people. In other words, he was a cat through and through.

Everyone else at the manor seemed intent on avoiding him as much as possible. It hurt, but Wil understood. These were the best of the best—masters, grandmasters, mages, and archmages. The biggest movers and shakers of human magic, and he was nothing more than a dumb, reckless kid.

He recognized so many of them. Rand Sandoval, one of the most prolific artisans in Calipan, spent plenty of time in the lounge chatting with others. He revolutionized rune work involving different metals and was a popular man. Niobe Jameson was one of the strongest in earth magic there was, and Jim Rance discovered a more efficient way of spellcasting for those who used power words extensively. Titans, all of them.

Whenever Wil came across them, his eyes would widen in recognition, and so would theirs. He dared not approach most of them, and they didn't approach him. They chatted with each other freely, and while he understood, it still stung.

So he spent most of his time alone, all of his other needs met. The library nearest to his quarters was his favorite place, and he quickly found a pile of books to go through while waiting for news about the investigation. The first was on the manor itself, and Morgan Marlowe's increasingly strange behavior as he cleared the land and built it from scratch.

It was dry reading with tons of stats on how many rooms and floors it had, the materials used to construct it, and a breakdown of some of the more obvious enchantments. Frustratingly, it didn't go into any real details, but it was enough to whet Wil's appetite. Next, he checked out books on magical geometry and leylines, hoping to learn more about his seemingly impossible feat.

Magical geometry was simple enough on the surface. Shapes, both two- and three-dimensional, held a lot of power in their structure when aligned correctly. The nature of runic magic was based on this study, with runic configurations that were shorthand for spells. After reading through the book, he had no idea what the subject could've meant when it came to the house's placement. So he moved on to leylines.

He discovered that he already knew most of the basics. They were rivers of power running through the world, and the ones in Calipan were known for being particularly strong. It was one of the many reasons for Albetosia's colonization, before Calipan broke away and continued their work.

They could be tapped into for power by individuals, and individual spells could be tied into them. When leylines were used, spells were more potent and took longer to degrade, but they were still only usable by wizards or magical creatures. The research began and ended at their discovered use. The only mention of trying to change a leyline had been one wizard blowing himself up in the attempt.

He had finished reading his third book on the subject when a dark-haired man a few years older than Wil approached. He wore a casual suit with a bow tie and had a sly smile. "Are you Master McKenzie?" he asked.

Instantly, Wil was on guard. This was the first time someone other than manor staff had come up to him. "Who wants to know?"

The man extended his hand. "Master Thomas Elliot, at your service. I heard people talking about you and thought I'd see what all the fuss is about."

Wil eyed the hand, then got on his feet and took it. "Was the talk positive or negative?"

Thomas made an exaggerated face. "Well, it depends. No one can decide if what they heard about you is true."

"That depends on what you heard. I'm all ears, Master Elliot. Tell me what they're saying." Wil released his hand and sat down.

"Call me Thomas, please." He plopped down on the plush, garishly purple armchair next to Wil. "Formalities have their time and place, but trading scandalous gossip isn't it. Is it true you killed Jefferson?"

Wil couldn't help but flinch. Of course that was the first thing asked. "He went rogue," Wil answered carefully. "He was trying to attack a foreign country and start a war against explicit orders."

"Then it's true?" Thomas looked delighted. "You did the world a service. If alcohol cost us anything here, I'd buy you a drink. He was a rabid dog."

Guilt was a funny thing. It didn't hit Wil like he thought it would. Rather than feeling remorse over Jefferson's death and his role in making it happen, the pain came from how easy it had been. The realization made Wil sick to his stomach. He felt worse over how fine he felt about it. It had been necessary.

"What else have they been saying?" Wil said, wanting to move on before he thought too hard about it.

"Nothing major. Just that you went a bit rogue yourself and somehow managed to broker a trade deal and peace with our former enemies. And that you also may have made a discovery that fundamentally changes how we understand leylines." He folded his hands over his chest and smirked.

Wil blew out a breath. "I didn't realize word would travel so fast. Especially when it's an active investigation. I shouldn't talk about it much, for my own safety."

Thomas waved him off. "That's where you're wrong, my friend. You should be actively campaigning to bring people to your side. These are the wizards and mages who will share their terribly important opinions about you to the big bosses who will be deciding your fate. Do nothing, and the only thing they'll know are the rumors making the rounds."

It made a certain amount of sense, and Wil hated it. With the way people had been looking at him, it brought him all the way back to his childhood, where the other kids would watch him, waiting for him to do something wrong. Approaching any of them and cutting past the awkwardness would be painful.

"And what's your angle on this?" Wil asked. "You're the only person who's come to talk to me and find out for yourself. I know that most of the people here are important, but, and I mean no offense, I'm unfamiliar with you."

Thomas chuckled, shaking his head. "Think nothing of it. I grew up near Cloverton and had private schooling. Until recently, I was apprenticed under Grandmaster Enrico Ferrovani. Perhaps you've heard of him."

Wil's eyes bugged out. "You worked with the man who figured out how to make a car powered by a wizard's own magic? That's incredible! I used some of his designs when making a flying carpet last summer. Are you a master of runes, then?"

Thomas shook his head with a chuckle. "Not at all. I'm great at them, but my specialty is divination. I'm excellent at conjuring visions of experiments after they happen, to better understand what went wrong and how. The way I see it, every discovery, every major innovation is a puzzle, and I have all the tools I need to find out how to fit everything together."

It didn't take long for Wil to connect the dots. "What's your interest with leylines?"

"Pretty key to producing faricite for making batteries," said Thomas, leaning closer. "As well as a great deal of time and raw work. As of now, we can anchor simple spells to objects and places, but they'll still wear down over time. What if we could dig deeper and tap into the leylines more efficiently, maybe even permanently?"

Wil nodded, taking a breath. "I'm not sure I should talk about it. Not until I'm more sure about how it works. Apparently, the last guy who tried to do that blew himself and several acres of land up trying." He still didn't understand how that happened, when his leyline had merely torn.

"How about we grab a drink and I shamelessly try to change your mind? You could be sitting on the discovery of a lifetime. Think of the money, the fame, and how many lives you could change if you shared your knowledge." Thomas stood, offering his hand.

"Funny order you have them in," Wil said, looking at the hand but not taking it.

"Everyone has their priorities," Thomas said, undeterred. "Mine happens to make personal gain and altruism line up perfectly. You or I could be rich and famous for our efforts, and the people of Calipan's lives will be easier. Everybody wins. Especially you, if you're willing to work with me."

"It's not that I'm unwilling to work with you," said Wil, finally taking the hand and using it to pull himself to his feet. "It's more that I need to know more before I can discuss it with anyone. It's for my own legal protection. I'm sure you understand."

"Of course, of course," said Thomas. "Doesn't mean I'll stop trying, but I'll stop for now. Good enough?"

Wil smiled. "I suppose it'll have to do. What do you have in mind?"

The other master wizard grinned. "How about we get drunk and drive around, and I show you Ferrovani's latest prototype?"

"You know," said Wil, "that sounds great."

CHAPTER 9

Fame

Wil had only gotten to drive a car a few times in his life. They had been during his last two years at the academy, when Ferrovani's breakthrough had been a hot topic among the students. The first time had been with a normal combustion engine. It had been a slow, rickety thing that shook violently and made Wil feel it was seconds away from exploding on him. Danger aside, it was a lot of fun.

The second car, one gifted to the academy by Ferrovani himself, had been on display for all the graduate students to try. The moment Wil sat behind the wheel and used his own magic to power it on was one of those memories that would stick with him forever. The feeling of awareness of all the little enchantments woven into every aspect of its design had been eye opening. Studying the car carried Wil through his final runic project.

Screaming down the far end of the grounds in Ferrovani's prototype Model F-Kappa blew both the other cars out of the water.

"Careful," Thomas warned him, but he was laughing. He had one hand on the handle on the ceiling and another on a mostly empty bottle of whiskey. "Don't flip us over!"

"I got this," said Wil, spinning the wheel. They briefly went up on two tires before the weight of the car slammed them back down to the ground. The spinning tires flung snow everywhere, making yet another messy pile for the groundskeepers to clean up. He'd feel bad about it later; it was too much fun to worry about now.

Every part of the car was alive and in the forefront of his senses. Whatever Ferrovani did with his prototype, it came with more inlaid spells than Wil ever would've guessed—everything from the basic runic configurations needed to make the car go to extrasensory information. With one switch pressed, Wil could sense everything within two to three feet of the vehicle and see it in his mind's eye.

It had been the only thing keeping him from clipping a frozen topiary animal early on in the drive. What a surprise it had been, going too fast and then suddenly seeing a six-foot tall bunny in his head with only seconds to swerve out of the way. That, along with the lights, sound muffling, silent running, and seat warmers had Wil ready to buy one of his own.

"You want to drive on the lake?" Thomas said, cutting through the gleeful fog in Wil's head. He pointed to the approaching lake, not quite fully frozen.

"Are you kidding?" Wil asked, laughing. "I'm not prepared to drown or freeze to death tonight, thank you."

"No, I mean it," Thomas insisted. He pointed to a switch on the dashboard, one of a dozen. This one was marked with three wavy lines for water. "It might be a bit draining, but it's fun. Trust me, I worked hard on the feature!"

Wil hesitated, then shrugged and went along with it. Why not? So far, meeting the divination master had been a welcome reprieve from silence and boredom. He grabbed the whiskey from Thomas and took a swig before flicking the switch.

The drain on his power, so far light but constant, intensified until Wil had to take notice. The car moved over the snow easier, and right before they hit the water, Wil was reminded of the sleds he had made. Then the wheels hit the water, and the car jerked and bounced on the surfaces, speeding through water and over small islands of ice.

Wil's senses went wild, detecting every chunk of ice as well as the fish in the water frantically swimming to escape from the speeding vehicle. The drain on his magic went from being incidental to something he knew he could only keep up for a couple of minutes before faltering.

"Hey," said Thomas, laughing as he looked out the windshield, "you're not allowed off the grounds, right?"

"Yeah, why?"

He pointed. "Because the lake is at the edge of the property, and I can see the other side now."

A flash of cold that had nothing to do with the weather pierced Wil. The end of the lake rushed to meet them. They no doubt had a tracking spell on him that would alert them if he left. He spun the wheel hard, willing the car to turn. Unfortunately, he didn't brake.

The wheels turned but the momentum carried him across a patch of ice, sending the car careening wildly alongside the shore. They spun, but the enchantments held, and the wheels never left the water. They kept spinning until they crashed into a snowbank on the edge of the lake.

Thomas applauded enthusiastically, careful not to spill a drop of whiskey. "Excellent stop!"

"But I crashed," said Wil. The drain lessened now that they weren't moving, but it lingered.

"Are you hurt?"

Wil shook his head, closing his eyes at the way the world continued to spin.

"Well then, it's fine! Anything you can walk away from, right?" Thomas elbowed him in the side. "But we should get this back to the workshop before we damage it. I can justify *some* wear and tear, but . . ."

Wil motioned to the steering wheel. "You want to take us back? I think the whiskey's catching up with me." It had caught up with him half an hour ago. He was comfortably drunk, right at the point where his last remnants of reason urged restraint.

"Nah. You're doing a fine enough job. Besides, I've been drinking more than you." To demonstrate his point, Thomas took another pull, wincing at the smoky burn. "Bring us back there, and I'll show you where I work."

When he got the car, Thomas had snuck off to the workshop alone and come back with it. That had been after raiding the cellar for some alcohol and the kitchen for snacks. Some of those snacks littered the floor, but if Thomas wasn't worried, Wil wasn't worried.

"Alright. How do I reverse again? Right, right," he said, remembering right as his new friend opened his mouth. Wil focused and let his instincts guide him. Combustion cars were notoriously fickle and hard to control, but this beautiful machine felt like it was made for him. It reacted to his every touch, and his connection to magic guided him.

They pulled back over the water slowly, then turned around, and Wil brought them back to land. Thomas flicked the switch back to off, and Wil let out a pleased sigh as the drain lessened. He had more than enough juice left to bring them back. He went more carefully this time, now hyperfixated on caution.

"What's it like working with Ferrovani?"

Thomas sighed. "Well, it involves a lot of people asking what it's like working with him. That part gets old sometimes."

"Sorry," said Wil.

"No no, it's fine." Thomas smiled ruefully. "I understand. He's a once-in-a-generation genius, and I'm just on his team. His name will be remembered forever, and I might be lucky enough to be a footnote."

"Is that what you want most?" Wil prodded. "Fame?"

Thomas took a long, deep breath. "Well, if you put a gun against my head and told me to choose, I'd probably pick fame, yeah. I make plenty of money, so I want . . . *need* recognition. What about you, Wil? If you had to choose between fame and money?"

Wil didn't have to think about it. "Not fame, but recognition. Everyone wants to be the next person to change the world. I don't want that necessarily."

"Easy for you to say," Thomas snickered, "having already changed the world and all."

"*Possibly* changed the world," Wil corrected. "Still have to wait to see how that shakes out. But I want to be known for the good I did for others. More than that, I want to do the right work that gets me recognition. It's not about being owed recognition, it's about earning it."

Silence reigned for the next minute. Wil didn't push and instead gathered all his focus to drive at a leisurely pace back to the manor. They passed by the uneven, jagged ruts his outbound drive had left in the snow earlier. Thomas spoke when the workshop came into sight.

"You can't be that saccharine, can you? No offense."

"None taken, and I can. I'm a simple guy, and I want simple things." Wil parked unevenly in one of the spots in front of the workshop. "I want my family and friends to be taken care of, and to live a calm, peaceful life, doing things I enjoy. Like you said, money is hardly a concern anymore, so why not focus on what really matters to me?"

"And what do you enjoy, then? What would you spend all your time doing if you had the option?"

Wil expected the same disbelief or judgment he usually got, but Thomas seemed genuinely curious. After recovering from the battle with Hugo and spending a few days here, Wil had had plenty of time to think about that exact question. It didn't take long to find an answer.

"If I could, I'd help the fae settle in on Skalet Peak and the forest and make sure things go smoothly there. I'd spend more time with my girlfriend and best friend. I'd focus on our business, and helping out anyone who needs it. Winter's the time of year older folks need heating spells laid over their homes or someone to help clean up for spring. I'd work on my craft, sharpen my claws, and see what I could do."

"Does that include leylines?" Thomas asked, grinning shamelessly.

Wil shook his head with a smile. "It might. I'm surprised it took you this long to bring it up again."

"Well, of course." Thomas took another drink of whiskey. He winced, then fumbled for the lid and screwed it back on. "I had to get you drunk and vulnerable first. Did it work?"

"Almost," Wil admitted. "I still can't talk about it yet. Hope that's not too disappointing."

Thomas laughed. "Not at all. There's plenty of time to wear you down. One way or another, I'll divine your secrets!"

They laughed together, and Wil thought about opening up, when he felt a familiar presence coming up. He had just enough time to avoid being startled when Isom landed on the hood of the car. Thomas jerked violently, gathering power. Wil put a hand on his arm and shook his head.

"It's okay," he said, eyeing the wampus cat. The jerk had dented the metal of the hood, and sat crouched, one eye glaring balefully at Thomas. "He's with me."

"Gods," Thomas groaned, clutching his chest. "That's a hell of a pet. Is he housebroken?"

Even from this side of the glass, Wil could hear and feel Isom's growl. A second later, his voice popped into Wil's head.

Do not trust this man. Isom's tail flicked behind him. *He's a predator.*

Wil opened the door a crack. "What are you talking about?" he said out loud. "*You're* a predator. Should I not trust you?"

"What's going on?" Thomas asked, alarmed.

Wil waved him off. "Mental connection. Long story involving Hugo's death. Ask me again later. Well? You're making a scene."

True enough, a few wizards had come out of the workshop to watch the wampus cat and the battered prototype car. Isom's ears flattened against his skull.

Enter his mind if you don't believe me. Take a peek, it's all there. He wants something from you.

"I'm not entering his mind!" Will said, perhaps too loudly.

"Um," Thomas started. He had one hand on the door but looked too frozen to risk leaving. "Maybe I should go. You two clearly have something to talk about. Am I safe to step out?"

Wil glowered at the wampus cat. "He won't hurt you. And you're right: he and I need to have a chat."

Thomas carefully stepped out on unsteady legs. He held the bottle of whiskey in one hand and the open door with another. "Tomorrow, after a long day sleeping in and recovering, I can show you around the workshop? That is, if your cat doesn't mind."

The tone was teasing, but it had an edge. Isom tended to bring that out in people. "Yeah, of course," said Wil. He got out as well. He pointed at the spot on the ground next to him and Isom got down, leaning against Wil. He sensed annoyance but also affection from the cat. "Tomorrow, then."

"Tomorrow. Night, Wil! Night, cat." Thomas saluted them with two fingers and wobbled his way into the workshop. Wil hoped he wouldn't try to fiddle with anything dangerous while drunk.

"C'mon, we're going inside," said Wil. "And then we'll have a long talk about not scaring off my friends."

Isom hissed. "Don't say I didn't try to warn you, Wizard." He padded off to the manor, leaving Wil behind.

With one last look at the workshop, Wil followed after him, thinking of his new friend. Of course Thomas was a predator. Most wizards were, and he made no bones about the fact that he wanted information. That didn't mean he didn't also want to be his friend.

CHAPTER 10

Bullworth

Chinis came for Wil the next day, waking him. The banging on the door echoed the throbbing in his head. Wil fell out of bed and half crawled his way to the door, opening it a crack. The mage's sleepy expression turned to amusement.

"Damn, McKenzie, you got any blood left in your alcohol system? Heard that Marlowe created an endless bottle and you wanted to prove him wrong?"

"Ha, ha, ha, also ha," Wil said, hanging on to the door for support. The inside of his mouth was a furry desert, and the lingering taste of burning and regret made him want to rinse his mouth out. "After damned near a week of being confined here, I finally had a little fun."

"Picked a hell of a night to do it," said Chinis, turning somber. "I'm here to escort you to the Ambrose Estate."

If anything could cut through the hangover, it was that. "I need a shower first."

"Yes," said Chinis. "You do. And also a cup of coffee and something greasy. Best hurry, though. You don't want to be late for this."

Although his tone was his usual drawl, Wil took his friend seriously. "Gimme fifteen minutes and I'll be ready."

With the water freezing cold to help sober him up, Wil furiously scrubbed everything twice, trying to keep his head on straight. Being summoned to the Ambrose Estate was either a good sign or a terrible one. Visions of being disappeared to the Bureau of Magical Investigation's Junk Drawer site, as Hugo had threatened, danced in his head. He shut off the water and dried off quickly.

He had enough sense to pick one of the nicer suits provided by the manor and checked himself in the mirror. He looked sickly and nervous, not at all a powerful young wizard worth this kind of trouble. A bang on the door shook him from his thoughts.

"Coming!"

The Ambrose Estate was another massive plot of land on the outskirts of Cloverton. Right when the city let out to the north, the home of Calipan's presidents sprawled out over enough ground to be its own neighborhood. Wrought-iron fences kept the public off the largest, most well-kept lawn Wil had ever seen. While there was snow on the house itself, the grounds themselves were a sea of green. All the snow had been carefully deposited in key areas, setting the stage for an entire village of ice sculptures.

"Have you ever been here before?" Wil asked with his face pressed against the window. Despite his nervousness, the place was as beautiful as Marlowe Manor in its own way.

"Oh, sure," said Chinis, not taking his eyes off the road. "I took the tour with my family after I graduated. But I haven't seen the big man himself, if that's what you're asking."

He drove up to a cul-de-sac where he then pulled over. The two of them got out and looked up the steps. The front doors loomed ominously over them, flanked by two armed guards. A well-dressed man with his hair slicked back met them.

"You are Master McKenzie, then?" He asked, looking Wil up and down. Without waiting for a response, he continued, "There are some ground rules you will need to follow before you're allowed entrance. Refusal to abide by these rules will result in your immediate expulsion from the grounds. Are you with me so far?"

"Um," said Wil.

"Excellent. You will not use magic of any kind around the president. If you do, his bodyguards will vaporize you."

"Okay, no magic, got it," said Wil, honestly glad for the anti-magic zone around parts of the capital. No wizard liked being shackled, but the difficulty made it easier to remember.

"Do not mistake anything the president says as an endorsement or friendship," the man went on. "Do not think to lecture or threaten the president for any reason. His bodyguards—"

"Will vaporize him?" Chinis supplied.

Wil snickered, but the man's sharp face twisted into a severe scowl.

"Don't say I didn't warn you," he said, shrugging. "Follow me." The man walked up the steps, and Wil scrambled to catch up.

The guards opened the doors, and they entered into a massive foyer with twin spiral staircases leading to a third and fourth story. Wil's guide ignored them and took a right, leading Wil past a series of austere and important-looking rooms. Another turn took them to an open park in the center of the house, where the president and his guests sat around, smoking cigars and drinking tumblers of amber liquid.

More importantly, Syl was among them. "Wil!" He called, setting down his drink and charging the wizard. Wil had barely enough time to throw his arms open and accept being hugged and picked up by the much stronger goatman.

"Syl . . . you're . . . okay!" Wil managed to squeak out between squeezes. He slapped Syl on the back, first to be friendly, then to signal his lack of air.

"Of course I'm okay," said Syl as he set Wil down. "I've spent the last few days drinking and playing games with your president. Fun guy!"

Wil blinked. It was then he saw President Bullworth coming up from behind, a drink in his left hand. The president was a fairly short, stocky man with salt-and-pepper hair and a square jaw. He didn't look small so much as what would happen if you took a burly man and made him compact. He came up and thrust his hand aggressively at a gaping Wil.

"Wilbur McKenzie, I presume!" Bullworth had a deep, boisterous voice with an accent placing him from the southeast. "Your friend Syl here's been telling me all about you. Pleasure to meet you, young man. I understand that you're to be commended. Or maybe executed." He let out a carefree guffaw.

Not far behind him was a pair of bodyguards wearing enchanted, tinted goggles, wands, and even guns. If Wil had to guess, they were the ones who would vaporize him should he cast a spell or act threatening. He took the president's hand and let his arm be shook ragged.

"It's an honor, sir. And I'd prefer the commendation if it's all the same to you." He flashed a weak smile, praying it came across as charming instead of scared.

He needn't have worried. Bullworth laughed with the same full-bellied gusto and released Wil's hand only to slap him on the shoulder. "Such cheek! I can tell we're going to be fast friends."

Between his nervousness and the lingering ghost of the hangover, Wil didn't enjoy the president's enthusiasm nearly as much as he might have. "That'd be nice, sir. Being honest, I got in over my head and did my best." That was the image he needed, right?

"Nonsense," Syl bleated. "Wil's just being hard on himself, like usual. He handled diplomacy like a champ. I can say with full fae honesty that I don't think any other human could've handled the situation as well as he did." He slapped Wil's other shoulder.

"You'll have to tell me all about it!" Bullworth threw an arm around Wil's increasingly sore back and led him to where the president relaxed, an entourage of workers and security orbiting him as they went.

The park was something out of Wil's dreams. It provided an easy way to move around to the opposite side of the estate and lent a touch of nature where they lived, a place to relax and catch your breath. At least, Wil presumed, when the president wasn't around.

In the span of one minute, Wil found himself sitting down in an opulent rocking chair next to the leader of Calipan, expensive and classy drink in hand, while the president talked his ear off.

"It's not any real secret our military's stretched thin," he said. "We've got a couple promising classes of recruits, but most of our men are cycling in and out on three different fronts. The last thing we needed was a fourth potential party to be at war with. And without your haste and vigor, I never would've met this charming son of a goat!"

Syl bleated theatrically, and the two dissolved into laughter and pointed at each other. "Results are what matter, right, Barry? Wil made things happen. It's silly there's even a question of his loyalty or intentions. He got the job done and everything's fine—what else matters?"

President Bullworth's laughter died down. "Well," he said, rolling his eyes like a slighted teenager, "*some* people are worried. Now me, results are what I care about, but killing a fellow wizard and making those kinds of major decisions without checking in?" He clicked his tongue.

"It was the only thing I could think of to defuse the situation," Wil said. Somehow, his nervousness disappeared. The experience of meeting the president and discovering he acted like an overly enthusiastic uncle was surreal enough to make him take a drink. "Mage Jefferson had it coming."

"It's true," said Syl. "At the first sign of a prank gone wrong, he tried to start a war. If Jefferson was alive, I wouldn't be."

"That's why I'll give you a medal or something," Bullworth said with a wave of his hand. "You did good, but you could be doing better. That's why I asked you here today. Is it true you have new information about those . . . what do you call them again?"

"Leylines, sir," one of his wizard guards supplied.

"Leylines, that's it! You holding out on us, son?" Bullworth's friendliness faded as he drew back.

"Not intentionally, Mr. President," said Wil, taking another drink. It gave him an extra second to think. "I don't have complete information. If I were to give bad information, it could set us back or cost lives. I'm willing to share what I learn when I learn more. I need to experiment first."

It seemed insane, telling one of the most important men in the world no. Wil understood then that they were going to bring the pressure down on him until he cracked. How long could he say no before he gave in? What would it end up costing him?

"Huh." Bullworth took a sip of his drink. His eyes remained on Wil's face, searching him for any weakness. "See, that's a reasonable answer. And I like to think I'm a reasonable man. What about you?"

"I try to be," said Wil, stomach dropping.

"Then it stands to reason that my best men, with all of the resources of the country at their disposal . . . Well, don't you think they could accomplish more than one brave, sharp wizard?"

Syl tried to change the subject. "With the amount your people will learn from us in the coming years, you'll have plenty to study. You're going to have such an easier time with portals."

"And that's fine," said Bullworth, voice now lower, colder. "But next year I'm up for re-election. I've taken some beatings over the past few years. All in service to our great country, but I've worked hard and suffered for the glory of Calipan. And in spite of that, I have many enemies nipping at my heels, looking for anything to take me out.

"I need wins *now*. And if I understand what those bookworms tell me, this could be the greatest win for our country since driving out Ilianto's settlers and taking our rightful place as masters of the continent. More than that, I want you to think about something, Wilbur McKenzie. What do you owe your country? I've broken my back for my people and fight every day to make a better world for us all. What else are you willing to do for your fellow citizens?"

So it came right back to this, from Mayor Sinclair's petty threats and demands of bribes all the way up to the president. Wil knew he shouldn't have been surprised, and yet he was. The appeal to his desire to help others threw him for a loop. It made him pause and consider his reasons for holding back.

The main answer was the fae. If Cloverton knew how to change leylines, then there would be no way for the fae to fuel their pocket world in secret. Wil had already exposed them and made the boundaries weaken. Who knew what kind of destruction or chaos could be unleashed if Calipan stopped playing nice.

The other was Calipan itself. The greatest advancements in science had all come from combat, disease, and death. Syl hadn't been wrong when he accused Calipan of existing primarily for war. The idea of them using Wil's discovery to hurt others . . . If anything could keep him from cracking, that would be it.

But that wouldn't be an acceptable answer to the president, who even now stared him down expectantly. No one believed Wil when his reasons were good intentions and good faith. So he thought of his friend Chinis and the argument they'd had in the Magical Madhouse. Wil put on a confident smile he didn't feel.

"Well, everything you said is reasonable. I do live to help my fellow citizens and our country. But as a reasonable man, I think you're forgetting something." Wil finished his drink, relishing the burn. It was smoother than what he had at home.

"And what's that?" Bullworth chuckled, but it held no humor.

"If I were to turn it over to your people, then I wouldn't get the credit," said Wil, "or the money that my discovery would bring in. It's in my best interest to discover things on my own and then sell it to Cloverton for a fair price. Isn't that what our country is based on? A man's labor and ideas are his own to profit from."

Bullworth looked like he swallowed something foul. "That is true, but I was told money wasn't something you particularly cared about. Are my sources wrong?"

"Oh no, he doesn't care about money, like, *ever*," Syl said with a laugh.

"Thanks, Syl," Wil sighed. "I don't, but a discovery like this is going to have far-reaching consequences. It's my duty to this country to make sure this knowledge is safe and can be used constructively. It's not a no. It's a not yet."

"Hmph." Bullworth poured himself another splash of whiskey. His eyes bored twin holes into Wil's soul. He still smiled, but it seemed predatory now. Wil found himself wanting to take a peek inside, but he took the threat of vaporization seriously. "Well, you'll have plenty of time to change your mind."

"I will?" Wil didn't like how that sounded.

"You will." Bullworth chuckled again, swirling the ice in his drink. "The thing about investigations like this, they take a while. And with something this important and delicate, I wouldn't expect to go home anytime soon. Take all the time you need, Wilbur. You're not going anywhere. We'll get that information out of you sooner or later."

Four Months Later

Bram Stevenson took off his glasses and rubbed his eyes. It was a bad habit he'd picked up over the last month as life continued to dogpile him. That wasn't to say things were bad. Other than not seeing or hearing from Wil for months, life was actually great. Better than it had ever been, in fact.

After things stabilized, it was Wiseman Brewing that helped keep the peace. Their steady mix of both human and fae customers and the relationships made over time created a lifeline in the community. People clung to it and shared drinks and medicine with their fae neighbors. Business boomed until he had no choice but to expand things. When Wil didn't come home, what else could he do?

More money came in than Bram ever expected to see, and it was on him to keep up the supply of potions and beer. He had employees now to follow his recipe for their drinks, but no one else but him could brew potions. After a long winter full of injuries and a bad case of the cold going around, supplies dwindled to nothing. He'd need to place several orders from different vendors and also arrange to pay his dozen workers.

"Hey, Bram, the Lanes are putting in an order for contraceptives and disinfectants," said Gerald the hobgoblin, shaking Bram from his thoughts. "They're not the only ones. Seems you humans got a case of spring fever."

"Dammit." Bram put his glasses back on. "Tell them we're not able to fill it for another week or two."

"We're running low, aren't we? What's the holdup? Isn't Darlene keeping up her end of things?" Gerald didn't sound accusatory so much as curious. Bram still got annoyed.

"Given her condition, she's due some leeway and patience. I'll go talk to her today and sort things out." Seeing her would ease his mind. Despite working together, it had been three days since Bram and Darlene had gotten a meal together and talked business.

"Right," said the hob, scratching under his drooping jowls. "We're also running low on a related potion. The one for men."

Bram sighed. Spring fever indeed. "I'll brew another batch of that right away. I think we should shut down the pharmacy for today. Is the brewery crowded as well?"

"What do you think?" Gerald snorted. It made his jowls puff up.

"We're running low on beef and bottles," Bram muttered, rubbing his temples again. He stood, his knees protesting loudly. "I'll take care of that as well. Don't be afraid to close early if we run out of anything."

"We're going to need to expand again soon," said Gerald. "We can't keep up with the demand."

Bram nodded and gathered up some papers on his desk. He put them in a folder that he tucked under his arm and left the downstairs office. On second thought, he popped out the back door and took the long way from the repurposed barn where they served beer and snacks. Billy-Ray and Elmer raised bottles in a silent toast. He waved at them and walked away from the bustling business.

The popularity had come as something of a surprise. It seemed absurd, how well they were doing for a new venture and with the controversy of the fae presence. Things weren't perfect now, but it seemed most of the town was tentatively pro fae. The younger half of town flocked to Bram's brewery and the McKenzie place. They even came to see Wil's house, despite him having been gone for months.

That's where Bram headed. Bram's home was on the northeastern side of town, not too far from the border with Gallard Springs. It wasn't generally a long walk to Wil's house, but with the streets so busy, the trip dragged on.

They had tourists now, and people were rushing to be the first to move to Harper Valley before the fae presence settled and trade picked up. The roads often had carts and carriages, and even the occasional car from Manifee City, wizard included. That had been the strangest thing to adjust to: Harper Valley now had multiple wizards.

None of them served the community directly, but they came to study and trade for faricite and fae baubles. One of them had even set up a rival potion-selling business, but Bram was relieved that the demand on their stock had gone down. Things had been nonstop for months now.

With a decent bit of luck, no one stopped Bram on the way there, though two people he didn't recognize stood outside Wil's house, one with a camera. They set the picture up. Bram stood in front of it right as it went off.

"Hey, what's the big idea!" A middle-aged woman snarled at him.

"I could ask the same thing of you!" Bram shot back. "Why are you taking pictures of my friend's house? Get the hell out of here."

"Ain't no law against taking pictures of anything we want," her wiry companion said with a sneer.

Bram raised up to his full height and cracked his knuckles. He smiled. In the past, he'd never have been this assertive, but the tourists were terribly rude and seemed to think the town was theirs.

"On second thought," the wiry man said, looking up, "we should pack up."

"Harold, you coward!"

Harold picked up the camera and walked away, refusing to meet Bram's gaze.

His partner followed after him, chewing him out the entire time. She looked over her shoulder at him one last time before they disappeared down the road.

Bram shook his head. He didn't know how Darlene did it. All the people who came to snoop around drove him nuts. There'd been three break-ins in the past two months. Things were hectic at the brewery, but no one dared trespass. He walked up to the door and reached for the doorknob, when it opened.

"Oh, hi, Bram." Mayor Bob McKenzie stepped out the front, closing the door behind him. "How're you doing today?"

"Tired, stressed, and irritated at the disrespectful new faces." Bram made a face and chuckled.

"I hear you," said Bob. "I'm up to my ass in people trying to suck up to me to speed up permits or property purchases. And that's nothing compared to the vultures trying to snatch up every house they can before folks realize what they can charge for it. Amazing how fast things change, huh?"

"Do you regret winning the race?" Bram had always wanted to ask but had never gotten a chance before then.

"Not at all." Bob let out a short bark of laughter. "Can you imagine how much worse things would be under Sinclair? He'd use this as a chance to get what he could before quitting rich. I'm glad it's me fighting for people. I'm not going to let anyone take advantage of my neighbors if I can help it."

Bram nodded, grateful for his friend's father. "What are you doing here? Checking up on Darlene?"

Bob's smile faded. "Yeah. I'm not sure I like her living here alone, but she insists, and it's not like we can force her to accept a babysitter. Best I can do is post a deputy near here in case anyone else tries to force their way inside. You still have Wil's most valuable books?"

"I sure do," said Bram, grinning like a fool. "It's been a joy going through them all. I may not be able to do much, but I've learned a lot and I think when Wil comes back, he'll be impressed. Any word on him coming back?"

"No," Bob sighed, "not yet. I've sent letter after letter, but almost all of them get ignored. They *finally* responded a couple weeks ago, telling me Wil is fine and that the investigation will be concluded when it's concluded. Basically, 'Stop asking,' but at least they're confirming he's alive and hasn't been sentenced or anything."

It didn't really make Bram feel better, but he supposed it was better than nothing. "I appreciate you asking. Is there anything I can do to make things easier?"

"Get me a few bottles of barley wine?" Bob laughed and patted Bram's shoulder as he headed off. "Come to dinner tomorrow. Bring Darlene if you can. Sharon's going to want to fuss over her and make sure she's okay."

"If I can," Bram chuckled. He turned and went inside without knocking.

Wil had never been too keen on decorating, but Darlene was different. She'd rearranged the living room to be more open and comfortable, better for hosting guests. Wil's office remained almost untouched, though the rarer books and the paperwork for his job were moved. The kitchen was now stocked, and the upstairs had a sitting area for reading in private.

"Darlene?" He called out. "You upstairs?"

"In the kitchen," she shouted back. "I'm coming."

"That's not necessary, I'll come to you, and— Oh."

Darlene waddled into the room, grimacing from the pain in her feet and back. One hand cradled her stomach protectively. As far as Bram was concerned, she carried the weight gracefully, but she was five months along and round.

"I'm pregnant, Bram, not helpless. Not yet." She made her way over to Wil's favorite plush armchair and carefully lowered herself into it. "What's up?"

"A couple of things," said Bram, sitting on the love seat opposite her. He took up the entire thing on his own. "But first, how are you doing? You getting enough rest?"

Darlene rolled her eyes. "I swear to the gods, if people don't stop asking me how I'm doing, I'm going to lose it. I'm not fragile, I'm not lonely, and I'm handling everything fine!"

Bram held up the folder he'd brought with him. "We're almost out of several key ingredients for productions, and I'm told that payday was a day late this last week."

Her expression fell. "Okay," she said with a sigh, "maybe I'm a bit behind. But it's not because I'm pregnant!"

"Then why is it?" Bram asked. "If there's anything I could be doing to help make things easier for you, I want to do it. I don't think you're helpless or weak or anything. I just want to help my friend breathe a little easier."

Darlene ran a hand through her hair. She'd let it grow out and it hung down around her ears, making her look more feminine than she had in the past, and older. "I'm frustrated," she said. "At everything. Nothing's wrong, but nothing's right either. We keep going on and on and doing well, but it isn't right. Not without Wil."

"Yeah," Bram agreed. "Feels like we're doing the same old thing while waiting for him to come back. But in your case, you can only wait so long before things get complicated. Are you mad at him?"

"For being unable to write to me or communicate with me at all?" Darlene laughed. "Of course I'm mad at him. I know it's probably not something he can help, but how can I not be mad? He should've been back by now. Gods, I could use a drink."

"I'm really glad you didn't take me up on my mutual abstinence offer," said Bram. "Not sure I'd be able to go a full year without alcohol. You have the patience and discipline of a saint. But seriously, what can I do for you? Not because you're weak, but because it would make me feel better to help."

Darlene thought about it and nodded. "I'm starving. Buy me dinner for three, and I'll see about filling out those orders tomorrow. We'll make sure people are paid on time this week, with a small bonus for their troubles."

Bram stood up and offered her his hand. "You got it. You thinking steak, burgers, noodles, or are you stuck on the same craving?"

She took his hand and let him pull her to her feet. "I hate how much I've been wanting fae food lately. It's so damned sweet, and it feels like you need to eat forever to get full, but that's what I want to do. Eat until they kick me out."

"Alright, then," he chuckled. "To the embassy. I wonder how many horrified looks we'll get over how much we can put away."

"Wish we had Wil's lost magic carpet instead of walking . . . hell. Wish we had Wil."

"I know," said Bram. "I do too. They can't keep him forever, right?"

Things hadn't been hard without Wil so much as incomplete. It had fallen to Bram to pick up the pieces and keep them going forward. It was something he'd been happy to do, even if he was unsure of himself. He wasn't a wizard, he could only brew potions. But he could help carry Darlene, just as she'd helped carry him.

Together, they'd survive for a little bit longer.

CHAPTER 11

Up in the Air

It had been a while since Wil was under the scrutiny of a master craftsman. Thomas would be the first to admit he was no Ferrovani, but he was still a master of enchanting. Over the last four months, he'd lent his professional expertise to Wil's ongoing project, and now came the time to determine whether Wil had succeeded or not.

Running his hand over the sleek metal exterior, Thomas hummed as he went over the enchantments one by one. Wil thought he had a strong wizard's sense, but it paled in comparison to the enchanter's. He could feel if lines were out of whack, or whether the metals and gem dust used in the construction would interact well. It wasn't stronger, just more refined, and he'd been at it for fifteen minutes.

"Would you say something?" Wil asked, wiping the sweat from his brow. The workshop was always sweltering, and their little corner was tucked in the back. Even with the windows opened, it was sticky. "Tell me what I did wrong. I'm going crazy here!"

Everything drove Wil crazy lately. Month after month of being stuck at Marlowe Manor took its toll. The only times he got out were to meet with Pierce and discuss the investigation, who almost universally told him a date had yet to be set for the hearing. And no, he couldn't communicate with Harper Valley at all. Wil missed home, and the workshop had been the best distraction.

"Well," Thomas said, patting the chassis, "I think that you've come a long way since you got here. Not everything is as streamlined as it could be. It's got your signature style all over it in how things are layered and interact. You're more creative than efficient, but . . ."

"But?"

Thomas grinned. "It'll fly. And it'll be fast and safe. More than likely."

Wil let out a sigh of relief. After over a month of designing and learning more about master-level enchanting, followed by three months of construction and refinement, his newest project was close to finished. Overall, he thought it looked nearly done.

The design had started as a bicycle that could fly, using elements of his carpet and the speeder sled he'd previously made. Further instruction and deliberations changed it into something Wil was proud of. The vehicle was designed after a diving hawk, wings swept back with lightning along its sides. The rider would sit on the back and control it with handles for both hands and feet.

It would be far more complex than driving a car and needed a few more tests, but this wasn't something made for mass production. This was Wil's pride and joy, the best thing he had to show for a third of a year stolen from him.

"I guess we better let people know it's time for another test, huh?" Wil lifted it and turned it to face the door that opened out to the grounds.

"Yep!" Thomas smiled wickedly. "Do me a favor and don't fall off. I have a lot of money riding on it being a success."

"Betting on something you have direct input on is unethical, don't you think?" Wil hit the button on the wall, and the door rose, showing the perfectly manicured lawn.

"What does ethics have to do with a decent payday?" Thomas laughed and went out to the rest of the workshop, where plenty of people waited on them.

After the first month with only Thomas as his friend, others had taken a chance to talk to him. Wil could honestly say he was outclassed by most of them in terms of skill or intelligence. But time among the magical elite gave them room to appreciate his strengths and friendliness. At this point, over a dozen of the cream of the crop had wagers on whether his Thunderhawk would crash and burn or not.

Isom met him on the lawn, licking his chops. After several incidents involving scared maids and serving staff, Isom was allowed to hunt in the woods. He went out a few times a week and indulged himself. Whatever he'd eaten that day, Isom hadn't been clean about it.

"It was a deer. A sweet little doe, who fought so her daughter could run away." Isom purred and stretched. "I toyed with her and—"

"Glad you had fun," said Wil. It was uncomfortable sometimes, how passionate and detailed Isom could be about his love of dismembering his meals. "You're not too full for a race, are you?"

Isom's eye sparked with interest. "You'll lose again, Wizard. Like you always do."

"We'll see, won't we?"

It took Thomas about twenty minutes to gather all the people who'd wanted to attend. A little under twenty wizards and mages came out on the lawn outside the workshop to watch. Wil sat on the Thunderhawk, legs splayed on either side to balance it. It had wheels on the bottom, but that's where the resemblance to a bike ended.

"What did you bet on, exactly?" Wil asked Thomas as he strapped his helmet on. "Perhaps I can make it happen."

"No way." Thomas feigned surprise. "Mr. Ethics talking about cheating at gambling? I'm in. Or at least, I would be if I wagered on anything rare. I bet that it would exceed all expectations and be a complete success. So be careful, don't crash, and if you can circle the grounds in under a minute, I'll . . . Well, I'll not only split the prize with you, but I'll help you with the patent."

"Patent?" Wil wrinkled his nose. "This is for me. This is going to be way too dangerous to let anyone have it."

"Not just anyone." Thomas held up a finger. "The military could use reconnaissance vehicles that are all-terrain. This would do nicely for highly mobile messengers. No violence, just helping out."

Wil shot him a look.

Thomas waved him off. "We'll discuss it later. I swear, you gotta start looking after yourself. The important thing is to take it easy and try to break the last flying machine speed record if it's not too much trouble."

"Tom," Wil warned before shaking his head. There was no discouraging him. "I'll do my best. No pressure, right?"

Thomas patted him and ran off to join the other spectators. Rand Sandoval was even there, watching with interest while he sucked on a fizzy drink through a straw. Most of the people were orbiting him, curious about his take on the reckless Mad McKenzie, as some had taken to calling him.

Isom sat a few feet away, four of his legs on the ground while the front two scratched behind his ears. "They don't care if you succeed or fail," he said. "They want something exciting."

"I know," said Wil. "So you ready to give them a show?"

The wampus cat puffed up importantly. "My audience awaits." After the initial shock, he'd proved to be surprisingly popular with some of the braver wizards. He enjoyed many succulent treats in exchange for conversation. The predator was starting to get spoiled.

"Then when you see me move, give me something to chase."

"I don't like being prey," Isom said haughtily.

"But you do love beef," Wil returned. "The better the show, the more you eat." Then he strapped on some goggles and leaned forward in the seat, resting on one leg as he took the handles in his hands. He breathed in and out and extended his senses for the enchantments, lying dormant until the circuits were completed and brought to life. Wil turned a key, completing the activation rune.

The Thunderhawk hummed to life, rising a foot off the ground. So far, so good. Wil made sure he was well balanced. Every little shift of his body or wrists made it list from side to side, ready to move. It wanted to move, and every second was like being poised at the height of a jump, ready to plummet.

That was the secret to this device, and what set it apart from the flying carpet. The Thunderhawk didn't fly using magic. It didn't actually fly at all. Wil's genius idea had been to propel it with earth magic. Using the magnetic core of the earth, he made himself perpetually fall forward, pushing against the planet.

"Here we go," Wil whispered. He twisted the handles and leaned in, and the Thunderhawk shot forward. Isom took off beside him, six legs powering him ahead of the new craft. The wind tore at Wil's clothes as he floated two feet off the ground now, moving as fast as a galloping horse.

Faster and faster he went until Isom trailed behind. The wampus cat leaped into the air and teleported forward, falling behind once more until he teleported again. Isom zigged in and out of Wil's way as the wizard laughed. The twist in his stomach never went away, and neither did the joy.

They cut across fields of emerald green, right by one of the flower gardens. Petals swirled in their wake, torn from the plants as he passed. Wil screamed as he went faster than the fastest train. The lake came into view. He twisted the handles and turned, body tilting sideways but clinging to the seat as he flew over the water, rending a turbulent line in the surface. He spun around and followed the boundaries of the property.

So many times Wil had come to the border and debated stepping over the lines, just to see what would happen. Would alarms suddenly scream? Would someone come after him immediately? Now here he was on a working vehicle he knew went fast over all terrain and would have enough power to take him across the continent.

He thought of Bram and how terrified he'd be to even think of riding the Thunderhawk. He'd be as excited as Wil for the construction and the work involved, but he'd never, ever fly it. Darlene would, but she would cling to him and scream the entire time, loving every second of it. His heart lurched.

Months with no word, no way to tell them he was okay. No way to check on them or his parents or anyone. The edges of the boundary whooshed by him, and the next corner came into view.

It would be so easy. He had enough strength and usefulness that he could likely make his way home, but they'd never stop hunting him. It wasn't worth it. Wil swallowed and turned around, pulling back and slowing down as he reached the assembled wizards.

He drifted to a stop in front of Rand, stepping off the Thunderhawk and kicking out the stop to keep it upright. Isom appeared into view a few seconds later, crashing along the ground and panting heavily.

You left me! he cried at Wil as he fought to gain his breath. He seemed happy enough, though, flopping down next to Wil.

Thomas ran up to him, laughing and grabbing him in a one-armed hug. "You did it, McKenzie! Well, almost. You were out there for like two minutes."

Wil thought of the border and the call to go home. He smiled and bowed to some of the applause and sharp whistles sent his way.

"Let's do it again, then. Double or nothing, under a minute."

CHAPTER 12

Words of Wisdom

The second time on the Thunderhawk, Wil pushed himself. Now that he had a feel for it, the Thunderhawk responded almost by thought. The sensation of holding on for dear life stopped being scary and became thrilling. Cutting across the lake practically turned him sideways before the baked-in stabilizing spell righted him. It was the only hiccup before he returned at fifty-three seconds to screams and applause.

"Just like that, Mad McKenzie casually breaks a record. Nothing to it." Thomas clapped obnoxiously, playing the crowd like a fiddle. "Is there anything in the world he can't do? Oh yeah. Be cool."

Wil dismounted, grinning in the face of laughter and jeers. He gave a mock bow and said, "There is one thing I can't do. Go home, apparently!"

He laughed, and everyone else did so, hesitantly.

"If I had to be stuck anywhere, I'm glad it's here," said Wil. "Getting to know some of you and work on this has been a dream come true."

"How much did that thing cost to make?" Rand Sandoval called out, taking another sip through his straw. He had slicked back jet-black hair and wore small spectacles on a friendly but unassuming face. Looking at him, no one would expect him to be one of the top wizards in the country.

"About forty thousand zynce," said Wil. "If I had to pay for the materials on my own, more like sixty thousand."

Thomas jumped in. "Let's call it forty. We wasted some material on early prototypes, and now you know what works and what doesn't. Forty thousand to produce. Do I detect a desire to invest, Mr. Sandoval?"

Rand raised his cup. "I don't know about investing, but I wouldn't say no to having one of my own. That looks fun, and I'd be so interested to look at how you made it."

Despite Wil's lack of interest in business, Rand appreciating his work made him want to squeal. He did his best to play it cool, shrugging and taking an offered drink from the manor staff. Spiked lemonade was perfect on a day like this.

"It's nothing you couldn't have done," said Wil. "We actually used a lot of your theory on alloys to make it happen. It took a particular mix to have the proper push against the ground while still being light and maneuverable. I wouldn't have thought of it."

"So how much to buy one off you?" Rand asked with a shameless grin. "I have my own flying devices, but none so exciting."

"One hundred twenty thousand seems a fair price, right?" Thomas interjected. He moved up to Wil and threw an arm around his shoulders. "Between materials, labor, and how rare they are. Wil and I are the only ones who know how to make it exactly like this, and this one's his baby."

"Tom, I'm not sure I'm going to have the time to—" Wil started.

"Sold!" Rand cried, thrusting a finger into the air. "In the meantime . . . can I ride it?"

After a bunch of warnings and instructions on how it worked, Wil and Thomas stood by as Rand climbed on and got moving. Very slowly. He went around in circles, whooping and screaming after he nearly fell off at one point. The rest of the assembled wizards cheered him on, while a couple knelt on the ground, petting a tolerant Isom, who half-heartedly swiped at them on occasion.

"I appreciate all your help," Wil said to Thomas, drinking more of his lemonade.

"There's a *but* coming, right?" Thomas chuckled.

"Yes. *But,* I am not sure I want to make things for a living. My job is serving my community and helping out with problems. It's not building things for the military and rich people." Wil turned to him. "Don't get me wrong, I don't think anything's wrong with that, it's just not me."

"It could be," said Thomas. "Not trying to force you to do anything, just expanding your horizons. You've got a lot of potential, and I feel like you try to hold yourself back for reasons others might uncharitably call silly."

"Others, but not you, obviously."

Thomas grinned. "I'm only saying, it doesn't hurt to explore your options and to take care of yourself. You had the money to build this without my help, but you could make this in two months next time. That's eighty thousand zynce profit split for an average of forty thousand a month. Which is like four times as much as you make, right?"

"Yes, that *is* great money," said Wil. "Not sure what point you're trying to make. That's a lot of money for doing something I want to do for fun and personal enrichment."

"That's what the patent is for," Thomas insisted. "Do it once, prove that it can be done and you know how. Show the way for others, and you gain a little trickle coming in for every major thing you do. Eventually, you have the money, the power, the connections to do anything you want. You'll have big name recognition, and with that comes influence.

"That's what I'm offering you, McKenzie. Influence. Wouldn't that have made your recent troubles so much easier?"

Wil paused. Time in the workshop and library had done a lot to distract him, but four months was a lot of time to ruminate. He had more than enough time to go over his actions and what he could've done differently or better had circumstances been different.

"It wouldn't have hurt," Wil admitted. "I thought Harper Valley would be fine if I let them see for themselves that the fae could be good allies and friends."

"Small towns are notorious for being slow to accept change. Trust me, I know. If you had more influence or used what you had more aggressively, things might've been smoother."

Thomas smiled the teasing way he did when he spotted weakness he intended to exploit. "Not saying you have to become a businessman. Just that you have to consider using everything at your disposal to get what you want. Influence lets you do it without violence."

Wil sighed. "And what do you get out of this? I'm still not giving up the secret to leylines."

"Wil, I'm hurt. Me? Ulterior motives?" Thomas shook his head sadly. He made it a whole three seconds before cracking. "I help you, you help me in the future. If not with that, then with something else. We make connections that could be useful later, and we enjoy ourselves while doing it. Unless you're trying to tell me you haven't enjoyed working with me. But then you'd be a liar."

"Yeah, yeah," Wil said with a chuckle. "It's been nice having a friend here. But I know you want more than that."

"I want to be on the front lines of discovery and change," said Thomas. "And I can see you're a man to be watched. Besides, you're such a sap I could basically ask anything else of you and you'd give it."

"You're not wrong. Hey, he's coming back." Wil pointed out to where Rand wobbled on the Thunderhawk.

He never went faster than about fifteen miles per hour and was unsteady on his legs when he got off. He staggered forward, fists thrust in the air as he cheered, and the others swarmed him. A few eyed the Thunderhawk, but no one was drunk enough to take it without permission.

"Think I should make a safer version for him if I do make one?" Wil asked. "One that doesn't go as fast and has more crash protections."

"Oh, definitely," said Thomas. "Him using one is the best advertisement. Everyone will want one, and then you can hire some workers who all build one part of it and—"

"Tom," Wil groaned.

Thomas held his hands up. "I'll wear you down."

They started off in the direction of the rest of the crowd until Wil saw Maddy running across the lawn their way. He stopped, and Thomas stopped a few seconds later.

"Master McKenzie!" Maddy called, waving an envelope in the air. "This message came for you, and I'm told it's urgent!" She closed the remaining distance and handed the message over.

Wil took it silently and ripped it open. His eyes went line by line. The message was short, simple, and threatened to knock him on his ass. He took a deep breath and read it again.

"Bad news?" Thomas asked after a minute.

"Kind of," said Wil. "Good news, bad news situation. The good news is the date of my hearing has been set. The bad news is that it's in two days. Tomorrow I'm to go into town to meet with Pierce one more time so he can finish preparing me, and then it's time to face the music."

"It's been wonderful having you here, Master McKenzie!" Maddy chirped obliviously.

Thomas swore under his breath. "They're really doing everything they can to put pressure on you, aren't they?"

"Seems that way," said Wil, folding the letter and shoving it in his back pocket. "I'll be okay. I made some mistakes, but everything I did was for the good of Calipan. And last I checked, we're still not at war with Faerie and have even had more visitors from Oakheart Spiral. That's got to work in my favor."

"You know what doesn't?" Thomas elbowed him. "Holding out on some critical, world-changing information. Give them what they want, and they'll let you go. I guarantee it. But," he continued, seeing the look on Wil's face, "I know why you don't want to. So how about we ditch this crowd and see what else you can offer them as a bribe?"

Wil hated how much sense Thomas made. If it came down to it, if it was keep this secret or die . . . Well, Wil was awfully attached to his life. There had to be a way for him to protect his fae friends and appease Cloverton.

"I appreciate it, Tom," said Wil. "I'm sure we'll think of something. Even if I have to sell the Thunderhawk to the military."

"Now you're thinking!" Thomas put his arm around Wil's shoulders, and together they went to grab the Thunderhawk and put it away. For better or worse, Wil wouldn't be stuck in Marlowe Manor much longer.

CHAPTER 13

The Tribunal

The past four months had dragged on, but not anymore. Now that Wil had a light at the end of the tunnel, the remaining time slipped away in the blink of an eye. The meeting with Pierce had been brief, and mostly consisted of Wil answering questions again. Questions they'd no doubt ask during the tribunal itself.

That night, he thought he'd be unable to sleep, but he closed his eyes, and after what felt like five minutes, he was woken for the day. Wil dressed in the best suit the closet had and grabbed breakfast. He spent some time with Isom, feeding him before their arrival in court. To his surprise, the wampus cat's testimony would be heard as well.

"Do not threaten anyone," said Wil. "Not even the joking threats that make people laugh. They will hurt us both."

Isom was too focused on his food to answer, but he got the impression of impatience and annoyance through their mental link. It was always closest when they were together, but Wil preferred to speak.

"I'm serious. Answer their questions and make sure that everyone knows Mage Jefferson was out of control and that he violated your person and nearly killed you."

That got Isom's attention. After that, he listened closely, and then breakfast was over and Chinis drove them over to the Cloverton Grand Court.

"This is it, huh?" Chinis asked. He didn't seem too fussed about being stuck in Cloverton for months. "Gonna miss that easy pay and seeing what you've been working on. If they decide to give you the axe, can I have your Thunderhawk?"

The ensuing good-natured bickering helped distract Wil until they pulled up to the courthouse steps. Chinis stopped the car and looked at Isom in the back seat. "Good luck, McKenzie. I'd be real sad if they punished you."

"Me too, man."

Isom kept close to Wil as they climbed the steps. The small crowd waiting parted for them. Largely, Wil believed, because of the wampus cat's near permanent toothy sneer. Things were fine until they made it to security.

"Any weapons or . . . What the hell is that?" A security guard looked at Isom with horror. "Why isn't it on a leash?"

"Try and leash me," said Isom, before Wil nudged him. "Ahem. I mean, I am here to testify in court."

The guards looked at each other. "I gotta check on this," the first guard said. "In the meantime, any weapons, magical instruments, narcotics, or any contraband you shouldn't have?"

Five minutes later they were through, and Pierce led them down wide, open halls to an office right off their courtroom. Between the dim lighting, the brownish colors, and the magic repression field, Wil was claustrophobic and anxious before they'd even begun. Pierce poured him a glass of water.

"Relax. The more nervous you look, the worse it's going to be," the old man said, sitting behind the desk. He went through his briefcase and brought out his notes. "Keep your answers as short as possible and don't let anyone bait you. Answer, do your best to sound dumb but helpful, and do *not* be baited."

"Okay," said Wil. "I can do that."

"Can *he?*" Pierce pointed at Isom.

Isom sat up straight. His mouth twitched, but he said nothing. Wil projected gratitude at him for the effort.

"I guess it'll have to do," said Pierce, rubbing his temples. "But there's one more thing."

Wil didn't need to hear that. "What?" he asked, more ready to panic than he would've liked.

"The president is here and will be watching over the proceedings." Pierce pursed his lips. "That means that the tribunal might be a little more . . . heated than we were expecting."

"Can he affect the proceedings at all?" Wil asked, alarmed. After that one night drinking and chatting, Bullworth had all but told Wil that he'd crack sooner or later and give them what they wanted. Would he make things worse on Wil?

"Officially? No. Unofficially? He has allies and enemies on the board. I don't know what game he's playing, but if he looks like he's supporting you, it'll divide people. Either way, you'll have to convince at least four people to vote in your favor."

A knock at the door made Wil's heart jump. A head peeked in long enough to say, "They're ready for you now."

"Well," said Pierce. "Are you ready?"

"Nope." Wil downed the rest of the water and stood. "But what choice do I have?"

The first thing Wil noticed was how incredibly full the courtroom was. The head table had seven people who would judge his actions and make a ruling on him. Since he was a wizard, two grandmasters and two mages sat in judgment. He recognized Jim Rance by sight, but the other three he knew by name alone. Rance, at least, wasn't one known for his bloodthirst.

Representing the nonmagical side of things were General Haken of the Calipan army, Minister of Foreign Affairs Allan Fengar, and Speaker of Congress Katherine Keene. They sat in an alternating pattern with the wizards spread out, and Keene sat in the middle. She'd be the one running the show.

Wil, Isom, and Pierce passed by a very full audience. Most were unfamiliar, but he recognized a few faces. Thomas had come to support him, and he gave Wil a quick wave before he went past the wooden gate. Isom sat upright on the floor beside him, sniffing the room and occasionally wincing at the psychic noise. Wil put a hand on the back of his neck to reassure him.

"Wilbur McKenzie?" Keene asked. At his nod, she motioned for him to sit. "You are here today on suspicion of treason, murder, and gross negligence. Over the past several months, our investigators have been hard at work sifting through hundreds of eyewitness accounts. Today we'll take your statement, and from there the final answer of what happened in Harper Valley will be determined. Do you or your defense have any preliminary statements before we begin?"

Pierce stood up. Despite being old and reserved, his voice carried well in the courtroom. "Over the course of today, you will discover that my client, *Master Wizard* Wilbur McKenzie, is innocent of these spurious claims. Wil's actions are those of a hero. Someone who wants the best for everyone, who acts first when lives are on the line."

"Yes," said Minister Fengar, "let's start with that. When you made your ill-advised trip to Faerie, did you not discover that the hostages were in no danger?"

"Sort of," said Wil. "It's a little more compl—"

"Yes or no, Master McKenzie."

It was then Wil knew exactly how this was going to go, and he wanted to be anywhere but in that courtroom. He took a deep breath and said, "Yes, they were safe."

General Haken spoke next. "So you were lured to Faerie under false pretenses?"

Wil opened his mouth to explain, then said, "No."

"Care to elaborate?" Keene's gaze bore holes in him. She wore a cold smile, like she was enjoying watching him squirm.

"As far as we knew, they had been taken and were in danger. It was only later we found out it was part of a fact-finding mission to determine whether to open diplomatic ties with us. To try again for peace after years of war." Wil reached for water and took a sip. That felt like a decent enough answer.

"Even though half of the captured people were children? Does that strike you as the actions of someone who wants peace?" General Haken scoffed, and a murmur went through the courtroom.

"It strikes me as the actions of a people who look human but aren't," said Wil as evenly as possible. "They often look like us, but they're not us. They asked questions and kept them in better quarters than they have in Harper Valley, with food and entertainment on demand. I don't agree with what they did, but I try to understand it and them. That's a hallmark of diplomacy, isn't it?"

Minister Fengar sneered. "Are you calling yourself a diplomat, Master McKenzie? With what experience?" Again, a ripple went through the audience. The minister in particular seemed to be against him.

"Well," said Wil, heat flooding his cheeks. "I did just negotiate a trade deal with our former enemies. Does that not qualify as experience?"

"Master McKenzie," Speaker Keene warned.

Pierce put his hand on Wil's shoulder. "Apologies, Madam Speaker, but I do believe my client's question warrants due consideration. I believe the record shows that out of the four dozen fae we've interviewed over the course of this investigation, they all speak overwhelmingly in favor of Master McKenzie."

"Why should we care whether our enemies praise us?" General Haken demanded.

Jim Rance cleared his throat. So far, the magical side of things had remained quiet. Now the rest of the tribunal looked his way.

"As an expert on the subject," he said, "I can safely say it matters a lot. Out of all the magical beings in the world, the fae were the ones Calipan and others have hurt the most. Through demons and devils, we've had numerous deals, good and bad, and maintained tentatively decent relationships. Elementals are simple and alien, and don't seem to resent when they are called upon to serve for a time.

"But the fae are the only inhuman people we've encountered who are like us, for better or worse. We wiped them out, or so we thought. For them to be willing to consider peace and to praise a human is unusual—it does merit consideration."

Wil nodded his way out of respect and gratitude.

"However," Rance continued, "we can't ignore the collateral damage. I would like to start a little closer to the beginning. I want you to tell us about the storm dragon and the leyline you altered."

Of course. Of course that's how it was going to be. No wonder the president was watching. Wil took a deep breath and tried not to let it affect him. They weren't going to give him much choice, but he could still make them work for it.

"Of course, Grandmaster Rance," Wil said respectfully. "As my previous testimonies have covered, a cursed dragon went across the country, bringing with it a terrible storm. When it arrived at Harper Valley, I . . ."

He'd told the story so many times now. What harm would it be to perform it one more time in front of the tribunal and the assembled audience? Maybe he could win in the court of public opinion.

CHAPTER 14

Capitulation

Wil realized too late that his story was much less impressive without the illusions he usually used to perform it. It didn't help that the tribunal interrupted him constantly to ask questions. Or throw accusations. After the first hour, it became a constant barrage against his battered self-esteem.

"What do you think happened in those two days you lost in Faerie?" Grandmaster Yensin asked, stroking his long beard.

"As far as I know, nothing bad," said Wil. The more he remembered, the more private the recollections became. "It was a bigger party than what humans typically throw, and I was a little occupied."

"How do you know you weren't compromised during that time? The fae are known for their ability to bewitch people!"

Wil swallowed. "No, I assure you, most of my time was spent either performing tricks, drinking, or . . . with my girlfriend, Darlene." A chuckle ran through the room.

The questions kept coming. "What on earth possessed you to gamble your life on a duel with an ogre? Or invite them to our world without any warning or preparations?" He answered them as best he could, but they rolled together until the tribunal started asking pointed questions about Hugo.

"According to your report, you freed his thralls, and they turned on him at your command. When did you come up with this plan?" Speaker Keene demanded. "That is not something one does on a lark. That's premeditated."

Wil looked to Pierce, who nodded. "His death wasn't premeditated, but I figured out how to disrupt his connection with his thralls. I kept that knowledge in mind in case I ever needed it. And then I needed it when he went rogue."

General Haken wasn't having it. "In case you needed to take out your superior. You wanted Mage Jefferson out of the way. You hated losing control of your illegal mission!"

"Hugo was unstable," Wil snapped, guilt warring with frustration. "I didn't want to kill him, but he gave me no choice. He threatened my friends and family." President Bullworth's words echoed in his head. "I should get a medal for preventing my town from being the staging ground for an unnecessary war, and you're seriously trying to frame me as the bad guy? This is a load of shit."

Wil surprised himself, but the lingering heat in his head and his shakiness told him he'd lost it. The spectators gasped, and Speaker Keene slammed her gavel down.

"Master McKenzie," she warned again. "Watch yourself. Am I clear?"

He nodded, anger broiling further, but he knew better than to push his luck.

"I think a short recess is in order," she said. "We'll return in twenty minutes." As one, the tribunal stood up, and the rest of the court followed. They went out a back door, while Pierce gathered his notes and they left, heading back to his office.

"That was foolish, McKenzie," Pierce grumbled. "I told you to not lose your cool. What do you call that?"

"Losing my cool," Wil sighed. "I'm trying. This is so damn exhausting. I'm not so good at sitting and being a punching bag for people who clearly want me pilloried."

"Only three of them want you pilloried," said Isom. "The four quiet ones are focused on how useful you could be. Though that doesn't mean they're happy with you."

Pierce's jaw dropped. "What are you saying?"

"Dammit, Isom, I told you not to read anyone's minds without permission!" Wil rubbed his eyes with a groan. "We'd be in so much trouble if they knew."

"I should say," Pierce said, looking disturbed for the first time since Wil had met him. "Why didn't you tell me your cat can read minds? These are not people who tolerate any slight or violation of their person or privacy. It might already be too late. I . . . I need to step outside and think." He stumbled out of the office.

Wil turned to Isom. "Did any of them detect you in their minds?"

"Detect?" Isom scoffed. "All but one of them were screaming their thoughts, repeating the same things again and again. I had no choice but to hear it all!"

"And the one who wasn't?"

Isom licked his paw and began cleaning himself. "It was more like a whisper. Like when your beefy friend gets lost in thought and mutters under his breath."

"You know his name is Bram," Wil said. He couldn't be too annoyed at the wampus cat. As loathe as he was to admit it, knowing what the judges of the tribunal felt toward him gave him something to work with. "So you're saying that the wizards are on my side, and the others aren't?"

Isom laughed his awful mrowling laugh. "None of them are on your side. They couldn't care less if you lived or died. The wizards would prefer to gain knowledge from you before they feast on your remains."

It all came back to that damned leyline. Wil poured himself some water and drained it. His entire body was tense and had been. It was exhausting. Right when he thought about laying his head on the desk and closing his eyes, there was a knock at the door. A second later, Thomas stepped in.

"They're really putting the squeeze on you, aren't they?" He said, taking the seat next to Wil. "I know it's rough, but you're handling yourself well up there."

"I keep losing my cool," said Wil, groaning and tugging at his hair.

"That's the right move," said Thomas, leaning forward. "You want to do that more often, I think."

"No one asked you," said Isom. He still hadn't warmed up to Thomas, but Wil was past caring. They ignored him.

"I don't know." Wil frowned. "Speaker Keene and the others seem to want my head."

Thomas shook his head. "It's a dominance display. They want to keep you cowed and off-balance. They're always harder on wizards than they are others because the council is often three or four wizards, depending on the case. Trust me, I've seen a few hearings like this, and you can't let them intimidate you.

"If I were you, I'd go harder. Show more strength, more personality, and less remorse. You look and sound guilty and like you know it. Each time you defend yourself, they bark and you give in. You need to go harder and make *them* look bad."

That sounded wrong, but Wil couldn't fully put his finger on why. He knew at least one reason. "Won't making them look bad end with them trying to punish me?"

"If their judgment pisses off enough people, they could be pushed out of power before too long."

Wil laughed. "Fat lot of good that'll do me when I'm buried in the Junk Drawer for my efforts. They might do it to me anyway if I don't give up the secret to leylines."

Thomas thought about it for nearly a minute. The clamor of people outside the office reminded Wil how little time remained in their break, and that Pierce hadn't come back yet. Whatever advice Thomas had, it was likely the best Wil was going to get before they went back in.

"I don't think you're going to get out of this without sharing that secret," he said. "So you might as well give it to them. But"—he held up a finger to forestall Wil's indignant response—"you need to do it on your terms. If that's what they want, make it clear you'll give it to them, but add a condition or a cost to it. Make it clear you're willing to play, but you will not *be* played. Make sense?"

Wil made a face. "After a fashion. So pound my chest and be loud about how right I am and then offer them up my secret to save my ass?"

"Yes." Thomas smiled apologetically. "Might as well ask for rain in a desert, right?"

"I don't know," Wil admitted. "I don't have any other strategies. The best I know is that the wizards on the council might be willing to vote in my favor when the time comes. So maybe I should do this. I don't want to, but I don't know how long I can hold out, or even if it's worth it."

"It would work," Isom confirmed begrudgingly. "They've been thinking about it often."

Thomas's eyes slid over to the wampus cat. So far, his best way of getting along with the cat was pretending Isom wasn't there and didn't say anything. It had worked well enough, but now he was interested. "If they're thinking about it and want it, you might be able to swing things in your favor. Be aggressive and be ready to jump on opportunity."

The door opened again, and Pierce stood in the doorway. He didn't look happy. "We're about to go back on. Are you going to be able to contain yourself and your pet?"

Wil and Thomas shared a look. "Yeah," said Wil. "No more outbursts from me. I'll behave, and we'll win them over."

"Fine," said Pierce. "Then let's go. We might have hours yet to go."

"Good luck," Thomas said, slapping Wil's back. He smiled slyly and slid past Pierce.

Wil stood up and joined Pierce. Part of him felt guilty over lying to a man who'd done nothing but try to help him, but Thomas was right. He wasn't gaining anything by allowing himself to be on his back foot the entire time. It was time to give them what they wanted, ready or not.

CHAPTER 15

The Best Defense

For the rest of his time in Cloverton, Wil would wonder how the hell he had managed to gather up the courage to perform. When they returned to the courtroom, the tribunal waited for him with harsh, unreadable faces. Knowing hours more of this awaited him hurt, made worse when they spoke.

"Kind of you to join us, Master McKenzie," said Speaker Keene. "Are you ready to continue, or do you perhaps need a few more minutes?"

Pierce forced a laugh and said, "Unnecessary, Madam Speaker. We're ready." He motioned for Wil to sit down, but he remained standing.

"I would like to make a statement," Wil said, the words sounding as if they came from another person. "You've asked a lot of questions, but not once have I gotten a chance to speak for myself."

"If you don't care for how we do things," said General Haken, "then you're free to file a complaint after. Otherwise, sit down."

"Actually," Jim Rance said, clearing his throat, "I for one would love to hear what Master McKenzie has to say for himself." He made eye contact with Wil and nodded. He knew, or at least suspected, what was coming. His sly smile said it all.

"We'll finish the hearing with it," said Minister Fengar, waving the wizard off.

"Or we can put it to a vote," said Rance. "All in favor of letting Master McKenzie speak?" He raised his hand and so did the other wizards on the tribunal.

The glare Keene sent their way made Wil want to turn tail and run, but Jim Rance smiled and bowed his head mockingly. Keene sighed. "You have the floor, Master McKenzie."

"Thank you," he said, throat suddenly dry. He gave in to his instinct and guzzled water first, to the muffled laughter of some of the audience. Pierce looked either irritated or disappointed in him, but Wil couldn't blame him. He cleared his throat and began.

"Over the past few hours, you've picked apart every decision I've made and questioned who I am. I get it, that's your job, and you need to find the truth. But the truth is, this entire hearing is a sham."

Oh gods, he was committed. A gasp ran through the room, and Speaker Keene's face twisted into restrained rage. He pushed forward before she could say something.

"There have been months now—*months*—of investigating and picking apart every single second of my story, and it always comes back to the same points. I went off to another world without telling anyone. I invited the fae to Harper Valley. I killed Mage Hugo Jefferson when he went rogue. And I brokered the peace this country is currently enjoying. Worst of all, I am withholding information.

"Out of those charges, the only one that has legs is my decision to go to Faerie in the first place and make a deal I wasn't authorized to make. If you want to punish me for those decisions, there's nothing I can do to stop you. But for you to act like saving lives is wrong is something I will *never* accept."

"Master McKenzie," Minister Fengar started, but Wil spoke louder.

"It was never about me saving lives or doing things without permission. It all comes back down to the information I haven't shared. This entire sham of a hearing is to pressure me and make me desperate for whatever deal you offer me."

More than anything, Wil wished he could turn around and get some support from Thomas, but his eyes darted to each of the seven members of the tribunal. Unsurprisingly, half of them were pissed. Jim Rance and a couple of his people, however, looked intrigued. Rance himself had his hands folded together, his chin resting on them.

"That's enough," said Keene. "You've spoken for yourself, and—" Her lips continued to move, but no sound came out. Wil blinked. That hadn't been him.

"Thank you, Katherine," said Rance. "Your dedication to law, order, and the truth is exemplary, but I think it's time to hear this young man out. If I'm not mistaken, he has yet to make his point."

"Jim, you can't be serious," General Haken growled.

"I am. We could put it to another vote if you'd like." He smiled innocently. Haken looked away, hate on his face. "No? Then please, Master McKenzie, continue. I for one am *fascinated* at this angle of self-defense you've chosen. Tread carefully."

That was it. He was right. Thomas had been right. This was a sham. Which meant that this was Wil's chance to present an offer of his own. He swallowed hard. He looked to Pierce, who shook his head. The meaning was clear: you're on your own, kid.

"Over the course of the last year, I became the second person to alter a leyline. The first died horribly as the land he was on exploded, leaving nothing behind but his shoes and hat. Which makes me the first person to successfully do it. It ripped and is even now pouring magic wildly into the area, changing the landscape and wildlife and making magic in the area more potent.

"I believe that it can be done better than that. I believe I know how to replicate it and improve on it. But I'm not just going to give out this knowledge for free, nor will I be pushed around or bullied."

You tell them! Isom's tail lashed behind him as he watched the proceedings. *They're as interested as they are angry.*

"If leylines can be torn, they can be changed. If they can be changed, they can be harnessed. And if we do, then we'll leave Ilianto and Albetosia in the dust, magically."

"That's a lot of ifs, McKenzie," said Rance. "What is it you're offering?"

"I'm offering to do the legwork," Wil said, pausing to take a breath. "I'll find out how it works, and when I know it can be replicated, I'll share what I learn. In return, I get the patent for it, funding for my research, and an assistant to help as well. And we stop pretending I'm on trial for anything other than theater. You will have your world-changing discovery, and I will get the credit. Most importantly, you people leave me alone."

Speaker Keene looked over at Jim, who stroked his short beard thoughtfully. He smirked, and apparently that was answer enough. The Speaker sighed and said, "Your manners and respect aside, you've given us something to deliberate over. We'll return in an hour."

Back in Pierce's temporary office, the old man read Wil the riot act. "You fool! What were you thinking, challenging them like that? You could be held in contempt or have them use this as an excuse to punish you!"

Wil backed up, shocked but not surprised by the anger. He held up his hands. "Isom told me—"

"Oh, the telepathic cat who shouldn't be allowed in this court told you." Pierce pinched the bridge of his nose. "I worked on this case for months to try to help you. And now you throw it away. For what?"

Isom growled. Pierce held still, but Wil waved the cat off. "I didn't throw anything away. I meant everything I said. This is a sham, and it was done to pressure me. How many people from Harper Valley did they interview? How many fae?"

"Dozens of each," Pierce answered, looking down. "They have the full story and are checking yours for holes."

"Yeah, right. Thank you for all your effort, Mr. Pierce," said Wil, heart thudding heavily in his chest. "But I think this is the only way out."

Pierce frowned, collected his things, and headed for the door. "I'll be back to escort you when they return, but other than that . . . I hope you know what you're doing, son. Your life's on the line." He left, only to be replaced by Thomas again.

"That was . . . incredible!" He went up to Wil and pulled him into a one-armed hug with a lot of backslapping. "Did you see the looks on their faces? They did *not* like being called out like that. I think you made your point well and didn't rub their noses in it *too* much. Well done, Wil!"

"Pierce didn't seem to think so," Wil chuckled.

Isom growled, "He wasn't on your side. His thoughts betrayed him at the end. It wasn't supposed to go this way. He was herding you, leading you to the kill."

Wil grimaced. That was the last thing he needed to hear, but it was out of Pierce's hands. It was out of his hands too. He had to hope his offer would be accepted. "Man, I could use a drink and a meal."

"When they accept your deal and exonerate you, dinner's on me," said Thomas. "It's the least I can do for the wizard I like, admire, and want to help out. Maybe not as an assistant. I prefer the term *partner*, but the details can wait."

Wil laughed and collapsed into the closest seat. He let out a fluttering breath and forced himself to relax. "You heard that and want the position, huh? I can't promise anything. I've never been involved in this kind of in-depth research before, though of course I was trained in it. Whoever ends up as my assistant is likely going to be responsible for a lot of recordkeeping while I do the fun stuff."

Was it bad that his original thought had been Bram? Gods, if they took his deal, he could go home and conduct his research there. He could examine that broken leyline more closely and dedicate himself to unraveling its secrets. And Darlene . . . His heart ached. She must've hated him by now, being stuck in Cloverton this long with no way to get word to her. Wil would enjoy every second of making it up to her if she'd let him.

"Funny enough, that's my specialty," said Thomas, undeterred. "I find things out and write them down for the benefit of the team. C'mon Wil, you can't seriously be thinking you'd go without me. Not after the last few months!"

Isom did his obnoxious, growling laughter and looked at Wil but didn't say anything, not even mentally. For the first time since that night Isom had called Thomas a predator, Wil gave real consideration to the words. Was it possible he was just playing the long game this entire time? That would take way too much dedication.

"Hey, I asked a few times, but I never got an answer," said Wil. "Why were you at Marlowe Manor for that long? You left for a few weeks here and there, but you were there almost the entire time."

Thomas laughed, looking down. "You caught me. I lingered there, befriending you so I could be a part of this grand discovery. Well caught, McKenzie. Is that a deal-breaker?"

"Be honest," said Wil.

The divination wizard rolled his eyes and took the other seat. "I am. I've made no bones about the fact that I want in on this, and I had some spare time. But it wasn't only out of selfishness. You were stuck here, and you needed a friend. And to be honest? I needed a break from Ferrovani. I've been doing research for him while here, but I want more than he's willing to give. There's no getting in the way of genius. I'll only ever be an assistant with him. I'd rather be a partner."

Wil took some time to think about it. Thomas was right, he'd been open about his interest from the start. And over the course of a third of a year, they'd spent a lot of time together. Before Wil had started talking to other wizards at the Manor, Thomas had been the only one to give him the time of day. It couldn't have been a long con and nothing more.

"The thing is, I'm going to be playing this as close to the chest as I can," said Wil. "I want to accept your help, and I probably will. But like you said, it has to be on my terms. I need to make sure that I'm in control of my project and of whatever information I give them."

Thomas nodded along. "Very true. I respect that, and I will leave you with one last argument in my favor if I may."

"You may."

He smiled and spread his hands. "I have experience. I know what goes into starting a project like this, managing the funding, and requisitioning the supplies you need for it. Not only that, but once you successfully replicate or improve upon your original blunder, what are you going to do with it?"

Wil fell silent. Those were all salient points, and he liked Thomas, but his gut told him to be careful. "We'll see how it goes," said Wil. "I'll definitely take any help you give me, but I've got an excellent group waiting at home for me. I think you'd be a great addition to our team, if you're willing to join on my terms."

Thomas clapped his hands and bowed his head in acknowledgment. "Perfectly understood. I want to discover new things, lend my expertise, and be able to put my name on it along with others. In the meantime, want to play cards?"

The hour turned into two before they were called back in. The three nonmagical judges looked as if they'd tasted something terrible. Wil tried not to look too excited as he joined Pierce back at the table.

Speaker Keene cleared her throat. "After much deliberation, this council has decided to accept your offer. In order to prove you're neither a reckless child nor a willing agent of the fae, you will show us proof that your story is correct by replicating it. To that end, you will receive funding, manpower, and access to any materials you need shipped in from Manifee City."

Wil grinned and looked back to Thomas.

"However," Keene's icy voice made every hair stand on end. "There is a condition to this offer. You will provide regular reports back to Cloverton, and you have three months to accomplish this. If you succeed, we'll consider your research as time served for your policy violations, insubordination, and questionable decisions. If you fail, someone will take over and you'll be right back here."

Three months. That was hardly any time at all when it came to major experiments. It took him nearly all four months to perfect the Thunderhawk, and that was under Thomas's guidance. In that time, he'd learned almost as much as he had during his time at the academy, and this was new territory. But . . . it wasn't like he had much of a choice.

"I accept," said Wil. "Give me three months, and I'll change the world."

CHAPTER 16

Good Luck and Goodbye

With the hearing no longer hanging over his head, Wil treasured having time to catch his breath and prepare. He'd gotten to postpone the consequences another few months down the road. All he had to do was replicate what he had done months ago by accident and make it useful somehow.

Wil, Isom, Thomas, and Chinis had to book it to avoid the swarm of people and members of the press who were barking questions at him. Flashes of cameras blinded him as they ran in the other direction, taking a side exit and slipping around the back of the building to where Chinis's car awaited them.

"I can't believe this," Chinis complained as he drove the clunky mechanical car away from the courthouse and, thankfully, outside the anti-magic suppression field. "If I were to accuse a court deciding my fate of being a sham, I'm pretty sure they'd lock me up and never let me see the light of day again. Must be nice, McKenzie. Must be nice."

"It beats a kick to the teeth," said Wil, laughing. He was in the back seat with Isom. Thomas, for some reason, didn't feel comfortable sitting next to the wampus cat. "And don't forget, my ass isn't out of the fire yet. They just turned down the flames."

"Details." Thomas waved him off. He sat twisted in the seat to face Wil as he spoke. "How do you feel about Ramenian food? I know this great place halfway back to the Manor."

Wil shrugged. At this point, anything he ate would be the greatest meal he'd had in months, so why not? Soon he'd be home. Everything else was a bonus.

So an hour later found the four of them in the back of a dingy ramshackle building with terrible lighting, strange smells coming from the back, and a surly, heavyset matron who gave them the stink eye the moment they walked in. Unsurprisingly, the food was incredible and served in massive portions. The Ramenians knew how to eat.

"So what's next?" Chinis asked, twisting some noodles with his fork and slurping them down obnoxiously. They'd all made a game of who could be the noisiest eater. "Gonna go home and do research, then?"

"Oh, no," said Thomas. "It's going to be way more involved than that. Figuring out the conditions of change and how to control it is just the beginning. After that, there are stress tests as well as finding practical applications for it. Three months isn't nearly enough time for . . ." He smiled sheepishly at Wil. "Getting ahead of myself, aren't I?"

"Yeah, I'd say so," said Wil. "I still haven't accepted you as part of my team." He schlorped his own noodles, keeping eye contact before he broke. "I'll be glad to have your expertise on my side again. But I need you to understand something before we begin."

"Oh boy," said Chinis. "Here it comes."

"I'm in charge of this venture," said Wil. "No no, don't say anything yet. I know how eager you are and have been, but we're going to do this my way. It means going at my pace and going in my direction. I'll gladly take your input, but to be clear: we're not going to be developing things for the military. No matter how well they might pay."

He doesn't like that, Isom purred in his mind. He chewed on massive meatballs on the floor, casually listening in as he often did. *He'll betray you if it means getting his way.*

Wil rolled his eyes. Isom's increasingly bad habit of reading minds had come in handy, but his observations were heavily colored by his own animal mind-set. Part of that was a cat's natural sense of haughtiness, mischief, and staggering bias. He never liked Thomas, so nothing the man did was enough.

"That's . . . okay," said Thomas, wincing but not complaining further. "No military applications. There's still bound to be plenty of things to improve on and profit from. We'll be advancing magical understanding to a whole new level. Good enough for me."

Which was enough for Wil, at least for the moment. "I've got a team of people I trust who help me with all my projects back in Harper Valley. They'll be invaluable to our efforts, and I miss them badly."

"Fantastic!" said Thomas. "What's their specialization? I know you work with earth magic and your raw power serves you well. I am of course a master of information and perspective, but do you have a metalworker or ritual person?"

"Uh, not quite," said Wil. "They're not wizards. It's my best friend, Bram, and my girlfriend, Darlene. I wouldn't be where I am without them."

Thomas paused. "Huh. What do they bring to the team?"

Wil didn't blink. "Darlene is an organizational mastermind, who somehow manages to keep us on track, more or less. Bram's one of the most methodical and curious people I've ever known. He's got no magic of his own, but he's been reading through all my books. I swear he understands some of the stuff better than I do!"

"Not difficult," said Chinis, finishing off his noodles with gusto. He set the bowl down on the uneven, splintery table. "You're not stupid, but you could never learn things that didn't come naturally to you."

"That's not true, I've improved a lot at runes and enchanting. With a really great vehicle to show for it." Wil raised his wine glass to Thomas and winked.

"That reminds me," said Thomas after he toasted Wil back. "Have you put any thought into what kind of budget you are looking for, what possible materials you'll want?"

Wil pushed his bowl away, covering one of the table's many holes. "I haven't. Not yet at least. That's the stuff I'm much less excited for. So yes, Thomas, to answer the question you haven't asked. I'm willing to let you take the lead on those things, so long as you teach me what you're doing."

"Partners?" Thomas prodded.

"Partners," Wil confirmed. "You, me, Bram, and Darlene."

"Right," said the enchanter, obviously not pleased, but understanding it was the way it had to be. So long as Thomas could accept that, he'd be a fine addition.

The rest of dinner passed by in a blur. After, Chinis drove them all back to Marlowe Manor, where Wil and Thomas stayed up late into the night talking. It continued almost as soon as they woke up the following morning, and the details came together.

It was another week and a half until Wil was allowed to leave. The time between was spent negotiating a budget, terms of correspondence, and the first initial batch of materials to be delivered to Wil's home in Harper Valley. The other items to be shipped were a few knickknacks Wil had made in the workshop, his new wardrobe, and everything else he couldn't fit on his Thunderhawk.

In what was possibly the best part of his homecoming, Wil had arranged for himself and Isom to go through the portal to Manifee City along with his new vehicle. Rather than catch a ride on a flying ship or a train home, Wil was going to ride his Thunderhawk and rough it for a couple of days. After months trapped in the manor, he was beyond excited.

By the time the day came, he and Isom looked out one last time at the Marlowe Manor grounds. Wil closed his eyes and felt around for the ring of leylines surrounding the property. He hadn't learned anything new about them in that time, but the manor's location was important. It had to be. Trickles of power flowed into the center, barely detectable but constant, like the waves at a beach creeping up the shore. Back and forth, push and pull.

Are we leaving or not? If not, I want to hunt one last time.

Wil started from his thoughts. He shook himself out of it. "Yeah, yeah, we're leaving. You going to be okay on the back of this thing?" Behind the Thunderhawk was a small, short trailer that would float behind it. It had taken some of their precious time to make it work, but there was no way Isom could sprint the entire way home.

Isom jumped onto the platform and turned a circle before lying down. "Assuming you don't do anything foolish or too fast, I should be fine. Our tests were . . . fine."

Their first test with the trailer had launched Isom out only a couple of times before Wil adjusted the enchantments to something more stable and comfortable.

The first time had startled the wampus cat. The next two had been a source of great fun. For Wil, at least.

"Then, shall we? Thomas and Chinis should already be waiting for us." Wil climbed into the Thunderhawk's seat and switched the keyrune on. There was no actual buzzing or vibration, but Wil's senses were awash with the enchantments coming to life. With a twist of his wrists, he spun in place, slowly dragging the trailer with it. And then he shot forward, hovering four feet off the ground as they headed to Cloverton.

At this point, Wil knew the way through the woods and back into the city by heart. Navigating the city itself wasn't much harder, given the military base could be seen towering off in the distance. Cars on the road honked at him as he turned up the power and flew the Thunderhawk a few feet above traffic. The metal of the cars underneath helped stabilize the vehicle and make it go faster, safer than everyone else. Mostly.

With all the towers of metal and clouds of smoke belching forth from factories and businesses, Wil couldn't say he'd miss the capital much. He had not gotten to explore it at all, and it didn't strike him as a missed opportunity. Turning into the military base was a welcome relief, though it made his heart flutter. Another few minutes, and he'd be a couple days' ride from home.

Security stopped him, not once, but at three different locations. More people swarmed the base than when he'd first arrived in the winter, and everyone was on edge. He found out as he and Isom met Chinis and Thomas in front of the portal itself. They weren't alone. President Bullworth and Sylano stood there, chatting, while the president's bodyguards' cold gazes followed Wil as he approached.

Wil dismounted cautiously. He made it a couple of steps before the president attacked him, grabbing his hand and giving it a violent pump.

"Wilbur McKenzie, the man of the hour!" Bullworth chortled. "I told you that we'd pry that information out of you."

Wil's cheeks burned, and for an instant he wanted to say something rude and insulting before sense tacked that down. "Yes, sir," he said, "but on my terms."

"On your terms indeed," said Bullworth. "You get the credit and the money for your hard work. It's the Calipan way, after all. I see you've got Ferrovani's boy on your side. With his help, I've no doubt you'll clear the terms and be exonerated on all charges. And if not . . . Well, surely there will be something to build on from what you find. I just wanted to wish you luck before you set off."

One final, friendly threat. Wil forced a smile and said, "Thank you, sir. And Syl, how the hell are you doing? You still the president's guest?"

Syl nodded enthusiastically. His time in Cloverton had him dressing in the local style, with an armless black suit on his chest and pants cut off before they made it to his hooves. His short horns had golden bands around them. It was the perfect combination of Calipan society mixed with fae chaos and Syl's habit of missing the point.

"We've gotten a lot done these past few months," said Syl brightly. "Another couple, and I can report to my father. We've established some rules of mutual tourism. We'll even be coming by Harper Valley in a few months to make a visit to Oakheart Spiral and show the president our hospitality. That'll be the next time I see you! Think your mom would be willing to cook when we drop by?"

"Cooking for her favorite goat and the president himself?" Wil scoffed. "She'd be delighted. Gods, I can't wait to go home and stuff myself."

"Then go with my blessing, Wilbur," said Bullworth with a smile that seemed almost genuine. "Just do what you do and work for your community, and everything will all be okay." He laughed again and wandered off, his bodyguards in tow.

"Bye for now, Wil. Give me love to Arabella when you see her! Tell her I don't miss her attitude or sneers."

Wil laughed. "You got it. Bye, Syl."

And then it was just Chinis and Thomas. "I appreciate you taking me around Manifee City and being the world's most lax guard," Wil said to his old friend. "I don't think I would've made it without your reassurances."

Chinis gave him The Nod and said, "Anytime. But I expect to stay at your place if I ever have a reason to visit. But I guess with your important research, you're going to give everyone a reason to visit, aren't you?"

"That's the plan!" Wil pulled Chinis into a hug and the two spent a minute seeing who could slap each other's back harder. Wil crapped out after four sharp slaps. "Come see me if and when you do."

When Wil turned to Thomas, he scoffed. "Look at me, last and least. Get a move on, McKenzie. I'll be along in a week with all the supplies we need. I'll keep you updated on any hassles, okay?"

"Appreciated," Wil said, shaking Thomas's hand. "And with that, it's time to hope that the Thunderhawk doesn't die halfway to home."

"Impossible," said Thomas with a shake of his head. "I helped work on it. The only way it stops working is if you wreck it. See you soon, McKenzie."

Human sentimentality is gross, Isom complained from the back of the Thunderhawk. *Can we hurry it up?*

Wil laughed. *We'll see how much you hate sentimentality after a side of beef, huh? Let's go.* He mounted the Thunderhawk and took one long look at the swirling portal. A nearby officer gave him the approval to go.

With a laugh, Wil drove through the portal, and onward to home.

CHAPTER 17

Homecoming

In some ways, going home on an airship would've been faster. It would've shaved an entire day off Wil's trip, in exchange for leaving a little later. He would've arrived at the same time, having done far less work. If he had traveled via airship, then Wil would've missed out on this feeling of pure freedom after months of being trapped.

The path from Manifee City to Harper Valley could be followed by the train tracks, and Wil and Isom rode the Thunderhawk over the rails the entire way. The vehicle was even smoother and faster over metal, and it had become second nature to move out of the way when necessary.

Not this time.

This is foolish! When just the two of them, Isom took to mentally projecting his words rather than shout them over the rush of wind. *Do you want to kill us both?*

"Maybe," Wil muttered, grinning as the train came screaming their way along the tracks. There was one more feature on the Thunderhawk that he had yet to fully try out, and these tracks were perfect for it.

At least let me off first!

"You can hop off at any time," Wil said, knowing Isom could read the words from him as soon as he thought them. Even his own mental defenses weren't quite enough to block out the telepathic cat. "But I'm doing this."

Your woman will be angry if you die before coming home.

It almost worked, but Wil bore down on the train. Closer and closer it came, so slow in the distance, then picking up speed as it got closer. Wil's own speed was about the same. If he didn't make it in time, then there'd be a harsh crash and a smear where he once had been. Three . . . two . . . Now!

Wil twisted the handles back simultaneously. The force pressing against the earth and keeping the Thunderhawk floating intensified and launched them into the air. Isom yowled in alarm and dug his claws into the platform hooked up to the back as they dropped.

The enchantment caught the top of the train and launched them forward, faster than ever before. Wil screamed in delight as they reached the Thunderhawk's top speed, and he had to hold on for dear life while Isom screamed in panic. The spells keeping them stuck to their seats held through the burst of speed.

When the train passed and they slipped back to the tracks, their speed cut sharply. Wil pulled them away from the tracks and glided over the land next to them instead. "You okay, Isom?" Wil asked as he moseyed down the countryside.

Don't ever do that again, Isom all but hissed at him. Wil chanced looking over his shoulder. The wampus cat had flattened himself against the floor of the platform, panting in lingering fear. Wil bit back laughter and nodded.

"Don't worry," said Wil. "We're almost home. Another hour or so." His heart soared.

The time spent sleeping on the ground and traveling all day had been just what Wil needed to reset before his return. No spending it waiting on a flying ship or the train. Every step he took, he wanted to do it himself. And while using the Thunderhawk taxed his magic and focus, it was a welcome change from the boredom of endless waiting.

Now that they'd passed Appleton, the tree on top of Skalet Peak was visible in the distance. Still small but growing bigger by the second. Wil increased the speed again, wanting nothing more than to see a familiar face.

It ended up taking another hour and a half, but Wil hardly noticed the extra time. Memories of his time at home bounced around his head. So many of them featured the people of Harper Valley giving him trouble over the silliest things, but he missed that. He missed them. If there was one thing he appreciated about home, it was that he was liked and respected but not worshiped.

Wil slowed as he hit the road leading north through town, parallel to the railroad tracks. He kept going until the road veered off to the east. He waved a hand in greeting to Candy, standing in front of Nancy Flanagan's dress shop. Her eyes lit up and she called out his name, which got the attention of others.

Just like that, he had dozens of people looking at him, at least half of them calling out Wil's name or else shouting, "Mr. Wizard!"

Many faces he didn't recognize, but his heart was overjoyed to see fae and human alike in the town square. He wove in and out of pockets, careful not to ruin his first day back by hitting someone. People had no trouble getting out of the way as he went by.

As much as Wil would've preferred going home first, he had duties to take care of. The relentless questioning had reiterated his need to follow policy and procedure. So he steeled himself and headed for town hall first.

Later on, he'd kick himself for his pessimism, but Wil wasn't looking forward to dealing with Sinclair again. The fact that the election had already passed and that his father could've won slipped his mind entirely. He came up with a half dozen scenarios where he'd have to tell the mayor off and declare his independence. He had sharp words ready on his lips when he entered and saw his mother behind the receptionist's desk.

"Mom? What are you doing here?" Wil asked.

"Wilbur!" Sharon McKenzie scrambled from behind the desk and launched herself at him. Despite being a petite woman, she cracked his bones with her hug. "Where the hell have you been?" She pushed him away and hollered up the stairs to her right, "Bob, come down here!"

A few seconds later, the light thunder of Bob coming down the stairs heralded the new mayor. Wil lit up and threw out his arms. Bob picked him up in a massive hug of his own.

"You're back home! Why the hell didn't anyone warn me?"

"Sorry," said Wil, breathing deep after he was released. "This entire thing has been a mess from the start. I wasn't allowed any messages or questions other than knowing you were all alive and okay. It's my fault. They were trying to pressure me, and it ended up punishing everyone."

"Then that sounds like a them problem," said Bob, expression darkening. "I'm guessing you didn't back down. Good on you, Wil."

Wil flushed and shrank away from his father. "I did, though. That's why they let me out. I cracked and gave them what they wanted. Or, at least, I will."

"Oh no," said Sharon, grabbing him in another hug. Wil couldn't complain about being hugged too much after months of the only affection being Isom lying across his legs when he tried to sleep. "Well, we don't think anything less of you, sweetie. What did they want?"

"Mind if I use the restroom first?" Wil asked. "It's been a long trip, and this is a long story."

Bob chuckled. "Take your time. I'll set us up with drinks in my office. Sharon, please keep all visitors busy."

"Keep them busy?" Sharon scoffed. "I'm going to be up in the office with you."

In the end, they recruited Isom to sit at the desk and play secretary to ward off anyone who wanted Bob's time while they spoke. Apparently, that had been a common problem lately.

"It's a nightmare," Bob said, rubbing his temples as he sat in his luxurious leather chair. He had three lemonades set out at Sharon's insistence. "I'm not saying I have more respect for Sinclair, but I can understand why he'd started to try to profit off the office. Everyone wants something, and you can't please them all.

"Ever since you left, it's been a full-time job juggling the wants and needs of people and keeping control of the fae situation. Which is doing a lot better now, by the way."

"Thank goodness," said Wil, sipping his lemonade. "Has the farm been okay with you two working here?"

Sharon laughed. "Arabella runs the farm now when she's not in Faerie. It's built up a lot more since you've been gone, and the only thing recognizable is the house. For now. Your father keeps insisting we don't change anything, but I think it's time to expand and modernize."

"I can't believe how much has changed . . ." Wil shook his head. "And I wouldn't have missed any of it had I given up what I knew. That's why they kept me. I wouldn't tell them how to change leylines, until the hearing. It started with . . ."

He launched into his time in Cloverton, of being bound to Marlowe Manor and using his time there to study everything he could about leylines and enchanting. He told them about his new friend Thomas and how it was his advice that got him home again, after the outburst in court. When he was done, Sharon looked like she wanted to hit someone.

"I can't believe . . . they took you away from us for a third of the year just to intimidate you? If I get my hands on those . . ." Sharon let out a garbled cry and wrung the air.

"Easy there, hon," said Bob, hand raised like he wanted to reach out, but he knew better. "He's home now, and that's what matters. And he's got time to find out what he needs to know to make this all go away."

Wil made a face. "I'm not sure it's going to go away, exactly. If what I've discovered is true, it's going to cause more change, fast. So I have to do this responsibly. There's a lot to do. I need to get Bram and Darlene together so we can start working as fast as possible. Gods, I missed them."

Bob and Sharon exchanged a nervous look. "Honey," said Sharon. "You might . . . You're going to want to go home and check on Darlene."

There were few things that could've spoiled Wil's mood, but the shared look of almost panic on their faces turned his blood to ice. "What happened?" he demanded.

"You should see for yourself," said Bob. "It's not bad, but . . ."

Wil didn't hang around to find out what that meant. He dashed out the door, down the stairs, and past a surprised Isom.

What's going on? the wampus cat asked, but Wil ignored him. He burst outside, scaring off the crowd that had gathered around his Thunderhawk. He mounted it and took off north, toward his house. Fear gripped his heart as he struggled to avoid thinking of what could've happened to his girlfriend while he was gone.

CHAPTER 18

Roots

Wil had never been this grateful to go so fast. Although the foot traffic was heavier than normal, Wil flew ten feet above them, twisting and turning to hug the path as he flew the Thunderhawk home. The distance was only a stone's throw to his house in the center of town, but it was enough for Wil's imagination to run wild.

Immediately, he imagined her moving on and finding someone else. It made perfect sense. After so long without word, it would've been easier to accept Wil either wasn't coming back or that he couldn't be forgiven for the absence. By the time he got home, he had a half-rehearsed apology ready to go.

He landed next to the front door and hopped off. Wil tried the door, but it was locked. Swearing under his breath, he forced it open with a burst of magic and went in.

"Darlene?" He called out.

A few seconds later, Darlene's disbelief shone through. "Wil? I'm upstairs!"

He bolted up the steps, heart going a mile a minute. "I'm so sorry I've been gone this long. I swear, I'll make up for it if you'll give me a . . . chance." He stopped at the landing of the second floor. Right outside the door of the guest room, she stood there in her nightgown.

Incredibly pregnant. Wil swallowed hard, looking up from her stomach to her face. Darlene smiled weakly. "Surprise," she said, wiggling her hands on either side of her bump. "I would've told you, but . . ."

Wil's knees wobbled beneath him. He clutched the railing for support, repeatedly swallowing a lump that wouldn't go down. "I . . . If I had known, I would've . . . How?"

Darlene raised an eyebrow. "Do I really need to explain the mechanics to you? You were there."

That shook Wil back to normal. Mostly. "No, I get *that*, I mean . . . We were so careful, weren't we?"

She laughed. "You were the one casting the spell, so I kind of had to trust you. So either you aren't as adept at preventative magic as I thought you were, or it happened in Faerie. During that time neither of us would've remembered to be careful."

The hobgoblin's party instantly came to mind. Three days of partying so thoroughly that they couldn't remember most of what happened. But the more time passed, the more bits and pieces returned to Wil. He remembered their last night there.

"Oh."

"Oh," Darlene echoed, crossing her arms over her chest. "And then you disappear for four months. What was that about?"

Wil winced. "I am so, so sorry," he said. Heat flooded his cheeks. His thoughts scrambled away from him, and he had to fight to find the words. "I shouldn't have been that long, but they kept me until I was willing to give in. I'm back home to study leylines to keep my ass out of the fire. If I'd given in earlier . . ."

Darlene's expression softened. "Then you wouldn't be your usual stubborn self. For better or worse, that's how I prefer you. But did you learn a lesson about how big you are compared to the full force of the government?"

"Yeah," said Wil. "I learned I need to grow bigger so I can swing back harder."

She stared at him for a second before she burst out laughing. "Get over here, you jerk."

Wil took a few tentative steps forward, his desire to hug his girlfriend at odds with his continued shock at her condition. And then she was in his arms, and he hugged her tight, careful not to crush her. She gripped him tightly, and then the tears started from them both.

Grief at the time lost, relief at being back together, and the shock of an uncertain future. Wil held his girlfriend, and the two lost themselves in one tight, vulnerable embrace. It was at least a couple minutes later when Wil whispered, "If I'd have known, I would've been back. They wouldn't have been able to do anything to keep me."

"I know," Darlene said. She broke away and rubbed her eyes. "You'd think they would've loved to tell you this, to put a fire under your ass."

"You'd think," Wil laughed breathlessly. "They're a hammer and think we're all nails. I . . . I need a drink."

"Me too," Darlene deadpanned. "But thanks to you, I'm stuck drinking tea if I want anything more than water. Even lemonade makes me uncomfortable. Well, it makes *her* uncomfortable."

It brought her condition right back into focus. Wil swallowed hard. "Then let's . . . let's get you some tea and talk."

"Okay," said Darlene. She punched his arm, "But you better believe you're making the tea and spoiling me for the next forever."

Wil smiled. "Gladly."

He helped her downstairs and made some sweet tea. The entire time, he told Darlene everything he could about being stuck in Cloverton and the hearing from hell. It was easier to focus on the past than the scary new future.

"Well, I'm glad you made a new friend," said Darlene after hearing about

Thomas and the Thunderhawk they built together. "You need more business-minded people in your life, reminding you when you make decisions that cost you money."

"Apparently. Seems like the only way out is to give in. If you can't beat them, join them, right? If it'll block the charges and keep me in the president's good graces, then maybe I *should* lean in that direction a little." He drank his coffee, wishing desperately to pour some whiskey in it.

But no, he had to face this with only his own courage. He couldn't avoid the elephant in the room. "Are . . . are you okay?" Wil asked after the silence stopped being comfortable. "I know it must've been hard without me, but like . . . are you doing okay?"

Darlene rolled her eyes. She settled in her chair, cradling her stomach. "I swear, everyone's acting like there's something wrong with me. I'm fine, Wil. I'm just pregnant. Thanks a lot, by the way."

"Anytime," said Wil. He chuckled weakly, but Darlene didn't join him. He looked down, staring directly at her bump. "I don't know how to react to this."

"It was a nasty shock to me too," she said, amused. "But at least I've had some time to get used to the idea. I guess the real question is, what do you plan on doing?"

The question struck him in the heart. "What do you mean, what do I plan on doing? I'm pretty sure we have to get married now, and—"

"Oh, we *have to*? Way to make the prospect sound appealing," Darlene scoffed. "I'll marry when I'm good and ready and not a second earlier. I don't care what some of the old biddies say about me. I'm young, my business is doing well, and I can take care of this baby with or without help and still do my job."

There was that fire he loved about her. Not once did Wil ever doubt a thing she said. If she wanted to raise their kid alone, she'd excel at it. But the thought of it distressed him worse than he expected.

"It'll be with me," he said. The next thought had his throat drying up and tightening. "If you'll have me, I mean. I don't think I'll ever be dragged away like this again. I plan on sticking around."

Darlene smiled, shaking her head. "Of course I'll have you. We already had the fun, so you might as well have to help me take care of the consequences. And I'm not . . ." She paused. "I'm still mad, but it's not at you, understand?"

Wil nodded. He reached over the table and covered her hand with his. It was strange. Everything was, but especially seeing Darlene so changed, and yet the same. She looked more tired and was obviously rounder, but she had had more of a spark in her before. A wave of affection threatened to bowl him over.

"Darlene, I promise I'll . . . I can't believe I'm saying this. I'm too young to be saying this."

"Wasn't your dad only a year or two older than you when Jeb was born?" Darlene countered.

Wil snickered. "And you saw what happened with him. But I promise I'll be around, and I'll be the best father I can be. And I will follow your lead on this. The more I think about it, the more I think I want it. I really want it."

"Well, that sure beats the alternative," said Darlene, shaking her head fondly. "So you've got three months to pull your ass out of the fire and produce some results for Cloverton. Do you have any ideas on how you're going to do things?"

Wil shrugged. "By the seat of my pants and a lot of luck. But I've got no doubt that with the three of us, we'll make it happen."

"Bram's going to be so happy you're back," said Darlene. "I think he's been struggling more than I have. He's done everything he can to fill your shoes, you know. People rely on him now."

"Bram? That's fantastic." Wil beamed, and more of the burden of the last four months faded away. "I'm going to need his help more than anyone's, I think. Thomas thinks that the key to making this work will be enchanting, and Bram's got a memory like a bear trap. I think it's time . . ."

"You don't mean!" Darlene played along, rolling her eyes.

"I do," said Wil. "It's time to go over to Bram's place and hold an immediate business meeting."

"Okay," said Darlene. "But let's grab lunch along the way. If I held anything against you, it's how damned hungry I've been."

Wil laughed, and his anxiety flared again but only for a second. The future was scary and uncertain, and he'd never expected to be a father so young, but . . . If the past four months had taught him anything, it was that life was unpredictable. You could either try to resist it or go along with it. Wil knew what he'd choose.

CHAPTER 19

The Gang's Back Together

Wow, things changed here, haven't they?" Wil looked around the Stevenson farm. Three of the fields were in use, with their beer's ingredients growing out in the open. The barn in the front quarter of the land had been replaced with something a lot bigger, with improved equipment and more tables and chairs.

More than that, there were people there, in the fields and in the brewery specifically. Most of them were fae, but everyone who saw him waved or cheered. Wil waved back as he took in how much things had grown without him.

"Yeah, after things cooled down, this became one of the new places for the more accepting people to come hang out and socialize with fae. They even serve food now." Darlene was red-faced and huffing for air as they got close. They paused long enough for her to catch her breath. "The past four months were just as busy as the months before that, if that tells you anything."

Guilt hit him again, but he swallowed it down. "I've got a lot of catching up to do with everyone. I'm glad my dad won the election. Did Sinclair drop out of the race?"

Darlene snickered. "No, of course not. He did, however, lose Mr. Carrey as a sponsor, and Sheriff Frederick got canned. Those two events, along with how well the fae helped clean up, swung the election in your dad's favor. Things are looking up for Harper Valley."

"I'll say." Wil took a breath, checked on Darlene, and then continued up to the house. He was about to knock on the door when Darlene tugged his arm and led him around the back to where the cellar doors were.

"He spends most of his time down there. I don't feel like going down more stairs, so meet me in the house, okay?" Darlene leaned over and kissed him and waddled back around to the front.

Wil knocked on the doors and then entered as soon as he heard Bram shout. The giant sat hunched over a workbench, stirring a vivid green potion counterclockwise, humming tunelessly.

"Whatcha brewing?" Wil asked.

"Oh, a lucid dreaming potion. Corey's been pestering me about it when he found out . . . I could . . ." Bram's head swiveled over to him. He was clean-shaven again, the terrible beard nowhere in sight. His eyes widened, and he stood.

The next thing Wil knew, he was scooped up in a bone-crushing hug. In hindsight, he should've expected something like this. He patted Bram on the side, gasping for air once he was released. "Damn . . . Bram . . . Happy to see you too," Wil huffed.

"After all this time, you just waltz in here and act like it's no big deal?" Bram demanded incredulously.

"Well, yeah." Wil grinned, and together they laughed.

"Did you go home? You should see Darlene first." The face Bram made reflected how Wil felt about it overall.

"She's here with me. I saw. I told her about what happened, so it's time I filled you in as well. Kitchen table meeting?"

Bram's eyes lit up. "I have a new brew too!"

Fifteen minutes later, it was the three of them sitting around Bram's clean but shabby kitchen. All the improvements were made to the brewery, and Wil was relieved that at least this hadn't changed. He went over everything that had happened to him as he nursed a vivid coffee stout.

Being back there with his closest friends, Wil found himself tearing up by the end. He knew he had missed them, but it wasn't until they were all together that Wil felt the months of crushing loneliness fade away.

"So that's the situation," Wil said, clearing his throat and wiping at an eye. "I have three months, and I'm going to need everyone's help. How much have you read up on runic configurations?"

Bram laughed. "How many books on it do you have? Ever since you showed me runes on our fences, I've been learning everything I can about them. Actually, I have a few things I made. I had been hoping you could empower them for me when you got back."

Wil shook his head in disbelief. "That's a lot of surprises to come home to. Alright, then we have some prototypes to make. Starting tomorrow," he added, noting Darlene's glare.

"Damned right," she said. "We may be on a time limit, but your stuff doesn't arrive for another week or more, and it's your first day back. You can at least pretend like you are happy to see us instead of diving into work."

Wil nodded. "You're right. I'm excited, you know? I got to do a lot of work while I was staying at Marlowe Manor, and it was . . . I missed you two, but it was some of the most fulfilling work I've done. And though I don't like being forced into it, I'm eager to tackle the challenge of seeing if we can make it work."

Darlene rolled her eyes and drank her tea. "Then you may discuss what you plan on doing for a little while. Afterward, we're celebrating your return by going to dinner. Am I understood?"

The two men nodded.

"Good. You may proceed." She magnanimously motioned for them to continue.

"Right," said Bram, drinking his own oatmeal stout. "What's our first step, then?"

"That one's going to be all me," said Wil, lighting up. "I'm going to go up the mountain and inspect the leyline I broke. Maybe even take notes and play around with it. Not like I can make it any worse, right?"

The two of them stared back at him. "I don't know," said Bram. "Can you?"

Wil shrugged. "It'll probably be fine. It took a *lot* of effort to break it the first time, and I don't think I'll have to worry about life-or-death circumstances distracting me now. I have a few things in mind I want to try."

"And then if you succeed?" Darlene prodded.

"The thing about leylines," said Wil as he set his drink down, "is that they're all about power. That's a lot of what magic is. Raw power of will that can change the world. When a wizard taps into one, it's like using a much larger reservoir of personal power but at the cost of it being possibly addicting and a bit rough on the body, right?

"Back when Hugo launched his attack on the rift, I tapped into it and blew the *Flying Calamity* out of the sky. It gave me the power boost I needed when I was running on fumes. It tore through me, and I needed rest, but it made me stronger while I did it. If we can find a way to make leylines less harsh, or to tap into them without having to channel them through our bodies, then that alone would change how we use them."

As they considered it, Bram chewed his lip thoughtfully. "That's why runes. You want to find a way to make the leyline activate them without you having to do anything, right?"

Wil nodded. "That's what Thomas and I are hoping for. It's not been successfully done yet, but we believe it's possible. And then you can take things like my sled or flying carpet, or my new Thunderhawk, and anyone could use them. And it'd allow us to recharge depleted artifacts more efficiently."

"Where's a damned notebook?" Darlene demanded. "I know you have a million of them here."

Bram got up and retrieved one and a pen from a drawer and handed them over.

"What're you doing?" Wil asked.

Darlene took the notebook and scratched a line with the pen to make sure the ink wasn't dry. "I'm going to start writing down possible uses and applications for this research. If you want Cloverton to get off your ass and leave you alone, you have to present them with something impressive, right? Someone's gotta be the organized one."

"Hey," said Bram. "I'm plenty organized. I've been keeping things running just fine, haven't I?"

"Anyway, what are some other things we can potentially do with this?" Darlene wore a little smile, not looking at Bram.

"Cars," said Wil immediately. They'd been increasingly on his mind since his trip. "The nonmagical cars stink and are liable to explode if they hit something. If we can find a way to make magical cars operate for nonmagical people, that would be huge."

"Cars," Darlene repeated as she jotted it down. "What else?"

They thought about it some more. Bram got an excited look on his face and said, "If you can affect the flow of magic and make it replenish artifacts, maybe we can make it channel magic into tools and even advanced potions. There are some high-end potions I can't do without casting spells. I've made do by using some help from the fae, but . . ."

Wil nodded. That had been something they'd talked about in the past, and something Bram was embarrassed about. He prided himself on getting good with potions, but the most potent recipes were out of his reach.

"For that matter," said Wil, "we can and should experiment with a lot of one-off spells. Wizards can use wands or crystals to store a spell at the cost of destroying the object with time, but you guys couldn't use those. Not on your own. I think that's the biggest thing we can hope for. Being able to bridge the gap a little bit between wizards like me and people like you."

Darlene jotted that down as well, then started a second page, pen practically a blur. Wil said nothing as she filled that page up, then realized everyone was watching her. "What?" she said. "I'm getting it all down and adding notes of my own. Some realism to go with your pie-in-the-sky idealism. And now I'm done. That's officially it for work talk today."

"You got it," said Wil. "Bram?"

Bram looked like he wanted to cry. "If we must," he sighed. "But think of—"

"Nope," said Darlene. "It's friendship and celebration time. Or else. I'm tired, cranky, and this is the first time in months I've felt alright."

"That sounds perfect to me," said Wil, looking around the run-down but comforting kitchen. "I've been gone a long time now. I want you to tell me everything that happened, no detail too small."

CHAPTER 20

River Run

After a few days of getting back home and enjoying reconnecting with friends, family, and the people around town, Wil took his Thunderhawk up the mountain.

It had been hard at first, not immediately going up to Skalet Peak and poking around. But Wil was committed, and Darlene insisted that they take a few days to themselves first. It didn't take too much to convince him to wander around town, say hi to the neighbors, and enjoy some home cooking.

He'd discovered that both Jeb and Sarah were away, off on their own adventures. Jeb traveled back and forth between the embassy and Faerie along with Arabella, and they'd be gone for another few weeks. Sarah was at school in Manifee City and had been for a month. Wil was surprised to find he'd flown by her school on the way back home without knowing his sister had been only a few hundred feet away for those few minutes.

Mack and Candy kept the Shack going, and not much had changed for them save for demand increasing as more and more people came to Harper Valley to see or deal with the fae. The extra population was the biggest complaint he heard when making his rounds about town.

Wil saw it himself a number of times. There were now half a dozen different wizards who were staying in town. Almost all of them had been excited to meet him and talk his ear off, and he had a slew of new names and faces to remember, but most of them had at least possessed manners.

Most of the tourists were fine if a bit obnoxious. As he, Darlene, and Bram had lunch, he heard one woman from Cloverton talking with her companions about how behind and like it was from another time Harper Valley seemed to be. They had to intervene before a man ugly-laughing at a farmer got his face rearranged.

Only four months, and everything was different. Not by much, but enough to make home feel foreign. As pleasant as it was to have a few days with loved ones, it was even better to start working. Wil flew the Thunderhawk through town, winding his way west past farmland and a neighborhood of tall, multifamily homes, now apparently at capacity. He approached the looming mountain, excitement flooding his veins.

Now that there was no mad mage trying to pick a fight, or threat of impending war, Wil got to enjoy the experience of going up the mountain at reckless speeds. For the most part, he kept to the footpath and didn't risk himself outside some incredibly sharp turns that almost capsized him. It was enough to be able to make the trek quickly and without tiring, and to enjoy even more of the changes in the forest on the way up.

There were homes, for one. The majority of the forest remained wild, though now with vividly colored trees and new creatures that looked almost but not quite like they belonged. The new mushroom homes in clusters of four or five around the mountain surprised Wil, but the guards placed throughout the woods didn't.

He only saw them because they let him, he was sure, as he made eye contact with an elf sitting high up on a tree's branch. She nodded to him and gestured higher up, as if he were expected. For all he knew, he was.

About halfway up, Wil drifted to the southwest and saw the river he'd created half a year before. There wasn't that much water flowing now. It was more a wild, deep stream carved into the mountain and winding all the way up to the peak, where it drained the rainy runoff of the lake. He slowed to a stop at the riverbank.

When Wil extended his senses, there was nothing special about the river in any direction. The land was disturbed long ago, but the mountain claimed and accepted those changes with time. It wasn't perfectly integrated, but it was like a healing scar. Wil powered the Thunderhawk forward slowly, following the scar upward.

As Wil traced the scar backward up the mountain, he thought back to the night. The rain and wind had blinded him, and he'd never been so afraid as he had that night, watching the flash floods pour down toward Harper Valley. Desperation had him do the only thing he could think of. He'd tapped into the leyline and used its power to enhance his own, and he ripped a channel in the earth.

Somehow, the leyline itself had ripped. Only moments passed, but the way it had felt at the time seared itself into Wil's memory. One second, he held all the power of the leyline in his hands, and it burned like the sun. And then something gave, and it had deflated. Like a sack of grain emptying out and spilling onto the floor, only without end.

Now, the leyline remained in the same state. Weaker down here, though the trickle of exposed magical energy still flowed down the mountain. Wil's heart warmed as he got closer to the source of all his problems.

Skalet Peak once had been a place where the people of Harper Valley could hike and camp. There was a single cabin that was property of the city, a lake, and plenty of places for families to visit and cook and enjoy nature, especially in summer. Now it belonged, once again, to the fae and housed their interdimensional portal to Faerie.

The standout detail was the tree, hundreds of feet tall and still growing, coming out of a new island in the center of the lake. The last time Wil had been up here, there were camps for guards and fae coming in and out to rest at, but now there were permanent buildings. Or what passed for buildings for the nature-loving people. They grew their homes out of trees, mushrooms, and oddly shaped rocks.

Wil slowed down once more, heart skipping a beat as he saw it all. Dozens of people were there, and several came toward him, headed for him but in no hurry to get there. There was Faerie and its siren call, begging him to return and drink in the magical air. He dismounted and decided to leave his iron-based vehicle far away from the sensitive fae, and he met a tall, hairy ogre.

"Hello," said Wil with as much friendliness as he could convey, "it's been a while, but I believe I'm still allowed up here, right?"

The ogre looked at him, sniffed, then nodded. "Yeah," he said in his thick, gravelly voice. "We recognize you, Wilbur McKenzie. What's your business here today?"

He was polite and even toned, for an ogre, but Wil recognized the quiet, insistent challenge. "I'm here to study the leyline," he said. "I made a promise to your leaders that I would do my best to better understand what happened, when I was able to come back."

"Hmm." The ogre grunted.

More fae came up to them until Wil was almost surrounded. He didn't feel threatened. He was stronger than he'd ever been, and close to Faerie. Even without his staff, he would be a force to be reckoned with. Besides, they loved him here!

"If now's not a great time, I can always come back later. I wouldn't want to be an inconvenience or a poor guest."

That caught their attention. As alien and capricious as they could be, they took hospitality seriously, and their nation collectively had an obligation to Wil. It wasn't enough to bludgeon them and take what he wanted, but it got the point across.

"What are you going to examine, Master McKenzie?" A gnome with a pipe hanging out of his mouth asked. "Perhaps I can be of assistance. I'm Connor, and I handle the wards here."

Wil lit up. "You're exactly who I need to speak to. Can I ask you questions about your wards and how you do them? Do they make use of the leyline, and do they function differently with the leyline in this state?"

A few of the fae fell back, seeing it was dealt with. The ogre lingered a second longer before he nodded at Connor and fell back. He kept his eyes on the two of them, but Wil stopped paying attention to him.

Connor chuckled and pulled his pipe out of his mouth. As far as gnomes went, he looked fairly young. Or, at least, not ancient, lined and with a thick gray beard. He jabbed the stem over to where logs had been carved into simple bench seats. "Come, Wizard, have a drink with me, and I'll be happy to share what I know."

Wil gratefully sat down and accepted some sort of tea. He brought it to his lips and was about to drink when he paused. "This isn't the type of tea that makes you party for a few days straight, is it? I'm still dealing with the consequences of the last time I had a bit too much fae indulgence unknowingly."

Connor shook his head with a laugh. "Just really delicious tea, perfect for aches and pains and a clear mind." He sipped noisily.

Wil took a drink of his own and nearly spat it out. Fae tastes tended toward either the extremely sweet or extremely bitter. This tea managed to be both. With a forced smile, Wil asked, "So, first question, I guess. Has the leyline changed much over the past few months?"

"Changed how?" Connor sipped again, a twinkle dancing in his dark eyes.

"Changed. Like . . ." Wil breathed out and extended his senses. It was like suddenly standing right next to a roaring waterfall and getting blasted by the spray and the sound. "It didn't used to be this forceful. When it tore, it changed to this, but I don't know if it's been steady this entire time, or if it's getting weaker, or . . ."

Connor cocked his head to the side. "Why would it be weaker? We're utilizing the leyline now and making sure it doesn't spill out too much into the valley below. The more we use and nurture the leyline, the more it will give back to us. With enough time, it might even knit back into one. I don't know what will happen to us then, but that's centuries away."

Wil blinked. When he'd asked before, the fae hadn't been particularly helpful or knowledgeable on the subject. "Does this mean that leylines have changed before?" he asked hopefully.

"Leylines are always changing," said Connor. "Never as much as this one did, but it'll heal in time as it continues to grow and wind around the world in its never-ending journey. And with it, it brings life and health."

That was the other hard part of trying to talk to the fae about leylines. To Wil and other wizards, they were a naturally occurring phenomenon that could be harnessed like a tool. To the fae, there was an almost religious reverence to them, even though the fae didn't worship anything as far as Wil could tell.

"If you were going to intentionally change leylines to make them look or feel different, or to change their flow, what would you do?"

The gnome's pleasant expression twisted. "I wouldn't," he said coldly. "I'd accept the gifts they offer and not be greedy or try to force them to be something they're not."

"That's the problem," said Wil. "My people can't use the leylines the way yours can. We need them to be different, and we're trying to figure things out right now. So we can be as good as you are at it."

The last line was pure flattery, but it worked. "You shouldn't try to be like us. You should try to be like you. Hmm. Close your eyes and reach for the wards. Go on." Connor replaced his teacup with his pipe again, puffing along pleasantly.

Wil did as he was told. With his eyes closed and senses opened, the leyline roared at him once more, spewing its familiar strength and power. At first, that's all he could sense, but then over time a few things popped out to him. Like dots of orange in a sea of red, hard to see but there once you knew what to look for.

It at once felt alien and unusual. Not hostile, but Wil couldn't tell much more than that. Fae magic of some kind, but it was anchored to the leyline, and that's what stood out to Wil.

"We can do this to an extent," said Wil without opening his eyes. "Tie a spell into a leyline. It helps for a while, but it's usually not this stable. What is it you do differently than us?"

"We don't try to force it," said Connor. "We accept it as is and use what it offers. That's not the human way. We take care of the leylines, and they take care of us. Simple as that."

Well, that wasn't helpful. Unless . . . Wil opened his eyes. "You're right," he said. "We're different, and we shouldn't try to be like you. No one else has done what I have, apparently, so maybe . . . It was nice sharing tea with you, but I need to go."

Connor inclined his head respectfully. "Then I am glad to share a drink and some words, Master McKenzie."

Wil had to force himself not to run back to his Thunderhawk. He flew back down the mountain, but not too far. The river he made waited for him, and the leyline was within reach. Wil flew down farther, keeping the river of power in his mind's eye until he could barely touch it. He made it about a third of the way down the mountain before stopping.

If he ripped it, he could fix it. Maybe change it. Wil took a long, steadying breath and reached out with his considerable magical strength. The leyline answered his call, a spark to ignite his fire. Wil brought his hands up and closed them together, and the river closed itself off. Drifting upward, Wil's mind was in two completely different worlds as he drove back up, sealing the river as he went, changing the landscape once more.

It wasn't until he was most of the way back up when he noticed the difference. The wild river of power seemed fast and impossible to grasp in his mind all at once, but that changed the longer he held on to it. Little by little it seemed to shrink, or else he grew. Wild magic cascading into Skalet Peak didn't stop. It thickened and intensified, becoming less of a wild sprinkler and more of a hose.

A sense of euphoria lifted his spirits, and he didn't know if it was overexposure to the leyline or the thrill of success. Upon getting back up to the clearing before the tree on the Peak, Wil's control gave out and he crashed three feet into the ground. He went rolling off the Thunderhawk and settled in a muddy patch, laughing his head off.

"Are you okay?" The suspicious ogre had run up to him and now made up half of Wil's vision, which made him laugh even harder.

"Okay? I'm better than okay. I did it again!"

A Patron's Favor

Thomas Elliot paced back and forth in his luxurious cabin on the train heading north to Harper Valley. While he would've preferred to fly, the amount of equipment, funds, and manpower required made the train less expensive and more efficient. It was that manpower that bothered him.

He wasn't the type of person to dwell on guilt or look backward. Oh sure, he was excellent at looking back and picking apart everything he experienced. His magic lent itself to that. But Thomas had no use for lingering in the past. Not when the future was so damned interesting and right within his grasp. All he had to do was be of value to the naivest wizard in existence.

Oh, Thomas liked Wil. Who wouldn't? He was like a puppy, enthusiastic and innocent. Even after everything that had happened. At first it had seemed an act, and he resented Wil for it. When he came to realize it was just how the illusionist was, it made him want to protect and arm him against the cruel world.

Wil was one of those people that proved how unfair and uneven life was. He had more power than brains, and he held himself back all the time. He blundered into a life-changing discovery and thought he'd be able to manage it all on his own. All while the jackals at Cloverton waited to pick apart and take what they could for themselves.

Of course, that included himself, but it was different. Thomas actually cared, and he wouldn't rob Wil. He'd latch on to his rising star and make sure he didn't make any stupid mistakes that would ruin himself or his research. There would be no theft or taking credit. No matter what his master said.

Thomas sat down on the bench seating and breathed, letting the smooth rocking of the train soothe away some of the stress. He needed a clear head to do the next spell. From the top of the desk, he retrieved a small book and a pen. He opened up to the first blank page and ripped a sheet out. On it he scratched out a series of runes in a simple circle array. Then he set it on the ground and gently let himself be a conduit for the magic script.

Grandmaster Ferrovani appeared in his cabin. He was a short, older Ramenian man with sharp, dark features. His black eyebrows stood out in stark contrast from his white hair and beard. He wore a permanent scowl, aimed directly at him.

Thomas crouched and turned the paper around, and the image of his master turned with it. The spell took some time to compile, and part of the difficulty was including himself instead of having it be from his point of view. Then he had to account for the actual time he was using as he peered into a pocket of the past, and extraneous noise and details. Divination wasn't easy, but he had a knack.

A copy of himself appeared in front of Ferrovani. Thomas grabbed his forgotten coffee from the desk and settled in as the spell continuously drew small amounts of power, swirling in the center of the room. Sound came in last as the scene started.

"What's the problem?" Ferrovani demanded, talking extensively with his hands. "You told me you were this kid's only friend. Surely, you've managed to ingratiate yourself to him at this point. I know you're too logical to be having second thoughts about this."

"I am," said the specter of Thomas. "It's fine. I don't have any problem getting close and making the work mine. It *will* be mine, I assume. No changing your mind and deciding for one last glorious achievement before you retire."

Ferrovani sneered. "My name is already eternal. I don't need this. I'm doing this as a favor to all my worthy apprentices. One last boost for all of you. Some will succeed and may be nearly as legendary as I am . . . And others will fail and get nothing."

"I'm going to succeed," said the specter insistently. "None of the others have put in the work I have."

"Work. Feh." Ferrovani spat on the ground. "Work means nothing if you don't know how to direct it. You've always been more of a follower, Elliot. What makes you think you've got what it takes?"

Thomas took a deep breath as he watched, mentally pausing the playback of the scene. The question haunted him. Ferrovani had never been an especially encouraging master, but he did have a way of getting under his skin.

"I've got what it takes because I know how to spot opportunity and how to work on a team, you arrogant son of a bitch," Thomas whispered. He wished dearly he'd had the guts to say it in the moment. The playback continued.

"Give me time, and I'll show you," said the Thomas from a few days ago. "My discovery will—"

"Your discovery," Ferrovani scoffed, pausing to cough wetly into his hand. "You mean this McKenzie boy's discovery. This simple farm boy who's accidentally contributed more than you ever have. Get it done, Elliot, if you want to win it all." And like that, he turned from Thomas and walked off.

The image of past Thomas glowered after the old man, lips twitching slightly. Thomas felt the same rage from the past renewed, sharpened by the clarity of time.

"No doubt you're giving everyone the same kick in the ass," Thomas said to the image. "But no one has the vision I do. I'll make it happen."

A knock at the door disturbed him from his thoughts. He stomped the piece of paper, and the spell ended. Just in time, as two men and a woman entered. "What is it?" He asked impatiently. "I told you not to bother me."

"We're almost there," said the earth wizard Gayle, a stony expression on her face. "We thought you'd want to know, and to see if there was anything you wanted to discuss before we pull into town."

Thomas took a deep breath. "You have your orders," he said. "I thought I went over them. But," he added, letting the breath out, "this is a perfect time for reminders. Firstly, to make sure you've been listening, do not ever talk to me in public when we're there. When I'm ready to make contact, I'll come late at night to you. As far as the subject is concerned, you are a rival team and have nothing to do with me."

"Obviously," said McGinnis, the surly mage they brought for security and dirty work, if it was necessary. It wouldn't be, but they would be prepared for anything. "We're not stupid, Master Elliot."

"Everyone's stupid compared to the great Master Elliot," said the final member of their party, a balding man with a gray goatee and an enchanted monocle over his left eye. "Didn't you know?" Mark scoffed, staring uncomfortably at the diviner.

Thomas frowned. "All you need to know is that I'll be reporting on our experiments. Every major update, every trick we try—it'll all get passed to me and Master Marfolk here for dissection and discussion. Then he and Gayle will work on prototypes. You should expect to see me once a week or so."

McGinnis grunted. "It feels stupid to ask, given this is a backward farming town, but is there anything we need to watch out for or be careful of? Or should I focus on securing the house and tapping McKenzies' place?"

"Not stupid, actually. For one, do not tap McKenzies' place until I have a chance to examine it myself. For another, avoid his pet cat."

"Aw," said Gayle with a wry smile, "is his cat protective?"

"Yes. And also seven feet long, hundreds of pounds of teeth and claws, and it can read minds. Take this seriously. We'll have a better idea of where we'll be after a couple of weeks of experimentation and study."

Mark snorted. "And our supplies?"

"It's taken care of," said Thomas. "I'm handling all the requisitions and the pay sheets. If he asks or pokes around, it'll be easy enough to convince him that it's a list of all agents out here and their costs. He *will* know you're here, and I will talk and complain about you, no doubt, but he shouldn't suspect anything. Anything else? No? Shoo."

The three wizards had no love for him, and that was fine. He didn't even want them on the mission. Thomas knew he could handle this his way, without having to be as crooked or shady about the matter. McKenzie trusted him, and so long as Thomas didn't do anything stupid, it would be fine.

More than anything, the goal was to do it right. Not because Thomas had any sentimental need to do things the right way. It was pure ego. Thomas was as much a researcher and engineer as any of them. Wil may have been a good guy, but he wasn't a real academic. He was a talent who needed guidance. It was a symbiotic relationship; the way things were meant to be.

An hour later, the train pulled into the Harper Valley station. Thomas calmly collected his luggage and loaded it onto a frame with wheels he'd built and enchanted. It rolled along behind him weightlessly as he exited the train.

Harper Valley was about what he expected. A bright, green, luscious place with people who looked stuck in the last century, living alongside a few pockets of modern sensibility. There were more people than Thomas expected, but then, it was a booming town now.

Wil and who had to be his friends waited for him at the train station. Wil waved and motioned him over, a floating sign with his name flashing blue and silver hovered above him. Thomas chuckled and made his way over there, extending his hand.

"McKenzie, you sentimental bastard. What are we, in school?" Thomas laughed. No, he wouldn't screw him over if he could avoid it. It would be like kicking a puppy.

Wil took his hand and pulled him in for a one-armed hug. "Always. School never ends if you're doing it right. Thomas, allow me to introduce my best friend, Bram, and my girlfriend, Darlene."

Thomas looked toward them. Bram was huge and had a wide, nervous, insecure smile on his face. Darlene looked tired and grumpy, as did most pregnant women in his experience. "A pleasure to meet you both. Wil's told me so much about you. But he left out something kind of big, I think."

Darlene shot Wil a look, making him cringe. "Yeah," she said. "He didn't know. And now he does, and if he ever leaves town again, I'm taking his house permanently."

"You already moved most of your stuff in there anyway," Wil protested half-heartedly.

Bram eagerly offered his massive hand. "Wil's been telling us about you. Enchanting is the other major craft, right? I've been huge on potions and want to do advanced alchemy, but . . ."

"Ah, yeah, a bit tricky with no magic." Thomas clicked his tongue sympathetically. "But I'm sure you do well enough. Potions were never my interest. I'm all about enchanting. Which reminds me, Wil. I managed to requisition a couple of cars to tinker with."

"We get to tinker with a car?" Bram let out a squeal that shouldn't have come from someone his size.

Thomas pursed his lips. "Yes, but we must be very careful. We've got one of each type, and I don't think they'll be happy to give us a third one too soon if we muck it up."

Bram straightened his glasses and drew himself up. "I've been doing a lot of reading on intersecting runic configurations, and I'd *love* to see what makes a car go."

"Wil, tell him about the development," Darlene said, still looking hard his way. "Your achievement yesterday."

That made everyone perk up. "I managed to re-create things," said Wil in a hushed tone, as if they were being listened to. "I went to the original leyline and managed to make it budge. I think we can do this."

"You're kidding! After only a week?" Thomas didn't know whether to laugh or cry. One week, and he'd managed to start things off right. He was either the luckiest man on earth, or else he had more going on under the surface. Thomas hated that he couldn't tell which.

"Yeah! So once you're settled in, we'll start playing around with the leyline on Bram's farm."

Thomas looked between the three of them. He didn't know why Wil needed his obviously jealous friend and pregnant girlfriend to function, but he wasn't going to question it. Things were already more promising than he'd hoped. He'd prove to Ferrovani that he had what it took to be the next great in the field.

"That sounds great," said Thomas. "But that can wait until tomorrow. Why don't you show me your favorite places around town? I'd love to hear more about your special potions, Bram!"

The big guy lit up. "Oh, I've been working on perfecting a potion for grief, one without dependency issues, right, and . . ."

Thomas didn't care. About Bram, or Darlene, or Harper Valley. But for a little while he could fake it and work. It was his greatest strength, being able to blend in and be part of any team. And he'd use every advantage he could. He threw an arm around Wil and let his new best friend lead him into town.

CHAPTER 21

Experiment One

Holding back and not showing off had come surprisingly easily to Wil. There was still most of the three months left. They had time to go around town. Wil showed Thomas Mack's delicious and greasy food, Main Street's increasingly diverse shopping options, and then his place for drinks and planning out the next day.

"I'm surprised this place isn't more enchanted," Thomas said when they were sitting around the kitchen table. "What did you do to it?"

Wil pointed around to different spots of the house, listing them off. "Not much, just some basic sensible things. Reinforced windows, fire-resistant frame and floors, a sensory thing to let me know if someone is on the grounds when I am in my lab or bed. I should do more, huh?"

"I don't know about that," said Darlene, eyeing their drinks. "If I'm going to live here permanently, it's nice to not have to worry about running into dozens of spells I have no control over."

"True," said Wil, "and I like to keep it simple. There aren't any leylines to tie my spells to here, so I have to recast them fairly often. Anything more difficult or complex would be a pain in the ass."

Thomas perked up. "I thought you said half the people living here have leylines on their property. You have none?"

He had to think about it for a second. The second turned into a few before he shook his head. "No, I don't think so. One of the many things I should do is reconnoiter the basin and map out all the leylines. As far as I can tell, the center of the basin near my house has fewer of them."

"My farm has two!" Bram said, a little bit tipsier than the rest by then. He knew his capacity and had started early at dinner. "A big one and a little one."

"Which is exactly why we'll be using his farm," said Wil to Thomas. "The bigger one is tied to the fields, which we're going to need to tear up and fiddle with if we're going to tweak the leyline there safely."

"I'm still a bit iffy on that," Darlene said, sighing and drinking her tea. "Didn't you say that one guy blew up when trying this stuff? I don't think the risk of exploding Bram's house is a necessary one."

"That does sound like a bad thing for experiments," Thomas conceded. "But Wil said he redid it already. What do *you* think the risk is?"

Of course Wil wanted to wave it off as not a worry, but the past while had made him rethink a lot of things. Of course it was easy to sit at his kitchen table and imagine everything working out okay, but he had to be safer. Wil drank his oatmeal stout and sighed.

"I think it'll be okay, but just to be safe, we should close the business for a day and make sure no unnecessary bystanders are around. Is that going to be okay, Bram?"

The giant thought about it, pushing his glasses up the bridge of his nose. "Should be. We might need to take a day to announce it'll be closed for the day after. We don't want to lose any more time than we have to. We *could* put signs around the property that we'll be closed on certain days for experiments."

Darlene chuckled. "It's a start, but what do we do about the people who think that doesn't apply to them? You're always going to get like ten percent of people who will ignore the signs and try to buy a drink or potion."

"Well, easy," Bram said. "Put up a couple repel spells or wards on the outskirts of the property. That should work, right? I've actually got a couple wards ready that need power."

Thomas stirred. "Did Wil make you some before he left? He told me the two of you assist him with a lot of projects."

"Knowing Bram," Wil said with a laugh, "he made them himself. They'll be more meticulously crafted than I'd make 'em. I'm telling you, it's rotten luck that he wasn't born with magic. He'd do better with it than any of us."

"I don't know about *that*." Bram tried his best to not look too pleased.

"I do," said Wil. "So, tomorrow we'll set up the grounds for preliminary testing until we can tell if we're safe from exploding. How's that sound?"

Everyone agreed. The rest of the evening was spent with drinks and swapping stories, save for Thomas, who tired early after his days of traveling and retired to his inn for the night. Wil drove Darlene home in one of the cars Thomas had brought with him, and they had a lovely evening together. Wil even managed to avoid talking about work or the future.

Darlene was right, and the hardest part of the day was setting up. They were at the farm right after breakfast, and already there were people lining up to buy medicine. Bram was already awake and directing his half dozen employees. Even with the barn closed and signs posted, there was still a line.

"Some people," Darlene muttered, standing with her hands supporting her lower back. "Disrupt their day at all, and they don't know what to do with themselves."

"On the other hand," said Wil, putting an arm around her shoulders, "if they're going to a brewery before noon, maybe their day should be disrupted a little."

"Big talk from you, as much as you drink."

"Jealous?"

Darlene sighed. "Gods, yes."

The wards Bram had made were excellent quality, minus the complete lack of magical activity to them. The lines were clean, and even a surprised Thomas had to admit that it was a good job. Funniest to Wil was the fact they were sandwich board signs with "Temporarily Closed, No Trespassing" written on one side.

"Did you design these to only function after being read?" Wil was delighted.

"Do you think it will work?" Bram asked, suddenly nervous. "Three-dimensional configurations are still a bit hard for me, so I tried to go with an Erskine Ring to focus it." He pointed to an inward spiral on the back side of the warning.

Wil turned to Thomas, who looked baffled. "Yeah, it's . . . it's clean. I'd only change the anchor rune used at the end there. This is a bit strong for the effect you'd need and might end up with people wandering around semi-intoxicated. But they *will* wander away."

That was good enough for them. They set the signs up around the edges of the farm, then Wil and Thomas powered them up. All that remained was cleaning up the fields themselves. One of the conditions Bram had set for using his property was that they had to quickly mature the crops and bring them in to be made into the next batch of beer. Only then could they tear up the fields.

With his focus in earth magic, Wil took charge of that and hastened their lifecycle. It took only minutes for the wheat and barley to grow to full maturation, and then Thomas helped move them to storage. Darlene sat and watched in the shade in a comfortable chair they'd moved out there for her. Now that there were no customers around, her job was to observe and take notes.

"So." Thomas clapped his hands together. Unlike the others, he came in clothes too nice for the job, and the warm spring day had him sweating through his shirt. "How do we do this, Wil? Moment of truth. Once is happenstance, twice is coincidence, thrice is a pattern."

Wil wiped some sweat from his brow. It was past noon, and after all the prep work and cleaning up the land away from the brewery for their experiment, he wanted lunch or at least a quick breather. Then again, he'd finally be able to share his wonderful accident.

"Open up your senses and touch the leyline first," said Wil. "Don't do anything with it, just wrap your focus around it and trace the bounds of the moving power."

"Oh." Bram deflated. "This isn't something I can do, is it?"

Wil and Thomas shared a similar look. On Wil, it was sympathy. On Thomas, pity.

"I don't think so," said Wil apologetically. "We can feel it with our wizardsense, and it's like seeing it but better. I know! We can dig out that pair of spectacles I made for seeing through fae magic. We could see the torn leyline with it, but I don't remember me or Darlene seeing normal ones. We can tweak it."

"I'll make a note of it," Darlene called from her chair. She sipped some lemonade and motioned for them to continue.

"Yeah, no problem," said Bram. "I'll leave you two to it, then." He didn't seem happy, but he took a spot next to Darlene and watched.

Wil hated that Bram couldn't participate this time, or in a lot of what they would be doing. And yet, he needed Bram's help more than nearly anyone's. As far as he was concerned, everyone on the team was crucial. It was a bad start that two of them had to sit out.

"So, open my senses and watch?" Thomas prodded.

Wil broke free from his thoughts and nodded. "Yeah. Close your eyes and search it out. Tell me what you sense."

He gave Thomas a second before he extended his senses. This leyline was familiar and answered his call immediately. It was one of two L-shaped rivers framing the farm. The weaker of the two was a ways off, on the other side of the house. The greater one, close to them, fueled the fields and thrummed serenely.

"It's not that big," said Thomas in a dreamlike tone. "Not as large as some I've seen. But it feels like trying to look at the sun or touch an electrical line. It's giving so much to the land around here, and it's . . . healthy. What else should I be noticing?"

"The shapes. Of this one and the other one." Wil breathed it in. They pulsed, one after another. An answer, and a call. "It's almost like it was one loop but broke up. They go around and drift off in the distance."

"Okay," said Thomas, a hint of impatience entering his voice. "And then what?"

"Watch."

Wil breathed in and tapped into the leyline. It answered immediately in its steady, thrumming pulse. The sensation of being struck by lightning passed through him, and he channeled it into the earth. Like so many times before, the Stevenson farm came to life under his touch, the dirt and soil vibrating together and parting, infinitesimal pieces of a greater whole on the move.

With a firm grasp on the greater leyline, Wil shifted the land around them. One section rose by ten feet, becoming a small plateau while a patch of dirt spiraled into a sharp valley. Every time Wil became a conduit to its power, it came easier. Shoving around so much earth was as simple as reaching out and molding the land with his heart.

Wil, the leyline, and the land itself, a dance with three partners. As Wil moved, he gently tugged, then firmly dragged on the invisible river of power. The land shifted and moved, and then so did the leyline. Slowly, Wil changed the direction, facing the flow toward its twin on the other side of the farm.

"Impossible," Thomas gasped, crouched for stability as the earth finally settled.

Wil released everything. The strain caught up to him like a rubber band snapping back, striking him in the brain. It had been a solid effort, and he proved his point. When he opened his eyes, the landscape was chaotic.

"Good job wrecking the fields, Wil," Darlene shouted. "Did it do what you wanted?"

"It worked," Thomas whispered. "It really worked!"

Bram watched with a thoughtful frown. "I guess I'll have to take your word for it."

Wil breathed in and out, catching his breath. He smiled and said, "I'll make those glasses next. We've got a lot of work to do, so let's get all the prep work out of the way so we can have some fun!"

CHAPTER 22

Dogged Darlene

One of the most frustrating parts of starting out was how stop-and-go it could be. After an initial success of changing the shape of the leyline, Wil and Thomas spent most of the day fiddling with it and kicking up dirt, showing that it could be done. Mostly Wil. Thomas wasn't as adept at moving the earth, a fact that turned his mood sour before too long.

Bram and Darlene waited by the side, asking questions and marking the answers down. Their first day ended with a laundry list of tasks they'd need to do before they did anything with their initial success. They parted midafternoon, and then the real work began.

Wil got to work on the specialized spectacles that would let Bram observe the leyline, to go with the pair Darlene already had. The old pair wasn't as clear as Bram's new pair, but they would remain more versatile. That took nearly two days of his labor.

Meanwhile, Thomas and Bram worked together to catalog and sort the materials they'd requisitioned and split the materials between Wil's house and Bram's. Thomas took one of the cars for his own use and grumbled about the likely necessity of a third or fourth one down the line. Another couple of days of work and that was squared away, ready for use.

By the time Friday rolled around, they were all but ready to actually get moving, with ten weeks remaining in their time limit. It was then Darlene revealed she had other plans than working that day.

"What other plans?" Wil had asked the night before, surprised. They lay in bed together, pleasantly tired after a hard day's work.

"Something unavoidable and a complete pain," Darlene said. She sounded embarrassed. "It's a doctor's appointment."

"Well, that's not so bad," he said. "Have you been feeling sick?"

She'd laughed and looked at him like he was slow. "For the baby, Wil. I have to get routine checkups to make sure I'm fine."

"Oh. Right, that makes sense. When is it?"

Darlene huddled under the light blanket as if she could somehow hide her belly. "Bright and early, nine a.m. It's probably going to be the same as last time. I'm fine, I need to eat more and rest my feet more. I don't have time for that."

"Don't have time to take care of yourself?" Wil scoffed. "No, you should relax more anyway. Especially now."

"Especially now," she echoed with a tinge of irritation. "I hate this. The change part," she added quickly upon seeing his face. "I have to uproot my entire life and change how I do everything for a year because of a night neither of us remembers. It's crap. I hate feeling so weak and helpless. And my feet and back hurt."

"I'm afraid of the change too," Wil admitted. "But I'll be here the entire time. And I might be able to do something about the foot and back pain. I could make you special slippers that help soothe your aches and pains and make you light on your feet."

"Right. With what time, Wil?" Darlene scoffed, but she relaxed. "Maybe come with me to the appointment? Doc Hawkins isn't the judgmental type, but he compensates by being *too* helpful."

"Of course." Wil threw an arm around her and got comfortable in bed. "I'll drive you there, we'll get a bite to eat after, and then we'll do something, just the two of us."

". . . Okay, that sounds good," Darlene said, slowly turning on her side, pressing up against him. Within a few minutes, she was asleep.

Wil cooked them breakfast and drove them to the clinic the next morning. Doc Hawkins was as energetic and friendly as ever, welcoming them both in with hearty handshakes and an offer of candy. Wil took him up on his offer, but Darlene passed.

"So make yourself comfortable, and I'll get started," Hawkins said as he grabbed his stethoscope. Darlene lay down on the examination table, Wil beside her, a disgruntled look on her face as she stared at the ceiling. The doctor slipped the stethoscope in his ears and put the other end on Darlene's chest.

He listened, humming as he moved it around and then down to her stomach. Smiling, he looked to Wil. "Everything sounds good so far. Strong, fast heartbeat. Would either of you care to listen?"

"Pass," said Darlene. "I can feel this thing in me at all times."

Doc Hawkins chuckled and offered the stethoscope to Wil.

He cautiously took it and slipped the prongs into his ears. As always, he marveled at the way the sound changed before noticing the deep, rapid flutters echoing in his head. Wil jerked, looking at an amused Darlene.

"Baby!" was all he could manage to get out.

"Yeah, that's what we're here for, son," Doc Hawkins chuckled.

Wil ignored him and focused on the sound of the baby, his baby, and the strong, indomitable heartbeat. As shocking as seeing Darlene had been when he first got home, being in the clinic made it real. Hearing the heartbeat made it real. His throat dried up instantly. In approximately four months, Wil was going to be a father.

"I . . . This . . . I . . ."

"Yeah, sounds about right," Darlene said, a small smile slipping past her grumpiness. "You see why I'm so stressed?"

Doc Hawkins laughed again. His lined face was as serene as Wil wasn't. "One of my favorite parts of the job is that look on your face right now. You haven't had time to get used to it yet, and coming into it this far along is shocking. But that face makes it worth it. Things are scary, but they'll get better. You're lucky the two of you have each other."

Wil believed it. He swallowed hard, nodding, then slipped the stethoscope off. "I . . . Yeah. It puts a lot of things into perspective."

On a hunch, he cast a small spell to sense life around him. Doc Hawkins was his usual rocklike presence, and Darlene was fiery and seemed to be flickering wildly. Deep inside her was a small flame, and he realized he didn't need to use this spell to sense the life in her. If he used his wizardsense, his child was right there. He was so engrossed in it he missed that the conversation moved on.

". . . and the like? Any new aches and pains?" Doc Hawkins had a pad of paper and a pen out.

Darlene groaned. "Nothing new, thank the gods. Everything's bad enough. Only thing that's been worse is I can't seem to go half an hour without needing to pee. Please tell me that doesn't get worse."

"Sure, I won't," said the doctor. He made it three seconds before chortling. Darlene and Wil joined in weakly.

"Then everything seems fine. Come back in a month from now, or if anything changes. Any weird pains that aren't gas, or any excessive bleeding or discharge, come in before then. Okay?"

"Sounds good, Doc," Darlene said, fighting to sit up. Wil took her hand and pulled her up.

"Then I'll see you later. Be safe, and congratulations, Wil." Doc Hawkins smiled and opened the door for them.

Back in the car, they sat without saying anything or moving for several minutes. All until Darlene winced, and Wil jumped to attention. "Are you alright?"

"Of course I'm alright," Darlene said with a sigh. "She's moving around, and it feels really weird." She reached for his hand and placed it on her stomach. Wil almost protested, then the first kick against his hand made him freeze.

The second and third kicks had him laughing. "That's so uncomfortable. I can't imagine what it's like on the receiving end of it. Gods, this is real."

"Yeah," said Darlene. "It's scary, right? I don't feel ready. I've got a million things to do, and there's no time to be slowed down by a baby. I'm . . . It's not that I don't want it, but I don't want this to define me. I'm supposed to be the smart, organized one. Not the one stuck at home taking care of a kid."

"You won't be," said Wil, taking her hand in his. He stared out the windshield, half looking at the front of the clinic, half seeing into space. "For one, we make enough money for a nanny."

Darlene shot him a look. "That's not what I mean, and you know it."

"I know," he said with a smile. "But I thought it might help. You'll never be stuck at home if I can help it. I need you too much, Darlene. I don't know if you've noticed, but I'm kind of an idiot and can't do things on my own. I may look like I have more power than you and Bram, but I'm helpless without my team backing me up.

"Without you taking care of every stupid little detail, I'd be stuck spinning my wheels endlessly. You're sharp, you're driven, you're fiery. You'll never just be a mother, stuck at home and living for your kids. I'd never let that happen. I need you."

Her grip on his hand tightened. She said nothing at first, swallowing in a way Wil knew was to hide a few unshed tears. He understood. After a long, deep breath, she nodded.

"I need you too. But I don't like it," she said, laughing weakly. "I don't want to need anyone. I always wanted to be strong and independent. I was going to run my own business and make it on my own. And while you were gone it . . . it felt like Bram and I were holding down the fort until you got back.

"And then *this* happened." She touched her stomach again. "And all I could think of was how badly I wanted you home. And the thought of you not coming back hit twice as hard. When I found out . . . It was the first time I was ever actually scared while you were gone. Thinking of doing it alone, and then being ashamed of that."

Back when Wil first came back, he'd genuinely thought Darlene to be one of the strongest, coolest people in town, and only now did he see how much effort she put into making that true. In all this time, he'd cared enough to make sure she didn't work too hard, but he'd never seen how hard she worked at seeming invincible.

"There's no shame in needing other people," said Wil. "Not even for the strong. Everybody needs somebody, right? No one is completely alone. And you should never feel ashamed of being scared or realizing you can't do everything on your own. If, for whatever reason I didn't come home, you would've been taken care of."

Darlene laughed, nodding. "I know. Your parents already made that clear. They're the best."

"They really are," Wil groaned. "But my point is, we're okay. We'll be okay. And you won't lose yourself or what you're good at. Without your logistics and planning, we'd be up the creek without a paddle. Even with Thomas here. No one can replace you, and I mean it."

She thought about it, and then her thoughts moved to the vehicle they were sitting in. "It'd be a lot easier, helping you and helping myself, if I could drive myself around instead of having to try to walk or catch a ride off a cart."

Wil's lips twitched. "Thomas isn't going to be happy about needing to order more cars, but clearly we need them both to get around and use for our tinkering. I'll happily give you the other one. I prefer my Thunderhawk anyway."

Darlene rolled her eyes. "You can have it. But you have to teach me to drive. Today, in fact. We can get back to work tomorrow. Today is all about making sure I stay as independent as possible, you got it?"

He smiled. "You got it, Darlene. Anything you need, it's yours. We'll grab the other car and get you going . . . right after second breakfast?"

"Yes." Darlene nodded and took her hand back. "Now let's get out of here before Doc Hawkins charges us rent."

Wil laughed and poured magic to turn the car on. He reversed and brought them back onto the dirt road and on to a good meal. They'd get back to work tomorrow. Ten weeks left, they had plenty of time.

CHAPTER 23

Work Never Ends

Further experiments over the next few days centered around changing the leyline, making little changes to the shape based on pushing around the land. No matter how hard he tried, Thomas had trouble with the raw power needed to make it work, even with the leyline's help. Before too long, it turned into Wil moving earth around while Thomas provided potential shapes and tweaks while they watched.

It didn't take long to make another pair of the spectacles for Bram, and he was there every day, eager to watch them work and make suggestions. Wil never hesitated to try out any of his suggestions. Thomas questioned them a few times but never pushed too hard against Bram's participation. It was just enough for Wil to notice, but not quite enough for him to be annoyed.

Unfortunately, shifting the earth around and changing the shape of the twin rivers of power on the Stevenson farm didn't accomplish anything. Over the course of those few days, Wil became more confident about his ability to do it, but not how to make it matter.

No matter how they twisted or contorted the leyline, they couldn't attach spells to it any more easily. They could bend and twist and pull, but at the very least it didn't rip open, and it didn't blow up the property. With that in mind, Wil couldn't be too disappointed.

That kind of block had been expected, and as Wil and Thomas toyed with that, Bram went back and forth between observing their attempts and doing some work of his own in his cellar. With all his customary care, he constructed a simple box with runic designs meant to fuel a simple spell. Thomas had laughed when he first saw it.

"Is that a music box?" he asked, delighted. "That was something my mother used to make when I was little, when she was learning how to enchant. But your wording is weird. Why do you have the runes for *void* and *hungry*? That's going to make it inefficient to power."

Wil understood immediately. "It's to try to coax the magic from the leyline into it, right?"

Bram nodded, wiggling in place with excitement. "It's the first big idea I've had! If it's designed to take power in, maybe we can establish a line or something when one of us is the conduit. Make it stick to the box."

"You mean one of *us*," Thomas said, referring to himself and Wil. "That's not an awful guess for not knowing how magic feels. It has potential." He stroked his chin thoughtfully. "Not bad."

Bram's face contorted silently. Wil saw embarrassment and gratitude fight to see which would win. He decided to push it over to gratitude by slapping Bram on the back. "Good going, as always. Let's give it a try. Thomas, would you like to do the honors?"

Thomas looked up from the illusion box he turned over repeatedly in his hands. "Hmm? Sure, I'll give it a try. Still getting a feel for the unusual syntax used here. It's not *wrong* per se, but . . ."

At receiving two unimpressed looks, he cleared his throat and held the box up. A few seconds later, a high-pitched tone came from the box. It wasn't actually music so much as a mockery of it through a few sounds it switched between, but it worked.

"This is about twice as difficult as it needs to be," said Thomas. "The configuration you used is strong. If it's going to work . . . Well, let's find out." He concentrated, and then the sounds cut out, but slowly. Thomas shook his head.

"Damn," Bram sighed. "Maybe if I tweak it a little, it might work better."

"Maybe," Thomas said unconvincingly. "It's a good thought, and it shows imagination and understanding I didn't expect."

"Wait," said Wil. "Do it again. Slowly."

The three men huddled over the crude magical music box, and Thomas activated it once more. It played its tuneless song and then tapered off into nothing. He shook his head again. "Nothing."

"Not true," said Wil. "One more time!"

This time, Thomas understood. "It's not shutting off immediately. It's lingering for a second, second and a half. It's not much."

"But it's something, right?" Bram asked. "It's more than we knew before. Do you two think this might be a direction worth pursuing?"

"We're not ruling anything out yet," Wil responded quickly before Thomas could say anything. "It's a possible direction to follow, and it's the only one we've got so far. But I think we're due for a break, don't you?"

They grabbed some sandwiches and sweet tea in the kitchen. The table was covered in notebooks, wood, tools, and some of Wil's old books on enchanting. They didn't clean up so much as stack the books at the empty fourth spot on the table and ate in silence, each of them lost in their thoughts on how to proceed.

They were most of the way done and finishing their drinks when Darlene came through the door, arms laden with a box filled with paper. "Hey, everyone. Wil, I just saw your dad, and he wanted me to give you these." She set the box on the table and pushed his empty plate out of the way.

"Thanks, Darlene, you shouldn't have," said Wil. "What are they?"

"Work slips," she said with a growing smile. "You've been gone for four months. Bram's taken care of dozens of slips since then."

"Over a hundred," Bram fake-coughed.

"Over a hundred slips, but now that you're back and have been back for a week, people are requesting your help once more." She leaned against his chair for support, supremely amused.

"Are you serious?" Thomas asked, half standing to get a better look at the haphazard stack of yellow papers. "We've got nine and a half weeks to go, and they want you to run errands for townies?"

"It *is* my job," said Wil. "And I've been neglecting it. I guess that's what we're doing after lunch. Bram, I hate to ask, but . . ."

"Say no more," said Bram, puffing up to his full sitting height. "I'm always happy to help. Besides, people got used to seeing me instead of you. I can knock half of these out without you."

"I don't mean to be rude," said Thomas, wetting his lips. "But if half of these can be done without you, should they really be tasks for the resident wizard? If some random guy can do them, couldn't anyone?"

It took Wil a few seconds to register what Thomas had said, and a few more to get over the surprise anger. Darlene recovered first. "Bram isn't some random guy," she said coldly. "He's put in a lot of hard work and study to be able to solve those problems."

"No, he's right," Bram said, eyes locked on the table. "A lot of them aren't too bad and could be done by anyone. I think people just want to feel special and like their problem matters and needs special care."

"Regardless," said Wil, "I would love your help. The sooner we can get these over with, the sooner we can get back to working on the main project. If you get done before me, then maybe spend some more time on the hunger runes and see if there's any way to tweak the meaning with the right configuration."

"Right," said Bram, standing up. He grabbed half the papers and tucked them under his arm. "I'll check these out and grab whatever potions might be needed from the cellar. See you in a couple hours?" He smiled at Wil and Darlene and left without looking at Thomas.

Darlene didn't let it rest. "I know you're a real wizard and all, but you don't have to be an ass."

"An ass? What? I said I didn't mean to be rude! Someone had to ask the question." Thomas adjusted his collar. Wil had never seen him on his back foot before. He seemed uncomfortable and nervous. "It has nothing to do with doubting your friend and more to do with the fact that he's not . . ."

"Not what?" Darlene pressed. "A wizard? Do you think that we're not capable of doing anything? Don't answer that. I've got some more errands to run." She kissed Wil on the forehead and left the two wizards alone.

"It's not like that," Thomas said after she left. He must've known how weak it sounded because he added, "I'm not prejudiced against the nonmagical. I just know how different our lives really are, what we're capable of. And if the people of Harper Valley are asking for that much nonmagical help from you, then maybe they don't need it that badly. Maybe they should ask less."

Wil stood up as well, unsure whether he was more irritated or disappointed. They were all things he'd thought in the past, in his guiltier moments. "You might be right, but after so much time away, I'm grateful to be home. And I'm grateful to serve my community too."

Thomas softened. "And that *is* a good thing. Not trying to act like it isn't. But . . ."

"But we've got work to do and a time limit," Wil finished for him, nodding. "Yes, that's also true. But I think we'll be fine. You can stay here if you want and continue to get some work done or maybe go home and take a break. I, however, am going to try to get as many of these slips done as I can before taking a look at Bram's idea."

He grabbed the half-full box of work slips and walked out of his best friend's house. Darlene had the car, and the Thunderhawk would be impossible to drive while carrying all of them. Even if he could, it went fast enough that they'd go flying without a sticking spell. A long walk would probably do him some good anyway. He was halfway down the lane when he heard his name being called.

"Wil! Wait!" Thomas ran up to him, slightly winded after a short sprint. "I'll come with you."

Wil raised an eyebrow. "Why?"

"Selfishness," said Thomas. "The faster we get the work done, the faster we go back to focusing on trying to make the world a better place."

"That's the thing, Tom." Wil held the box up and jiggled it. "We *are* making the world a better place. For these people. The only difference is scale. No one should be too big to help their community. You don't have to help if you don't want to. If you come along, I don't want to hear any complaints, understand?"

Thomas grimaced but nodded. "Alright, I can do that. What's our first stop, then?"

Wil reached into the box and fished out a slip. "Our first job is helping Mrs. Bartleby with her mouse problem."

"You're joking."

Wil eyed him.

Thomas held up his hands. "Okay, okay. Helping Mrs. Bartleby with her mouse problem. Lead the way."

CHAPTER 24

Rodent Roundup

Mrs. Bartleby was beside herself when they arrived.

"They won't stop stealing from me!" Mrs. Bartleby cried when she opened the door and invited the two wizards in. "Those rotten little jerks!"

Her home was standard for Harper Valley's non-farming population. It was a small two-bedroom house with an open living room connected to a small kitchen. Snug, cozy, and more than enough for the empty nester. She was a frumpy, nervous woman with thick spectacles, gray hair, and conservative clothes twenty years out of date.

"Err. You mean the mice?" Thomas asked, looking around as if he expected someone or something else.

"Of course I mean the mice," Mrs. Bartleby huffed. "They've been insufferable for months, but this time they've gone too far. They've taken my late husband's wedding ring and made off with it!"

Wil nodded sympathetically. "And we'll do what we can to get your husband's wedding ring back, and make sure this doesn't happen again. Do you have any signs of the mice disturbing things or taking them? Do you know where they nest?"

Mrs. Bartleby didn't take her eyes off him as she pointed to a corner of the kitchen. Wil smiled and said, "Wait here and let me take a look, okay? Thomas, if you'll come with me."

Although the kitchen was open and there was no separation between them and Mrs. Bartleby other than the distance she allowed them to keep, Thomas whispered, "Since when do wizards stop mice theft?"

"Ah ah, that sounds like complaining," said Wil as he looked around. It was a standard, drab-looking kitchen, clean but with no life to it. It wasn't hard to find the hole in the wall where the mice made their lair. "Here we are." Wil crouched to the ground and sniffed.

"Sorry," said Thomas, sounding anything but. "I appreciate you wanting to help anyone, but this is mice, right? This would be a perfect task for Bram, wouldn't it? Set out some poison and—"

"Set out some poison?" Mrs. Bartleby was outraged. "And risk my poor Mittens getting into it and dying? I think not!"

"Mittens?" Thomas mouthed to Wil.

"Her cat," Wil supplied. "But she's right, no need to kill all the mice when we can communicate with them. I just need something to anchor myself to. My rodent is a bit rusty. Hey, can you see into the hole better than I can?"

Thomas took a deep, long suffering breath before nodding. "Yeah, not a problem. A simple scry, add on a bit of night vision . . ." He fished a pad of paper out of his trousers and began writing down simple runes along the paper. Crouching down, he ripped out and stuffed the paper into the hole and then sat cross-legged, eyes closed.

Wil waited patiently and wasn't disappointed. Thomas's eyes remained shut as he spoke. "Surprisingly roomy in there, past the initial tightness of the hole. If I go along it, it branches off along the walls. There're droppings here, so I think it's safe to say she's not wrong about the mice at least. A little deeper and . . . Huh. Well, there's the wedding ring. Want me to nab it?"

"Yes, please," said Wil.

Thomas nodded and reached out with his hand. The sounds of scrabbling in the walls heralded the ring as it bounced around and popped out the front and into the wizard's waiting hand along with a ton of dirt, dust, and fur.

"Good job. Gross, but nice work." Wil took the ring from Thomas, who brushed his hands off on his pants. "Here's your ring, Mrs. Bartleby."

"Oh, thank you, thank you." She clutched it tight to her chest. Her eyes watered, while her smile made the lines around her eyes increase. "But how do we know the damned mice won't steal it again? They've been breaking into my locked jewelry case, and nothing seems to stop them."

Thomas muttered, "We could always gas the house, and the problem's solved."

Wil shook his head. "I don't know how much experience you have with mice and other pests, but unless they gnaw their way through, they're not going to get into a jewelry box. Did they chew their way through?"

Mrs. Bartleby shook her head vigorously. "No! They picked the lock, I swear it."

"Right," said Thomas. "Lock-picking mice."

"I'll check it right now," Wil said before Mrs. Bartleby could take exception to Thomas's tone. "If you don't mind me going into your room, of course."

Her room looked exactly as Wil had pictured it. Neat and orderly, with the same lost-in-time quality the rest of the house had. She'd not been the same since her kids grew up and her husband died, and nothing here looked like it had changed in the better part of a decade. The jewelry case on her vanity was open, with the tail and back legs of a mouse hanging out of it. It continued rummaging without noticing either of them.

Thomas made a face and looked at Wil, who suppressed laughter. Wil held up a finger and concentrated on one of his more complex spells. When he spoke next, it came out as squeaks and chitters to Thomas, but sounded normal to him.

"Hello, small friend, are we the interruption?" he asked, the words sounding stilted and off to him. He'd not communicated with a rodent in a while.

The mouse jumped into the air with a squeak. It landed and turned black eyes over to the two wizards. It trembled in place violently.

"Do not afraid," Wil continued. "Friends of no harm you."

"Wil, what the hell are you saying?" Thomas asked. His voice jolted the mouse out of inaction. It took off running, dropping to the ground.

"Give chase!" Wil shouted in mouse before leaping forward. He reached for the mouse right as it approached a crack in the wall. He pulled it back using magic. It flew straight into his hand, where it twisted and fought to either get away or bite him badly enough to make it so. Too late. Wil had it floating in his palm, spinning in place.

"Stop! Stop! Do not like the spin, please!" the mouse chittered at him.

Wil held the mouse still. "Why must thievery, small brother?"

The mouse stopped trying to attack him and sat in his palm. "Is shiny and pretty."

"What is it saying?" Thomas asked.

Wil cleared his throat and switched languages. "I'm asking him why he's stealing, and he said it's because the things he steals are shiny and pretty. Pretty relatable, honestly."

"So?" Thomas prodded. "You got the culprit, you got the ring back. What more is necessary? Just bop the mice or drive them out elsewhere, and we can move on to the next work order, right?"

"Might not even have to come to that. If the mice leave here, they're going to go somewhere else. Once, I helped Darlene's dad clear out mice from their basement. They ended up going elsewhere in the house and to the fields outside, but the wards kept them from the food there. Could do that, but there are a lot of houses here. I think I'm going to check something else first."

Clearing his throat, Wil switched back to his iffy version of mouse. "Gray lady here wants the family exiled from house. No thievery or gone into cold. Understand?"

"No," said the mouse. "You talk odd."

Yeah, that was fair. "Have you a daddy leader?" Wil grimaced. That couldn't have been right. To his surprise, the mouse chittered in acknowledgment.

"Yes. Mik is daddy and leader. You want to talk to Mik? What's in it for me?" The mouse groomed himself in a way Wil perceived as smugly.

Clearing his throat and switching back to normal, he said, "Thomas? Would you ask Mrs. Bartleby for some fruit? And maybe some bread. I've got an idea."

Ten minutes later, Wil sat on the floor in front of a succulent spread of meats, cheese, bread, and fruit. Thomas stood behind him, radiating impatience, irritation, and incredulity. On the other side of the feast was Mik and three dozen of his family. More than Wil had expected, and way more than most would have been comfortable having in their walls.

"I am here, Human. Speak now, or . . . ?" Mik addressed him. He was a dark gray mouse with a long, naked tail.

"Eat now," said Wil, gesturing at the food.

No one waited for their leader's permission. They swarmed the bread and fruit first, while Mik took his first pick of meat and cheese. Wil wasn't typically the type to enjoy watching others eat, but the speed in which they devoured everything fascinated him.

"Not complaining, but how is this going to help?" Thomas didn't look as entertained.

"Getting them in a good mood first. Watch."

As the mice finished the feast, Mik crept closer to Wil. He looked as if he didn't fully trust any human, even one who fed him. "What do the humans be wanting with us?"

"I want to help you. If you stealing, old lady will want you gone. Don't steal, maybe she is to be a friend."

The mouse cocked his head to the side quizzically. "Old lady want treasures back? She can feed us! More like this."

"I'll see what I can do. If you'll all come with me."

Thomas waited somewhat patiently for him to finish. When Wil stood again, Thomas asked, "So, what's the plan, then? And the purpose of this?"

"Watch and see," said Wil, going back into the main room. He was trailed by all the mice. They fanned out all over the nearby furniture and got comfortable. "Mrs. Bartleby? It appears the mice love your trinkets and treasures."

Somehow, Mrs. Bartleby avoided screaming. "Well, I know *that*," she said.

"Yes, but they're willing to offer a trade," Wil said. "If you feed them some bread, meat, and cheese once a day, they'll not only leave your treasures alone but will return what they've stolen. And not only that, but I think I can convince them to help keep your floors cleaner." He spread his hands, smiling apologetically. "It's one of the best offers I've heard an animal make, so you might want to take them up on it."

Mrs. Bartleby looked at him as if he grew a second head. "Why on earth would I agree to that? That's my food. Those're my treasures!"

"Sure," said Wil, "but they need a place to live too. If you do this, then you're making a deal with a mouse family to share the place and for them to have no reason to get into your stuff."

"How do I know they'll keep to their side of things?" Mrs. Bartleby demanded.

Wil shrugged. "Animals are pretty simple, but they aren't known for lying much. Besides, these are very smart mice, and I think they'd appreciate a comfortable place to stay and raise a family. If you do this, maybe they can even be out in the open, and you won't be alone anymore."

Mrs. Bartleby froze. "I won't?"

Ten minutes later, they walked out of the house, one work slip down. Thomas was beside himself.

"How in the hell did that work? Why did it work?" He asked, laughing in disbelief. "You made it sound like you were doing her a favor by not getting rid of the vermin."

Wil shrugged, not quite sure how to explain it. How did he tell someone results oriented that sometimes, you didn't have to solve problems if you could sidestep them? Thomas was no fool, but things had to make sense for him.

"The way I see it, she's a cranky older lady who needs something to fuss over. The mice are simple and just want food and to not be attacked. Make it clear they won't be attacked and that she'll have roommates . . . I will bet you a thousand zynce that we could come back in a week, and she'll be happy and things will be okay."

Thomas eyed him suspiciously. "I'm not sure whether I want to take that bet or not. Let's . . . That's one job down. How many left are there? Will they all be this . . . unconventional?"

"Hey, bravo for not complaining more," Wil said with mock applause. "It's spring, so a lot of them have to do with allergies and helping with farms. This one seemed the easiest. Really, you don't have to keep coming with me. If you'd rather not waste your time, you could take today off or even work on your own."

"No, I can't," Thomas sighed. "You've got me curious now. And the more of these you get done, the less we'll have in the future, right?"

"Right."

Thomas reached into the box of work slips and pulled one out. He read it, making a face. "Carl the bull's having stomach issues."

Wil groaned. "Not again. Pick another one, we'll do that one later."

They did have other, better things to do, but there was a comfortable familiarity in running around town and solving problems. If nothing else, it would work wonders for his sense of accomplishment. With the clock working against them, he needed every mental boost available.

CHAPTER 25

Community-Minded

Thomas didn't complain too much more over the next few stops. They dropped by the Manson residence about a haunting. It turned out to be wind going through a hole in the walls, especially when someone opened or closed the front door. They took care of that one in ten minutes, and they moved on to the Poyle family, who had a terrible feud with the Spaceys that got better or worse depending on the season.

Thomas had been the one to come up with the solution there. They were next-door neighbors and could often be heard shouting at each other at all hours of day and night. Through a tricky bit of layered spells, he managed silence from each other but not the rest of the world. They left with the hope that the lack of perceiving each other's voices would usher in peace.

After that was Erin Davis, who'd had a break-in two nights before. The sheriff and deputies were stretched thin with the increased population and tourists and had shifted the responsibility to Wil now that he was home. Again, Thomas had an easy solution and conjured a vision of the culprit in the middle of the act.

Wil had captured that vision in an illusion he stuck to a piece of paper, handing it to Erin afterward. "Give this to the sheriff and tell him I sent you this time. If he continues to give you guff, I'll get my dad to lean on him a little. How's that sound?"

"That sounds excellent, Mr. Wizard, thank you!"

Three hours of working on different small cases, and they'd earned a break. Wil brought them to a place that specialized in one food only. Crane's Chickporium, or CC's, was the best place in town for fried chicken, and the two dug in with gusto once they got their plates.

"Still a bit confused about the work?" Wil asked, dipping a chicken strip into honey mustard. "Now that we've been at it for a while, I mean."

"Yes. I am so confused. And tired. Walking around town and being reasonable around upset people is . . ." Thomas made a face. "Why would you do that to yourself? Why does Bram want to do this so badly? You both have a business that has to be more rewarding *and* less demanding."

"Yeah, probably," Wil admitted. "But that's not the point. The point is helping people. No matter how small their problems may seem. Might feel like a waste of time to you, but for those people? Their days or weeks are made better by getting a bit of help with something they can't do."

Thomas chomped a strip in frustration. "Half the tasks," he said after he'd finished chewing, "are things they could've done on their own."

"Maybe, but everyone needs a bit of help now and then. Even if it's not with something concrete, just having some help makes it feel like someone cares and is looking out for you." As he spoke, Wil realized he'd never truly verbalized it before. It felt good.

"Maybe there are other cities or positions that could use me more, but if I did that, who'd look out for Harper Valley? It's easy to say that it is . . . *was* a Podunk farming town, but when you know every face in the community, it changes things. Besides, are you sure you can't think of any other reasons why I might be so insistent on making appearances around town?"

"Hmm."

Thomas took his time thinking about it. That suited Wil. They ate in relative quiet. There was only the hollering of the front counter lady to the cook in the back, the hiss of oil, and a quiet mutter from the other people in there.

"Is it image work?" he finally asked. "Just making yourself look good?"

"Kind of," said Wil. He leaped on that angle. "I'm a pillar of this community. It took me time, but the majority of these people trust me. Or at least, I hope they do. When the time comes to change things, they'll be more willing to listen to me and take my suggestions. And more than that . . ."

Wil leaned in close. "The more we know about what kind of problems they are having most often, the easier it gets to think of possible solutions. For example, I know that every winter here, people will want help with warming their homes. So if we were able to harness the leylines better, we could make it so every house is warmed by them."

Thomas shook his head. "I know you're not stupid, but it's strange to hear you being both saccharine and deliberate about things."

"Deliberately saccharine, perhaps?" Wil smiled.

"I suppose that's one way of putting it. But you know what I mean!" Thomas brushed crumbs and grease off his hands and onto a napkin. His brow was furrowed, like he was trying to work through something difficult. "This is the first time you're talking about helping others has made real sense and sounds like a plan instead of a bad habit."

"Thanks, I guess." Wil finished off his food and chased it with lemonade. "I like getting as many goals done at one time as possible. In the long run, altruism almost always makes more sense. You don't have to be a bastard in order to be smart or contribute to the world. Don't have to be a wizard either."

Thomas winced. His sharp-featured face showed a mix of regret and irritation. "I didn't mean it like that," he said.

"Then how *did* you mean it, Tom?" Wil pushed his plate away. He wasn't angry, or even bothered. He'd had hours of hard work to push the anger out of his head, leaving only curiosity.

The other wizard set his food down and sighed. "It's . . . I appreciate how much you care for your friends and respect your town. You're right in that wizards aren't any better or worse than nonmagical people. You know how it is, spending your life around other wizards and then going back to the rest of the world. You get used to being able to relate to everyone around you and have them understand you.

"I respect Bram and Darlene. Darlene especially. But it's impossible for them to truly understand what we go through, and what we're capable of. And sometimes, that gets all-encompassing to me. I don't think they're not capable in general, I just get stuck on knowing they can't do most of what we do. But their work is important too.

"Again, especially Darlene. I don't know what a goober like you did to land a sharp woman like that, but oof." Thomas pulled on his collar, feigning heat.

Wil laughed and kicked him under the table. "I'm still trying to figure that out. But I try not to take her, or Bram, for granted. They're smart, strong, good people, and I guarantee you they'll pull their weight. You don't have to like them, but I won't tolerate you disrespecting them."

"I understand," said Thomas. He returned to his food, grabbing the last few bites and dipping them in a thick white dressing that stunk to high heavens. "And I was telling the truth. Darlene's sharp and is handling all the stuff I'd ordinarily have a hand in. It's a relief to be able to focus on the research itself."

"And Bram?"

Thomas sighed. "He's goofy, excitable, and wishes he was a wizard very, very badly. He's so jealous of us. Of you."

"He is not," said Wil, a flush coming to his face. "He wishes he had magic too, but he doesn't hold it against me or anything."

"Not yet. Look"—he finished up and pushed his plate back—"I admit I could be wrong about him, but I feel like he's going to get in the way more than be helpful if we're not careful. He's smart, and he has access to your books, but he doesn't *understand*. It's all guesswork to him. And in an important research mission like this, it can be a liability."

Wil figured it was about as much as he could hope for. If things didn't work, then at least he could say he tried. "Good enough. But Bram *will* surprise you. In the meantime, we've got more work ahead of us. You good to continue?"

Thomas stood, grabbing both their plates. "Are you kidding? I'm looking forward to it. More chances to help the little guy and figure out how to make money off them later. It's the perfect public relations scam position."

With a roll of his eyes, Wil got up. They threw away their trash and left Crane's Chickporium behind. He wondered how Bram was doing, though it was probably fine. He'd managed for months without Wil, what was another few hours? Tomorrow they'd get back to working on the leyline, and hopefully heads would be cooler then.

CHAPTER 26

Potential Prototypes

The good thing about working with a small team was that they were always in communication with one another, and everyone saw the progress pile up. The hard part was it was just them, working on every tedious task in turns. They often had to take breaks while another of them worked on a part. Occasionally Wil wondered about the extra people he swore Cloverton would send, but their absence was a relief.

The other problem was a lack of progress toward exploiting leylines. There were advancements and victories. A week in, Wil had managed to link the two smaller leylines into a bigger, stronger one. The unified leyline was stronger than the previous smaller ones had been combined, and it now ran the length of the property.

Although it was bigger and stronger, they were no closer to making it power the small devices they'd prepared. Which led Bram and Darlene to focus on alternatives. A week after the merging of the leyline, they all gathered in Bram's cellar for a presentation.

"This," said Darlene, as she stood behind a covered table, "is what we've been working on. And by *we*, I mean mostly Bram, with me logging things and suggesting different approaches based on his notes and Wil's books."

"We're *delighted* to show what we have," Bram said beside her. Like usual, he looked like an overexcited, overly large child. He had yet to do one of his little dances, however. "Even if we somehow can't accomplish our goal, this should still be a great addition to the hallowed halls of major discoveries."

"If we somehow can't accomplish our goal, then I might end up disappearing forever," Wil joked. No one laughed.

"What have you got for us?" Thomas asked after the ensuing silence lingered long enough to grow awkward.

Darlene nudged Bram and ripped the cover from the table, revealing a handful of knickknacks and gadgets. The most notable of them was the metal box with an emerald-green glow coming off the top, but there were also a couple of minor spellboxes and one small chest with runic configurations covering the surface, and an odd metal dial on the side.

"Fantastic," said Wil. "What are they, and how do they work?"

Bram held up the first spellbox. "This one is pretty simple and kind of based on wands anyway. When activated, it projects an illusion. This other one plays a song. Simple stuff, right? I spent a lot of time looking up runic configurations and how they work, and after my brain melted, it gave me a few ideas. If runes are words of power, then configurations are like sentences, right? That's how you described it to me once."

Thomas made a sound. "That's a simplified version of it, but not a bad way of putting it. Configurations are linked runes that come together to do certain effects based on the shape of the greater rune the configuration spells out. It is as much about the collective as it is the individual. Which is why so much trial and error goes into finding the best configurations."

"Wait," said Darlene, leaning against the table for support. At six and a half months along, standing was more of a strain and tiring than it had been. "If that's a configuration, what's an array?"

Wil answered this one. "Arrays aren't as intricate but often have more power and . . . weight, for lack of a better way of putting it. If a configuration is a detailed sentence, an array is like shouting a single word or a short sentence. It's talking about what you're going to talk about to make it clearer." He stood and picked up one of the spellboxes. He pointed to the symbols carved into the wood.

"If you take a look here, the arrays along the border are simple but effective runes for things like *containment, sound,* and . . . a complicated, modular rune that measures things. And then the more delicate, intricate configurations in the center of each side talk about things like conditions and specifics."

He closed the lid on the box and poured a bit of magic in it. "Open this."

Darlene took it and examined it closer. She popped the lid open, and from the box came an uncomfortably loud moo. Rolling her eyes, she looked at Bram.

"What?! It was simple." Bram laughed and took it from her. "Well, not really, but it works! And there're a million different conditions or ways we can change the illusion."

"Works normally, yes," said Thomas. He was always good at keeping them on track. "What about with the leyline? What have you done to aid in that? Curious, not accusing."

Wil sat back down. Darlene looked irritated at the question, but Bram cleared his throat. "We're getting to that. But first, look at this." He pushed the small chest to the front. "Just an ordinary chest, right?"

"It's obviously not, but go on," said Thomas. Wil laughed, and Bram took a second to compose himself before continuing.

"We were talking about heating and cooling for the seasons, right? Well, this is my first attempt at making an icebox . . . without the ice!" Bram framed the box with his hands and wiggled his fingers while mimicking the sound of an excited audience.

"That'd definitely be useful," said Wil. "That's bound to be a lot more complicated than an illusion box. Don't feel bad if it takes a couple of iterations to work."

Darlene jabbed a finger in his direction. "Hey! No being pessimistic in the middle of our presentation. Poke holes in it later, after we're done."

"Can we test it out, then? Show us how it works." Thomas looked more interested in this one. "We already can do something similar with magic by tying a spell to runes and renewing the spell every so often. How is this different?"

Bram ran a finger along the dial. "So, you have all the necessary runic configurations to detail out not just cold, but temperature variation. So if we were to tweak it, it could also run hot. But in this case, we take this dial . . ." He twisted it, and both the dial and a ring of metal around it rotated.

Wil and Thomas both leaned in closer to inspect it.

"Oh," said Thomas. "Rotating modular runes. That's more complex than I was expecting from you."

"Yeah!" said Bram. "I got the idea from Wil's Thunderhawk and some sleds he made. Getting it right will still take some time, but as you can see, each rune is a specified temperature. Sort of specified. The runes we're using for settings are things like *rain*, but a very specific type of chilly rain. Or *snow* and *blizzard* for our coldest setting. We do have one setting for *gentle sunlight* to compare and contrast."

Wil wasn't as surprised about this one. Bram had bounced ideas for it off him the entire time. It made the futile days tapping the leyline more enjoyable, and now Wil got to share in the excitement. "Good job," he said to Bram.

"I really don't mean to be raining on the parade all the time, but that's if it works." Thomas turned to address them all, his lip curled in restrained frustration. "They're great ideas, and I'm willing to bet these will be viable products once we've ironed out all the issues. But what does it have to do with the leyline? Is that what the final object is?"

Darlene took a deep breath like she did when someone tested her patience. "Yes," she said, slowly exhaling. "This is a battery. But not just any battery. According to Wil's books, faricite can be used to help fuel long-term enchantments, right?"

"Yes," said Thomas. "Faricite batteries are already a thing."

"What about ones you can reuse? Ones that get recharged by the leyline with less strain on the wizard focusing the magic?" Darlene's smile was as smug as it was justified.

"Go on," said Wil, as if he hadn't helped rehearse it. "How are we going to make it easier to recharge?"

Bram took off his glasses and cleaned them on his shirt. The cellar was always dusty, but he often did it when he needed to think, as if the act of cleaning his glasses would make him see more clearly on every level. "I believe that for now, we can use a specific runic configuration to always be seeking to draw in magic. Using runes for *hunger*, *feeding*, and *power*, as well as ones for *gift*, *exhale*, and *touch*."

Thomas's eyes lit up. "Those are borderline contradictory, but . . . depending on the array you use and the specific configurations . . . That could work. Wait, you're saying that it can power things up by touching them?"

Without saying a word, Darlene held up one of the spellboxes. She closed the box and set it on top of the battery. It stayed there for a few seconds before she opened the lid. It mooed loudly for all to hear.

Wil's heart soared. They didn't know if it would be reusable yet, but this alone was an astounding discovery. Thomas staggered back a step, then collapsed into his seat. Darlene laughed at him.

"That good enough for you, Tommy?" Darlene grinned, standing tall with her hands on her lower back. "Surprised a couple of nulls managed to make it work?"

"I'd never call you a null," Thomas protested.

Darlene grasped the still mooing box. She lifted the chest and stuck it inside, then moved the battery over to the icebox. "Care to do the honors, Bram?"

Bram, sensing the tense mood, said nothing but twisted the dial. Metal on metal spun around until the rune for *blizzard* completed. Then he leaned against the box, and they waited.

"Seriously," said Thomas. "I don't like that term. You two have done a great job, and I'm sorry if I've said anything unintentionally insulting."

Wil stepped in. "Look, things are tense, and we're all still adjusting to each other." He winced at how that sounded. He wasn't fooling anyone. Thomas didn't fit in as well, but he was trying. That had to count for something, right? "The most important thing is we have not only a potential success, but a direction."

Darlene nodded and muttered an apology under her breath. "Do us the honors, Bram. Let's see what happens when Harper Valley's smartest man puts his mind to something."

Bram turned the dial back to neutral, then opened the chest. He reached for the spellbox, then jerked back with a yelp.

"I think we do have a success," said Darlene. "So here's one more for you, Thomas. If this battery . . . or the next one; let's be honest, it could take a few tries. If this battery works, I want to stick it in a car."

Thomas chuckled. "That's Ferrovani's next move. He's going to put in batteries so that wizards can drive without taxing themselves. This . . . this would not only put more cars in the hands of people, but it would also make for safer driving, if all the sensory spells and similar work for nonmagical people.

"Honestly, you two have done an incredible job." He didn't sound shocked so much as surprised. His normally smooth, collected face twisted into discomfort. "And all the while, Wil and I have only made one breakthrough of our own. We've only got eight more weeks until we have to be ready, and we're off to an incredible start. And as Ferrovani's apprentice, I think I'll be able to help with that, if you'll let me."

"That could work," said Darlene. "If you can watch your mouth. You *did* get me a car. Now I want one that isn't as loud, smelly, or rough to drive."

"That could be arranged," said Wil. A huge weight he didn't realize had been there lifted from his shoulders. "Then all that remains is seeing if we can drain the battery, then refill it. And then . . . Bram, how about you and I work more on your modular heating?"

This time Bram did do a little tippy-tap on the ground. "Yes! I have so many ideas I want to try out!"

Wil loved it. If this mission had taught him anything, it was that he wasn't nearly as creative or observant as he thought he was. Thomas obviously knew more about enchanting than Wil did, and Darlene was cunning, but Bram surprised him. Runes could be tricky, with a single word having sometimes ten different symbols, all representing a different meaning. He had difficulty with them, but Bram proved to be a natural.

"Then we'll try them all," said Wil. "Good job, team. We've got this!"

CHAPTER 27

Audience Participation

One of the weirder adjustments was their unintended audience. On days when they experimented, they closed the brewery. After the first few times they stopped warding off people, they drew the attention of the people of Harper Valley. They gathered around the property, watching from the other side of the fence as Wil moved earth around for hours on end.

After reshaping and connecting the two leylines on the property, the land was an incredible mess. Grass and growth were gone, replaced with disturbed dirt and exposed stone. There were hills and dips and a weird obelisk of hardened earth in the middle of a small island inside of a ten-foot dip. It didn't make sense to Wil why those shapes were necessary for the contour of the leyline. No doubt it made even less sense to the spectators.

Sense or not, they came every day, opened or closed. When open, they'd walk around, whispering to each other. A few had asked Wil why he did what he did, but the wizard shrugged and said it was classified. That had been fun the first few times. Now, on a day when they were hard at work trying another shape, an audience hovered around the fences.

"I could get rid of them," Isom offered from atop the obelisk, which he considered his new bed. "I wouldn't even have to hurt them. A bit of stinky breath, a devastating roar, and they'll scatter. It would be *so* fun."

Wil paused his efforts. A wave of loose dirt spilled over, losing its shape. The leyline ran lower, invisibly brushing up against the earth instead of floating above it. If nothing else, he could take a few days and see how it would affect plant growth. It worked on Mr. Carrey's farm, with all the beanstalks now tied to the leyline.

"Maybe if I eat in front of them. Just give me some delicious beef ribs with some sauce. I'll eat, really messy-like, so they stop watching." Isom wasn't going to drop it.

"That's really not necessary," said Wil, brushing sweat from his brow. "When we close up for the day, we'll put the wards back up. No one's breaking in when we're not around."

Isom slipped off the obelisk, landing with a heavy thud in the dirt. "How do the wards not affect the Beefy One?"

Wil took a deep breath and sighed. It wasn't going to happen today. Not with all the distractions. Between Isom, the sound of distant conversations, and the strain of throwing so much earth around, working didn't sound too appealing. "They don't affect him because of a charm I made for him that's tied into the wards. Makes him immune. Do you want to terrorize people so badly?"

"Well," said Isom, licking his chops, "I'm bored. I need to hunt, eat, or sleep, and I'm not tired. Fix this!"

"It does seem to fall on me to make sure you get enough enrichment," said Wil. "Every responsible pet owner needs to take care of their *cute widdle pets*."

Isom went from playfully insolent to snarling in seconds. Wil burst out laughing and launched himself at the cat. Isom reared up and caught Wil with his middle set of legs. The two collapsed to the ground and wrestled around. Isom snapped dangerously close to Wil's neck and ears while Wil scratched every spot he could reach.

A minute later, they were sprawled out on the ground, distant laughter in the air. Wil laughed breathlessly, patting the wampus cat on the side. "Let's stop for now and get some food. And you can come too if you can agree to behave in public."

"Beef ribs?" he asked hopefully.

"Even better."

After a long shower, he, Bram, and Isom drove over to Mack's Shack. Mack was one of the many business owners in the Le Guin Basin who needed to expand their operation after the treaty was signed. His long, sprawling diner now had two more wings built on either side of the original, curving around. As busy as it was, there was always a place for Wil and friends.

Candy led them all the way around the side to the corner, where the fewest people would bother them. Mack himself came up to shake Wil's and Bram's hands. "Gentleman," he said in his gravelly voice. "Where's your better half, Mr. Wizard?"

"She's working with Thomas on integrating the battery with one of the cars," said Wil.

"We split up into two teams to get more done," Bram added helpfully, pushing the table out so he could fit in the booth. "They'll be in before too long."

"You know pets aren't allowed in here, right?" Mack joked, pulling out a pad and paper.

"You're free to try to remove me," purred Isom from the ground.

"I like living too much. What can I get you?"

"Monster Burger," said Bram, rubbing his hands together.

"Monster burger and a steak if you have it. Extra rare." Wil peeked over the half wall into the kitchen. "We're actually working on something that might interest you, Mack. How'd you like to have magic equipment?"

The middle-aged cook stroked his salt-and-pepper beard. He was a powerfully built man, with a neat white apron covering the start of a belly. "I mean, I wouldn't necessarily be opposed. What would make it better than what I've got already?"

"You wouldn't need to buy firewood anymore," said Wil. "We could make you a new grill that takes up half the space and burns cleanly without any waste. And we could get you a new, better icebox. No more ice shipments. You'd have everything you need to be self-sufficient, for the most part."

Wil wasn't 100 percent sure they could deliver on it, but something they had discussed had been needing a direction, a smaller deadline ahead of the big one. The deciding point for him was the leyline about twenty yards away, in the middle of trees and grass where nothing had been built up. Whenever they succeeded at their goal, it would make it easier to replicate it here.

"Well," said Mack after thinking about it, "I'd be willing to give it a try, but only if it's reversible. If it turns out old Betsy's better than whatever you've got, I won't want to keep it."

Bram sat up straight with uncustomary pride and said, "Of course. But you'll want to keep this. If we can finish this and it works, you'll be the first person in the world to be using our new system."

Mack tapped the pen to his pad of paper. "Then I'm looking forward to it, boys. I'll send Candy over with some sodas and get started on your food."

Bram waited until they were as alone as they could be in a crowded diner before saying, "I've been working hard at tweaking the runic configurations to work better, and I think I have a couple of really promising options. The hardest part is the moving parts for dials and making sure the runes complete and trigger when aligned properly."

"You're doing a great job," said Wil. "This is where my brain goes fuzzy and I have a bit of trouble following along. A good chunk of building my Thunderhawk was learning what all I didn't know. Still took three out of the four months I was there. What we're doing might be smaller and less complicated, but we basically have to reinvent the wheel to make it work."

Bram bloomed with pride. "Thanks, Wil. I'm trying. This has been really hard, but also some of the most fun I've had in a while. More than just your deadline, I want to think that maybe I have a future in this. Even with no magic."

Candy came by with an orange and a grape soda, setting them down with a friendly wink. "Any chance of seeing Syl anytime soon?" she said hopefully.

"He should be this way in a month or two," said Wil, taking a sip of orange soda. "He'll be happy to stop in for a 'borgor' or two."

Candy laughed. "He does like his borgors. Holler if you need anything!"

Returning to Bram, Wil said, "I think it's possible even without magic. You're going to have a harder time of it, but . . . What?" Wil cocked his head to the side. Slowly Bram's gaze slid off Wil and to something behind him.

"Those three people," Bram said with an odd expression on his face. "They were at my place. They've been coming to my place to watch occasionally."

Paranoia gripped Wil instantly before he laughed it off. "A lot of people have been watching us lately. What's so special about them?" He craned his head over his shoulder to get a look.

"They're not from around here," he said. "And I'm pretty sure they're wizards."

That got his attention, and Wil got out of the booth. They stood at the entrance. An older man with a short, trimmed goatee and a monocle, a meathead-looking guy with resentful eyes, and a dark-skinned woman with a stony expression. They stood out, even among the other recent arrivals, and Wil had no doubt they were wizards.

They met his gaze, and the meathead smiled. He made right for him. The other two exchanged sharp looks, then followed. Wil crossed his arms over his chest and waited for them to approach.

"You following us?" Wil wasted no time in asking.

"Sure are," said the meathead. "We've been watching your progress. You're doing really interesting work, throwing things around for hours on end. What's it supposed to accomplish? We've all been wondering about it, but Gayle here especially wants to know how you make it look so damned easy."

Gayle sighed and rolled her eyes, but she didn't correct him or tell him to shut up. The other wizard, the one with the monocle, chuckled. "It's been interesting, watching the leyline move. They said you could do it, but I didn't believe them. You make it look easy. Is that why you're changing the landscape?"

"What is it you want from us?" Wil demanded. His pulse quickened, but he tried not to let his surprise show.

"Better make it good," said Bram, standing. As gentle as he was, Wil appreciated how much he was starting to lean into his intimidating appearance when needed. "We're not the kind of people to mess around with."

"Oh, no doubt," said the guy in front. "My name's McGinnis. We're fans of yours, you could say. We wanted to come over and have a chat, see what the fuss was about."

"And now you're leaving," said a voice from behind them. Wil looked past the three to see Thomas and Darlene standing behind them. It was the first time he could ever remember seeing Thomas look angry, and that was an understatement. "And you will not come back. If I see any of you trying to poach our research, I'll have your heads. Do you understand me?"

"Oh, don't worry about that, Master Elliot," said the bearded one. "We were just saying hi before we grabbed a bite to eat."

"Eat elsewhere."

Gayle scoffed. "You don't get to control where we do and do not eat."

"No," said Wil, "but I am the resident wizard, and my father is mayor. If Thomas doesn't want you here, I don't want you here. If you leave now, we'll just call this a slightly rude encounter and forget about it without any trouble."

"As you like, Master McKenzie," said McGinnis, mock bowing. "It was a real pleasure to meet a new legend up close and get a gauge of you."

"You're weird and have outstayed your welcome," said Darlene. "Get lost." She brushed past them and stood in front of Wil.

"As you like. Good luck in your endeavors," said McGinnis. They trailed out of the diner.

"What the hell was that?" Darlene asked Thomas. "He knew you. And Wil, but he seemed to know you."

Wil eyed Thomas but said nothing. After a few seconds, Thomas shifted uncomfortably. The anger left his face, replaced by resignation.

"I should explain, then. I need a drink."

CHAPTER 28

Competition

They all huddled around the diner booth, Darlene cramming in next to Bram for the increased stomach space. Thomas sat next to Wil, as stiff as a statue, save for the occasional twitches when he'd been still for too long. Isom sat on the ground, watching the people around him with the familiar overstimulated expression that came from being around too many people.

"Well?" Darlene asked after she and Thomas put their orders in. "You want to explain? Explain."

"I know them," said Thomas. "Not well, but they also worked for Ferrovani. As far as I know, they're still working for him. They're some of the others Cloverton sent to spy on you."

"Fat lot of good that'll do," said Darlene. "We haven't really discovered anything concrete yet, and you guys just warded Wil's and Bram's houses. We'd know if they tried to get access to them, right?"

Wil nodded, taking a sip of his soda. "I'm not the best at intricate wards, but even someone like me can manage a few basic perimeter alerts and traps. I have to be careful because of how many lookie-loos come around. I often have to fly past people who want to talk, but only a few have tried to get in. They've failed, obviously, but other wizards could be trickier to deal with. What can you tell us about them?"

"Not much," said Thomas with a sigh. "I know who they are and what they're good at, but I don't know how they operate. They were on a different team. I know that Gayle is an earth wizard and metalworker, and Mark is excellent with enchantments and breaking down their construction. That last one, McGinnis, I don't know at all. He must be new."

"Well, that's all awfully convenient," said Darlene, giving him the side-eye. Working together the past few days had helped her dislike Thomas less, but the fact was she still didn't care for him. "If they were here to spy on Wil, why would they walk up and introduce themselves? That seems like a bad idea."

"I don't know." Thomas pursed his lips in frustration. "It doesn't make any sense, and it makes me wonder what the hell it is they're planning, or if they just decided to take a stupid risk to tweak your nose."

"Is there any chance it might be benign?" Bram asked but with no conviction.

"Or at least not entirely hostile? How many other groups of wizards do you think Cloverton sent?"

That was the worst thought of all. There were about a dozen wizards in Harper Valley now, last Wil checked. He could ward off or handle three of them, but if all of them were determined to get through his security and try to take their work, there wasn't anything Wil could reasonably do to stop it.

"What do you think, Thomas?" Wil prodded after the wizard had fallen silent. "How many people are spying on me?"

"I don't know," said Thomas. "I only know for sure that those three are. Ferrovani must want one last discovery under his name before he retires. I can't think of any other reason they'd be sent here, other than to maybe annoy me."

Candy came by with their drinks and Isom's steak. The wampus cat eyed the redhead with interest. She set the plate down a couple feet away and slid it over to Isom, who snapped the meat into his mouth and tore off chunks. They'd need to clean the area thoroughly. Wil mouthed an apology to the waitress.

Darlene sipped her tea, eyes locked on Thomas. "And you're not still working for Ferrovani too, are you?"

His face contorted with rage. "I *hate* Ferrovani. I want to make it without him. I want nothing to do with those three jackasses that came here, and I hate that they're here."

Right from the beginning, Thomas had been up front about wanting to work with Wil on his discovery. He'd never lied about it, even if it had been dressed up in jokes or convincing arguments. Wil hated what he did next, but paranoia gnawed at him.

Isom? Is he telling the truth?

The wampus cat looked up from his rare steak. His face was covered with the meat's juices, and he looked a fright. Isom sniffed the air and returned to the last few bites of his meal. *Yes. He hates the other humans and wants to break away from Ferrovani.*

"I believe you," said Wil, earning looks from all his friends. "I know how much you've chafed being under his name and fame. We can do that together. We just have to work harder now to prevent discovery."

"And," Bram added, jiggling nervously in his seat, "we need to, you know, actually make a discovery worth stealing. Everything we've done is great, and I think that our batteries and fusing leylines or moving them could prove to be huge game changers. Especially since today's leyline adjustment worked. Some of those seeds we planted are already sprouting."

"They are?" Wil perked up. "Excellent! If nothing else, we can use this to improve farming yields a considerable amount. I can include that in my next report to Cloverton." Some, not all, of the anxiety lifted. They had enough to possibly make Harper Valley the produce capital of the world if nothing else. That had to be worth something.

"We need more than that if we're going to win a possible race," said Darlene. "We need something concrete, but this is a direction. And we need to keep an eye on them."

"She's right," said Thomas. He bowed his head. "Sooner or later, they're going to get in the way or cause trouble. We can't ignore them. But we have something on our side. We know that if they're going to try replicating our progress, they're going to need a leyline to work with."

Bram lit up and slapped the table. "That's right! There are only so many places they could work in town. They'd need a place they can rent or buy that has a leyline and is out of the way but close enough to be able to move around and keep an eye on us. Wil, weren't you going to map out all the leylines in town?"

Wil slumped backward, groaning. "Yeah, I've been meaning to do it, but we've been so busy."

"Well," said Darlene with a grin, "no time like the present, right? You've been looking for an excuse to go flying anyway. Driving on the road with the rest of us peasants has been eating at you, hasn't it?"

"You're not wrong," Wil mumbled. "About wanting to go flying, I mean. We've been so damned busy, I haven't had as much time for de-stressing. Although this would still be work."

Bram tapped the table excitedly. "This is a perfect test for the ley-lens. It works up close, but we can see how far away you can see with it."

He'd been insistent on the name of the spectacles that allowed the viewer to see leylines represented as glowing rivers of light. Wil preferred to use his wizardsense, but that was a good way to crash and get himself killed. So he nodded and said, "Good idea."

Candy arrived with their food, killing all conversation. Wil and Bram both had ludicrously large burgers, smothered in onions, pepper jack cheese, bacon, and house BBQ sauce. Darlene had been craving protein lately, so she got the meatloaf, while Thomas had a simple shaved beef sandwich with au jus to dip it in.

"After lunch," said Wil, picking up his burger and watching it drip sauce, melted cheese, and grilled onions. "If I don't need a quick nap, of course."

"Of course," said Darlene.

"Right," said Thomas.

"Well, that just makes sense." Bram alone could hold the burger in one hand, and he did so, taking a small, dainty bite.

CHAPTER 29

Beans on High

Wil loved flying and hated having to be careful. Wearing the ley-lens forced the wizard to slow down and take his time. Getting an accurate map of Harper Valley had proved impossible, but they had a pretty good approximation of the entire Le Guin Basin tucked away in a special compartment of the Thunderhawk, along with Wil's staff.

The nature of his job meant flying a few hundred feet and stopping to get a feel for the leylines in the area and mark them down. There was a lot of ground to cover, and the project ended up taking several days. Bram joined Thomas and Darlene in working on the faricite batteries, matching them up with the prototypes they'd been working on.

Marking the map wasn't unpleasant work by any means. It meant a lot of stopping to chitchat with people along the way, showing that he wasn't always sequestered in his tower or on Bram's farm. He took it as an opportunity to eat out for every meal as he flew around Harper Valley, looping around the borders of the town before sweeping west and east, going from north to south.

He discovered two things. The first was that Harper Valley had way more leylines than he'd ever realized. There weren't enough for everyone to have one of their own, but every major location Wil actively sought out had one nearby, which led him to the second thing he discovered.

Wil didn't just mark down where they were, he marked how powerful or big each one was, and the condition of the land around it. Universally, the strongest leylines were in the healthiest stretches of land, or places with a unique geographical feature like an odd copse of trees, certain rock formations, or uniquely shaped ponds or rivers splitting properties up. The leylines were undeniably tied to the land.

That much had seemed obvious, and with their experiments on the Stevenson farm, they'd all but proved it. Now it gave him another thing to ponder. Did leylines gather around the land, or did the land form around the leylines and then shape them afterward?

If there were answers, Wil was sure they'd come to him eventually. Until then, they haunted him as he filled out the map and came to a conclusion. He found eighty-four leylines in Harper Valley and the mountains to the north and west. It didn't account for all of them in the basin, but Gallard Springs would come later.

"Afternoon, Mr. Wizard!" Old Gilbert Sully said as Wil filled out one of the last marks on the map. "What're you up to?"

Wil looked up from his map, wiping a line of sweat from his brow. Spring was well on its way to summer, and staying still meant heating up. "Just riding around, getting a feel for the land for my experiments. How are you doing, Mr. Sully? You adjust well after getting back from Faerie?"

The old man laughed. "Wish I was back there, but they ain't taking any permanent immigrants right now. That big tree is something else, and their wine is sweeter. Makes me feel almost young again."

"I can always talk to them," said Wil with a growing smile. "I know they'd listen if you want to go back so badly. Hey, I have a question. How's Mr. Carrey been since I've gone away? Is he still mad about the beanstalks?"

Gilbert barked out harsh laughter. "Not at all. He brags about the beanstalks to anyone who will listen. How he's got the best, most healthy farm in the entire basin. Why?"

Wil moved beside Gilbert and held out the map. He tapped a blank spot in the southwest part of town. "He's my next stop, and he and I have had a contentious relationship in the past. I want to know what to expect when I get there."

"As far as I know," said Gilbert with a sigh, "he's got plenty of reasons to be happy with you. He's richer than ever and getting insufferable. Think you can do something about that?"

"Not legally."

"Damn. Well, I'll let you get to it. I'm meeting up with Jimbo Jones for lunch." Gilbert patted Wil's shoulder fondly and turned to leave.

"Wait," said Wil. "How would you like a ride there?"

Gilbert paused. "What? On that flying death trap of yours?"

"Yes, my Thunderhawk."

The old man grinned. "You're damned right I would!"

It was only a short ride, but Gilbert's screams of glee as they tore through the air twenty feet above the ground made him sound like an excited kid. Wil was more than happy for an excuse to ride around for fun before he faced up the basin's wealthiest farmer. When he dropped a shaky, unsteady Gilbert off, he had to steel himself before continuing.

The Carrey farm had once carried all of Harper Valley's staple crops in higher volumes than everyone else. Now, it had only one crop. The beanstalks were tall enough to be seen from any part of Harper Valley, some of them brushing up against the lowest clouds as they wandered across the sky. As Wil got closer, he saw most beanstalks had scaffolding to help workers get up and harvest beans the size of people.

Wil flew over one fallen beanstalk and parked in front of Mr. Carrey's house. It was more formality than anything, but he slipped into his wizardsense and felt the leyline. It had always been one of the biggest and healthiest of all Harper Valley, but four months later it had grown. Now the magical energy surged through the land like raging rapids.

Fierce and fast, it flowed from one end of the farm to the next, strengthening as it passed through the beanstalks that had consumed several fields. Wizardsense always skewed Wil's perceptions, and feeling the leyline was like staring into the sun. He didn't have to suffer long. After a few moments, the pointed sound of the clearing of a coarse throat shook him out of it.

"Wizard," Mr. Carrey said, limping his way to him. Despite it being a warm spring day, Mr. Carrey looked like he belonged in winter. Already old, stooped, and leathered from decades in the sun, he now needed a cane to get around. "Is there something I can do for you?" He always sounded suspicious, but now more than ever.

"Hello, Mr. Carrey," said Wil. He held up his map. "Just going around and doing a survey of the magical properties of the land here. I'll be out of your hair before too long. How has business been?"

Mr. Carrey puffed up. "At first, I wasn't too happy about what you did to my farm, but look at it now! Your ma was right, and now I'm making money hand over fist. I'm making textiles, and I got a military contract for my endless beans! They're turning them into rations for the southern front. Everything's going pretty damned well for me, I tell you!" He gave a creaky laugh.

"That's fantastic," said Wil. "I'm happy for you. You've gotten quite the blessing here. The beans are really interesting in that they're in a feedback loop. The healthier they get, the better the leyline gets, which makes the beans healthier. You might have one of the best farms in the country, in fact."

"Damned skippy!" Mr. Carrey laughed again. It made the lines on his face crinkle and deepen even farther, and he looked more like a goblin than ever. "I'm the luckiest man in Calipan."

Hard not to be, with magical plants from Faerie overproducing tons and tons of food and plant fiber for cloth. The last time Wil had been there, he'd tried to kill the beanstalks or change them, but it had been impossible. An idea hit him.

"Hey, do you mind if I run a little experiment on it?" Wil asked, rolling the map up and tucking it into the Thunderhawk's inner compartment. "I think I might be able to get you even more beans."

Mr. Carrey's eyes lit up so fast Wil almost felt guilty over preying on the old man's greed. "Absolutely. I'll admit I may have been a bit cranky the last few times you were here, but you've done alright by me. Have at it, Wizard."

Wil retrieved his staff. With a second to stretch and roll his head along his shoulders, he limbered up and readied himself to embrace the overstuffed leyline. Once more opening his senses, he touched the leyline.

Even the barest brush against it was like holding out his hand to catch a train as it passed. Wil gasped and was almost taken under. He steadied himself and pulled, mentally grasping the beanstalks with his power. Wil twisted, and the colossal stalks bent sideways, twirling in around themselves. To the wizard's surprise, the leyline twisted with it.

He gasped again and let go. The leyline was so intertwined with the beans that it took less effort to shift it around.

"What's wrong?" Mr. Carrey demanded. "Did that help the beans? You gonna make them grow more?"

"Yeah," said Wil absentmindedly. "Grow more. Just a second."

This time he knew what to expect. The leyline drew him in, but Wil mentally planted himself in the ground and yanked on the beanstalks. The river of power shifted but didn't stop. Wil let his instincts guide him as he pushed on one beanstalk and pulled on another, tying them together. It was so much easier to do it here, Wil wanted to laugh.

But it still wasn't a solution. It didn't change anything on its own. He could move and change things, but how did he make it work independent of a wizard's touch? As he mulled it over, the plants corded together and twisted, making tight spirals. They grew, and the occasional fifty-pound bean flew off and thudded in the dirt below.

It was so easy Wil found himself making shapes in the leyline, zigzagging over the property like a lightning bolt one moment, then in a circle. It was the circle that gave him the idea. If the leylines could be moved around, and it was all just magical power coursing through its set path . . . Yes, it could work.

It only took a minute to get a feel for how the changes to the skyscraping beanstalks would affect the leyline. In that time, he came up with the right shape in his head and did his best to guide it. With one last loop of plant matter, the leyline settled into the shape of a rune: *feed*.

Wil opened his eyes, breathing heavily. Sweat covered his face and made his clothes cling to him. It was harder than he'd realized, but now that he had completed it . . . There! The nearest beanstalk shifted, thickening. Beans the size of his fist swelled and grew bigger than Bram before falling off.

"It worked!" Wil cried as more and more beans fell to the ground. "I did it!"

"Hurray!" Mr. Carrey crowed. "More beans!"

More beans indeed. Wil leaned on his staff for support as he looked all around the property. Beans fattened and fell off the stalks, and they didn't stop. It started slowly at first, picking up speed as the leyline poured its power into the land, spelled out by the rune. *Feed*. It did that, feeding and growing the plants at an accelerated rate with no end in sight.

Faster and faster, until it rained beans.

"Um," said Mr. Carrey, as his hired hands ran screaming from the fields. They had to rush to avoid being crushed from falling beans. Then beans fell on the roof of the house, punching holes through it. "Too much. Too much, stop it!"

"Right, right!" Wil blinked and then produced a silvery shield above his head before beans crushed them. He grabbed on to the leyline again and yanked on the stalks. The rune broke, but power continued to make it rain beans for another several seconds before it tapered off.

It was early enough that no one had been truly hurt, but not in time to save Mr. Carrey's house from being pummeled to oblivion. Wil shifted his shield, and beans slid off the side like a miniature avalanche. One came dangerously close to rolling into Mr. Carrey, but the old man didn't notice.

"My house . . ." he groaned. "My . . . my house!"

"Well," said Wil, wincing. "At least there's enough beans to pay for the damages, right?"

It wasn't the first or even second time Wil had to leave the Carrey residence in a hurry, but he didn't let it get to him. He had what they needed to succeed.

CHAPTER 30

Eureka!

Wil couldn't get back soon enough. After the second time nearly clipping someone, he poured more power into the Thunderhawk and skipped the roads entirely, soaring two dozen feet above farms and backyards and then later Main Street itself. The wind blew through his hair, so fast that even his racing heart had trouble keeping up.

Logically, he knew his discovery wasn't going anywhere, but after weeks of spinning his wheels with nothing to show for it, he needed to share the breakthrough with the rest of the team. The brewery came into view along with the normal bunch of customers. At Wil's approach, those hanging out in front of the open barn doors waved at him.

He half-heartedly waved back and parked in front of the house. The Thunderhawk had no sooner sunk to the ground before Wil jumped off and ran into the house. Darlene and Thomas sat at the cluttered kitchen table. Loose papers with diagrams and lists of materials were everywhere, in the stage of chaos that came before Darlene set everything right.

"Wow, where's the fire?" Darlene asked, not getting up.

"You okay?" Thomas asked. He did stand up.

"I did it," Wil said. The words felt like victory, so he shouted them loud and proud. "I did it! I was at Mr. Carrey's farm, and I did it!"

"That's great," said Darlene. "What did you do?"

"I made the leyline do something!" Wil paused. "And I also kind of destroyed his house a bit in the process."

"How?" Thomas looked as intrigued as he did horrified. "Did it explode?"

"Sort of. It rained beans!" Wil looked around the room. "Where's Bram?"

"Dealing with customers," answered Darlene. "What do you mean it rained beans?"

"I'll explain later. You guys get one of the batteries and a prototype and bring them outside. I'm going to change the leyline into something usable!"

That got their attention. Darlene hoisted herself up with a little assistance from Thomas. The Cloverton wizard looked skeptical but calculating, as he often did when presented with complicated new information.

"On it," said Thomas. He offered his arm to Darlene. She eyed him before taking it. They headed for the door. Wil rushed out first, letting the flimsy screen door slam. He'd apologize later.

Outside, more people had gathered near the barn. They'd become used to the experiments and time spent away from the brewery and apothecary Bram had set up. They weren't happy about it, but there was nothing to be done about it. Now, with Wil rushing in, many of them knew they were about to be kicked out again.

"C'mon, McKenzie," skinny Lonnie MacDougal groaned upon seeing him. "Can't we have today to drink?"

"How would you like year-round cold beer without having to buy ice?" Wil asked.

Lonnie's eyes lit up. "That sounds pretty nice," he said.

"Then clear out and let us work, you damned lush!" Wil closed the distance and playfully shoved the other man. "You're going to love what we're working on."

Bram came out of the barn. When working on their project, he was found in the same battered pair of faded overalls with holes in them. In his roles as brewer and proprietor, he looked almost a proper gentleman in a casual suit and bow tie. He'd started dressing better since Thomas had come around, more like the wizard than himself.

"What's going on?" Bram asked, throwing an arm around Wil and leading him away from the barn. "Am I going to have to close? This is really not a good time for it." He looked over his shoulder at the dozens of faces peering from the barn and area around it.

"It'd probably be safer if they went home," Wil admitted, "but so long as those three wizards aren't around, why not have an audience? They can all bear witness to our success. We're going to make history."

Bram looked more nervous than excited. "Then maybe we should get them a safe distance . . ." He released Wil and went back to the barn. "Alright, everyone out for a moment. Wil's about to throw some earth around, and we don't want anyone getting hurt."

A murmur of discontent passed through the crowd.

Bram sighed. "Free drinks if we succeed!"

They tripped over each other to get out of the barn and up the drive where they usually watched when they weren't allowed to drink. He waved for them to keep moving as he rounded up the last of the stragglers.

In the meantime, Thomas and Darlene (mostly Thomas) dragged up a couple of their spellboxes, the box Bram designed to freeze things, and a faricite battery. Darlene sat in the chair they left out for her, waiting patiently as Wil grabbed his staff and got to work.

After telling Thomas to watch the leyline closely, Wil centered himself in the field. After a few weeks of playing around with it, the entire property was an uneven mess with clumps of grass and plants scattered all over the disturbed loose soil. The leyline itself was stretched out across the property. He didn't move it yet.

"So I got to the Carrey farm and saw the beanstalks tied into the leyline," Wil said, loud enough for Bram and Darlene to hear. "And when I moved the stalks, the leyline moved. So I tried something, keeping in mind they were connected. I changed them into a specific shape. One that matches the one on the battery."

Thomas inhaled sharply. "That's it? That's all we've been missing?"

"What?" Darlene looked between them with clear impatience. "Dumb it down for the nonmagical among us."

"Runes," Bram said. "You changed the leyline into a rune!"

Wil bowed his head, more pleased with himself by the second. "How did we not think of that, right? I put in the rune for *feed* and—"

"Which one?" Bram and Thomas asked simultaneously to Darlene's snickering amusement.

"The command," said Wil with a chuckle. "The ambiguous one that could either be eat or feed someone else. I did that, and suddenly the beanstalks got out of control, growing faster and raining beans down. They pummeled Carrey's house before I could stop it."

"That sounds like a great way of getting sued," said Thomas. "But if we do, if this works, it shouldn't be a problem. Gods, if this works, then we'll be the richest people in the country. What're you waiting for, McKenzie? Show us!"

Without further ado, Wil took a deep breath and channeled power through his staff, then tapped into the leyline. After weeks of moving the earth around, it had become second nature to him. The earth rumbled, then dipped all around them. The plateau surged up and then twisted sideways, forming an arch in the land. The leyline moved with it, and Wil followed his instincts.

He had to stretch the leyline to its limit before it bent and formed the series of loops and spikes in a spiral that formed the *feed* rune. When Wil opened his eyes and looked around, the fields were a series of rolling hills with a twenty-foot valley that went on for two hundred feet. All around the house itself, rocks and dirt were pushed up like a protective guardian. But if Wil wasn't mistaken, the rune was complete.

Thomas wasted no time in taking the icebox and setting it in one of the untouched patches of grass remaining. Bram ran back to the house and came back with a glass of water, which he stuck in the box. He closed it up and turned the temperature down to as cold as it could get. And then, they waited.

"So," said Darlene after a few minutes of waiting. "What exactly are we looking for here? We probably look a bit crazy to all our adoring fans."

Sure enough, the people who hung around were whispering to themselves. Weeks of Wil and Thomas reshaping the land, what could they have thought about it? No one had answered any questions, especially not after the wizards confronted them a few days back.

"Well, the freeze function drains the battery superfast, so I guess it depends on how fast the battery drains and if the leyline recharges it," said Bram. He nudged the box with his foot. "The highest setting is called blizzard for a reason. It must take a lot of magical power to get that cold."

Thomas cleared his throat. "You did a really great job with that," he said. "In this case, I think the less efficient configuration you have works in our favor. It wears down faster, so now all we have to do is check. You want to do the honors, Stevenson?"

Bram looked surprised but pleased. "I would, Master Elliot." The giant knelt by the box and turned the dial back to neutral. He opened it up, and frigid air made him flinch back. Inside was a block of ice with some shattered glass sticking out.

"Don't mean to beat a dead horse here, but again, good job, Bram." Wil gave him silent applause. "You're an asset."

Bram flushed. "What about the battery?" he asked.

Wil reached out with his senses and laughed.

"What's so funny?" Darlene demanded.

"It's full," said Wil. "If it was drained at all, it's already full again."

Silence.

It was Bram, of course, who let out a victorious cry and jumped in the air. He broke into dance, Wil joined in, followed by a reluctant Thomas. Darlene called out a high-pitched "WHOO" and got to her feet. Their audience burst into cheers and screams of their own. They may not have known what was going on, but Wil appreciated their enthusiasm and encouragement.

Darlene, as always, looked to the future. "Any land with a leyline can have magic powering their homes and businesses. *We* can make it happen. Wil, you're saved!"

Wil felt lightheaded. With under half their remaining time left, they had what they needed. All that remained was refining it and creating projects as proof. "Great job, everyone! But we've got plenty more to find out. Like how far this can get from the leyline itself before it stops working. And then we're going to need access to another leyline to compare and contrast."

Darlene groaned. "Relax, Wil, and enjoy it with us for a second."

He could do that.

Dissent in the Ranks

As far as assignments went, McGinnis had seen worse. Spending time in Harper Valley in a cozy little cottage on the outskirts of town would've been a great vacation if it wasn't so damned boring. After his time as a mage in the military, sleepy farm towns weren't his shot of whiskey.

It wouldn't have been so bad if he wasn't stuck inside for most of it. McGinnis had been hired to provide security for the group as well as be the one to lead the raids and sabotages. So far, there had been none of that, or anything resembling action. It was him, Gayle, and Mark waiting around for whatever scraps Thomas decided to send them. Was it any wonder they'd gotten bored enough to disobey orders?

"Stop it," said Mark, not looking up from his book. "You're going to wear a hole in the floor." He sat at the kitchen table, a mostly finished cocktail in front of him. The cottage they rented was largely one big room, with three small bedrooms for some semblance of privacy. It still meant spending too much time together.

McGinnis paused, then grunted. "At least that'll mean I've accomplished *something* on this assignment. Who wants to sit around, doing nothing?"

"Me," said Mark. "I greatly enjoy receiving steady pay for catching up on my reading. Besides, it's not like we've done nothing. Gayle and I have accomplished a lot. I suppose it's different when you're being paid to effectively be useless. My sympathies."

The mage growled. He considered setting the enchanter's book on fire. That might get him a good fight or problem to focus on for a while, but . . . the repercussions would be too much. "I haven't been entirely useless. I've done my share of spying."

"Oh yes." Mark finally put his book face down on the table. He finished his cocktail in one gulp before smirking at McGinnis. "Watching them work along with the rest of us and feeling out for whatever wards McKenzie has. You want to tap the place and be more active, don't you?"

"Gods, don't *you?* Forget for a second that you're getting paid to read old romance novels," said McGinnis.

"Hard to forget when I'm this happy about it, but go on."

"Don't you feel like your talents and time are being wasted? Watching that dumb kid throw dirt around for a couple of weeks while you and Gayle try to replicate and keep pace is dull. That McKenzie kid is toothless. I'm not needed."

"Then perhaps you should resign and let us work instead. I'll happily split your pay with Gayle. Maybe a bit more zynce will remove the stick from her ass." Mark always sounded cheerful, no matter who he insulted or pissed off.

McGinnis ground his teeth but forced a smile. "All I'm saying is that we could be doing more, and my talents are being wasted. Why must we wait for them to make the discoveries first? All you've done is copy their work."

That got through to the older wizard. Mark stood and cleaned his monocle with a nearby cloth. He focused on that, chewing over his words before speaking. "What we've done so far is analyze what they've come up with so we can follow their process based on Elliot's reports. There's no point in coming up with our own ideas until they've given us something to use.

"Half the job requires patience and discretion. Perhaps they should've left you behind after all. You seem like every other mage, ready to throw a spell first and think things through never." Mark set his monocle back with a smirk.

McGinnis growled once more. "Oh yeah?" he challenged.

"Yeah," said Mark. "Problem?"

"No, not really," said McGinnis, sighing and taking the other seat at the table. He buried his hand into his cropped orange hair and massaged his scalp. "You're not wrong. I hate waiting, and here I am waiting twice. Waiting for those dumb kids to give us something to work with and waiting for Gayle to get here with our godsdamned food."

The front door opened. Mark turned to McGinnis with glee on his face. "Complaining always works, it seems. It's about time!"

It wasn't just Gayle. Their direct superior came with her, pushing past her and going straight for McGinnis. "What in the hell were you thinking?" Thomas Elliot snapped at him. "I told you to not approach them."

"Why are you singling me out?" McGinnis demanded. He looked to the other two wizards for help, but Gayle didn't like him, and Mark was always entertained by others' pain. "We all got fed up and had a chat."

"He already chewed me out," said Gayle, holding a big basket full of covered meals from the local pub. She pushed past Mark and set the food on the table. "I already regret following you into the diner and going along with it."

That traitorous bitch. "We all went," he barked.

"We followed you," Mark said in a singsong voice. "Had to make sure you weren't going to do anything as stupid as pick a literal fight with them."

"That's exactly what you did," said Thomas. For being a lanky, overdressed man in a stupid bow tie, he managed intimidating passingly well. McGinnis didn't fear him, but he respected the steel in his voice. "Worse, you picked a fight with me. Did you consider that you could've blown my cover? They got suspicious *immediately*."

"I wanted to get a feel for them," said McGinnis. His head heated up, and the weight of everyone's eyes on him pushed him into a corner. "You hired me for security, and there's nothing to be afraid of. The rumors are true, aren't they? McKenzie is weak."

Thomas took a deep breath. He smiled. "You're an idiot. Do you have any idea what he is capable of?"

"You mean that crap about him washing out of being a mage?" McGinnis scoffed. "I believe the washing out part, at least. No way he could've handled being a mage."

Mark snickered, earning the ire of both men. He held up his hands and stepped back. "We've watched him play with several acres of land like it was modeling clay. For weeks now, he's been throwing around magic like it was nothing."

"That was through the leyline!" McGinnis couldn't believe what he was hearing. "Any of us could do that if we were permanently latched on to one."

This time Gayle shook her head. The quiet, sullen earth wizard was the person he got along with least, but she at least kept it professional. "Have you ever tapped into one? It's more draining than you think, and after a while, it feels like it's burning you inside out."

"Funny how you all seemed fine with it at the time. Guess I get to be everyone's scapegoat, don't I?" McGinnis crossed his arms over his chest. If he was fired, it wouldn't be the end of the world. "You're all as bored as I am."

"Make no mistake," Thomas said, whirling around. He leveled an eye of contempt to each of them in turn. "I am not happy with any of you. I'm this close to ending this entire ridiculous mission right here."

"But Ferrovani," McGinnis started.

"Isn't here, and isn't my boss anymore," Thomas snapped. "You are here because he and I both agreed that this discovery is too important to leave to one lucky amateur. The truth is, I could just as easily take it from here and do fine. I'm tempted to do it."

"Then, if I can be so bold to ask," said Mark, "what's stopping you? Keeping in mind that I would prefer to have continued employment and the same stake in the project as before."

Thomas shook his head but raised a thick folder. "Ferrovani has decided he wants a piece of this. If I refuse him, he could make things difficult for me. So I am obligated to keep you fools around. But you're right. Things have been boring. Now they aren't. We've succeeded, and the notes are here."

"Really?" Mark perked up. "We can do our jobs now?"

"What was the big revelation regarding the leyline?" Gayle asked. "I'm assuming that's the nature of this breakthrough."

"You assume correctly," Thomas said. Then he hesitated.

McGinnis knew what that look meant, and he changed his previous appraisal. If McKenzie was weak, so was the stuck up Master Elliot. The bastard was having second thoughts about it.

"Well?" he asked. "What's the news then?"

With a sigh, Thomas slapped the folder down on the table. "It's simple but not easy. You have to shape the leyline into a rune, and it channels power through a link to the land. As the power flows through the shape, it constantly pushes that command out into the world. It's a call, waiting for a response, and we've developed a way to answer. We developed the answer first, and then found the call."

"This is fantastic," said Mark. "Assuming Gayle can accomplish what McKenzie has, I can begin working at once!"

"What about me?" McGinnis asked.

"Depending on whether or not you can behave," said Thomas, "they'll need your expertise to design and implement security measures based on this emerging understanding of magic."

"You want me to make weapons," said McGinnis. That changed things. The weeks of waiting around, reading and rereading the notes that bastard Elliot sent every week were over. No more staying a few weeks behind the local yokels.

"And defensive measures," Thomas said. "In fact, I'd prefer you to focus on defensive measures rather than offensive. Consider it a way of lying low and not drawing unnecessary attention to yourself until we're ready to move. I do *not* want Wil or his friends to have any reason to remember or recognize you."

"That can't last forever," said Gayle. "They'll know when we start carving up the land like they did. It's going to take me time to get used to doing it. Which I assume I am now allowed to do."

"Yes. It's time to move forward. The race begins. You will have your own work and my notes of theirs to work with. Make it count, and do not—*do not*—give me reason to end this."

Thomas looked around once more, disgust plain in his eyes. McGinnis knew it was only halfway directed at him. Poor little rich kid, having second thoughts. Whatever. He'd been around long enough to know how to play nice for a while. He gave a nod and kept his mouth shut. For now.

CHAPTER 31

Now We're Cooking

It took them another two weeks before they were ready to implement their design and test it out elsewhere. Surprisingly, it wasn't building a new grill and figuring out how to scale up their icebox that took up most of their time but getting permits and Mack's consent in writing to be processed before Wil could alter the land.

Of course, they did both at the same time, but between Bram and Thomas working closer together and a string of work orders to fill out, the days passed by in a dreamlike daze. One by one they disappeared, and their deadline loomed closer and closer, albeit with far less dread. They likely had enough to give Cloverton, but Wil couldn't shake the feeling that he still needed more.

"Are you ready?" Wil asked Darlene as she slipped on a disgustingly bright maternity dress in their bedroom.

Rather than be ashamed of her growing size and inability to fit into her favorite clothes, she'd made a habit of choosing loud, obnoxious colors and maintaining her short, spiky hair in different wild styles. He loved that she took everything in stride and faced the world with pride. Darlene was here, her clothes didn't fit, and she was happy with herself.

"Almost," she said, pulling the dress down. After admiring herself in the mirror, she turned to Wil to ask, "Does this dress make me look fat?" It was accompanied by an over-the-top pout.

"I'm pretty sure being almost eight months pregnant makes you look fat. The dress is . . . something, though."

Darlene turned around, twirling bright purple and blue flowers against a pink background. "Gotta look my best for our great success, don't I? Mack's life is going to be changed forever."

Wil pulled her into a hug, breathing her in. "You're just saying that because you've been craving meat lately."

She pushed him away, laughing. "So what?"

Wil drove them to Mack's Shack, where Bram and Thomas were already hard at work. Mack and Candy stood together out front, talking to Bob and Sharon. Wil parked beside them in the area that had formerly been for carts and carriages. He helped Darlene out and they came up.

"Hey, you two!" Sharon pulled them both into a big hug. "You have no idea how excited I am for this. How are you feeling, sweetie? Any pain?"

Darlene laughed. "Every day. My feet hurt, my back hurts, everything's sore and bloated. She won't stop kicking, but at least the puking's over."

"You keep saying she," said Wil. "I'm telling you, it's going to be a boy."

Bob shook his head. "Don't count on it, Wil. If she says it's a girl, it's a girl."

Mack cleared his throat. "If this doesn't work . . ."

"It's going to work," said Candy as she slapped Mack's arm. "Wil's good at what he does."

"Aw, thanks," said Wil. "Your confidence means a lot to me."

Darlene groaned, rolling her eyes. "Aw shucks," she said. She thickened her accent and kicked the ground. "I'm glad to have helped."

Everyone, including Wil, had a good laugh. He kissed Darlene on the cheek and stepped inside. The Shack was devoid of people save for Thomas and Bram working together in the back. Here, Thomas truly had a chance to shine. As bright as Bram was when it came to magical theory, he wasn't much of a handyman.

"Wrench next," said Thomas from his position on the ground. "We've almost got this."

They'd torn out the big wood-burning stove nicknamed Betsy that Mack had been using for going on twenty years. In its place was a sturdy, shiny sheet of metal three feet wide and ten feet across, sticking straight out of the wall. It was supported by four thin legs spread out along the outer edge, stabilizing it. The metal was a dull, almost reflective silver in color, with an upraised lip before dipping down to four equal sized sheets of metal, each connected to a mechanical dial in the front.

"Are you sure there won't be a problem with having the runes on the bottom?" Bram handed the requested wrench to Thomas. "It looks so plain with them out of sight."

"Better them out of sight than easily damaged or messed with," said Wil. Both of them jumped, then looked at Wil. "That's going to be the hardest thing moving forward. Making sure we can fit the runic configurations in a place where they won't get nicked or changed at all."

Thomas patted the bottom of the stove. "Everything looks good here, and it's covered by a plate that I've attached to help protect it. We're more likely to break the dial than anything else. Those are a pain to make, but when we go into full operation, we can outsource that to someone else."

Bram chuckled and shook his head. "You can't help yourself but to jump right to the end, huh? We haven't even turned it on yet, and you're already thinking years down the line."

"I'm a divination specialist. And while I may not be especially good at predicting the future with magic, I *am* still good at predicting the future. And we're done!" Thomas tightened the final nut and slid out from under the grill. "We already set up the new and improved icebox. The Freeze-it, we're calling it."

Wil helped him to his feet and ran his hand along the new stove. It was funny, how much time they'd spent on this and the Freeze-it. It hadn't been hard to get the assistance of one of the local metalworkers, Anthony Bahks, to help them with the measurements and use of some of his equipment. Carefully engraving the proper runic configurations into the metal and making sure only the right parts of the oven would heat up were trickier, and then there was making sure there were slots for batteries.

The Freeze-it had been similar. Mack's meat storage room had been emptied and then lined with its own sheet of metal. They'd almost encountered resistance when it came time to slot the batteries in to its side, as it involved cutting holes in the wall, but Mack didn't need *that* much convincing. At every step of the way, Wil's greatest contributions seemed to be his reputation in the community, and his raw magical strength.

"Then I guess I better do my part, right?" Wil said.

"Well, given we've been slaving away over this project for hours, yes. Get your ass moving, McKenzie!" Thomas made a shooing motion, and Bram joined in a second later. They couldn't be called good friends yet, but they'd made an effort at getting along, at least.

"Alright, alright," Wil said. He backed away from them, ducking melodramatically as they leaned in to shoo harder. Once outside, he stopped to kiss the back of Darlene's head again as he headed behind Mack's Shack to the small patch of unused land in the middle of town.

They were lucky in so many ways. It would've been a choice place to build another business or even some housing. But while Harper Valley grew faster than ever before, developing the unused land was still a slow, long-term process. Another few months, and Wil might not have had the freedom to play around and reshape the region.

The leyline came alive at his touch and filled him with power. It snaked across the land in a wave parallel to Mack's Shack along a small tree line. Wil let go and abandoned himself to the process. After moving leylines around for two months now, it had become second nature. The ground shifted beneath his feet, trees moving along as well, roots and all, carried with the dirt.

The zigzag of the leyline stretched and turned itself around, forming a loop at the end of a line. Wil pivoted, guiding the stream of magic along as it circled in on itself, forming the rune for *feed*. In the future, they'd experiment with others, but it was what they had for now. The land settled, and he released the leyline.

When Wil opened his eyes, he winced. It wasn't as drastic as the damage on the Stevenson farm, but developing the land here would be problematic. The trees had moved and formed a circle, with rocks spiraling inward into an upraised spire of land. For a fifty-foot radius or so, the land wouldn't be able to be easily changed, lest they disturb the leyline.

"Did it work?" Bob asked Wil as he came back around front. "I heard a bunch of noise back there. Sounded like some trees split in half."

"No," said Wil, "they just walked around some. The leyline feels right to me, and it should be able to power anything within half a mile or so of it. So all that's left is trying it out and making sure everything is safe."

"Excellent!" said Sharon, clapping her hands once. "I think we could all use a bite to eat. Especially Darlene."

Darlene looked irritated, but then shrugged and nodded her agreement. "It's going to be a relief when I go back to eating normal amounts of food. You could stand to go on a diet with me, afterward," she directed at Wil.

"Me?" Wil asked, feigning hurt.

"Not on my watch," said Mack. "If this works the way you say it will, you eat for free here forever. You'll never be in want of good food. Let's go check this out!"

One by one they all poured in to where Bram and Thomas waited, sodas in hand. Wil escorted Darlene in, his arm thrown around her shoulder. She leaned into him, and they waited as Mack went up to the stove.

"The dials work like this," said Thomas, gesturing to the stove. "There are five different settings based on the heat you need. The first one can be summed up as a food warmer, the last one is the temperature needed to boil water, and the middle are . . ."

"Somewhere in the middle?" Mack asked, making a face. "I know my way around a stove. It might take a little bit to get used to it, but no problem. Candy, you want to get me today's lunch?"

Candy crossed the line separating customers from employees and went to the storage room where Bram waited. He held up a hand and pointed to the dial at the door as well as the bar keeping it shut.

"First thing you have to know is that you want to set the Freeze-it to neutral before you open it. You do *not* want to enter this thing when it's too cold, or get stuck in it. This setting right here?" He pointed to the most prominent marking on the dial. It was a partial rune, not a number. "This is a simple freeze, and you shouldn't need to adjust it much more than this. But this . . ." He moved his finger over to the other prominent marking, on the far side of the dial.

"This is blizzard. It's really good for flash freezing things, but it takes a lot of power, and I repeat, you do not want to be caught inside while it's on. I don't think you'd last long." Bram clapped his hands together and leaned against the doorway. "Any questions?"

Candy stood there frozen, one hand halfway to the handle. "Is this thing safe?" she asked.

"It's safe if you and everyone else take all the proper precautions," said Wil, coming up to the demarcation line as well. "We kept it simple on purpose, but you shouldn't let anyone back here to mess with it until we collect enough data."

Candy's hesitation stretched on another few seconds before she nodded. She touched the bar locking the door, then stopped and set the dial to neutral first. She opened the heavy metal door and shivered at the blast of cold air that escaped. With one more nervous look, she dipped inside, grabbing a box and darting back out.

She set it beside their new stove, and Mack turned on the stove to the second highest setting. He held his hand out over it and his mouth formed a surprised O. "It's working!" He licked his finger and tapped the stove, pulling it away instantly. "It's warming up fast too. You're sure this won't burn my place down?"

"If we did our job right, it won't heat anything but the metal in the center. Which will of course radiate heat in the area, but Bram is already working on a solution to that."

"Oh yeah?" Mack's head craned over his shoulder at Bram. "Like what?"

The giant brought his hands up and wiggled his fingers. "Like maybe some kind of heat sink up on the ceiling, siphoning heat in the area and making everything around it cooler as it vents the heat through the roof."

"Imagine that in the summer," said Thomas. He straightened his bow tie, looking pleased with himself. "You are in a position to be the first nonmagical person to have an entirely magical eatery in the world by the time we're done."

"I don't know about that," said Mack, "but I'm open to more improvements. For now . . . you want rare or medium rare?"

"What if I say well done?" Thomas asked with mischief in his eyes.

"Then I say get out," Mack returned with a wolfish grin.

The kitchen erupted with laughter. Bob and Sharon took stools at the counter, while Wil and his team grabbed a nearby booth. Mack pulled out some frozen hunks of ground beef already formed into patties and threw them onto the new stove. The sizzling hiss was the sweetest sound they'd heard in weeks.

"So, success," said Darlene, taking an offered drink from Candy before the waitress joined Mack back in the kitchen.

"Success!" Bram echoed, raising his bottle of grape soda in a toast.

"Success," said Thomas, a small, contented smile on his face.

"So," said Wil. "Now what?"

CHAPTER 32

Darlene's Dreaded Dinner Date

D o we have to?" Darlene asked as if it hadn't been her idea.

"Pretty sure we do," said Wil from the bed. He pulled on one sock, then the other. "You were excited for the opportunity a week ago."

Darlene groaned and lowered herself onto the mattress next to him. When she'd first moved in to watch after the place while Wil was gone, she'd taken one of the extra rooms as hers. Now Wil found himself sleeping in there most nights, even if most of his stuff remained in his bedroom tower.

The room reflected Darlene's tastes, full of bold, bright colors painted on the wall in abstract designs, while every piece of furniture, from the big bed to the dresser and bookshelf all were in the only places they could be. It was neat, clean, and casually stylish. The more time Wil spent in there, the more he realized how much he wanted her to do the other rooms and bring some life to his—their home.

"That was a week ago," she said. "It seemed like a good idea at the time, but now I don't want to. I'm pregnant and cranky, you have to cater to my whims." She laid down behind him, and Wil could hear the pout without seeing it.

"Pretty sure each time I've tried to start something by noting your pregnancy, I've gotten fussed at. This seems like a bit of a double standard, to be honest. You're not scared, are you?" Wil continued to get ready. He pulled on his rarely worn dress shoes and tied them tight.

"No, not really." Darlene sighed. "Not of either of them, anyway. Maybe I am scared of what we've never had, what I'll never get. That it'll hurt when nothing changes."

Wil nodded in understanding. He lay facing her. Luckily, she was too focused on their upcoming plans to tell him to get his shoes off her bed. "Then I think the best thing you can do is to not try to cling to the past. I see how much this hurts you and has always hurt you. Maybe don't focus on what you don't have but what you *could* have, if you give it a chance."

Darlene grumbled, but visibly relaxed. "You know," she said, none of the playful petulance to be found, "you're going to make a good dad."

Wil's heart skipped a beat. "I hope so," he said. His eyes flitted down to her stomach. They'd spent so much time working on their experiments and projects, and he'd been grateful for it. The more exhausted he was, the less time he had to think about the future and how unprepared he was for it.

Sure, he'd read some basic books, but no book could ever prepare him for the gravity that would come from being responsible for a new life. Darlene didn't seem any more ready than he was, but it was different. She was sharp, driven, and always had a good idea how to approach any given situation. Wil just did his best and powered through.

"You will," Darlene reassured him. "If nothing else, you'll be better than my father was. I don't see you obsessing over money and how great you think you are."

"Well, no," said Wil, lips twitching. "If I were to get lost in how great I am, you'd be right there to knock me down several pegs. It's one of the things I appreciate most about you. You aren't impressed by me."

Darlene laughed. "That's not true at all. I'm impressed by you all the time. I'm very much a fan of you."

"Oh, is that so?" Wil grinned and leaned in. Darlene met him halfway for a slow, soft kiss.

They'd been dating for a little over a year, and it still astounded Wil that the girl he'd had a crush on as a kid was now his girlfriend and soon to be the mother of his child. Not only that, but she was his best friend, his partner. The weight of those four months away gripped him again, filling him with an irrational panic that it all could be taken away again.

"You okay?" Darlene whispered after they'd broken away.

"Yeah," said Wil. He smirked at her. "We *could* stay home tonight and enjoy a bit of quiet. Just the two and a half of us. Say the word."

Darlene's expression contorted into the agony of indecision. "Argh. I want to. But we can't, can we?"

Wil shook his head. "Afraid not."

"Then fine," she said with a melodramatic sigh. She tried to sit up and faced some difficulty. Wil hopped up and offered his hand. "It's not fair, you know. You get to dress up and look impressive, while I'm stuck in *this*."

"I thought you liked your maternity clothes," said Wil. "You picked them all out, and they're your favorite colors."

Darlene grumbled, "They're still shapeless and ugly. I'm not worried about it. Let's get this over with."

Wil chuckled. "You act like you're going to your death. It's dinner with your parents. Relax, and if your dad says or does anything stupid, I'll hex him. Deal?"

She deflated in relief. "Yeah, deal."

Wil hadn't been back to the Johnson residence since helping Darlene pack and take her things when her father had kicked her out for starting her own business. If that didn't paint a picture of the man, Wil didn't know what would. He'd left after threatening Jonjon, only later to offer him a lucrative trade agreement over the course of negotiating peace with Faerie as an olive branch. As frustrated as

Darlene was, she wasn't going to keep her child out of her parents' lives. He could respect that.

He kept telling himself that on the drive over as Darlene fidgeted in her seat nervously. They arrived right as the sun dipped halfway past the mountains to the west, casting the Johnson residence in an orange glow. Arm in arm, they walked up to the door and, after a second's hesitation, knocked.

Twenty seconds later, Angelica threw open the door and let out a piercing sound before throwing her arms around them both.

"Wilbur, Darlene! Darlene, I've missed you!"

Maybe it was unkind of Wil to notice Angelica seemed less drunk than usual, but she had more energy than he'd seen in a long time. He hugged back, and Darlene said, "Hi, Mom. You just saw me the other day!"

"That was different," Angelica insisted. "That was in passing. It's so nice finally having you home again!"

Darlene pulled back, holding herself protectively. "But this isn't home any-more, right? Dad made that clear the last time we spoke." The last time Wil knew of them being in the same place together had been when Jonjon had been turned into a toad and Wil had administered the potion to turn him back to human.

"I, uh . . ."

"Darlene and I have made a great home together," said Wil. "You should see some of the things she's improved on. Maybe after tonight, depending on how things go, we can do the hosting sometime."

Angelica blinked, looking from Wil's hopeful expression and Darlene's con-flicted, pent up anger. "Yeah, yeah, of course. But for now, why don't you come in? You're looking good tonight, Mr. Wizard."

Their house was much as Wil remembered it. Big, full of all kinds of unneces-sary, expensive furniture, and set up around a big plush chair Jonjon sat in. He had a drink halfway to his mouth when they entered. "There you two are. Was beginning to think we'd have to start dinner without you." He laughed, a sound like a mix between a honking goose and the braying of an ass.

"Maybe you should have," Darlene muttered before Wil squeezed her hand. She may have been the one to suggest this mending of fences, but everything her father said and did put her on edge.

"How's business been, Jonjon?" Wil asked. "It's been like half a year now; that exclusive contract must be in effect by now."

Jonjon's face lit up. He had sharp features and dark hair like Darlene, but none of her natural spark or her blue eyes. Moments like this, the resemblance became uncanny. "Oh, you have *no* idea."

"That'd be why he's asking," Darlene said. "You're doing well for yourself, right, Dad? Faerie wine's been flying off the shelves near as fast as he can stock it. That's what Mom was saying, at least."

Jonjon stood up. He was half a head shorter than Wil. "Angie's right! Wine, paintings, books. I'm thinking I'm gonna need to buy the building next door just to be able to keep my stock separate. It's a damned shame you left when you did, Darlene. I really had to scrape the bottom of the barrel to find enough people to replace you, and now we're about to boom."

Silence. Wil looked from Jonjon to Darlene. His girlfriend's face was red, and everyone but her father seemed to realize she was about to blow up. Wil thought about it for less than a second before he got there first. "Are you saying that Darlene was bottom of the barrel?"

"What?" Jonjon froze. "No, she's the best I ever had. I was hoping to pass the business on one day. I was saying there aren't any good workers in town. The only people I could find were a bunch of dumb kids who don't listen and don't want to do any real work."

"Maybe we should save the business talk for after dinner," said Angelica. She tried, at least.

"Funny, we haven't had any problem finding workers," said Darlene. "You know, for my own successful business."

Jonjon groaned. "Look, you know I'm not good at talking."

"And yet you can't stop yourself from doing a lot of it," Darlene spat back.

"You should know better than to take it personally!" Jonjon said. "Gods, you have to take everything the wrong way, don't you?" The humor drained from his voice. Everyone saw the situation souring. All it would take was an apology and backing down. Two things he wasn't capable of.

"You're right, I should've known better." Darlene sighed and turned to Angelica. "Thanks for having us over, Mom. I'm not feeling well anymore. Maybe later this week, you and I could grab lunch. I could show you some of the things we've been working on."

"Oh, come on," Jonjon cajoled. "Don't be that way. I'm bad at talking, and I stepped in it. Let's have dinner, and things'll be better."

Wil shook his head. "No, I don't think so. You came out swinging, and she was already worried about coming. You couldn't make it five minutes without insulting her. No, we're leaving. Thank you for cooking, Angelica. I'm sorry we couldn't enjoy it. Darlene, let's go."

"Now look here," Jonjon raised his voice and took a step forward. That was a mistake.

Wil stepped in front of him and made eye contact. He didn't need to go all the way in for Jonjon to freeze in place with a blank look on his face. Wil left him a little present for later, then backed up. The man remained staring into space when Wil took Darlene's hand and led her out of the house and back to the car.

Once inside, Darlene sniffled. Wil threw an arm around her, and the dam broke. She hugged him as tight as she could and cried for a minute. Angelica came out of the house, but a shake of Wil's head warned her away.

"I'm sorry your dad's a jerk," said Wil. "We don't have to see him much. If you just want to invite your mother over and make it clear he's got to apologize first before the invitation is extended, we can do that. The important thing is you tried. He doesn't deserve it, but you tried."

The sniffles dried up before too long. Darlene raised up, wiping away tears and snot on the bottom of her colorful baggy dress. "What did you do to my dad? At the end there."

Wil shrugged. "I implanted a nightmare. For the next week, he's going to have some really weird dreams involving losing you because of running his mouth. Either he gets the message and apologizes, or he doesn't, and we don't worry about him again."

Darlene took a deep breath. "He's never going to apologize. But mom was . . . She looked and sounded good."

"Bram told me she's been buying a lot of potions, trying to wean herself off drinking," Wil admitted. "She's trying. And that's all we can ask, right?"

She chuckled. "Yeah. Yeah, she's trying, and maybe it's not too late."

After silence threatened to choke them again, Wil leaned in closer. "You know what else isn't too late? We can go have dinner with my parents instead. They made extra tonight."

"How do you know?" Darlene asked. Then it hit her. "You expected tonight to go bad."

Wil shrugged. "I thought it could happen, and if it didn't, I still would've stopped by for a smoke with dad."

Darlene laughed and shoved him. "Cunning. I like it. Yeah, Wil, let's go have dinner with your parents. You're lucky to have such a great family."

Wil turned the car on and backed up. "They're your family too, now. No matter what happens, you're one of us."

Darlene said nothing, but she looked happier than she had all night. Good enough. All their experiments aside, all their shared work, it was great, but he resolved then to have a different priority. Darlene and their kid first. He'd spend the rest of his life making them happy if he could. Smiling, Wil drove to the embassy and his parents' house.

CHAPTER 33

An Enchanted Life

Now that they had working prototypes to give to Cloverton, the past two months of effort finally caught up to everyone. They agreed on a week-long break to rest and recover before they threw themselves into refining their new inventions. After spending a few days alone with Darlene, Wil went for a ride on his Thunderhawk to check in on his best friend.

After this much time, Wil was finally getting used to the new layout of the land. He'd helped Bram fill out the new valley on the south side of the property with water, giving Bram a new lake. It had been another experiment, seeing if the addition of water would affect the leyline at all. If anything, it made it stronger.

Wil parked beside that lake and admired his work. All they needed now was to fill it with some fish and they had the perfect spot to sit with a few beers and enjoy a lazy day. He had a sneaking suspicion that the addition of more life to the land would make the leyline healthier.

He shook himself from his thoughts. This was supposed to be a day off. Wil had never been good at turning off when he had a project to complete or a goal to reach, but the enforced rest had turned out to be necessary. Now, at the end of the week, his thoughts strayed back to work.

The brewery was bustling, and Wil ignored it for now. While Bram spent a lot of time among his customers, Wil had an idea where to find him. He made for the cellar, chuckling as he faced something new.

"You *have* been working hard, haven't you?" Wil said aloud. Bram had managed to install a fairly complicated ward on his cellar doors, projecting the intent to wander off. If Wil hadn't been an adept mind mage, it might have worked on him. He opened the doors and ventured down.

The cellar had been divided into three different stations for the three of them to work on their individual projects. The stations were in each of the three corners, with the fourth dedicated to a mountain of crates and boxes with hunks of different metals and parts they'd discarded. All things considered, the workspace was normally clean and organized.

Now, it was a chaotic mess with half-finished prototypes scattered along the different station's tables. Bram sat on the ground like an overgrown kid, with a faricite battery and several metal doodads between his legs. He looked up with a wild look in his eyes.

"Uh, hi, Bram," Wil said, looking around. "I see you're making good use of your enforced time off."

"I have too much to do," said Bram. His voice was strange. He always sounded anxious and breathy, but never this urgent. "I took a couple days off, but there's . . . so much!"

Oh no. His best friend had cracked. Wil pulled up a stool and sat in front of him. "There is. It's a marathon, not a sprint. We don't need to do it all immediately. We've earned a bit of a breather, haven't we?"

Bram shook his head vehemently. "We've only scratched the surface. There is no telling how far our projects will go. We only have the next month to do our best before others get their grubby hands on this discovery and start developing as well."

"Maybe," Wil allowed, "but we'll still have the credit for it. No one will be able to think about leyline power without thinking of us."

"Thinking of you and Thomas," Bram muttered. He let the dial he'd been holding clatter to the ground. "I'll be a footnote."

Wil laughed and hated himself for it. Judging from the look on Bram's face, it was one of the worst possible replies, but he couldn't help it. "If I have my way, your name will be just as big as mine. If not bigger."

"Yeah, right," Bram scoffed.

"I'm serious," said Wil. "I wouldn't have been able to do any of this without you. *We* wouldn't. We might've landed somewhere similar between my strength and Thomas's experience, but it's been your ideas that we've been working on. That's not a coincidence."

"You're only saying that to make me feel better," said Bram. "Which I do appreciate, but I know it's not true. We've been working on mine because they're . . ."

"They're what?" Wil did his best to suppress his desire to laugh. "They're brilliant. Even Thomas, who's been doing this for a living for six years now, is impressed by your quick grasp of configurations. Anyone can learn arrays, but a working configuration with any degree of complexity is hard. What's this really about, Bram?"

His eyes dropped to his lap, and his ears turned red. It took him nearly a minute to speak, and when he did, he sounded on the verge of tears. "Nothing I do matters without you and Thomas there to make it happen. It doesn't matter how smart I may or may not be when I can't use magic."

There it was. Wil knew his friend could be envious of him, but it had never been this bad before.

"There are so many things wrong with that," said Wil. "I genuinely don't know where to start. Actually, I do." Wil jerked a thumb over his shoulder in the direction of the cellar door. "I didn't help you with those wards. And I don't think Thomas did either. You set up magical wards completely on your own."

Bram shook his head. "It took faricite batteries to make it happen."

"With your special touch that makes those batteries refill themselves at the leyline. Batteries that we've developed together."

Wil didn't have a problem giving Bram the validation he needed, or boosting him up during a dark time. He'd do that any day of the week without question. The hardest part was making it clear Wil took it seriously when it baffled him. How could his friend not know how essential he was?

"Bram," Wil tried again. "All I've really contributed to this project is my brute force strength. I knew it was possible because of an accident. Thomas and I could design and develop some good tools and machines together. It wouldn't be the same. You're creative and have the touch, and Darlene knows what people want and need.

"When it comes time to celebrate and bask in our victory and assign our credit, I'll likely be the face of the group. It was my problem and project to deal with, and it'll be me getting the focus at the end. But I promise you, my friend, that I am going to be singing your praises the entire time."

"You will?" Tears of relief shone in Bram's eyes.

"Bram, I'm going to tell people you're going to be the next Ferrovani."

He burst out laughing, wiping at his eyes. "Now I know you're just trying to make me feel better."

Wil shook his head vehemently. "No, I'm serious. You're starting out. *We're* starting out. Give it ten years, and you'll be bigger than I will be. I mean it."

Bram was silent again. His eyes were locked on the battery between his legs and a piece of paper with a series of runes in different colors on them. He picked up the battery. It looked so small in his hand. "I wish I had magic too. Real magic. This is great, but anyone could do it."

"And that's what makes it so important," said Wil. "Anyone could do it because *you* did it. You made it clear that the gap between wizards and the nonmagical population isn't as wide as we thought. Tell me something. What have you been working on the past few days?"

Bram looked up, a crooked smile on his face. "I was looking at ways to make my house better. And the brewery too. And potions. I want things to be cool in the summer and warm in the winter, and I think I can make it happen. If I do, that's another thing we can give people. There's *so* much around the house we can improve to make peoples' lives more magical. To make them better."

He groped for a piece of paper covered in runes and depicting a drawing of a toilet. "Think of what we could do for water reclamation and purification! That long stretch of badlands between here and Kappala would be less harsh to live in."

"Bob the Plumbing Wizard reborn," Wil muttered, unable to stifle the laughter this time.

"What?"

"A wizard I knew. Made big improvements to pipes and water flow. It can be done, and he'd love someone to talk to about it and share notes." Wil drummed his fingers on his knees with excitement. "I could probably contact him and get him to chat with you. What else have you got? Tell me what you'd do if you had unlimited time and resources."

Bram thought about it. He stood up, groaning with the effort it took to heft himself back to his feet. When he straightened, his back let out a sick crack. "Wards against nightmares for children. Better boundaries for ranchers, fences that repel predators and keep livestock in. Think of what we could do for sheep herding if we had a way to collectively attract them on command."

"That's a hell of a start," said Wil, but Bram wasn't done.

"Everything we could do with electricity or coal, we could do with magic. More, even!" Bram paced back and forth, head down, words coming out a mile a minute. "All we need to do is find a problem, find a spell to fix it. And imagine what we'll be able to do when we're able to expand the range of leylines."

"Whoa now," said Wil, "not even sure if that's possible."

"They said changing leylines was impossible too," said Bram, pivoting to face Wil. He manically gestured with his hands. "I started that book by Marlowe you brought back. It's all right there, I think. How else would so many spells anchor to the same place without something breaking? We just need to crack what he figured out!"

Wil nodded along. "It probably won't be me figuring it out," he said. "I'd put money on you doing it. Do you see your worth yet?"

Bram lowered his hands. "I . . . I don't know. Maybe? I know there's so much more to go, and I don't want to rest. I want to get there before others do. And maybe I *am* smart and good at this, but . . . once those other wizards get a chance, then what hope do I have of keeping up?"

Wil slid off the stool and went up to his friend. He put his hands on Bram's arms and squeezed. "You're going too fast for me, and Thomas is pleased with your progress and is mostly just checking your work and helping polish it at this point. Bram, can you do me a favor?"

"What's that?"

"Come out and have a few drinks with me. Leave all of this behind for two more days, and we'll get back to it. You did a lot of work already, and when we pick it back up on Monday, we'll go over these notes and see what we should focus on next. But for now, let's go have some fun. Let's eat too much and listen to Lonnie talk about girls who definitely didn't give him the time of day."

It didn't matter if it was his words, his tone, or the look on his face, Bram nodded. He let out a breathy laugh as he hunched and minimized himself. "Yeah, we can do that. I'm being a bit silly, aren't I?"

"Not at all," said Wil. "You're driven, and you've got something you're insecure about. I'll spend as much time as you need making sure you know how much we appreciate you, buddy. But for now, let's drink and you can talk about some of those ideas there."

Bram smiled. "Yeah. I think I'm going to do everything I can to upgrade my house, use it as a basis for experimentation. But we need more batteries."

"We'll figure it out." Wil patted Bram's shoulder and nudged him toward the cellar door. "Now c'mon, I want some more of that coffee stout."

CHAPTER 34

Correspondence with Cloverton

The worst part of the mission, in Wil's opinion, was having to periodically provide progress reports. He understood why they were necessary. If he was in their position, he'd want a close eye on him as well. Knowing that didn't stop him from being annoyed at the hassle of it all.

At least he didn't have to leave the comfort of his home to fill them in. They'd given him a two-way journal like they had with Hugo, and once every couple of weeks Wil wrote in it and communicated with whoever was on the other side. Wil had asked for their name once, but he was told it didn't matter and to give the details of his experiments.

In truth, Wil never told them everything. It very well could have been another in a long line of stupid decisions, but until now, he hadn't had anything concrete to tell them other than his success at manipulating leylines. Now as he looked at the last message written, he struggled.

Master McKenzie, we appreciate the difficulty of your experiments, but after nearly two out of your three allotted months have passed, we're growing impatient. If you have any reports to make, now would be the time to make them. Some people are beginning to wonder if you're working on it at all, or maybe, instead, thinking of making a break for it.

We don't want to assume the worst, but until you give us something we can work with, we might be forced to cut spending, cut supplies, and instead send someone there to audit your work.

That had been the last time he'd heard from them, two weeks ago. It had been right before he and the others set up Mack with the stove and Freeze-it. Now was the time, he supposed, to talk all about that and hope that the people back east would keep to their bargain. A dark part of Wil wondered if they would use this as an opportunity to steal his research. Maybe take it and throw him to the wolves anyway.

He wouldn't have put it past them, but it was pointless thinking of everything that could go wrong if he was unlucky or careless. It was time to finally fill it out . . . after he ate.

Wil cooked himself and Darlene some grilled breakfast sandwiches and settled into his increasingly outfitted kitchen. When he first moved in, he'd only had the bare essentials, but Darlene furnished the house in his absence.

"This is delicious," Darlene moaned as she devoured one of her two sandwiches. "Too delicious. What are you putting off?"

Wil laughed. "Biweekly update. I don't wanna."

Darlene shrugged and took another bite before drinking some iced tea to wash it down. "Doesn't matter, right? If you don't give them updates, they might take you away again. And if you end up disappearing because you didn't feel like telling them what we've been up to, I'll be upset."

He grunted his acknowledgment. "It's such a pain. And they always act like I'm trying to hide stuff."

She raised an eyebrow.

"Okay, but can you blame me?" Wil sighed and set his sandwich down. "We're close. We just need to—"

"We're not close, Wil. We're there. Our products work and we can replicate it. What else do you want?"

Wil thought about it. "I want to have a presentation so big and grand that their jaws drop. I want them to be so impressed they stop trying to screw me over. I want something so undeniably impressive that I can have some peace of mind and we can really start a life together."

Darlene chewed it over. "We've already started a life together, dummy," she said. "Unless you were stringing me along this whole time."

"What? Of course not, I . . . Oh, very funny." Will shook his head as Darlene laughed.

"It's been a while since I've been able to make you nervous. And here I thought I'd lost all my power over you." She smirked, but Wil detected a hint of truth in the statement.

"Never," he said. "I'm forever under your spell. It's been going strong for twelve years now, and I don't see that ending."

Her face reddened, and she looked down, pleased. "And don't you forget it. So, what're you going to do?"

Wil groaned. "Tell the truth, probably. I've already gotten in enough trouble for keeping things from them. I'll get it over with."

"Attaboy."

After lunch was consumed and dishes cleaned, Wil retreated to his office where he sat at his desk and stared at the journal for another ten minutes. Sighing, he opened it and readied the matching pen.

Greetings, Cloverton!

It wasn't the most professional way of starting his report, but at this point they realized who and how he was. But the green ink in the paper gave way to the blue of his handler as they responded.

Greetings, Master McKenzie. What do you have to report this time?

Wil bit his lip. This was his last chance to lie or obfuscate. Darlene would be mad at him if he did.

I've succeeded in my mission, Cloverton. I've managed to change the leyline and exploit it in a way that can be replicated and used to fuel machinery. When representatives come in a month, then we'll have a full presentation ready as proof. My team and I have worked hard on this and are proud to share our work soon.

There was a pause, and Wil could imagine the disbelief from whoever was on the other side. Two months of dodging questions and making excuses, and now this.

Elaborate, Master McKenzie. Give a detailed report and leave nothing out.

So Wil did that, more or less. He started from Mr. Carrey's home, detailing the way he'd twisted the beanstalks up and changed the leyline, to the destruction of Mr. Carrey's house. He paused to ask if it was in the budget to help pay for repairs. The handler ignored him and pressed on with their questions, such as what he'd built so far.

Our initial focus has been practical applications. We've built leyline-powered stoves, a new form of an icebox we're calling Freeze-it that serves as a cold storage room. Illusion boxes, lights, and we're working on adapting the cars I requisitioned for our new faricite batteries. They all work, and we will be able to show them off soon. With further time and resources, we can come up with even more things to impress.

There was no answer at first. Wil wondered if he'd said the wrong thing, or perhaps the right thing. Then again, sometimes the handler fell quiet, possibly to pass on information and receive instructions. It didn't matter; it made Wil anxious every time he had to wait. This time, the handler made him wait nearly ten minutes. He'd been seconds away from writing more when the blue ink appeared in real time.

Congratulations, Master McKenzie. President Bullworth would like to pass on his well wishes and support. Quote: I knew you could do it, son. Arrangements are being made for a trip to Harper Valley to inspect your work, as well as for the president to make a trip to Faerie. Upon a successful demonstration of your experiments, you will be granted a full pardon for your missteps.

That was a relief. All they had to do was wait a month and everything would blow over. Not that they would ever stop. Their team was too hungry for more, too ready to keep working and get as far ahead of the competition as possible. Now that they knew there were spies in town, it was a relief to know that they were too late. He wrote back.

That's great to know, Cloverton. I'm very relieved. I would also like to make it clear that I could not have done it without the help of Master Thomas Elliot as well as Abraham Stevenson and Darlene Johnson. The four of us together are responsible for these breakthroughs, and they should receive a full share of credit with me. Abraham and Darlene are nonmagical, but their contributions were key to the development of this project.

That was important, and he'd fight for it if he had to.

Understood, Master McKenzie. We have one more request. In the remaining time allowed, you are to turn your attention to possible military applications. If you can create a new working weapon to use on the southern front, your efforts will be well rewarded. It would show us you are reliable and your honor and conduct beyond reproach.

Wil dropped his pen and rubbed his eyes. Of course they'd ask for weapons. Several different possible responses ran through his head, each one as nonthreatening and polite as possible. All while his irritation grew and then ignited into anger.

No, Cloverton. I will not design weapons for you, or for anyone. These inventions are meant to make the world a better, happier place. If you want to develop weapons, there is nothing I can do to stop you, but it will never come from me.

Pause.

That is unfortunate, Master McKenzie. We are prepared to offer you a lucrative, exclusive contract if you are willing to reconsider. Your current efforts are enough to get you out of your legal trouble, but with as divisive as your case has been, you should consider doing everything in your power to work on your image and usefulness. Think of your time at Marlowe Manor, Master McKenzie. Four months of your life gone, all because of your stubbornness and pride.

Wil stared at the journal in disbelief. They were threatening him. Again. Do what we say, or we'll give you trouble. Anger surged in him, like cold lightning directing him to act. He took a deep breath and thought about it. That was a fight he couldn't win, and he knew it. Thoughts of Darlene and the baby kept him from telling them exactly what they could do with their proposition.

I do not make weapons. I do not hurt people if I don't have to. I can't give you what you want, but I can instead see what can be done for defensive options. Depending on the leylines on the southern front, we might be able to develop extra powerful or durable warding, or even mask entire bases from sight. If that's not enough, I have the designs for a potential all-terrain scout vehicle.

He hated to do it, but maybe the Thunderhawk design would appease them. Thomas's insistence that it would do him good to patent and sell it came to mind, and he hated how right the jerk had been. He'd been right about many things involving the work, and he'd finally started to get along with Bram and Darlene. Maybe his advice was right, and it would help.

Your proposal is acceptable. We'll contact you in two weeks to give you more details about the president's visit. Once again, congratulations, Master McKenzie. You not only have changed the world, you've clearly grown wiser. The president says that he'll see you in a month.

Wil slumped over his desk. He'd done it. The worst of the danger was over, and now he had plenty to look forward to. And hey, reporting in hadn't been too painful this time. Maybe things were looking up. He took a deep breath and stood.

"Hey Darlene," he called out. "Wanna go for a drive? We've got one day left. Let's go to Gallard Springs and enjoy a hot spring."

Darlene poked her head into the office, eyes bright. "That sounds fantastic! I could use a good soak."

He beamed at her. They were in the homestretch now, and Wil planned on enjoying every minute.

CHAPTER 35

Family Dinner

On the night before their work resumed, they gathered for dinner at the Faerie embassy, located on the McKenzie property. It astounded Wil how things had turned out and that his family had been so willing to give up their farm and embrace a future of change and diplomacy. When Wil had made his decision, they didn't hesitate.

Now, six months after the disastrous Midwinter Feast that had ended with Wil's imprisonment, it didn't feel like home anymore. The land may have belonged to the McKenzie family, but they'd all but given it up in the name of peace and friendship. Along with the new man-made lake, the two massive trees serving as apartments for the fae, and the fallen tree they used for restaurants, there was now a central building in place of their old wheat field. At sunset, it was lit up from behind by a burnt orange sun.

"Knowing you for about half a year now, I still have trouble believing this is all because of you," said Thomas. He gawked openly, marveling at the difference in architecture. Fae homes were grown and shaped naturally, working with the environment rather than conquering it. The central building looked like a tree had grown from it, rather than the other way around.

"If it makes you feel any better, same." Wil slapped his back and joined him in admiring things. A nearby pixie called out his name. Wil waved at a small group of fae cheering him on.

"They seem to like you," Thomas remarked.

"What can I say? I'm a likable guy." Wil grinned. "Is there anything you would like me to show you about the land before we go to dinner? Anyone you'd like to meet?"

The enchanter smirked. "From everything I've heard, that elf princess is supposed to be beyond gorgeous. Any chance of setting us up?"

"She is easily the most attractive woman I've ever seen, and she's also a bit stuck up, bratty, and dating my brother last I checked."

"Must be nice, McKenzie," Thomas said with a sigh. "Must be nice."

"If you listen to him, she's a lot of fun but also demanding. Unfortunately, I think they're both back in Faerie at the moment. I should be able to see her tomorrow, during my trip to Oakheart Spiral." Wil began walking, and Thomas followed.

"And you're sure I can't come along?" Thomas tried again. "You know I won't cause any issues. I won't speak at all if that's what it takes. I need to see Faerie."

Wil shook his head. "After what happened with Hugo, they are incredibly selective about which wizards they allow in."

"Wasn't that your call?" Thomas said.

Wil walked faster. "Maybe, but it was the right call, and they agreed with me. Best that we give it some time. After we show off for the president, maybe that'll give you enough clout to be on the short list."

Thomas jogged to catch up. They came across a split in the path. One way led to the McKenzie house, dwarfed by all the buildings around it. The other led to the fallen tree. Wil led them there. "I still can't believe the president himself is coming to check our work."

He shrugged. "He's kind of pushy, but if he's happy with us he'll probably be friendly. And a bit obnoxious."

"Look at you, unimpressed with meeting the president. Again. Oh, no big deal, he's a bit of a bully, but you'll manage him." Thomas shook his head. "Must. Be. Nice."

Wil nudged him. "Shush. I'll introduce you and talk you up. By the time I'm done, he'll forget about me and focus on you."

"Somehow, that sounds worse."

"Then there is no pleasing you." Wil stopped to shake hands with a golden-haired centaur. After exchanging pleasantries, they headed into the restaurant.

It was, like many things in the embassy, bigger on the inside. They'd managed to take a huge tree and make it even roomier and usable than Wil could've dreamed. The ceiling was a good ten feet above the ground, with glowing lights of all colors every so often, casting the cozy room in a kaleidoscope of pulsing lights. Tables were built right into the tree, along the sides, with some additional tables scattered out in the open. There were dozens of humans and fae alike dining. At one of those open tables, their party waited for them.

Bob sat at the head of the table, as was his right as patriarch of the family and mayor of town. Sharon was at one side with Bram on the other. Wil sat down at the other head, Darlene to his right and Thomas to his left. Bob raised a hand in greeting. "What took you two so long? Bram and Darlene were about to order without you."

"I was not," Bram insisted. "I said maybe we could get something to start."

"I would've ordered without you," Darlene admitted. "In a heartbeat." She had a mug of something blue and fizzy in her hands, and she took a drink.

"Luckily, no need for that," said Wil. "Thomas and I were working on the car. We've been having some problems with the extrasensory spell on it, and it's been giving people headaches."

"We got that sorted out," Thomas added, adjusting in his chair until he got comfortable. His eyes darted around at everything and everyone, drinking in the sights. "Now we need to make it a button you press. Nonmagical people have trouble with dealing with extra senses."

Bram nodded enthusiastically. "The first time I tried to drive with that on, I nearly barfed."

"Maybe don't say that at the dinner table, Bram," said Sharon, but she smiled.

"Right, sorry, Mrs. McKenzie," he said.

"I've been meaning to ask, Mom, how often do you eat out now instead of cooking?" Wil grinned at the way Sharon's face dropped.

His mother groaned and covered her face with her hands. "It's gotten so bad, but I've been busy! After your dad won the election, he needed someone he could trust to help him out. And then there's also being the go-between for the fae here and now . . . I think I've cooked twice in the last month."

Everyone but Thomas made a loud "Ooh" at her confession. He laughed along, eyes still darting around. He was a friendly, relaxed man most of the time, but it seemed like whenever he was around anyone Wil truly cared about, anxiety hit him, and he clammed up. Not a lot, just enough for Wil to notice.

"Well," said Bob, "it's kind of hard to resist when we live right here and they never charge us anything for it. I always insist, but they won't hear anything of it."

A sprightly elf woman who could've been thirty or three hundred came up to their table. "Welcome, honored guests," she said, bowing her head respectfully. "How may we serve you tonight?"

"We're all hungry as hell," said Bob.

"Well, in that case, can I recommend the King's Feast?"

Wil's eyes lit up. "What's in that?"

The elf, upon recognizing him, favored him with a warm smile. "A sampling of all our meals. Perfect for a group this size. You'll go home fat and content and dreaming of more."

A quick look around the table showed it sounded good to everyone. Darlene spoke up for them, saying, "As long as you bring us food and fast. I'm liable to eat Bram if I don't get something in me now."

"I would taste terrible!" Bram protested.

"Not according to Isom," said Wil with a pleasant smile. "He says you'd taste like beef. A high compliment from him, actually."

His friend paled before laughing it off. The elf woman bowed once more and disappeared into the back before Wil could ask for whatever Darlene was drinking. Oh well, there'd be other chances. His mother got his attention again.

"Are you excited to go back to Faerie?" she asked. "What has you going there again?"

Bram bounced in his seat. "Our experiments!" he said. "We're making really good progress, but faricite batteries are hard, and we're running out."

Wil nodded. "I'm going to see if I can make a trade for some faricite directly and also see how they're doing. Six months after possible war, I want to make sure things are going well over there before President Bullworth comes to town."

Darlene's face darkened. "He's the one who kept you there for four months?" she asked in an icy tone.

"Basically, but nothing to be done about it. Probably best if we don't try to pick a fight with the most powerful man in the world." Wil laughed, shrugging. In truth, his anger at being stuck in Cloverton had largely faded. He'd never get back that time, but he made the best of it.

Thomas shifted in his seat. "The president and some of the grandmasters at the hearing have a vested interest in seeing this through. And they're not alone. My former master, Ferrovani, is champing at the bit to have a hand in this."

"Yeah," said Bram, pointing at Thomas. "He sent some people to spy on us."

"Just to be clear," said Thomas, as everyone's eyes turned to him, "I didn't, Ferrovani did. I don't want them there, but they're spying on us for sure. Or at least trying to."

Bob cleared his throat. "Do I need to see about encouraging them to leave town?"

"Couldn't hurt," said Wil. "But maybe don't use your power like that just yet. We don't want anyone to accuse you of being biased or furthering your agenda."

Sharon made a face. "Too late for that, sweetie. It's all part and parcel of being a leader. We've had to make a few less than popular decisions, and it makes people talk."

"You're right, Wil," said Bob, though he took his wife's hand in his. "No use throwing my weight around if they haven't broken any laws that we know of. But maybe I'll have the sheriff keep an eye out for them."

"Good," said Darlene. She turned to Wil. "And you'd better get back within a few days. If you disappear on me again . . ."

Wil shook his head with a chuckle. "No need to worry about that. I'm going to go in, say hello, inquire after the council's health, and then make my request."

"Do me a favor while you're there?" Bob said. "Ask Jeb to come and visit for a few days. It's been like a month since we've seen him."

"You got it," said Wil. "Anyone else have requests while I'm in Faerie?"

It turns out, they all did. The rest of the table talked over each other, and Wil had trouble keeping up with it all. He smiled and didn't bother to slow them down. He was looking forward to Faerie, but he found himself deliriously happy then. Just him, his best friends, and his parents, enjoying a night together chatting.

Could it get any better than this?

CHAPTER 36

Back to Faerie

Bright and early the next day, Wil had breakfast, kissed Darlene goodbye, and flew up the mountain with Isom at his side. Going back to Faerie was a treat, but he couldn't help but worry that going in and asking for a favor might be tacky or rude. They may have liked him there, but there were limits, and he didn't want to cross them.

Finally, an excuse to run and possibly do violence! Isom trotted behind him, occasionally jumping into the air and disappearing only to reappear several feet ahead and keep going. Together they wove in and out of the trees, making a game of it. With as busy as Wil had been, the wampus cat would finally get a chance to alleviate his boredom.

If it's still a week in there to a day out here, maybe we'll get a chance to go hunting together. As much as Wil didn't care for senseless violence, he'd never deny his companion's need for the fresh meat and the thrill of the kill.

Isom said nothing back but accelerated, leaping straight into the air. He blinked out of existence and reappeared twenty feet in the air, scrabbling to climb over a rock jutting out over the path higher up. Wil took his time and careened around rocks and trees. Now that he'd gotten used to it, his Thunderhawk handled like a dream.

The rest of the ride up the mountain was relaxing until he sensed Isom's excitement and alarm. That's when Wil remembered the security at the rift and how they'd react without him to vouch for Isom's behavior. He put on a burst of speed.

When he arrived at the peak, Isom had the fae panicked. Some ran after him, but most ran the other way. Wil drove by, mentally commanding Isom not to hurt anyone. For the fae, he conjured a ball of light and sent it floating to the center of the clearing. It hung in the air before it exploded in a silent flash of searing light.

"Stop!" Wil cried out in a boosted voice that echoed off the sides of the mountain. "He's with me, and we're not going to hurt anyone."

The nearest fae was a troll in petrified bark armor. He glowered at Isom before turning to Wil. Isom, for his part, looked about as gleeful as any cat causing trouble.

"This wampus cat is yours?" the troll demanded.

Wil got off his Thunderhawk, hands raised up to show he wasn't a threat. His staff remained in the Thunderhawk's compartment, and he saw no reason to bring it out. "He is. He's a mischievous little jerk, but he's bound to obey me. He won't hurt anyone unless they hurt him first. He thinks if he baits someone into starting a fight, he can have fun. Isn't that right?"

Isom declined to speak, instead stretching out his body and digging his claws into the dirt. He looked unconcerned.

"You're here to go to Faerie?" the troll asked. Wil nodded. "Then make sure you keep him close. The guards around Oakheart Spiral are less understanding than I." He growled at Isom and knucklewalked back to his post.

All around the clearing, the fae recovered and went about their day, although the guards kept a close eye on them. They knew in advance he would be coming with a companion, but even knowing it was coming didn't prepare one for a rampaging predator. Wil snapped his fingers and pointed to the ground near him. Isom trotted over to him without a care in the world.

"Stick with me and don't threaten anyone, for Pete's sake."

"Who's Pete?" Isom tilted his head to the side.

Wil got back on the Thunderhawk, and they went through the rift in a mushroom ring at a relaxed pace. More than anything, he was grateful that the rift was nothing like going through portals. One second they were in Harper Valley, the next Oakheart Spiral loomed over them. The air was rich with magic, and Wil drank it in, already feeling himself buzz with power.

The last time he'd been there, the leader of the ogres had thousands of troops ready to mobilize for war. It had been part of a combination of plots trying to escalate both sides to war, narrowly avoided. Now the plains around the great tree had signs of human settlement. The Calipanian embassy, if Wil had to guess. He stopped by there first, and Isom ran joyfully around his old home.

He carefully parked the Thunderhawk in a stable housing horses, small dogs, and a big, broad-snouted lizard. After grabbing his staff, Wil stepped out of the final open stall and looked to the nearest elven attendant. She was short and had silvery hair and sharp features awash in curiosity. "Is it alright if I leave this here while I meet the council? This is for visiting diplomats, right?"

The elf girl nodded. "It is!" she said in a delightfully squeaky voice. "Do you want us to wash it or do anything special to it?"

Wil shook his head. "Don't let anyone touch it or take it out. Tha— It's appreciated." Four months of not having to watch his language, and he almost put himself in debt to the first person he saw. He chuckled and wandered out, whistling for Isom to join him.

The rest of the embassy area looked like standard fae construction, but more closed off and less open and airy. It was one of many differences between their people, and Wil always liked seeing how they could offer consideration for the other. He raised a hand in greeting to a couple of fauns chatting outside the main building. They smiled at him and waved enthusiastically.

Isom came and fell into step behind him. He scanned with his one good eye, getting a look at everybody. His tail flickered behind him.

"Too loud?" Wil asked.

"Not at all," Isom purred. "I can't hear the thoughts of fae. Excellent!"

"Excellent? I thought you liked listening in and violating others' privacy?"

"This means I am now perfectly built to hunt humans for prey," Isom boasted. "It might be my calling now. Are you sure I can't eat anyone?"

"I've made myself clear by now. Only if they attack one of us physically or magically, or if someone trespasses. Even then, disable them, and I'll decide if you can eat them or not. For now, stay close." Wil put a hand on the back of Isom's neck affectionately.

It took half an hour to enter the capital. Flying would've been faster, but it was better not to bring a machine made of steel and iron to the fae capital. Besides, Wil enjoyed the chance to walk up to the tree and soak in how tiny it made him feel. The top stretched up past the clouds, with only a few branches visible before disappearing into tufts of white and gray. There were balconies and homes built right into the side of the tree, spiraling upward. Wil magically enhanced his vision and peered into an open window, where an ogre and a dryad were locked in heated debate of some kind. There was an endless number of interesting sights, and Wil promised himself he'd linger the full week if he could.

Isom's warning growl brought him back to earth. Wil dismissed the spell and looked down in time to stop walking before he crashed into the last person in line to get in. It was a young gnome woman, looking up at him suspiciously.

"What's your story?" she said in a high-pitched voice. Her eyes drifted down to the wampus cat.

"Here to meet with the council," said Wil. "I have a favor to ask them."

"Oh, is that all?" she scoffed. "You might be waiting for a while. Traffic going in is worse than it's ever been. All because you humans are coming by."

Wil and Isom shared an amused look. "I feel pretty responsible about that," Wil admitted, "but that ship has sailed. Maybe things will get better in time."

"Hmph."

She spent the rest of the time ignoring him. Every minute or so, they moved a few steps forward until they were in the shade, where a breeze sent a bracing chill down his back. It felt like the end of winter and the start of spring. After Harper Valley's blistering summers, it was a much desired change. Finally, they came up front to where security was inspecting every party and pack.

"You," said a hobgoblin as he pointed a short spear at Wil. "You're the wizard we were waiting for."

"That's me," said Wil. "Hello. I believe I'm expected in the council chambers?"

The hobgoblin's cheeks puffed up and back down. "You are. If you'll come this way . . ." His eyes flitted to Isom.

Wil nudged his cat, and they followed after the squat man, cutting past several groups slowly making their way to the open center of the tree. As much as he wanted to stop and gawk, he followed their guide past locked doors and down a curving flight of stairs to a basement. "In here, behave; you know the drill."

The portal waited for them, swirling chaotically. Wil took a long, deep breath and ran through. That familiar sensation of being stretched over the course of a couple of miles threatened to overwhelm him, but holding his breath helped. He managed to avoid screaming when he came out the other end, into the familiar council chambers.

It was exactly as he remembered. A recessed center was ringed by five thrones, and seating for an audience behind him. Only two of the seats were occupied, but Wil had expected at least Skalet to be missing from the meeting. Arabella, the beautiful but haughty elf princess, lounged in her throne. A few feet away, he recognized Syl's father from a memory the faun had shared with him.

King Martinus the Silenus greatly resembled his son save for his big belly, extra body hair, and golden ring through his right nipple. Syl tended to wear some amount of clothing, while his father had vines and plants protecting his modesty: an impossible task. He too lounged on the throne, putting on an unfortunate show. Wil wasn't sure he wanted to know if it was intentional or not.

"Greetings, honored council," said Wil, bowing his head respectfully. "And a great pleasure to meet you, King Martinus. I count your son among my closest friends."

Martinus raised up, laughing right from the belly. "I'd expect nothing less from my boy. He's got a good heart and wants to be everyone's friend. He has yet to understand that not everyone can be."

Thinking back to the beating Syl received at the hands of the former sheriff, Wil shook his head. "No, he understands that now. And he still chooses friendship first. You should be proud of him."

"I am," said the fat satyr. "Every day."

"Hello, Princess," Wil said, turning to Arabella. "Have you got tired of my brother yet?"

The smirk on her face could only be described as scandalous. "He's fine when he's not talking. Luckily, I can find plenty of use for his mo—"

"Never mind, don't want to know," said Wil, winking at her. They shared a laugh, and he treasured seeing a glimpse of the real Arabella when she dropped her guard. She wasn't always the brat she pretended to be. "Has Gallath been well? Who have the Wee Folk chosen to replace Timothy Twist?"

"Gallath is busy today," said Arabella with a sigh, "but we've gotten a lot done over the last year."

"Only one year?" Wil cocked his head to the side.

"We've sped up our flow of time," King Martinus said. "If we're going to deal with humans, we can't be advancing seven times as fast. We're down to twice as much time passing."

"Damn," said Wil, "I was looking forward to lingering here, if I am welcome."

"Of course you're welcome here." Arabella made a face. "I imagine you'll want to have dinner with Jebediah soon."

"If I have to," said Wil, and they laughed again. "I'd like that. I'd love to make this a social call, but I'm afraid I *am* here for a request."

"Of course you are," said Martinus. "But that can wait until the rest of the council is here. It *must* wait until the rest of the council is assembled."

"I see," said Wil. "That makes sense. How long will that be?"

King Martinus stood and stretched. "Tomorrow. For now, I think I'd like to spend some time with you. Pick your brain about things."

"What about food?" Isom piped up. Wil had nearly forgotten he was there but chuckled at his predictable one-track mind.

"That's a good point," said Martinus. "FOOD! NOW!" He clapped his hands twice, and servants burst into the room, carrying with them a feast.

CHAPTER 37

The Satyr King

Wil knew that his friend Sylano loved to party. There were enough stories passed on about fauns and satyrs that talked about their propensity for hedonism, and the three-day rager celebrating a hobgoblin wedding anniversary was proof of that. But that had been in the middle of nowhere, and semi-improvised.

King Martinus had to have planned this. There was no way he had dozens of servants on standby with food and drink and music to play just for his own benefit. Right? They came from the open doors in the council chambers, carrying every kind of meat Wil could think of and several that were unfamiliar. Fruits piled high on platters were served by dryads wearing . . . Well, if a Calipan politician had this kind of service, they'd never hear the end of it.

"Um," said Wil, frozen in place as tables and chairs were set up in the recessed center behind him. Isom's ears flattened against his head, and he looked around wildly.

"Be welcome, Master McKenzie, and enjoy our hospitality. If anyone deserves a party, it's you!" King Martinus's voice boomed over the clamor of the setup. Musicians gathered to the left and right of the council thrones and began playing a loud, bombastic tune that was all boisterous swagger.

The satyr king got off his throne and joined Wil, throwing an arm around his shoulders. He guided them to a table filled with smoky-smelling meats still on the bone. "I've heard the stories of how you wrapped everything up and took down not only Grimnar but Timothy Twist as well. Do you have any idea how much that's shaken things up here?"

"No," said Wil. "It's one of the things I was hoping to find out during my trip here. I've been worried about the aftereffects this entire time. Are things okay?" He eyed the meat, then went ahead and threw a piece to Isom. The wampus cat snapped it out of the air and crawled under the table with his prize.

"Okay? They've never been better!" Martinus guffawed and slapped Wil's back. He was starting to hate when people did that. "We're alive again. For the first time in centuries we're looking to the future instead of remaining bogged down by the past. There's plenty of time for your people to disappoint us, but we have *hope*. And that's all thanks to you!"

It was always strange, getting complimented or thanked for things like that. His first instinct was always to downplay it and try his best to not sound like an arrogant jerk, but Wil couldn't deny his impact on the situation. He shrugged and laughed weakly. "I lucked into most of it, to be honest. I want the best for everyone, and for no one to get hurt."

Martinus released him and grabbed one of the pieces of meat. He took a bite and then, unfortunately for Wil, talked with his mouth full. "Luck or not, we have more of our people wanting to travel and see Calipan again, and others are excited to host humans coming our way. The world has changed in our absence, and we get to see more of it. What was your request going to be, by the way?"

Will took his own piece of meat and tried a taste. His eyelids fluttered shut. The flavors danced around his tongue, demanding another bite. Then he remembered the question and said, "Me and the other humans who helped us all out, we're making brand new magical machines to help those without magic. But we need faricite, and a decent amount of it."

"Is that all?" Martinus laughed, spraying food. Wil wiped it away discreetly. "I'd be more than happy to gift you as much faricite as you need."

A thrill went through Wil before he remembered what gifts could cost in Faerie. "That's incredibly generous," he said. "But I could never accept such kindness without showing it in return."

Martinus dropped the meat onto a platter and held out his hand. A servant popped up to give him a goblet. He drank deeply and motioned for Wil to get a drink as well. Before he knew it, Wil had meat in one hand and an incredible blackberry wine in the other. He couldn't help but feel trapped by the king and caught along in his desire for revelry, but he also couldn't complain.

"I thought you might say that," said the satyr. "Arabella's talked my ear off about you, and Gallath has as well. For as much as that dour boy talks at all, I mean. The fact is, you saved my boy's life and did all of Faerie a service. Thank you, Wil."

That familiar feeling of Obligation hit Wil, skewing the power balance between him and the king. It wasn't power over Martinus so much as a promise of a debt to be repaid. "That's not necessary, Your Highness. I would've done it regardless."

"Doesn't matter," he said. "You'll get your faricite, no problem. For tonight, I want to share with you all of Faerie's hospitality and fun."

"That sounds nice," said Wil, "but at least let me return the favor with some kindness. When I go home, I think I might be able to repair the leyline and let you guys control the way to and from Faerie more easily."

"Sounds good to me. Here's to you, Master McKenzie! Friend to Faerie!" Martinus raised his glass and drained it before hurling it at the wall. He and everyone assembled cheered at the sound of exploding glass.

"Here's to the king of the Woodlands, friend to Calipan!" Wil joined him, savoring the wine as best he could before he, too, hurled his glass.

Memories of his last fae party screamed a warning, but Wil trusted in his friendship to protect him from harm. If worse came to worst, maybe he would come home a day or two late. After that, things got blurry. One drink turned into two turned into four. His new best friend King Martinus kept his glass full and dragged him across the council chambers.

He met dozens of enchanting fae in a short amount of time. He couldn't remember names, but there was the satyr poet whose work gave Wil renewed life. After that was a dryad woman who made an art of cultivating flowers and fruits on command from her body. By the time an impromptu unarmed duel happened between an ogre and a troll, he was comfortably drunk.

"Look at them go," King Martinus crowed. "I could watch big guys hit each other for days!"

"I should've brought Bram," Wil said, clinging to the satyr for balance. "He would've loved to come back. And he misses Gallath. He doesn't say so, but I can tell."

Martinus nodded sympathetically. "Imagine how good it would be for our people. A marriage to seal our new relationship!"

"I don't know if they're ready for marriage, but—"

"I could preside over it! We'll have contests of strength, and a play, and . . ."

It became easy to forget that the satyr was royalty. He and Wil made their way across the room, topics changing every five minutes to whatever attracted the king's attention. Isom kept pace, stealing food at every step of the way, occasionally chasing gnomes and goblins before catching up.

The hours melted by, and his fear of losing time came true. It was well past sunset when Wil came to. His vision swam, but he became aware that he was staring directly down over the railing on one of the branches outside. Vertigo made his stomach and head roll and he stumbled backward.

He collided into someone soft and sweet smelling. He giggled as she caught him and spun him around. Arabella had a sly smile on her face. "Well, well, well. It looks like you do know how to cut loose. King Martinus share his favorite wine with you?"

"And food, and conversation. He's a lot of fun! How are you doing, Ara-Arabella." Wil swayed in place, trying to still the world. "You having fun too? This is your scene, right?"

"It is, and I am. I wanted to find you so someone could say hi." Arabella whistled a complex tune Wil couldn't have imitated if he wanted to. A few seconds later, Jeb came outside, clad in gold and white armor.

"Jeb?" Wil looked him up and down. His brother looked taller and stronger than ever, more confident, and most of all, proud. His armor made him look older and more dignified, while the sword at his side made Wil laugh. "You some kind of knight now?"

Jeb frowned. "That's right," he said. "I'm a knight of the Wild Glen now, sworn to protect the princess from all threats."

"Wow, Arabella, you domesticated him!" Wil laughed obnoxiously, but he threw his arms out and grabbed his big brother into a hug. "You look good, Jeb. I take it that life in Faerie is treating you well?"

His brother sighed and hugged him back. "I get to attend all kinds of fancy balls and events, I get into some good brawls, and I'm wielding a magic sword! I even got to defend the princess from a dragon!"

"Really?" Wil's eyes widened.

Behind him, Arabella cleared her throat. "It was just a drakeling, not an actual dragon. But yes, you did a good job defeating it. No one got hurt, and you even got a new toy out of it."

Jeb drew his sword and held up the hilt for Wil to see. When his eyes focused on the spot, he gasped. The hilt was the drakeling's blue claw, wrapped around a fine silver blade with Arabella's crest etched in. "That's so cool!"

"He plays with it every chance he gets." Arabella came around to Jeb's side and leaned her head against his shoulder. She wore a small, pleased smile Wil couldn't remember ever seeing before. It reminded him of an owner doting on a beloved pet.

"I can't believe I'm saying this," said Wil, "but you might have a more exciting, more interesting life than me at this point. Look at you!" He slapped Jeb's armor. "You're fighting drakelings and traveling. I'm working in Bram's cellar to make things to sell to the government."

"Aw, don't sell yourself short, Wil. You could do with some peace and quiet for a change, and you've done enough. You invent anything good?"

Wil snickered. It grew into a chuckle, then unhinged laughter. "Yeah, Jeb, I sure did. I invented a new way of harnessing magic power in a way everyday people can use it. Things are going great. Bram's brewery is huge, and we're outfitting it with our inventions soon. Darlene's pregnant and only has like a month to go. And I have a new friend, named Thomas, I met in Cloverton. He's a master enchanter and together, he and Bram are unstoppable."

Jeb raised an eyebrow. "Damn, sounds like everything's going your way. I can't believe you're gonna be a dad. You even gonna have time for a kid?"

The question hit him like a ton of bricks. Wil had thought about it often, and the constant realization that he'd be a dad terrified and thrilled him. They'd spent so much time working, trying to race the pregnancy and get it done. Maybe he could afford to back off and relax.

"I am," said Wil. "Nothing's more important than family. By the way, Dad says you need to come home and visit! There's no way you gave me crap about that and then went around and did the same thing."

"That sounds like him," said Arabella. "Perhaps he'll get better as I further domesticate him. Declan's been handling the embassy well, but I'll dedicate some time in Harper Valley and let your brother come home."

Wil shook his head. Here she was talking like she owned Jeb, and all his brother could do was grin like a fool. Whatever, that was none of his business. He opened his mouth to speak but a hand came down on his shoulder.

"There you are, Wil!" King Martinus chortled and shook him playfully. Wil fought to stay on his feet as his vision went out and his balance went upside down. "Getting a breath of fresh air, I see. C'mon, the party's just getting started. I've got more wines to show you and the *loveliest* collection of nymphs to share them with. Voices sweeter than sin."

The thought of more alcohol made Wil's stomach turn. He opened his mouth to protest, but the satyr king pulled him along by the arm. He looked over his shoulder at Jeb and Arabella. She grinned wickedly while he gave Wil a mocking wave.

"I'm taken," Wil managed to say before they went from the quiet of the balcony to the cacophony of the party. The king cackled like a maniac. Wil fished an anti-hangover potion from a pocket and quickly quaffed it.

Wil had a feeling he'd need a couple potions to survive the night.

CHAPTER 38

Turf War

Two days later, Wil returned to Harper Valley and fixed the leyline.

After several months of doubt and fear that he wouldn't be able to do it, it came together in a matter of minutes. That wouldn't have been such a bad thing if there wasn't an audience for his efforts who expected something big and world changing.

King Martinus, Arabella, and half their retinues gathered on Skalet Peak to watch Wil fulfill his promise of fixing things and giving them better control. They made an event of it, complete with food and drink everywhere, though Wil suspected the satyr king brought a feast with him everywhere.

Wil stood in the center of the clearing, and Isom waited with the king. He had to be more careful now, with the camps and now permanent settlements littering the mountain clearing around the lake. Closing his eyes, he reached out for the chaotic leyline and let himself be caught up in it.

Awareness of the mountain flooded him as he reached out to the land. He called, and it answered like an old friend who'd been waiting for him. The earth rippled, each wave stronger than the last. The camps and houses shifted and creaked but mostly held, while the waves continued to the lake. Instinct told him exactly how to change things, and he embraced it.

The lake widened as earth first fell into it and then gathered to form sloping hills above the recessed water. More time in Faerie and a deeper connection to the leyline, almost a relationship, made the task the simplest it had been since Wil had stopped Skalet's cursed storm. The island in the middle of the lake widened as it rose above the water, the tree pushing up into the heavens.

Wil tugged, and the two pieces of the leyline lined up and melded into one. The flow of raining power diminished. The rift and the land itself were still saturated in magic, but the flow had slowed to a near stop. If he had to guess, he would've called it ninety percent healed. Time would do the rest.

He raised his fists in the air, and the assembly cheered. Wil had enough time to brace himself before King Martinus enveloped him in a big hug and lifted him into the air. Déjà vu. Balance became an ongoing struggle, but he was stuck on the satyr's shoulder.

"He just keeps on giving," Martinus crowed. "Master Wilbur McKenzie, friend to all of Faerie!"

After that, things got a little embarrassing. After another hour of celebration and exploring the renovated landscape, Wil and Isom finally took off down the mountain. The king and rest of the council would come to Harper Valley in two weeks when President Bullworth and his entourage came to verify Wil's findings.

A couple days of partying and then flying back home had Wil in the best kind of mood, bright and optimistic. It was nearly spoiled when he arrived home to find Thomas and Darlene in the middle of an argument on the porch.

"Why are you defending them?" Darlene demanded. She stood with her hands supporting her lower back. It was her default stance these days when she couldn't find a place to sit, or when she was mad. "You really want to let them spy on us?"

"I'm saying we don't have a choice other than upping our security and making sure they don't get anything else from us going forward."

Wil climbed off the Thunderhawk. Isom had lingered in the woods for a bit longer, finding some prey before he came home. It was probably for the best. He couldn't imagine walking into a scene like this and the wampus cat not using his mind reading to fan the flames.

"What's going on?" Wil asked as he climbed the steps to the porch. He threw an arm around Darlene's shoulders and pulled her close. She vibrated with irritation, and he saw fear on Thomas's face. He'd never admit it, but Darlene scared him.

"Your friend from Cloverton is defending the assholes spying on us," Darlene spat.

"I am doing no such thing!" Thomas was on his back foot, frustration tinting his words. "I'm saying that there are no legal avenues for us to get back at the people doing this. All we can do is prevent it from happening again."

"Again," Wil said through a deep breath, "what happened?"

Thomas and Darlene started speaking at the same time. At a sharp look, Thomas fell silent, and Darlene answered, "Those three wizards who confronted us at Mack's have been watching us closely. And now they have gadgets of their own based on our designs. They're demonstrating them every day and selling them, getting the word out about them being the ones to discover this."

A bucket of ice water upended itself over Wil's head, chilling him to the bone. All his good news and hope evaporated in an instant. The look on Thomas's face told him that Darlene wasn't wrong or exaggerating by much. "Is this true?"

Thomas nodded, swallowing hard. "And your girlfriend thinks that I'm helping them."

"I didn't say that," Darlene snapped.

"You didn't have to! You wear your suspicion like one of your ugly dresses." As soon as the words came out of his mouth, Thomas realized it was a mistake.

"You try finding something good to wear while pregnant!" she all but screamed. Darlene's face was a brilliant red. Rather than go on, she turned to Wil and said, "It gets worse. Ask your new best friend over there what we found."

Thomas closed his eyes and took a deep breath.

"What else is there, Thomas?" Wil asked quietly.

"Weapons," said Darlene. "They're making enchanted guns and bullets."

Wil was not the type of person who felt much anger. He knew he was forgiving to a fault, and he had very little desire to change that. The problem with not dealing with anger often was how hard things were when it became the only thing he could think about. Wil took a deep breath.

"What."

Thomas flinched. "They're making weapons with our research. And they're selling them in town."

Wil nodded. "Where are they?" His tone was flat, pleasant even.

Darlene looked at him funny. "Are you going to tell your father?"

"Where are they?" Wil repeated.

Thomas's eyes widened. "You need to be careful, Wil. Whatever you're thinking or feeling right now, we need to play it smart."

"Where. Are. They." Wil's heart lurched in his chest. That sense of coldness never left him, it only got colder until it burned him from the inside out. "I just want to talk with them."

Darlene and Thomas shared a look, and she softened. "If we tell you, do you promise to do nothing but talk?" she asked carefully. So much for her earlier anger, Wil wanted to point out.

"No, I'm going to make them realize what a stupid idea this was," Wil said. "When I'm through with them, they're going to have nightmares for the rest of their lives if they don't pack up and leave." The words tumbled out of his mouth, faster and faster until he realized he was trembling.

"Okay," said Darlene, "I changed my mind. Let's talk to your dad, and maybe Thomas can do something to prove they spied on us, and we can use that to—"

"I'll tell you," said Thomas, "but only on the condition that I come with you. Let's not do something that will land us before another tribunal."

Wil nodded once. He turned around and mounted his Thunderhawk. Thomas came up behind him, reluctant to hold on to him while this angry. Darlene carefully climbed down the steps, then waddled out in front of them.

"Promise me you won't hurt them physically," said Darlene. "Nothing that can get you arrested. Deal?"

"Deal," said Wil.

He didn't need to hurt people to assert himself. It was a lesson he should've learned with Hugo early on. So many people in the world, they didn't back down when you asked nicely. They only stopped when you made them stop. It wasn't a mind-set he wanted to have, but they had crossed a line. It was one thing to eventually make weapons with this technology. Wil had no control over that. But to take his hard work and then steal the credit while making *weapons*?

"They've set up shop on the north side of town," Thomas said behind him. "The neighborhood before the town ends and the road out begins."

They blasted off, keeping at ten feet above the ground as Wil pushed the Thunderhawk as fast as it could go. Harper Valley melted around them. Thomas shouted something, probably a plea for restraint, but all Wil could focus on was getting there.

The place they were at was one of many places Wil had surveyed a few weeks before. He knew the area fairly well and hated that the trio of wizards had been right under his nose when he passed by. They had to have laughed at him when he left. Wil pushed the Thunderhawk harder. Thomas clung to him for dear life as they blazed over the town to the gasps and calls from people beneath.

The three wizards had set up a booth outside their rustic cottage. A quick dip into his wizardsense, and Wil saw the leyline behind it, twisted into a familiar rune. A crowd of about twenty people had assembled in front of the property. Behind the booth, there were piles of straw with targets painted on, covered in little holes. Smoke billowed up from one of them.

The redheaded meathead of the three held a rifle in his hand. The dark-skinned earth mage handled money, while the monocled man was surrounded by little gadgets and faricite batteries of his own. The crowd parted for Wil as he drove right up to the booth. He got up and retrieved his staff from its compartment. Purple light shone from the wood.

"Ah, Master McKenzie," the man with the monocle said. "We've been expecting you one of these days. See anything you like? Anything you want to buy?"

Thomas pushed past Wil, putting himself between the two. "Mark, don't do this. You three have crossed a line."

"And what line is that?" McGinnis strolled their way, cradling his gun. "The finish line? We sure did. We got here first, and now all of Harper Valley will know that while you may be big for here, you ain't nothing compared to real wizards."

Wil saw red. Without thinking about it, he tapped into the leyline. McGinnis felt it, and his smirk dropped, then the earth rumbled and swallowed him up to his neck. Mark opened his mouth to protest, then he was swallowed as well. A gasp went through the crowd, and they backed up.

"Stand down, McKenzie!" the final wizard shouted. When Wil tried to submerge her as well, the land fought him. Not enough to stop her from sinking up to her knees, but she didn't go any deeper. "Don't make me . . ." She struggled to stay above ground.

"Wil, you can't do this," Thomas said, but Wil ignored him. "You'll hurt Gayle if you keep pushing. You're stronger than her."

Wil looked down on McGinnis, blistering rage consuming him. He took a deep breath and released the magic pulling Gayle down. "Let me make something clear. I don't know how you stole our information, and I'm not sure I care. You do *not* sell weapons in this town. Not on my watch."

"You don't get to decide that," McGinnis growled. "The cat's out of the bag. We've started, and there's no stopping us now. Unless you're gonna fight us in front of all these witnesses. We both know you don't have the guts."

For the first time, Wil became truly aware of the people watching and whispering from a distance. No one wanted to get in the middle of a bunch of feuding wizards, and he couldn't blame them.

"I wouldn't be so sure about that," said Wil. "I don't need to. Look into my eyes . . . McGinnis, was it?"

Wil didn't have to go deep to do as he promised. All it took was a thought, an idea, and the knowledge of how to make McGinnis do all the work for him.

The mage recoiled. "What did you do to me?"

"Leave town. All three of you. Leave town." Wil pointed his staff at a pile of altered guns. The smart thing to do would have been to take one of them for study, break down exactly what kinds of weapons they were marketing. Instead, he blasted it with lightning until all that remained was burning wood and metal slag.

Wil got back on his Thunderhawk, heart pounding. He looked over to see Thomas bent over, whispering something in McGinnis's ear. Then he straightened up, kicked dirt in the mage's face, and got behind Wil. They flew off.

After a few minutes, Wil had cooled down enough to ask, "What did you say to him?"

"I told him that if he wasn't careful, I was going to encourage you next time. I should've put an end to those three's shenanigans early." He paused. "I'm sorry I haven't. Their spying is my fault."

Isom's warnings echoed in his head, but Wil pushed them back.

"Don't beat yourself up about it," said Wil. "This just means it's time to get back to work. If they bother us again, they'll regret it."

Wil didn't like being angry, and as they flew home, he tried not to regret it. They started this fight, but after Hugo had nearly ruined everything . . . Wil would finish it if he had to.

CHAPTER 39

Summer Showers

The anger lingered long after Wil felt it should have moved on.

To be fair, he dealt with it in the best way he knew how: he visited his father and confessed to burying his rivals up to their necks in dirt, threatening them, and breaking their stuff. He'd left out implanting a nightmare. After the fact, there was a bit of shame at his actions, but overall Wil felt good about what he'd done.

"That was stupid, Wil," Bob told him in the mayor's office. He sat in the over-sized plush seat, filling it in a way Sinclair never could. He was also more honest than Sinclair had ever been. "That could cause both of us a lot of problems."

"I know," Wil groaned. "But they're showing off and selling *weapons*, Dad!"

Bob slid a small jar of candy over. Wil knew he was about to hear something he didn't like, so he took a piece of hard candy and put it in his mouth. Sucking on a sweet while his father lectured him made him feel like a teenager again.

"That's not illegal, son. Calipan's always allowed the sales of guns." Bob took a piece of his own and sucked on it. "We may not like it, but that's not something we can do anything about without overreaching."

"And what about them spying on us and threatening us before?"

Bob shrugged. "You should've filed a complaint that day if you wanted a trail of their behavior. You shouldn't have let it go. I know this isn't what you wanted to hear, but I can't help you if you don't help me. Not without proof. As it is, if they complain or file a report against you, they'll have the upper hand."

Inside, Wil boiled, but he understood. His temper had gotten away from him, and now he was on his own. "I understand," Wil said around the candy in his mouth. He rose to leave.

"If you do get proof that they're violating your privacy, stalking you, or trying to hurt you, then we can do something." Bob stood as well. "Work with me, and I'll do what I can. Until then, I have to take care of Harper Valley, and that currently includes them."

Wil left city hall annoyed and further worked up. When he returned home, Darlene waited for him on the porch. He got a couple of cold drinks and filled her in on what had happened. To his surprise, she laughed.

"You had to do your nightmare thing," she said. "You really like doing that, don't you?"

"It's mostly harmless! And you said no hurting them physically," Wil protested.

Darlene gestured wildly at him. "And then you moved the earth to entrap them and keep them uncomfortable, so you ended up doing both."

"They were fine," said Wil. "I was just making a point."

"Oh, a point. Do you think upon receiving it that they'll leave, or . . . ? Look, I'm not mad at you. I'm frustrated and a little scared, I guess. What happens when they retaliate?"

Hugo's face popped into Wil's thoughts again, smug and mad. Some people, when they pushed, you had to push back twice as hard. Maybe a couple days of nightmares would make that bastard think twice. If that didn't work, there was always . . . He swallowed, and realized he was shaking.

Darlene noticed, and her expression softened. With great effort, she got up and slid over on the bench next to Wil, pressing herself up against him. By reflex, he threw his arm over and drew her close. "You okay?"

"Yeah, yeah . . ." Wil cleared his throat and tried to project confidence. "I think maybe there's some lingering trouble with . . .things that happened before I left." Oh, so now he couldn't even say it. Shame flooded him.

"You don't handle anger well," Darlene said. "I hate seeing you like this. Look, we can beef up security for the house, right? Protect here and Bram's place with spells, wards, whatever, and we can make sure it doesn't happen again."

Wil nodded.

"Good," said Darlene, "because my mom sprung something on me. Your mom too."

His stomach twisted in anxiety. "What's going on?"

"This might be a bad time for it, but we've got people coming by in a couple of hours. I highly recommend you have a drink or two, maybe smoke some staggerleaf, and take today off. Maybe get out entirely if you don't want a bunch of mother hens squawking and trying to impart their wisdom."

Dread filled Wil. They were about to have a baby shower.

Instead of leaving, Wil did as his girlfriend suggested and let himself relax, enjoy a few drinks and a few bracing puffs while the occasional person walked the road past his house. It was hard to stay angry on a lovely summer day with a cold beer in hand. Besides, maybe he could skip the festivities if he sat out here.

Angelica Johnson drove up before too long, parking in front of the house. Of course the Johnsons were among the few people in Harper Valley with the newest model of car. She got out and pulled a big box from the back seat, clearly struggling.

Wil knew the right thing to do would be to rush off the porch and help her, but he was lazy and still the smallest bit annoyed. So instead, he pointed at the box and exerted a little will and power. The box lightened to the weight of a pillow. Angelica heaved a sigh of relief, and Wil didn't even have to get out of the rocking chair he'd moved to.

"Heya, Wil," Angelica called out. "Surprised to see you here. You going to be here for the shower?"

He waved his hand and the front door opened for her. "I sure am. Here and nowhere else. You ladies can have all the fun you want without me. I promise I won't make a peep." Wil puffed on his pipe, blowing rings out into the summer afternoon.

Angelica laughed and walked in the front door. The faint cry of "Mom!" trickled out to him, but Wil chuckled and kept on rocking. Soon he'd need another beer.

After Angelica, Robin came with a bulging pack over one shoulder. She had been one of his former classmates and a good friend of Darlene's throughout the years. Wil couldn't say they were close, but he vaguely liked her and had helped her family with a fox getting in the henhouse almost a year ago. He waved at her.

"Looking relaxed, Wil. Gonna give anyone a hand, or are you going to be a bum?" She grinned at him.

Wil responded by puffing and blowing smoke at her. A quick, precise flick of his fingers formed the smoke into a single word: *no*. Robin laughed and walked through the open door.

People trickled in as the day went on. More former classmates, a young woman who Wil believed had worked at the general store with Darlene a while ago, Angelica's sisters, and then, naturally, Wil's mother. She was accompanied by Wil's least favorite relative.

"Wilbur, sweetie, there you are!" His aunt Linda rushed up and invaded his personal space. Her hands went right to his cheeks and threatened to rip them right off his face. "And the mustache and goatee, I like it, I like it. I'm still used to thinking of you as just a teenager and—"

Wil looked past her to his mother, silently begging for her help. Sharon looked as instantly exhausted as he felt. Aunt Linda was a good example of how hard it could be to love your family. With her talking a mile a minute only a few inches from his face, he felt less than charitable.

". . . and of course, your mother was jealous of me, and—"

"Aunt Linda," Wil interrupted her. "Lovely to see you. Please, be welcome and enjoy a drink inside on this hot day." Please, for the love of gods and demons alike.

She released his face and backed up to an acceptable foot away from him. "Aw, you're such a sweet boy. But we *must* talk soon. I've got all kinds of wisdom to share about raising kids."

"C'mon," said Sharon, putting her hand on her sister's shoulder. "Wil's already having a bit of a day and could use some quiet." She gave him a pointed look before leading Linda inside.

Wil groaned. Right as he'd managed to forget about his previous bad mood. Aunt Linda had a way of doing that. He finished off his beer and went inside to use the toilet.

They'd decorated his house in pink and blue with a huge banner featuring a stork carrying a wrapped up baby from its beak. It said "Darlene McKenzie's Johnson's Baby Shower" in rainbow letters. Darlene sat in the middle of the living room with a stack of wrapped presents beside her. He raised his eyebrow and nodded toward the sign.

"Mom thought we were getting married," Darlene said with a laugh. "Or that maybe we already had. By the time she realized, it was too late."

"Want me to fix it? I'm going to fix it." Wil twirled his finger in the air. Simple illusions didn't take much focus or power, so he made it look as if there was no crossed out name, and then, just for fun, he made the letters wiggle. And then the stork flew across the banner in the background before it managed to break free of the banner and circle the room, a two-dimensional bird doing a three-dimensional loop.

"Show-off," Darlene teased. "Do more. Our house is honestly kind of boring for you being a master illusionist."

"Oh really? Really? Okay." Wil looked around and decided to have some fun. To the walls he added several babies crawling around and burbling nonsense. He made the stork chase them and added them to the banner, then he moved on to her stack of presents. Wil had to rely on his imagination for a lot of it, but every present she opened would have a baby crying, laughing, or otherwise making a sound.

The ceiling fan, he gave a touch of frost to disperse over the room, making it cooler. Out of pure mischief, he put a few mind-altering spells on the couches and chairs. Whoever sat in them would gradually feel more relaxed. One of them he designed to put someone to sleep if they stayed too long, and he added another one to a chair he mentally assigned to his aunt. And then, just because it was obnoxious, he created a spinning orb that projected colors to the walls and rooms as it passed.

"Better?" Wil asked.

Darlene hummed and then nodded. "For now. But by the end, we might have you perform for us."

"I'd love that!" Robin came out of the kitchen with bowls full of fruit. She sat down in one of the sleep-enchanted chairs and turned to Wil. "Remember how you used to do whatever you could to entertain us after school? You'd make dancing lights, or make people sound like cows, and one time you set the schoolhouse on fire!"

Wil's cheeks burned. "I'm still grateful no one tattled on me. Got away with saying it was Billy-Ray smoking that did it."

Darlene laughed. "I worked really hard at keeping people quiet, thank you. If you got in trouble, there'd be no more shows."

"Absolutely. On that note . . ." Wil saluted them and disappeared into the bathroom. After he washed his hands and came back out, he grabbed another beer and a hunk of bread with seasoned butter and cheese and slipped out the back door. He found his seat again and relaxed.

He opened his beer and brought it to his lips, when his aunt's head popped out the door. He froze, and she took her opportunity.

"Hey, love, can I take this time to talk about something serious?" she asked.

Wil swallowed. "I'd rather not, actually! Maybe later."

Aunt Linda sat on the bench across from him and made herself comfortable. "Having a baby changes things."

"I know, Aunt Linda," he said. "I'm pretty well prepared." He dreaded what came next, and his aunt didn't disappoint.

"No, you don't understand. Things will get harder for you and Darlene, and if you're a real man, you'll make sure they're both provided for. You're going to have to work harder than you ever had to before."

Gods. Wil wondered if it would be unethical to hypnotize his aunt into leaving him alone. He decided against mind magic and settled in for a slog as she moved on to diapers and complained at length about her third husband and his unwillingness to be a parent. Wil drained his beer and prepared himself for pain.

CHAPTER 40

Transportation for All

Getting back to work was oddly difficult. After a week of either relaxing or doing diplomatic work, going back to a slow grind took willpower. As much as he hated to admit it, Wil was grateful that Bram hadn't allowed himself a real break. When the time came to act, he was already in motion. The only thing he'd been waiting on was the shipment of faricite to come through.

"That's . . . How much is this worth?" Wil asked, staring at the cart stacked high with the glowing green crystals. The fae had packed them in as tight as they could, and nothing had fallen out of place during the ride down the mountain and through town.

"You want actual numbers?" Thomas asked, staring at the pallet. "I could probably do the math with enough time, but the answer is a lot. If we went through all this in a year, I would be surprised."

Darlene walked up to it. The faricite was still piled higher than she was tall, and it cast her in a soft green light. "We already knew the fae love Wil, but this proves it. With as expensive as faricite is, we're going to need to find a way to make our products affordable. Or not need faricite. Is that possible?"

"Probably," said Wil. "That's what I'm working on now with one of the cars. C'mon, let's get all of this into the lab." With a careful spell, he levitated the pallet and moved it to the back of Bram's house. Thomas rushed forward to open the door and then took half of the stack as well so they could fit it through the cellar doors.

With the faricite in place, their lab was more cramped than ever. At this point, they would need to take some of their projects outside and work on them out in the open. When Thomas said as much, Wil thought of their rivals building weapons off their work and shuddered.

"Only if we can close it in," he said. "Maybe ward it further."

"So we need our own garage," said Thomas. "Kind of a problem if we want one fast, but we can throw something together that'll be fine for working on the cars. It's better than having them out in the open and begging people to steal them. I'll get on that."

Like they'd done many times over the past couple of months, they split the work up. Thomas and Darlene went into town to get a long overdue garage built, while Wil stuck with Bram, and they worked on the cars together.

Every so often one of Bram's employees would run in to ask a question, or a customer would venture up to the improved wards and call out distracting questions. A lot of people demanded their customary potions from Bram, who had to break several times to get something from his personal stores or even brew up some of the simpler medicines and tonics on the spot.

Out of all of them, Wil worried about Bram the most. He never slowed, never stopped, never did anything but work, read, work, pop his head up for air in the brewery, and work. It was much the same for Wil, but the wizard didn't push himself as hard as Bram did. He at least had a girlfriend and had to make appearances around town. Nothing held his best friend back from dedicating everything to their various projects. No one but Wil and Darlene ever seemed to notice how much he threw himself into everything.

"Hey, Bram?" Wil asked from underneath the car. They were in the back, a few hours later, and the other two still hadn't come back.

"Yeah?" Bram had just come back from the brewery, and he slowed to a stop nearby, panting.

Wil continued etching out the finished part of the *feed* rune on the underside of the car. It would join others and hopefully be their next big advancement. The more usable devices they had, the better. He needed to overwhelm and impress to get the government off his back. When he was done, he slid out from under the car.

"When the president and others come, there's going to be representatives from Faerie. Do you want me to make sure Gallath is there?"

Bram's face colored instantly. "That's . . . not necessary. He's made it clear that things can't work. Too much distance, too much responsibility. Too much." His hands twitched, like he wanted to crush something.

Wil nodded and sat against the driver's door. "Sounds like he's scared. And like you're scared too."

"Right, this was a good conversation, but let's turn back to the car."

"C'mon, Bram," Wil said, a little annoyed. "I don't say this to be a jerk, but you're often scared of things, and I don't want to let you ruin a good thing because you think it won't work out. If nothing else, we can get you a date with someone else."

Bram growled and threw his arms up in the air. "What does it matter? We're hard at work and—"

"Well, that's just it," Wil interrupted. "You work too hard. And it's great for us, but I want things to be better for you. More balanced, you know?"

"I took the damned break like you asked," said Bram. "Mostly. I spent two entire days reading and eating a lot and not doing any work. It was stressful."

On the one hand, it was great to see Bram sticking up for himself and pushing back instead of backing down. On the other, he either didn't see Wil's point or was deliberately ignoring it. "And that's great, but you jumped right back in. And you need something for yourself when you're not working. It's not like you care that much about the money, right?"

Bram looked like he'd been slapped. "Of course I don't really care about the money," he said. "It'd be nice to have more and not ever have to worry about losing my home again, but I'll be fine. I'm fine right now. Your last pep talk was great and all, but I'm okay. Just because you've been all goo-goo-eyed over Darlene lately doesn't mean . . . Sorry, not going there."

Wil nodded. "I appreciate it. That would've been some crappy deflecting. But you're not entirely wrong. I'm happy, and I want that for you too. You seem lonely. If not Gallath, then let's at least set you up with *someone*. What's your type?"

The summer heat could make any argument, no matter how big or how petty, flare up into something personal. Wil was glad it didn't happen, but seeing Bram's growing annoyance, he knew he'd best stop soon.

"Muscles, good sense of humor, and confident. Gallath, basically." Bram sighed and sat on the ground next to Wil. "If it'll make you feel any better, invite him. The worst thing that happens is he says no. Now, can we talk about the damned car? What else do we have to do?"

That would cheer up Bram's mood. "I think we're about good to give it another go," said Wil. "I just put the batteries in, and we need to give them a test. I think my latest enhancement should make a huge difference."

"What's that?"

Wil grinned like a fool. "I put the *feed* rune in a Thompson Configuration and made sure it connects to all the moving parts. I think this might work."

Bram grunted as he stood. "I'll give it a shot. Still not that comfortable driving. They're too small, you know? But I'll give it a try if it means you lay off my love life."

"For now," Wil allowed, and then he, too, stood. He got into the passenger seat, motioning for Bram to go around and get in. He did so with a roll of his eyes and a lot of effort. Once inside, he had to hunch over the steering wheel and suck his gut in a little.

"So, I turn the switch and . . . ?" Bram's eyes darted around nervously.

"And then you push down on the pedal when you want to go." That had been one of the harder things to work on, and Thomas had put hours and hours into it. A wizard could control the speed of their car, but nonmagical people would need something special and familiar.

"Right, right." Bram took a deep breath. He flicked the switch. Nothing happened. He flicked it back and forth, then raised his eyebrow as if to say "Now what?"

Wil reached out with his wizardsense. No magic flowed through the car's frame, although it should. On a hunch, he slammed his fist into the console. The circuit completed, and the car came to life with a low, barely perceptible hum.

"Ahh!" Bram cried as they started rolling forward, right for the fence. Wil grabbed the steering wheel and yanked it to the side. The car rolled around until it lumbered across the chaotic landscape.

"Ahh!" Wil agreed, laughing with joy. "Guess what, Bram? I lied about putting the batteries in!"

"You what?!"

Wil pointed, and Bram avoided driving right into his new lake. It was a missed opportunity to see if the amphibious mode worked as intended. "Yeah, this car is driving without faricite batteries. And it seems to be doing just fine. How's it feel? Try any of the features?"

"Um . . ." Bram looked around the dashboard. He flicked a switch marked with an open eye. A second later, he made a distressed sound and veered to the right. Wil turned it off.

"Yeah, the extrasensory setting is weird. It's easier when you deal with a wizard's extra sense."

"This is incredible," said Bram as he drove in tight, lazy circles on his front lawn. People in the brewery came out, as they often did when the experiments were conducted in public. "But what's the point of doing it without batteries? Once we get out of the range of the leyline, it'll be useless, won't it?"

Wil shook his head. "Not if we can increase leyline coverage. Imagine a line going across the basin, powering everyone's houses. And along that line is a train powered by magic that goes across. We get a couple of intersecting lines, and suddenly you can get to anywhere faster. No need for a car or a horse anymore, and it leaves plenty of walking room around town."

Bram inhaled sharply and pulled out of the circle. The car leveled out, heading straight for the gate. Wil waved his hand and threw the gates open in time for them to go through and up the drive. "Are you serious?"

"We just can't stop winning," said Wil.

Bram laughed and continued away from his house. "You're unbelievable. *We're* unbelievable! We have to see how far this will work."

"You read my mind!" Wil slapped Bram's shoulder, then recoiled as the car swerved for a second. They both laughed and continued up the lane.

As timid as Bram could be at times, their continued success buoyed him, and before long, he enjoyed driving. He gradually picked up speed until even Wil had to tell him to cut back. But before he could, the car drifted to a lazy stop.

"Well," said Bram, "I guess this is it. How far away from the leyline are we?"

Wil closed his eyes. "About a mile. Your leyline is pretty strong, though, and we won't know how much range any of them might have until we test it further. But it would cover a lot."

"And there has to be a way to expand a leyline's reach," Bram said, a familiar mania entering his voice. "Like in that one book on Marlowe Manor you brought back. Those leylines are far off but still affect the property, right?"

Wil was taken aback. "That's right. But to be honest, I have no idea how in the hell he managed that. Do you?"

Bram shook his head. He opened his mouth to speak, when the honking of a horn made him jump and squeak. Darlene and Thomas were in a car right next to them. Bram lowered the window and said, "What was that for?"

"What're you two doing out here?" Thomas asked. "We were on our way back. We've got someone who can build us a garage in just a couple days."

"Notice anything?" Wil called out.

Darlene groaned. "Spit it out."

"This car has no batteries, and I'm driving it," said Bram. "We now know how to make things that don't need a big battery attached to it if it's used in a close enough proximity!"

Thomas looked impressed, but Darlene let out a frustrated cry. "Right when we get all that faricite. Great timing."

Intruders

In his many centuries of existence, Isom had never pledged himself to anyone's service. Not before Wil. The idea of a proud and fierce apex predator serving anyone had been absurd.

Until it wasn't.

Right from the beginning, Wil smelled different. Seven hundred years had passed in Faerie before the rift opened. Which meant that it had been about seven hundred and thirty years, give or take a decade, since he'd last eaten a wizard. Even so, the memory of the time he'd earned the ability to teleport short distances remained strong. That wizard had been among the best of his time, but his power paled in comparison to Wil's. He wasn't easy prey, which made him the perfect prey.

Until he wasn't.

Rather than get ambushed and eaten quickly, he'd fought Isom off and delivered a nasty blow that took a few days' rest to get over. After that, the wampus cat approached it cautiously, waiting for another chance to strike. And each time he tried, he lost.

Normally that wouldn't matter much. In the wild, losing a fight could mean dying, and no matter how much Isom threatened the wizard, he only ever got driven away. Which led to a realization: Wil was a stronger predator, and he treated it like a game.

Isom wasn't stupid, but he wasn't much of a thinker either. Following the humans back to Harper Valley hadn't been a choice so much as a compulsion. He and Wil had unfinished business. That's what he told himself, at least.

Truth was, he had been curious. What kind of apex predator didn't finish off their opponents and went around doing things for the weak? Wil and his kind were obviously *social* creatures and functioned as a colony, not unlike some of Isom's cousins, who hunted in packs and took care of each other. So he watched the wizard, following out of sight in order to better understand him.

That never happened, but instead he saw the other wizard come into town and throw his power around, acting every bit the fighter Isom craved pitting himself against. At least, he thought so. When he challenged Wil at the feast, it had been as much out of frustration as a desire to fight and prove to himself what he had suspected since their first meeting: Isom couldn't win.

It hadn't mattered. There was a joy in the fight, in playing with someone who was evenly matched or better, knowing that no matter how many times the game went on, it wouldn't end. It was an opponent who wouldn't kill but would at least play. For the first time in his long life, after years of hunting and fighting, Isom found a friend.

And then, trapped after losing once more, Isom was helpless after the mage Hugo broke his mind.

He didn't like thinking of that time, where life was like a dream controlled by someone else. It had been like watching himself from the outside, unable to affect anything or even scream.

And then Wil had saved him, but not only that, he allowed Isom his revenge and then healed him. After he recovered, what else could the proud wampus cat do but dedicate a few decades to the first person who had embraced him without bending to him at all?

Sure, Isom gave the wizard as much trouble as he could. It was fun, and he needed all the meat and stimulation he could get. The wizard was great about letting Isom run around and hunt in the woods, but the wampus cat ultimately cared about his oath and his duty.

Which brought him to tonight, when Wil and his pack went for yet another celebratory dinner. Isom didn't fully understand the point of what they were doing, but it made them happy, and it made them vulnerable. They left, and it was up to him to guard their home against all intruders, as he did most nights he wasn't hunting.

The three-story den had tons of people coming by at all hours to gawk and bask in his master's seat of power. The majority of them could be scared off by a growl, or a whisper in their mind. Isom had all kinds of places to hide and stalk in, from the roof of the house to the trees surrounding it, and even a few choice places along the road, behind brick walls where plants grew and framed the walkway.

He'd been lightly napping behind one of these walls when a trio of people approached Wil's house. The moment they came into Isom's range, his eyes shot open, and he listened in.

. . . stupid wizard, thinks he can get away with . . .

This is a bad idea. We're going to get in trouble, but after what he did . . .

His home doesn't have much in the way of defense. This should be easy.

Slowly, Isom peeked his head over the wall. Three humans stood in front of Wil's house, looking up at it: an older man looking around nervously, a beefy one Isom immediately wanted to taste, and a stony woman who had a permanent glare. Three wizards, all blatantly thinking about trespassing on Isom's territory. Wil had been very clear about what he could do while defending the house. The wampus cat licked his chops in anticipation.

"How long is this going to take?" Mark hissed to McGinnis. "We don't know how long they'll be gone, and we shouldn't be here anyway. Elliot is this close to pulling the plug on things as is."

"Please," McGinnis scoffed. "He's all talk. We're doing good work, and he can't afford to lose us now. Not when the president and others are coming. If we can get inside, maybe we can destroy their notes and any evidence that they got there first. And it'll serve that bastard McKenzie right for what he did to me."

"Maybe you shouldn't have antagonized him," said Gayle. "Seems to me you had that one coming."

"Whose side are you on, Gayle? You don't want to be here, you can leave!" McGinnis snapped.

"I didn't say that," she muttered. "He shouldn't have embarrassed us like that."

Well, this was perfect. Isom almost wanted to thank them. Instead, he jumped up to the wall and then leaped through the air. He disappeared from view right as Gayle's head shot around to look where he'd been. He reappeared in the branches of a tree above them and pondered who he should take out first.

"What was that?" Gayle hissed.

"What was what?" Mark looked around frantically. He repeatedly stroked his short beard. He was the weak link, Isom decided. He wouldn't be a threat, but if he took him out early . . .

"It was nothing." McGinnis turned around. "You're imagining things. The wards haven't been activated. It'll only take me a few minutes to break through them. Just shut up a minute and let me work." Ooh, he'd be distracted.

Isom resisted the urge to purr. Only one of them was wary enough to be a bad target. One didn't care, and the other reeked of fear. He bunched up his muscles, ready to strike.

All three of the wizards inhaled sharply. As soon as Isom made up his mind to strike, they reacted, much like Wil did. Just as they looked up, Isom jumped and disappeared into another tree. The branch he'd been standing on swayed violently.

"There's something wrong here," Mark said. "Tell me you didn't feel that."

"I felt it," Gayle confirmed. "Something's watching us."

"It's an illusion." McGinnis laughed suddenly, as if catching on to a joke. "McKenzie's a master of them. I bet he has more than just wards here. Be careful about what you see or hear, it's probably there to scare you off and isn't real."

Isom couldn't have been more delighted. Prey that helped him stay hidden. He watched in amusement as the three tinkered with the magic tied into the house. As a member of the fae, he could vaguely sense that there was magic tied to the house, but not the nature of it. A few minutes later, that magic disappeared.

"There we go. As good as he is, those wards were child's play," said McGinnis. "I don't expect anything dangerous here. He's not half of what people say he is."

"And yet he got under your skin," Gayle muttered. McGinnis didn't respond other than to go up the walkway to Wil's house and magically unlock the door.

Well, that was Isom's cue. He jumped and disappeared, only to land on the roof. He went in through the tower bedroom's open window and stayed low. He slunk through the door and crept down the stairs to the second story as the wizards entered.

"His office is over here," Mark said. "I'll check that out."

"Gayle, you should check the basement," McGinnis said. "I'll poke around upstairs. Be back here in ten minutes with whatever you find."

Splitting up would make it so much easier to deal with them, but Isom wanted a challenge. He crept up to the top of the stairs and inhaled deeply. The taste was always the real cost of using this ability, but the chaos and fear it caused was worth it. He exhaled a poison fog down the stairs, settling at the landing where the wizards waited.

McGinnis opened his mouth to say something and got a whiff of the poison. He coughed, at first light and surprised but then deep and racking as he couldn't breathe. The other two were no better, though Mark managed to cover his mouth with a spell to filter the poison out. Gayle was already running out the door.

You shouldn't have come here. Isom delighted in the way they jerked as his words entered their minds directly. Their thoughts turned to fear, and then they dismissed it. Just another McKenzie illusion. Isom leaned into it and let out his loudest roar, rattling the walls with his call.

"Wait . . ." Mark said, voice distorted by his spell. "That's not an illusion. That's . . ."

Isom appeared in front of him out of nowhere. He landed on the wizard and tackled him to the ground. His middle paws wrapped around the wizard's front while his front claws raked lines into his sides. His teeth snapped right in front of his face, and he roared again, mentally crowing as the wizard relieved himself on the spot.

Heat bloomed to his side and then seared his skin. Still coughing, McGinnis projected a flame his way. Isom leaped to the side and disappeared, and the flames danced over a screaming Mark.

Isom reappeared outside, where Gayle waited. Her eyes were wide, and she tried to catch him by opening the earth around him, but he knew that move already. He leaped up and pounced at her. Right as she raised her arms to defend herself with a hissing, violent glyph in the air, Isom teleported behind her and crashed into her. He sank his teeth in her shoulder and shook violently.

Fear and blood, the best tastes in the world. The wampus cat's heart sang as he gnawed on her bone. Then another blast of fire came out, and he jumped away, projecting his voice behind McGinnis. "Do you still think I'm an illusion, Wizard? I'm going to drink the marrow from your bones!"

And then he disappeared again, landing on the roof above them. In the dark night, he blended against the pain. He watched and waited as McGinnis helped Gayle up. The stony-faced woman breathed hard, nearly hyperventilating as she cradled her wounded arm. Isom enjoyed her taste while she looked around in terror.

"Get ahold of yourself," McGinnis barked. "It's just one weird cat. How bad could it be?"

Mark staggered out of the house. "We need to leave."

"No!"

Isom helped them along by breathing another blast of poison down on them. They weren't prepared again, and Isom jumped down. He chomped down on Mark's leg and dragged him to the ground.

Coughing and hacking, McGinnis and Gayle looked up in time to see Mark disappear into the house as Isom dragged him in. His scream cut off suddenly, replaced by hideous laughter right into their minds.

Isom didn't need to be able to read their thoughts to know when they gave up. McGinnis and Gayle ran from the house as fast as their legs could take them, while the wizard underneath Isom gathered the power for a spell. He released his leg and wrapped his fangs around the wizard's throat.

We're going to wait a while, you and I. Isom purred, letting his teeth carry the vibrations against his prey's skin. *You shouldn't have come here. But I'm so glad you did. Please, struggle. I'm so hungry.*

CHAPTER 41

Friends and Fame

Wil was amused to find that he wasn't the only one who couldn't put work out of his mind. Here they were, just over two weeks until their presentation, and their newest breakthrough meant that they all fought over who could dream bigger. Which wouldn't be so bad, if they weren't out in public at the classiest place in Harper Valley.

Danson's Steakhouse was usually a place for dates, with its dim lighting, pleasant ambiance, and quality food. The four of them grabbed a table together in the back, with an order of drinks for everyone who wasn't pregnant, and about ten pounds of rib eyes. Wil would take a raw steak home for Isom later. The wampus cat's behavior had been good lately.

The same couldn't be said for Bram's and Thomas's—they had placed diagrams out on the table in between partially cleared plates. Thomas prodded a spot underneath a picture of one of their cars. "If we've got vehicles that run purely on the leylines, that frees up room where the batteries would go. You're mad if you think we shouldn't make the most of the room we have."

Bram groaned loud enough to disturb people at a nearby table. They shot them dirty looks, but Bram replied with the same fire. "They should still have batteries as redundancy. There's no telling when something could go wrong, and we want them to still work in case an emergency happens. Besides, do you really want to stress the machine with that many nested runes?"

"Oh, so the newbie is worried? Why not ask an expert? I'm waiting." Thomas didn't break eye contact, even when he took a petulant drink of beer.

They had finally gotten to a point where they could joke about the difference in experience without hurting anyone's feelings.

"Why *don't* we ask an expert? Let's invite Ferrovani over, then."

Wil leaned over to whisper in Darlene's ear, "I could listen to them fight all day."

"I couldn't," said Darlene. "Break it up, fellas. Before I have to splash some cold water on you."

Bram and Thomas glowered at one another. Despite how much of a teddy bear he was, Bram had a face made for intimidation. Eventually Thomas snickered, and the tension broke with the table's laughter.

"That one hurt," said Thomas. "Ferrovani's an ass, and I'm glad to be done with him." His smile faded, and he had a faraway look on his face.

"You imagining telling him to kiss your ass?" asked Wil.

Thomas chuckled and nodded. "Exactly. I think that I'm going to do that soon, before he comes for the presentation. He still bothers me, and he very badly wants a piece of what we've done. I think I'm going to make it clear that he and his spies are done here."

Darlene raised her glass of sweet tea. "Should've done that weeks ago, but better now than never. Think we should do something to run them out of town before the presentation? Something other than giving one of them a nightmare and melting their guns, I mean. We don't want to get arrested, or worse: notably not arrested because of nepotism."

Wil winced. Now that he'd lost his temper and lashed out, guilt consumed him whenever he thought about it. The spies weren't on the same level as Hugo, and he needed to calm down and let go. It didn't mean he wanted to. "We could always speak poorly about them in the brewery and around town, make them pariahs."

Thomas shook his head. "I'll deal with them tomorrow. When I'm through with them, they will leave town. I . . ." His mouth snapped shut, and he wrestled with himself over something.

"What's going on?" Bram asked, nudging Thomas. "You what?"

Thomas cleared his throat. "I've been working quietly, figuring things out about them. Collecting dirt, reaching out to others. They won't be a problem anymore. I guarantee it. And for what it's worth, I'm sorry that I haven't done it sooner. They should never have gotten an opportunity to make weapons, and I take full responsibility for that."

"Why?" Darlene's eyes narrowed. "It's not like you invited them here to town, right?"

"Right," Thomas said, eyes dropping. "I didn't want them here, and I told Ferrovani that. But like I said, tomorrow I'm going to put a stop to all of it. I'm actually glad we're talking about it, because I have something I've wanted to say."

Wil looked around the table. Thomas had their rapt attention. He cleared his throat and began.

"I appreciate being part of this team. More than I can say. This is exactly what I needed, and I didn't even know it. For years I worked alongside the masters, never really appreciated for my contributions. I thought that being on a small team like this, I'd instantly rise to the top and show how brilliant I've been all along."

Thomas made a disgusted face, and they all laughed. "That didn't happen, because I'm not. Working with you made me realize that I function best as part of a team, and that I didn't know nearly as much as I thought I did. You've impressed me beyond my ability to convey it. So I wanted to thank you all, for the honor of letting me work with you.

"And so, a toast. To friends and fame, may we all be flush with both." Thomas raised his beer.

"To friends and fame," said Bram as he raised his drink, "in that order, preferably."

"Friends and fame," said Darlene. "And a ridiculous amount of money from our success."

"To friends and fame," Wil said. He raised his beer and they clinked their drinks. "May we continue to make each other better as we go on."

They drank and settled back into their chairs with contented sighs. Wil sought out Darlene's hand and ran his thumb over her palm. Just a couple weeks away from an end to all their worrying and struggles, and he could hardly believe it. It was too soon, but it also wasn't soon enough. If Wil could speed up time and have it be tomorrow to get it over with, he would in a heartbeat.

But they still had time to iron out any last issues and finish up Bram's latest designs. Which reminded him. "Hey, Bram, how close are you to finalizing the coffin?"

"For the last time, we're *not* calling it the coffin," said Bram. He threw his napkin onto his empty plate and relaxed. "That's too morbid, and it's the opposite of what it will do."

"But you have to admit," said Darlene, "it kind of looks like a coffin. And you do put dying people in them. The snail coffin has a ring to it. Snoffin, maybe."

"I don't want people to associate it with actually dying!"

"Bram, Bram." Thomas put his hand on the man's shoulder. "You *want* something memorable and controversial, trust me. The snail coffin is a great way for people to ask what the hell it means."

Wil drummed his fingers on the table. "The Time-Stretcher," he said. "It's like a magical medical stretcher, and it stretches out each second as long as possible. What could be better?"

Their latest creation utilized a time bubble. The knowledge how to do it had come from the fae as Wil left Faerie. The Time-Stretcher was a large box with enough room inside for a person. Whenever the box was closed and locked, time stretched on inside. One second inside was a minute outside. Their final creation before their deadline would revolutionize trauma care.

"Dammit, that's good," Thomas admitted.

"I can go with that," Darlene conceded.

"And it's nearly done," Bram said. He had that familiar, manic look in his eye when he talked about their projects. "It's so funny, how much easier it is to stretch time like that than to speed it up. That first version broke the batteries, even with the connection to the leyline. All we need to do is make sure that there's enough air and motion stabilizing to help prevent the time bubble from collapsing. It'll be ready in time."

"Alright, enough already," said Darlene. "We've had a good, productive day and a nice celebratory dinner. We're going to go back to work tomorrow, but I'm fat, full, and sleepy. I think it's about time for Wil to roll me on home so we can listen to the radio and de-stress."

"De-stress, huh?" Thomas waggled his eyebrows, earning some groans. "I think that's a good idea. I'm tired, and I have a lot to prepare for tomorrow. But more importantly, dinner's on me." They cheered, once again earning the ire of their neighboring diners. Wil didn't care.

Ten minutes later they were in their car with Wil driving. Darlene was too far along now to comfortably fit behind the steering wheel. They drove on at a leisurely pace with the windows down. Darlene stuck her head outside the window and breathed in the summer night. Wil activated the extrasensory mode and watched his girlfriend.

Everything about that day reminded Wil of how blessed he was. He could honestly say he had a good life and things were going his way. Which was, of course, reason to worry. Wil chuckled at his paranoia and put it out of his mind, focusing on moving past the light foot traffic on the way back to their house.

And then the foot traffic thickened past the point of being able to drive.

"What's going on?" Darlene asked.

"Good question," said Wil. He popped his head out the window and honked the horn. It cleared a way through scowling pedestrians, and he jumped at the opportunity. The problem only got worse the closer they got to home. "I have a bad feeling about this."

It took twice as long to get home, and then Wil saw the problem. Or rather, he felt the problem as soon as he got close enough to sense Isom and the pure glee coming from the predator. Wil jumped out of the car and ran up the drive, pushing past the concerned onlookers.

Isom lay on top of one of the three wizards, teeth wrapped around his neck. He waited patiently for Wil, tail flickering like a snake's rattle.

Look what I caught. He and the others tried to break in while you were gone. They work for your friend Thomas. Can I eat him?

CHAPTER 42

Betrayed

Wil stood there, shocked.

Did you hear me? Isom made eye contact, growling lowly as the wizard in his jaws whimpered and went limp. He was the oldest of the three spies, and he looked and smelled terrified. Wil almost felt bad for what he had gone through, but the wampus cat repeated the pertinent fact. *They work for your friend Thomas.*

"Yeah, I heard you," Wil muttered, glaring at the wizard.

"What did he say?" Darlene asked, looking back and forth between Isom and the people on the street watching. "And what're we going to do about this?"

"Might let Isom eat him," Wil muttered.

"Please . . . please don't . . ." the wizard said. His monocle was on the ground and broken. "I'll do whatever you want, please . . ."

Wil turned to Darlene, all the night's joy lost. "Isom said that this bastard here, and the other two, are working for Thomas. Sure makes tonight's speech make more sense, now that I think about it."

Darlene said nothing, but her face turned a bright red. She pointed right at the wizard's face and said, "if you want to get out of this, you're going to answer every single question we've got. We've got half a mind to let you get eaten and then turn Isom on the others!"

Isom rumbled with approval. His prey whimpered and trembled. That was enough for Wil. "Let him go, Isom. If he tries anything, you can take him down. But no eating him until I say so."

Although he didn't say anything, the wampus cat projected supreme disappointment and irritation. But he did as he was told and carefully extracted his teeth. The wizard's neck was covered in saliva and welts where Isom's fangs had dug into his flesh. Wil offered him a hand. The wizard took it and let himself get pulled up.

Wil led them inside, but a mental command had Isom sit at the front door and guard them from any possible intrusion from either the man's allies or any of the bystanders. Certainly, one of them had contacted the sheriff. That meant they only had so much time to get offers before he was arrested and beyond their reach.

"So, before we start, you realize this was stupid, right?" Wil asked as they went to the kitchen. He got water from the sink and let it accumulate in the air, held aloft by magic. Water wasn't his specialty, but he could handle a few gallons.

"Profoundly stupid," Darlene added. "And not just coming here tonight but trying to spy on us at all. We didn't want any trouble, but you're in for it now."

The wizard nodded, still trembling. "My name is Mark. I'll cooperate, I promise. Please don't hurt me!"

"As long as I get some answers, I won't." Wil said. He then directed the water to crash into Mark and soak him to the bone before he turned off the sink. "That's for the pee smell," he added.

Mark nearly crashed to the ground again, but he held himself up with the wall. He dripped and looked more miserable than before, but it was hard to feel too much sympathy. Darlene took pity on him and directed him into one kitchen chair, while she took the other. Wil turned on the light and paced.

"How long have you been working for Thomas?" Wil asked.

Mark's eyes darted between the two of them. "We don't, strictly speaking, work for Thomas."

"Ferrovani," Darlene said. "Thomas is still working for Ferrovani, isn't he?"

A sour pang went through Wil, a mix between embarrassment, anger, and hurt. It only got worse when Mark nodded. "I suppose I shouldn't be surprised," Wil said. "Thomas was up front about why he was interested in me right from the start. He saw I was lonely and trapped, and he made himself my friend. Even when I knew it was possible, I . . ."

Darlene took over for him. "How many times have you or your associates tried to break into either here or Bram's house?"

"This was the first time we've made a real attempt," Mark answered. Every so often he swallowed hard and looked to Wil with fear in his eyes. "Before now, we've looked from afar and probed your defenses a bit. Nothing that would trigger your alarms or trip your wards, just enough to see what you've got. We wondered why it wasn't more protected. I guess we don't have to wonder anymore."

Wil went into the cabinet and got himself a glass and the whiskey. He hadn't drunk much with dinner, not enough to impair his ability to drive, but now he needed a drink. He poured himself two fingers and then after a moment poured a second glass for Mark. He wasn't fighting them yet.

"Th-thanks," Mark said, taking a sip and wincing.

"Tell me how it went," said Wil. "Tell me all the ways my friend Thomas is betraying me."

Mark gripped his glass tighter. "Every week or two, he'd show up with copies of your notes and give them to us. We'd study them and practice with the leyline out back. It was mostly boring until you cracked it. As soon as you cracked it, we got the notes and got to skip ahead to working on things that Cloverton wants."

"Like weapons," said Darlene. She looked as angry as Wil felt, but they both managed to keep it together. "So you had everything you needed. Why break into the house at all? You could've kept going as you were, and we wouldn't have done anything to you. No worse than a nightmare or two," she added, eyeing Wil.

"That's . . . that's why," Mark said. He shrank in his seat and took another desperate sip of whiskey, as if afraid Wil would take it away if he didn't like what he heard. "After you hurt McGinnis and destroyed our weapons, we were all a little sore. And McGinnis is a dumbass, but he's insidious and good at getting people angry. So we thought we'd . . ."

"You thought you'd break into my house, take anything that might help with your experiments, and make it clear that I wasn't safe in order to get under my skin," Wil finished for him. "How's that working out for you?"

Mark finished his whiskey and coughed. "Not well. You're not going to hurt me, right?"

"Of course not," Darlene scoffed. But then she saw the look on Wil's face and fell silent. Mark followed her gaze and he paled.

"I don't know about that," said Wil. "I could do horrible things to you, and there's nothing anyone would be able to do to fix them. I'm one of Calipan's best mind mages. I could trap you inside your worst memory and slow down your perception of time. I could remove your ability to understand language, cutting you off from the rest of the world forever."

Darlene gaped at him, and her reaction made Mark tremble worse. "I, uh, would greatly appreciate it if you didn't do any of those. Please."

"Well, that depends, now doesn't it?" Wil smiled pleasantly. "When the sheriff comes by, are you going to confess everything?"

"Yes, yes, I will confess anything you want!"

Darlene understood then, but it was clear she didn't approve. Her glare bore into Wil, but he ignored it in favor of staring Mark down.

"Wise. I don't want to have to do any of that, but something happened recently. You've heard about what happened to Hugo?"

Mark nodded.

"I don't tolerate any attacks on me or Harper Valley anymore. Confess, and at the first available opportunity, you're going to get the hell out of my town and never return, or I will do any number of horrible things to you. Am I understood?"

Mark nodded with more enthusiasm.

"Excellent," said Wil. "Go out the front door and sit next to Isom. He's going to keep an eye on you until the sheriff arrives."

The spy paled at the suggestion, but he nodded and slunk away from the table and out the front door. Wil got an impression of malicious joy from Isom, and for once he didn't dissuade the cat from his little pleasures.

As soon as he was gone, Darlene turned on him. "What the hell was that, Wil? Where did those threats come from?"

"He invaded our house," Wil said. His voice was rough, and he realized he was holding back tears of rage and frustration. "He and the others. It's not enough to try to steal our work, but they invaded our *home*. They're making weapons based on our research, and my supposed friend is responsible for all of it."

Darlene braced herself on the table and chair and fought to stand. She staggered over to him and hugged him. Wil clung to her and helped keep her steady, even as he began shaking.

"I know that," she said gently. "And I'm mad too. I know what this means to you Wil. They deserve to get their asses kicked for all of it. Thomas especially. Weapons? He looked you in the eye and promised no weapons, and he was lying the entire time. We'll get them, Wil, but we'll do it the right way. We don't need to hurt anyone. I'm . . . a bit scared. For you, not of you. You're not the type to want to hurt others."

"I didn't used to be," Wil whispered. "Ever since Hugo, I . . .When we're working, things are fine, but I get angrier than I used to. I don't want to be pushed around or let bastards like him push other people around. I hate being this way, but I hate how people hurt others more."

Darlene squeezed him. "I know. But you're strong, Wil. How many times have you told me that the strong have a responsibility to watch themselves and not hurt anyone weaker than them. You're better than this."

"I want to be, at least. You're right. And . . ." Wil pulled away. He wore a sad smile. "I wouldn't have done it to him. Not really. But for the moment, I wanted him to think that I would. If he confesses, then it worked. But I'll stop with the nightmare thing."

"Thank you."

Isom sent a mental warning several seconds in advance. Wil went to the front door and opened it right as the sheriff went to knock. Sheriff Harrington was a strong, good-natured man in his mid-thirties who wore a big hat.

"Master McKenzie," he grunted. "It looks like there's been a little trouble here."

Wil nodded. "There has, Sheriff. My house was broken into by three rival wizards, and my pet defended my property. I wish to press charges, and our friend here has promised a full confession and to cooperate with you."

Sheriff Harrington looked at a cringing, soaked Mark. "Alright, then. I hate to take up your time after what's been a trying night, but I'm going to have to ask some questions of you and Ms. Johnson first."

Darlene joined Wil at the front door. "We're happy to help, Sheriff. Anything to make sure our home is safe again."

Wil saw his future for the next few days. This was what his father needed in order to act, so maybe they'd finally be rid of their problem once and for all. He wasn't looking forward to having to confront Thomas.

CHAPTER 43

Get Out of My Town

Neither of them rested well that night, but Darlene got to sleep in as Wil went down to the jail and talked things over with his father. Dealing with the sheriff had taken a couple hours, and then they gave Isom his steakhouse treat before going to bed. Wil had woken up about three hours earlier than he had wanted and took the Thunderhawk out for the day.

His father was already at the jail and talking with Sheriff Harrington. In his short time as sheriff, the jail had become less oppressive and more in line with what you'd find in the city. Mark Marfolk sat behind bars on a bench, staying wisely quiet. When they saw Wil in the doorway with his staff and dressed in his official capacity as town wizard, their conversation stopped.

"Wil," his father said, coming up and hugging him. "They told me their side of things. You did the right thing here, but this is clear retaliation for your messing with their operation. You're not blameless here."

"I know," said Wil, eyeing Mark in the cell. The prisoner kept his eyes locked on the ground like he was pretending not to exist. "But what I did was genuinely harmless. What would have happened if Darlene had been there and neither me nor Isom were there? They might've hurt her. *He* says they were just going to rob me and vandalize the place, but that leader of theirs is unstable. There's no telling what he'd do, all because he was angry at me."

Sheriff Harrington cleared his throat. "There's no arguing that, Master McKenzie. But you should understand that they could potentially press charges against you as well. We want this to end as cleanly as possible. I would greatly appreciate it if you would let me handle things. Your reputation precedes you."

Wil nodded, ignoring the heat rising to his cheeks. That was a valid complaint, and he knew it. "Of course, Sheriff. I'll do whatever I can to make this easy for you. When can we expect the others?"

"Any minute now. Can I get you some coffee?"

Wil gladly accepted and sat at his old desk in the corner with a mug of frightfully strong coffee. He nursed it over the next twenty minutes. His father and the sheriff chatted while they waited, talking about the other townspeople and a few tourists who had damaged an inn and tried to skip town to avoid paying.

Right as he considered getting a second cup, the door opened and the other two wizards were marched in, hands cuffed behind their backs. Wil grabbed his staff and stood. McGinnis made eye contact, and Wil saw the man's desire to hurt him even without having to read his mind. This was personal, and it wasn't going to end here.

Gayle, on the other hand, looked embarrassed. As if she couldn't believe she were stuck here with the others, and she totally wasn't at fault. It almost made Wil laugh, but he stayed silent and let the sheriff handle things.

"So, are you two going to try to deny breaking and entering, or are you going to make things easy on me?" Sheriff Harrington hooked his thumbs into his belt and waited.

"No, not going to deny it," said McGinnis. "Why should I? I was looking for a cure for an affliction Master McKenzie placed on me. Are you going to arrest him for that?"

"Mm. No, I don't think so," said the sheriff. "We could charge him for it. Just like we could charge you for this. But if you're willing to have an adult conversation, we can handle this like men. And a lady," he added, nodding at Gayle.

"If it keeps me out of jail, I'll do whatever you want," she said. "I see that's what Mark did, at least. You alive in there, Mark?"

"Alive and mostly intact," said Mark. The older wizard stood and pressed himself against the bars. "No thanks to you two. You left me to die by McKenzie's cat!"

Wil cleared his throat. "He wouldn't have killed you unless you seriously harmed him," he said. "He's well trained and was ordered to hold any intruders there for my return. Which he did. As for the nightmare I planted? That was wrong of me. Blasting your pile of guns, though? No regrets."

McGinnis surged at him, but the deputies grabbed him by the cuffs and yanked him back. "Those took hours to make, asshole!"

"Good," said Wil.

"Dammit, everyone," Bob said. He didn't raise his voice often, and Wil immediately shut up. Even McGinnis winced, though being handcuffed and unable to defend himself had something to do with it.

"If it were up to me, I'd let you all brawl it out. I'd put good money on my son cleaning your clocks, and it'd be satisfying to see. But as there is no doubt about what occurred, the sheriff and I have decided to offer you three a deal. You won't be arrested or charged with anything, and you will be free to go. So free to go, in fact, that you should get your things and leave town and never come back.

"In exchange, you forget your grudge. Pack it up and take it with you. With any luck, none of us will ever see each other again."

"And what about our damaged goods?" McGinnis demanded.

"You mean the ones you built from stolen research?" Wil asked. "Given to you by a man I thought was my friend. A man who promised me no weapons. Those goods?"

McGinnis sneered. His face was a splotchy mess, and magic charged the air.

"Yeah, those ones. The ones that are going to make us a fortune and keep us employed rather than just throwing together a bunch of junk and trying to sell it to nulls. *We* have a future. You may have gotten here first, but our weapons will eclipse anything you do as far as Cloverton is concerned.

"So sure, I'll take your deal. We'll take our stuff and leave. We've already won. All we have to do is finalize our magnum opus before the president comes. We don't have to be in this boring town to do it."

Sheriff Harrington stared daggers at him, and his hand balled into a fist. Bob looked at McGinnis with undisguised disgust. They all seemed to be waiting on Wil's reaction. The funny thing was that Wil didn't feel anything about it. He didn't care about McGinnis in the slightest. All his anger and hurt were somewhere else, and the petulant ravings of an embarrassed man meant nothing.

"If you ever come near me or my friends again, there is nothing in the world that will protect you from me," said Wil. "Now get out of my town."

Without much further ado, Harrington released Mark and had his deputies escort them from the jail and back to their cottage. They had three days to pack and leave, which soured Wil's enjoyment of getting the last word in, but it would have to do. During those three days, he and the others wouldn't be able to relax or progress in anything. They would need the time to hurt and grieve.

Wil remained at the jail, waiting for the hammer to fall. It was almost noon when Thomas entered the jail. He was as pale as a ghost and kept his eyes on the ground.

"Yeah," said Wil, "I wouldn't want to look at me either. You and I have an uncomfortable talk ahead of us. I can handle this one, Sheriff, if I may."

Harrington nodded. "Only if you're sure this won't end in violence."

"If it does, then I will have deserved it," said Thomas, cracking half a smile. "I waive my right to press charges."

"That won't be necessary. C'mon."

They walked out of the jail and down the road. Thomas said nothing, and Wil suspected he appreciated more time before they got to the point. Or maybe he dreaded it, and stopping for ice cream was a torture he may or may not have deserved. Either way, Wil needed something to boost his mood.

They sat on a park bench in the hot midday sun with ice cream sundaes, the sounds of birds and children playing nearby. "How long, Thomas? Was it the entire time? Was any of our friendship real or just manufactured for your scheme?"

"It's complicated, Wil. I'll happily explain it to you if you're willing to listen, but the short of it is the friendship was real." Thomas took a bite of vanilla and chocolate fudge. "And the spying wasn't my idea. I was pressured into doing it, and I deeply regret it."

Wil breathed deeply. It wouldn't do to laugh in his face. "You have to know, that's not that comforting. I mean, I'm glad you regret it, but that doesn't make me feel better. If that's what you were hoping for."

"I was. Damn."

Part of Wil wanted to shout and growl and roar and maybe cry a little. It hurt, and speaking became difficult. He was in control, and it was miserable. "Explain it for me, please."

Thomas swallowed and took a moment to prepare himself. "I was at Marlowe Manor when you arrived, and I was genuinely curious about you and interested in working together. As time went on, it got back to Ferrovani. He didn't care for me staying and keeping you company as often as I did, until the explosive end of your tribunal.

"He saw my proximity to you and bribed and threatened me in the same breath to spy on you. I should have . . . I should have led him on and lied about doing it, until it was too late for him to do anything about it. I should've done that." Thomas laughed bitterly.

Wil nodded as he ate his ice cream. "Yeah, you probably should have done that. Or maybe told me about it and seen what I could've done to help. If you had come clean about this at any time before last night, we could've worked things out."

Thomas winced. "I tried last night. I was building up to telling you all about it, and I was going to tell them to get lost and destroy their copied notes. But then that idiot McGinnis decided it was time to get back at you."

Wil laughed suddenly. Thomas gave him a funny look, to which Wil said, "I just thought that if Ferrovani was really that rich and accomplished, he'd have better hired help."

Thomas laughed as well. "The thing is, they're good at what they do. Mark and Gayle are almost as good as me and Bram, and McGinnis is more imaginative than you'd expect. They're used to much harsher conditions, with more competition, a deadline, and sabotage all around. I think they went stir-crazy here."

Wil's laughter cut out. "I'll take your word for it. They broke into my house, Thomas."

"I know. I'm sorry, Wil. I can't undo things, but I can promise you that I want nothing to do with them anymore. If you can forgive me, I'll prove myself twice over." A manic, desperate gleam appeared in his eye. "I was trying to do the right thing, and I swear to you that the last couple of months have been the best. Please, let me have another chance."

Wil wanted to, more than almost anything. It would be so easy to shrug it off and welcome Thomas back in. There was no way their friendship wasn't real. Even if it had started fake, it felt real, and they'd accomplished so much together. But Wil knew he forgave too easily, and he couldn't think only of himself.

"They broke into my house. They're making weapons. *You're* making weapons. It was the one thing I asked of you, and you lied to me." Wil took one last bite of ice cream before throwing the dish into a nearby trash can. The sweetness offset the bitterness he felt. "I could've forgiven you if it weren't for that."

Thomas inhaled sharply. "Wil, please . . ."

"It's not just for me, it's for Bram and Darlene too. They deserve better than this."

"Well, let's ask them!" Thomas tried to smile. "Make it a group vote. Let me state my case to everyone, and if you don't want me, I'll leave."

Wil stood up. Thomas trailed after him in a daze. "This is my decision. I can't trust you. But I need you to know that we're not going to pretend you had nothing to do with our success. You'll receive a full quarter of the credit and the money, as we agreed upon. But as of now, you're no longer part of the team."

He started to walk away, when Thomas called after him. "What am I supposed to do now?"

Without turning around, Wil said, "It doesn't matter to me. Go work with your other team. Make your weapons and double-dip on discovery, like you wanted. Just do it away from me. Goodbye, Thomas."

Regrets And Repercussions

Thomas sat on the bench for a while after Wil left, ice cream all but forgotten. It was easier to sit there and feel crappy than to take the next step forward. He didn't care for any of the available paths, and he found himself thinking of how he could have done it differently. For a good fifteen minutes, he sat on the bench with people passing by, imagining a world where he hadn't screwed up so badly.

There was comfort in letting himself pretend. It was the empty comfort of saltwater to a man dying of thirst, but he still drank it down until it hurt and he wanted to throw up. The more he thought about going back and telling McGinnis and the others to leave early, the less he had to reckon with the fact that those idiots were all he had left.

Go work with your other team.

The very idea sickened him, but it wasn't wrong. What else was left? If Wil rejected him, there was no way Bram and Darlene would accept him. They'd fall in line behind Wil, and that left Thomas with . . . what? Running back to Cloverton? He'd still get his credit as part of the team, but how could he sit back and let them finish up without him?

There would never be a day in his life that Thomas would have to work. That was true before he'd come to Harper Valley, and knowing how their discoveries would change the world meant riches beyond his wildest dreams. It didn't matter. His name would be attached to the greatest magical innovation since they'd first learned runes from demons. That was slightly better, but still not enough.

Thomas stood and threw his melted ice cream in the trash and trudged away from city hall. He didn't know Harper Valley too well, but he let his feet carry him down the road as reality sank in and weighed him down.

It was absurd how wrong the day was. The sun shone too brightly, everyone he passed looked happy, and it was hot enough to make Thomas take a moment to cast a minor spell to follow and cool himself with a miniature flurry of frost. Here he was, having thrown it all away, and the world kept on like nothing had happened. Thomas laughed bitterly and continued down the road.

He found himself at a familiar place. Mack's Shack was busier than ever, and Thomas had to go in and take a look at his handiwork. He immediately regretted it.

"Master Elliot!" Mack called out before he'd made it two steps in. "Here for a free burger?"

Thomas's cheeks colored. "No, thank you. I just . . . I wanted to see how the stove and Freeze-it are working for you."

"Ahh," said Mack knowledgably. "Your periodic check-in, huh? Everything's gone real well. I accidentally started a small fire when I forgot one was on, but we handled it. And the Freeze-it." Mack grunted his supreme satisfaction. "At first, I thought I'd leave it on blizzard, right? But then that actually accumulates snow. So now we use blizzard to flash freeze the new stuff and then snow for keeping things frozen.

"All in all, they're working like a dream, and I'm saving so much money on fuel and spoilage. I owe you and Wil a lot." Mack leaned over the counter and extended one gnarled, hairy hand.

Thomas took it and welcomed the pain as the cook crushed it. "I'm glad to have helped. I normally work on cars, so this was a fun challenge. Wil and the others have a bunch of other things they're cooking up as well. They're going to change the world."

"They?" Mack cocked his head to the side. "Not you? You worked on this too, right?"

It would've been so freeing to confess his sins and accept Mack's anger, but more customers came in, and Mack's eyes slid over to them. Thomas smiled. "I did, but I might head home early. Next time I'm in here, I'll take you up on that burger."

"Anytime, Master Elliot. Anytime."

As he went back to his rented home, Thomas noted all the leylines he passed. It was incredible how many were in this basin, and that had to be worth studying as well. Maybe not by him, but someone could take their research and run with it. Everything could be improved, and even his own contributions would eventually fall by the wayside of time.

The rented house was like a lot of Harper Valley: small, cozy, charming, and out of time. Between access to Faerie, the railroad, and all the leylines, this town was already blowing up. Another year or two and this house would probably be replaced with something bigger, or maybe apartments. He went inside and packed his belongings. It didn't take long.

Go work with your other team.

Well, hell. What did McKenzie know? Thomas plopped himself down at the kitchen table. Did Wil really think that they would get a chance to do research without others sticking their finger in the pie? Did he think that he would just invent a new way to harness leylines and then get a trophy for his efforts? The world didn't work that way.

The more Thomas thought about it, the angrier he got. For over half a year now, he'd gotten close to Wil and had to put up with his saccharine optimism and ideals. It was endearing, until it wasn't. Now, poised to leave town and forced to report on his failure to Ferrovani, he hated everything about it.

Why the hell couldn't they move past this? It's not like McGinnis and the other two idiots had managed to do anything special. Weapons were going to be made. Might as well make them the right way so that no corners were cut. You couldn't change the way a country was headed; you could only aim and do your best.

Wasn't that what he'd done? Thomas buried his face in his hands. And then he laughed at an inane thought: would he get in trouble if he took one of the cars? Screw it, he was the one who requisitioned them. They could do without one. Everything he'd taken with him fit in the back seat. He drove off, heading north. He'd drive to Kappala and then take the train east. It would give him time to think about it.

Go work with your other team. Make your weapons and double-dip on discovery, like you wanted. Just do it away from me.

No, there was one thing he had left to do. Thomas wasn't normally an angry person, but some things he didn't let stand. On the north end of town, off the main road, was the cottage he'd come to once a week for the past two months. Three deputies remained out front, the trio's babysitters until they left town. They parted for him, giving him inscrutable looks as he went inside.

The three of them were already packed and sat at the table with the remnants of a bottle of whiskey between them. "What the hell were you idiots thinking?" Thomas demanded.

"Oh, hey, Master Elliot," said Mark, lifting a shot glass his way. "This one's to you." He still looked shaken and hurt from his encounter with the wampus cat.

McGinnis stood on unsteady feet. His face was redder than usual, and his brutish attitude was somehow worse. "I thought that I'd maybe get something since you skipped last week's meeting. I thought maybe I'd scare him a little or take something valuable in exchange for the stupid dreams ending."

"So, you weren't thinking at all," Thomas said.

"Give it a rest," Gayle groaned. "We've lost, and we're out of town as soon as we finish getting our stuff together. And thank goodness. If I never have to spend another second in Harper Valley, I'll be happy."

"We've lost? Just like that?" Thomas stormed over to the table and snatched the whiskey. He took a pull from the bottle and regretted it, but it helped his appearance when he slammed it back down. "Now we don't have to hide. We can do things in the open. Not here, but Harper Valley isn't the only leyline-heavy place in the Le Guin Basin."

"Are you serious?" Mark gaped at him. "We're officially being run out of town. And I'm pretty sure everyone in this room hates everyone else."

"What do you hate more: each other or losing?" Thomas's heart pounded in his chest.

"Losing," Gayle admitted.

"Losing," McGinnis muttered.

"Each other," Mark said cheerfully. "But I can put that aside if it means a better paycheck and not having Ferrovani pissed at me."

"Leave the old master to me," said Thomas. Wil, Bram, Darlene. If they had given him a chance, he would've moved the heavens to prove himself. But Wil decided to give him the boot. Well, he'd regret it. They'd all regret it.

"For now, we're going to move over one town, bribe the mayor, and start full production on weapons and shielding. McGinnis, you're going to keep your damned head down, or you're out. Am I understood?"

"Perfectly." McGinnis lied with zero skill. He'd be trouble later, but for now, Thomas needed all the help he could get.

"Then get your stuff, and let's go. Daylight's burning, and we have just over two weeks to embarrass McKenzie and the other townies. When the president comes, we'll have all eyes on us instead of them. Understood?"

The trio shared a look. "Agreed."

CHAPTER 44

Looking Forward

It wasn't the most considerate thing he could have done, but Wil disappeared for a few hours. The time to think and breathe was more important than Bram or Darlene in that moment, and he promised himself he would apologize later. For now, he needed to fly.

It started out as an excuse to go fast around the edges of the farms, jumping the occasional fence or wall. Isom caught up to him partway and ran alongside the Thunderhawk, though he kept mercifully silent. As sadistic as he could be, he could literally feel Wil's pain.

By the time he got to the edge of town and saw the deputies in front of the cottage where Ferrovani's lackeys were, the anger had mostly faded, but the hurt had not. People always told him that he was naive and thought too highly of people. Maybe they were right. Hadn't the last year proved how alone he was?

He continued east until he came to the border with Gallard Springs. Wil stopped and pulled out his map of the basin. He never had finished it. Well, now was as good a time as any. It was simple work, and things could brew on the back burner while he lost himself in the repetition. He wouldn't do the entire basin, just map around the edges and explore a theory.

So, on he flew, marking down each leyline he came across. Gallard Springs was rockier and less good for farming. Little outcrops of houses sprouted from the ground while simple roads wound their way around rock and stone. Even on the outskirts, there were hot springs along the mountains. The leylines were especially potent there.

The east side of town sloped upward to that mountain range, an eastern twin to Skalet Peak. As he and Isom went up, Wil wondered if that was a dragon's home as well. Exactly as he suspected, the very top of the mountain had a leyline. And so on and so forth, through the eastern foothills and the wide open range south, leading to Appleton, he marked them down.

Once he was satisfied, he flew home at sunset, where Bram and Darlene waited on the porch.

"Where the hell were you?" Darlene barked, though Wil knew her anger wasn't really at him.

"I needed to clear my head," said Wil as he went over to his rocking chair. Even if she had been mad at him, Darlene had his pipe ready for him. He packed a bowl as he said, "Are you two okay? How about you, Bram?"

Bram took up an entire bench on his own, and he currently sat slumped over with his elbows on his knees and his head in his hands. "I'm not happy," he said, chuckling at the understatement. "I know things were a little rough at first, but we'd started getting along. By the end, he stopped being surprised when I knew stuff."

How much had Thomas's casual derision of Bram's efforts added to his self-esteem problems? Wil puffed deeply on his pipe. Maybe the anger wasn't entirely gone.

"I don't think getting along now changed anything," said Darlene. She wore her irritation openly. "He wasn't going to change just for us. We were useful idiots."

Wil sighed. "He told me that he was going to call it off, before this happened."

"Sure," said Darlene. "Easy for him to say after he got caught."

"What if he meant it?" Bram asked, eyes darting between the two of them. "People can change. I did."

"What? You want to give him another chance?" Darlene asked.

Bram stiffened. "I don't know," he said after a few seconds of silence. "I want to say yes, but . . . He had a lot of time to talk about this. We're so close to the end. We could've kept him on a short leash."

"And what could we have possibly done to make sure he wasn't still betraying us?"

Wil sighed and let his friends argue. He didn't know what was right, so he could hardly expect them to. The fact was, he'd made the decision, and it was over. And he didn't regret it. Not much, anyway.

"Wil, what do you think?" Bram asked.

"Like I told him, I would've accepted his apology if he hadn't made weapons. Now I don't know what to do, but I know I can't do it with him around. I think there's not much time left, so we might as well focus on our last few projects. The Time-Stretcher, the car, and maybe seeing if we can charge the batteries with more than just the leyline."

Bram nodded. "Right back to work, then. I can agree with that."

"I can't," said Darlene. "Aside from the fact I'm tired, cranky, my feet hurt, and I'm mad, we need to deal with this. We can't go 'Oh well' and act like nothing's happened. It's not healthy."

"What more is there to say?" Wil took the final puff of his pipe before cleaning it out. "Our friend wasn't really our friend, and now he's going to have plenty to present on his own as well as with us. He's going to be the star of the show."

"And why does that matter?" Bram asked. "Don't we have enough to keep you out of trouble? Who cares if he ends up having more to show off. Isn't it more important to make good works and have them readily available to the world?"

That sounded nice, and Wil didn't disagree, but . . .

"Screw that," said Darlene. "He doesn't get to come out on top of this. You're right. We'll go back to work tomorrow, and tonight, we'll sharpen our claws and come up with more."

That sounded good. It sounded right. "He used to tell me that his biggest regret was always standing in the shadow of bigger men. Well, he's going to have to get used to it. No double-dealing or spying is going to keep us from the top!" Wil jumped out of his chair, and so did Bram. Darlene struggled.

"So I propose dinner, discussions, and detoxing from the day. Who's with me?"

They were not the type to turn down dinner, especially Darlene.

The next day, they went back to work in Bram's cellar, and . . . nothing went wrong per se. They showed up, fiddled with their inventions, made notes of more, and the day ended. Something was missing. Everyone knew it, but no one wanted to be the one to voice it.

So the day after, Wil took a break and went flying again. He mapped out the rest of the Le Guin Basin's leylines in Gallard Springs and collapsed at night with his project almost complete. When he woke up, he gathered his friends to show his findings.

"I don't see anything," said Darlene from her chair. He had hung the map up on the wall after copying it, and they looked at a ridiculous number of marks all across the basin. "Are they in a shape or something I can't see?"

Bram stood by the map, stroking his chin. "No real pattern to it other than all over. What is it we're supposed to see?"

Wil tapped his finger on the map, then swirled it around the edge of the map in a slow, lazy spiral moving inward. He stopped on a beanstalk marked *Mr. Carrey*. "The highest concentration of leylines is around the edges, but the strongest ones are *around* the center. And then here in the center of the basin, there's nothing. Except for my house and the road going north, but no leylines."

Darlene made eye contact with Wil and then did the most exaggerated shrug imaginable, but Bram understood.

"Marlowe Manor!" Bram gasped.

"Marlowe Manor," Wil confirmed.

It was a testament to Darlene's patience that she took a deep breath and said, "You two enjoy doing that to me, don't you?"

"Yes," said Bram.

"It's less that I like keeping you out of the loop and more that I like being dramatic, and Bram gets me." Wil spread his hands with a sheepish grin.

Darlene motioned with her hands for them to get on with it. Bram jumped at the chance.

"Marlowe Manor is in the center of a bunch of leylines," said Bram. "The location was chosen for its density, right outside the capital. The manor is enchanted down to its foundation and known for slow decay of the magic and strong ambient magical energy in the area. They don't fully understand why, but scholars believe that its location is responsible for it."

Like usual, Bram recited it like he was reading it from a book. Darlene nodded in understanding, then had a question. "So if that's the case, and you're in the middle of an entire basin full of leylines, why do you have trouble making spells stick to our house?"

Wil pointed at her. "That's the big question, isn't it? There's probably something I could do about that if I tried. I'm not entirely sure how. I suppose I could try to make that the focus of the next two weeks. Bram's got the Time-Stretcher, I could have this, and Darlene could have the car."

"Just one problem with that," said Darlene. "I'm so far along that I can't easily get under the car or do anything with it without Thomas."

That punctured their good mood. No one wanted a reminder of what they'd worked so hard to avoid talking or thinking about. Darlene sighed and fixed it.

"It's fine," she said. "What we have works, and I have a lot of other work I can be doing. Despite the brewery and apothecary part of the business being closed half the time, we still have employees to pay and people to reach out to. I'll handle that, while you two get to do the fun stuff."

"You could come with me," said Wil.

"No no, don't worry about me," said Darlene in a long-suffering voice. "I'm only eight months pregnant and have trouble getting around."

Bram cracked first, laughing at the look on Wil's face, followed by Darlene's pleased smirk. Wil shook his head with fondness.

This was more like it. They didn't need Thomas. It had been the three of them long before it had been the four of them, and they had this. Two weeks to go, and Wil intended on making good use of every single second.

CHAPTER 45

Sister's Situation

A much needed distraction came in the form of Sarah's return home from school for the midsummer break. Her train got in at noon, and Wil drove his parents from the embassy to the train station, silently wishing he could go faster than a crawl.

"Slow down, maniac," said Bob from the back seat. "We ain't in a rush." His aversion to cars was of great amusement to Wil. He had gone much faster on their horse Percival when they'd been younger.

Sharon laughed and shook her head. "Relax, hon. You saying you don't trust Wil to be careful?"

"I've seen that thing he flies around on. The boy is reckless."

Wil cleared his throat. "'The boy' is right here, and he is also a good driver. I have the extrasensory spell on and can feel people coming from a ways off. Relax and enjoy a lazy Sunday drive." Still, he slowed down.

During his trip to Faerie, it had been nice to see and talk with Jeb for a bit. The closer Wil got to the train station, the more he missed his sister and her catlike personality. She deserved the opportunity she had to go study art and make a real career of it, and he couldn't wait to ask her all about it.

They arrived ten minutes early, with enough time to get drinks and for Wil to set up an illusion of floating words saying "Welcome Home, Brat." He'd wanted to write something far more insulting or vulgar, but his mother hadn't let him. He may have been a powerful wizard, but she was Mom, and he trembled at her power.

The train came sliding in with a loud whistle, puffing smoke overhead. As much as Wil loved trains, maybe he could improve them. He shook himself out of the mind-set and waved his hand. The illusory letters grew and bounced in place. The first people off the train saw it and laughed, but it took another five minutes before Sarah came into view.

On the surface, nothing was different. She still had short, blond hair and piercing blue eyes. She was nineteen now and still resembled an overgrown kid to Wil. But there was a sharpness that hadn't been there before, a confidence and swagger that was brand new. She sauntered over to them with her luggage dragging behind her.

"Oh look, the feds let you go. What did you have to give up?" Sarah asked.

"Sarah!" Sharon groaned, but Wil didn't mind.

"My dignity and pride, mostly. It took a while to get through it all, and now I've made a discovery that's going to make us the richest family in the country, if not the world."

Sarah sniffed. "Apparently you got to keep some of your ego after all. Anyways, let's go home. Or whatever counts as home now." She walked past him and slashed her hand through the illusory letters before hugging her parents.

Wil blinked. That sounded way more bitter than he'd expected, and the look on Bob's face said he felt the same way. It wasn't the time to bring it up. Wil joined in the hug behind her and took her luggage for her. They headed to the car soon after, where she joined him in the front seat.

"Pretty nice, right?" He asked as he ran his thumb over the steering wheel. "We managed to grab a few from Cloverton to help with research. This one got tweaked a lot by Darlene and Thomas . . ." His throat tightened.

"Huh," said Sarah. "Yeah, it's not bad. There's tons of cars in Manifee City, and it's really easy to get used to them. Any chance I can get a car too?" She fluttered her eyelashes at him theatrically, flopping over to goofy once more. That was more like it.

"I could probably be persuaded," Wil said before hitting the switch to turn the car on.

Once more he took his time and enjoyed the early summer afternoon with the windows down. The air streamed through and left a light roar in its wake. Loud enough to be pleasant white noise, but not so loud they had to strain to speak over it.

"Things picked up after the election, but we're keeping things relatively smooth going, even with the fae changing things up and Wil's spy problem. We haven't touched your room, though, so you'll be right at home," Sharon said.

Surprisingly, Sarah didn't say anything, not even a sardonic jab or feigned disinterest. She nodded and stared out the window. Wil thought he understood. Returning to Harper Valley after leaving changed how you looked at the place and the world. He'd gone through the same thing after a much longer gap between seeing family. Even she would be affected.

Although she did scoff when the lane going to the McKenzie's home, now the Faerie embassy, had a line to get in. Wil had to slow down for a mix of fae and humans coming in from town to explore the diplomatic services, meet a friend, or grab a bite to eat at their incredible restaurant. By the time they got to the house, Sarah groaned, and Bob chuckled appreciatively.

"Yeah, it's a bit of a pain sometimes, but we're pretty happy about it. And we're even more happy to have you home. Anything you want to do before dinner? Take a nap, maybe?"

"I napped on the train," said Sarah. "I guess I'll go walk around where our fields used to be. Kind of weird they're all gone. I kind of like the look of this better, but it's a pain." She stepped out of the car and headed for her room. Wil grabbed her luggage and floated it behind him as he followed.

He deposited the luggage on the floor in front of her small bed. It had been months since he'd been in there, and before she'd left for Manifee City, everything changed. The one thing that didn't change was the fact that the walls were covered from floor to ceiling with her art, as well as the occasional picture cut out from a book or newspaper and pinned to the wall.

Sarah threw herself on the bed with a huff. Wil stood there awkwardly for a few seconds before he finally asked, "Is everything okay? You seem moodier than usual."

She turned away from him, facing the wall. "School's hard," she said, with none of her usual playful whine.

"Don't I know it," said Wil. He risked sitting on the edge of the bed. "Do you want to talk about it?"

"With you?" Sarah scoffed. "Yeah, right."

Wil chuckled and patted her leg. "Mom and Dad will crowd you and be concerned. But you're my bratty little sister. I'm only doing this out of big brother obligation, so you can be secure in the knowledge that I only care so much. I'm the perfect person to talk to."

Sarah rolled over. "You might have a point. The problem is, I don't know where to start."

"Well, what do you like about school? What's giving you problems? I thought you'd be happy at an art academy. Did something happen?"

His little sister's face screwed up as she thought about it. "No, nothing happened. Not any one thing at least. There are a couple people I don't get along with. One of the teachers deserves to have her bad wig set on fire."

"Yeah, I had a few similar teachers," said Wil. "I don't recommend actually setting it on fire. They get touchy about that."

Sarah laughed and sat up. She hugged her knees to her chest and looked over them at him. "I guess . . . I thought I was good."

"You *are* good," Wil insisted. "I get to cheat with magic. Your drawings genuinely look better to me than my illusions."

"Yeah, but everyone at school is good. Being good doesn't matter anymore, you know? And it's so damned hard." She nibbled on her lip while she decided whether to continue. "I just want to draw and get better at it. If I could spend all day playing around and making things, I'd be happy. But they want me to learn history and different kinds of art that have nothing to do with me."

That made sense, and Wil had once had similar complaints when he went to school. Now he had to communicate that without sounding smug or too knowing. Sarah would hate that. He took a deep breath and blew it out.

"There's a method to their madness. Schools today are more up-to-date and modern than they've ever been, and I think they're trying to make sure you get a chance to understand and try a bunch of different forms of making art. For example, when I first went to Saint Balthazar's, I thought illusions were useless. Everyone likes to joke about that. But I fell in love.

"Don't think of it as being forced to do things you don't want to do. They're opportunities to try new things and see if you might like it better. Are there no classes you like more than you expected?"

Sarah sighed but thought about it. "Sculpting and painting. Those were pretty fun and extra hard. I really liked getting my hands dirty, and it was tricky to get things to look how I wanted them."

Wil lit up. "That's perfect, though. That's a trifecta of skills. You draw out an idea, sculpt it, paint it, and bam, you have something special."

"Gods, you sound like Professor Lynne," Sarah groaned. She swung her legs over the edge of her bed. They sat side by side for a little while before she inclined her head. "Thanks, I guess. Does it ever get less tiring?"

Wil shook his head. "Not even a little. You get used to it, and it gets easier. The first year is the hardest, except for years two, three, and four."

She shot him an unamused look. "Five and six were easier, then?"

"They were." Wil stood up. "C'mon. You're home. Or what used to be home. It probably feels different than it used to. Let's do something fun, or take a nap, or whatever. Anything you want."

Sarah took a long look around her room, as if seeing it for the first time. "It does feel different. I'm fine, but I don't think I want to spend time here right now. Even if I *do* want a nap. I don't know, let's get ice cream or something. You know, Wil, you might not make a terrible dad."

"Thanks," said Wil. He shook his head and opened the door. "Ice cream sounds great. It's my treat."

"As well it should be, rich boy. I'm a starving artist, and I'll be in debt before I graduate."

Wil laughed, and they went downstairs. Maybe after the dust settled and the presentation was over, he'd see about paying for her education, even if she didn't want him to. She had all the potential in the world, and if he could do anything to boost his family and give them the best chance possible, he would. She deserved it.

Even if she was forever a brat.

CHAPTER 46

The Presidential Preparations

Days later and Wil had no idea how to leverage his position in the middle of the basin to utilize all the leylines around him. It was hard, theoretical work and the only person he could've asked about it had died decades ago, alone and insane. After racking his brain to try to understand how it all worked, Wil felt his own sanity slipping. The solution, of course, was work orders.

It was as impossible to be done with work orders as it was to comprehend whatever the hell Marlowe had been smoking when he designed his manor, but at least he could make headway with the former. Wil put away his battered copy of *Mysteries of Marlowe Manor* and put on his work overalls. Harper Valley needed him.

First it needed him to sort out a property border dispute, which was easily done with some wards and free beer for both the feuding neighbors. Easy. Then it turned out that parts of the road through town had bad potholes, and their increased carriage and car traffic faced difficulties with damaged wheels and shocks. No problem, moving earth was what Wil did, and the potholes were not only filled in, but the roads reinforced and leveled out to make transportation smoother. Then finally, he helped change the water level of the river to avoid the flooding of lowland farms. All in a day's work!

By the time he broke for lunch and returned to the book, Wil was that comfortable level of weary that meant he could take a break without feeling guilty. Of course, that's when he got the most important work order of the day.

"Sweetie?" Sharon had knocked on the door but walked in anyways, as parents did. She walked into his office and sat down at his desk with him. "Could I trouble you for a favor?"

"Of course, Mom." Wil put his book down again. If he had to choose between being annoyed at having his work disrupted or grateful that he didn't have to brave the book again, he'd choose grateful. "What can I do for you?"

"It's not for me, it's for the mayor's office. We've got time to get it done, but I figured you could help us do it for cheaper, much easier. Any money we can save means our taxes go further, right?" She laughed.

"Yeah, no problem." Wil smiled. "So what do you need me to do?"

"Grow a lot of flowers."

Wil waited for the other shoe to drop. When Sharon said nothing else, he said, "That's it? Just grow some flowers?"

"A lot of flowers," said Sharon seriously. "We're arranging for the welcoming ceremony for the president and others, and there was a dispute over who was going to provide floral arrangements and decorations. Your father has been so busy juggling other things that he dropped this ball, and it's up to me to get it in the air again. Which means it's up to you!"

Wil laughed. "Yeah, that's understandable. I got to visit the Ambrose Estate's gardens, and those will be hard to top. In fact, I suggest not even trying. Do you have a plan for what you want for the arrangement, or can I come up with something?"

Sharon pulled out a rolled up picture from her purse. When she unrolled it on Wil's desk, he saw the picture had been drawn by Sarah. It showed two scenes in miniature: the train station and the fairgrounds, both covered in flowers and with banners and the like. Wil looked over it, nodding as he went.

"You don't need me to do any actual decorating, right? Just, what, grow flowers to maturation and maybe keep them in a sort of stasis so they don't die over the next week and a half?"

"Yes!" Sharon tapped her finger on the picture. "We have a list of the flowers we need, but some of them are out of season. It's what caused the dispute between the two florists who were bidding on the job. They *could've* filled our request, but they were asking for a lot of money for it."

"As opposed to me, who is salaried and will do anything you guys ask of me," Wil said wryly.

"Exactly! Besides, I know how much you love working with the earth." Sharon smiled. "Are you going to try to tell me you don't want to do this?"

"No, ma'am," he said. "Gather everything you need, and I'll meet you at the train station tomorrow, and we'll get started. Is there anything else I can help you or the mayor with, Mrs. McKenzie?"

His mother laughed and stood up. "Yeah. Is Bram's party still next weekend?"

In the middle of all their hard work and planning, Bram had it in his head to dedicate his remaining time to not only perfecting the Time-Stretcher, but also to redoing his brewery and house to take advantage of the leyline. His home, they had decided, would be proof of concept for the house of tomorrow. And naturally, that meant throwing a big party to show it all off.

"Should be," said Wil. "We're really looking forward to displaying all our work and getting an initial impression before the group from Cloverton shows up. The place is currently a mess, though."

Sharon laughed. "Can't be worse than when we all put it together. Glad to hear things are going so well for you two. Is there anything your father and I could be doing to help you in the final stretch?"

Wil gestured to the picture on his table. "You're already doing it. The better an impression the entire town makes on Bullworth and his advisors, the better it looks for me and my decisions leading up to this point. I *should* be fine by now, but . . . better safe than sorry, right?"

The talk with his mom ended up being the highlight of the day. He finished four more work orders after lunch before coming home to Darlene and spending time with her. Before bed, he read more of *Mysteries of Marlowe Manor* and wished he had a chance to go back to the property and examine the leylines there. There had to have been something there he could learn from.

Work orders continued the next day, and he managed to knock another three down before he showed up at the train station to find his mother already there with several bulging burlap bags of seed. Wil had the picture his sister drew on him, and he hugged his mom in greeting.

"There's a problem," said Wil when he felt the area. "There's no leyline to tie this to, so I might need to make stops here every few days to make sure the growth is even and not, you know, explosive or dead. The fairgrounds have one, though."

"Is that too demanding?" Sharon asked, unsure of herself. "If we need to do this closer to the time, then we can postpone it another week."

Wil looked around the train station. Other than being cleaner than the train station in Manifee City, it was ordinary and badly in need of some decorations and life. Plants would do a lot for the place, and his brain itched with possibilities.

"I can work with this," he said. "We can use a faricite battery and a basic spellbox to care for the plants and keep them in a sort of stasis for the next week and change, once I get them grown to the proper age."

Sharon clapped her hands together. Thanks, Wil. I appreciate you *so* much!"

The work could hardly be called that. Wil was glad he didn't get paid by the job. It would've felt wrong to charge for making plants grow and prettying up a place. By the time he'd finished growing all the flowers and vines around the train station's main building, he wondered why he didn't fill out parts of his week doing it with all the public buildings in town. Between him and Sarah, they could make Harper Valley so much more aesthetically pleasing.

He stood outside the train station, admiring his work. His mother, or the two feuding florists, or whoever, had designed it based around Harper Valley's natural wildflowers and some of the most commonly grown crops, like bundled wheat and, to Wil's amusement, some of Mr. Carrey's beans.

Apparently, the old man had complained to Bob at length about Wil's antics, but his father knew how to deal with cranky old men. Wil promised himself he'd pay for the damages and to rebuild the house after the presentation and getting paid. Without those beanstalks, he might never have found the answer so easily.

"Why beans?" A nearby boy of eleven or twelve asked. He gawked at the display of "Welcome to Harper Valley!" framed by two beans bigger than he was.

Wil saw his chance to have fun and grinned. "Well, once upon a time a greedy farmer abused the generosity of the fae, and his farm got overrun by magic beans. Now they're his main crop and part of town history. Where you from?"

"Kappala," answered the kid. He looked Wil up and down. "Who're you?"

Wil stroked his short beard and posed dramatically. "I am the master wizard of Harper Valley! Call me Wil." He produced a glowing green fire, which he rolled back and forth between his hands.

The kid scoffed at him. "My uncle's fires are, like, three times bigger than that."

"Oh, your uncle is a wizard?" Wil stood with his hands apart and produced a second flame, this one purple. A second later, they both ballooned in size, becoming the size of carriage wheels each. "How about this?"

"Not bad, I guess," said the boy. "What else can you do?"

"Oh, just not bad? Okay, okay." Wil nodded melodramatically, then dismissed the fires. He twisted his arms together in a slow, ridiculous build up. Every detail of the kid's appearance, from his black hair to the field of freckles on his cheeks, Wil re-created them into an illusory double. "What's your name?"

"Jake," said the kid. His jaw dropped, and he hesitantly leaned in closer. His eyes remained wary.

The illusion waved enthusiastically. "Hi, my name is Jake!" it said in his voice. "I like eating boogers, and my feet smell bad."

"They do not!" Jake shouted, but he busted up with that uninhibited, surprised laughter that kids had.

"Yes, they do," the double said. Wil twisted his hands again, and the illusion soon mimicked every motion he did, half a second later. "They stink because I love dancing!" And sure enough, he directed the illusion to dance like a lunatic while Wil hummed a goofy tune.

Jake clapped, which finally drew the attention of his parents. They came up behind the boy, his father an image of what he'd be in twenty years. He put his hands on Jake's shoulders and said, "Who's your new friend, Jake?" His voice had a wary edge to it.

"That's my son," said Sharon as she came up beside Wil. "He's the town wizard, and I'm the mayor's wife. Welcome to Harper Valley!"

"O-oh," said Jake's mother, visibly relaxing. "Well, nice to meet you two." She and Jake's father pulled the boy away. He frowned and looked over his shoulder at Wil as he was pulled away.

"Was it something I said?" Illusion-Jake said before disappearing.

"Naw." Sharon wrapped an arm around Wil's shoulders. "Parents are protective, and wizards can be scary."

"He said his uncle is a wizard," said Wil. He watched the family's retreating form for a while. Something in his stomach twisted, a pang he didn't understand.

Sharon noticed and turned toward her son. "Got something on your mind, kiddo?"

Wil chuckled and lowered his face. The flush came on, right on schedule. "I . . . I think I might want kids."

"Well, that's good timing," said Sharon with a wry smile.

He rolled his eyes and said, "You know what I mean. I'm not prepared, and I don't think I ever will be, but I like kids. And I'm having weird feelings right now about it."

Sharon squeezed his shoulder. "You might not be prepared, but you're ready. Make sure to talk about it with Darlene. She needs to hear it. For now . . . are you done for the day?"

He nodded and looked over his work. "Bram and I will work on a way to keep the plants in stasis. But that'll come later. I think I'm going to go home to Darlene and talk a bit."

His mother reached up and patted his cheek. "You'll be a good father, Wil. I know it."

CHAPTER 47

Runic Renovations

Throughout all their time experimenting, Wil genuinely felt bad for how much damage he did to the Stevenson farm. By now, the land was unrecognizable, though he did enjoy the new look. It was a lot like his parents' house, now forever changed due to his interference and needs. Wil asked, and people gave without a moment's notice.

It would be so easy to dwell on that for hours and hours and hate himself for it. Sometimes, it was tempting. When he'd brought it up to Darlene the night before, she'd set him straight in that sharp way she had.

"Everyone who did this, did it freely because they trust you. If you question that hard enough, that means you're questioning their judgment and not trusting *them*."

He had no reasonable argument against that.

But just because he accepted that his loved ones trusted him enough to donate to his causes, didn't mean Wil had no intentions of making up for them. He couldn't undo the changes, but he could clean up and make things as easy as possible for his parents and for Bram. With that in mind and two days until the party at Bram's place, Wil flew there after lunch.

He knew Bram would already be at work, but he underestimated how far along he would be. The brewery was closed for the next couple of days until the party, but some of his employees were active. It turned out the fae had decent carpenters, who could work without growing their buildings from saplings, and half a dozen trolls and ogres worked on construction of a new, larger brewery close to the Wil-made lake on the southwest part of the property.

Still more worked at cleaning up around the house itself, and a hobgoblin stood over a pit filled with weeds and detritus. He burned it with conjured flames, laughing occasionally as the flames danced wildly. Luckily, most of the grass and plants on the land had been cleared out when Wil reshaped the earth. One of the many things he'd hoped to correct, but it looked like Bram was tackling everything at the same time.

Wil left his Thunderhawk at the start of the lane and walked through the construction. Now that he was closer, he could see the garage Bram and Thomas had built to house their surplus faricite. That was finished and right beside the cellar, with one of their cars parked next to it. Bram stood nearby, arguing with a goblin.

"I'm telling you, when I'm done with everything, it's going to be freezeproof *and* fireproof. I know you guys don't like or trust runes on account of their connection with demons, but you trust me, right?"

"Most days," said the goblin in his high, nasally voice. His pointed features looked malicious much of the time, even when mildly disagreeing. "Now? Questioning it."

Upon spotting Wil, Bram motioned for him to come over. "Back me up here, Wil. Runes are perfectly safe, right?"

Wil forced himself to keep a straight face. "I don't know about *perfectly* safe."

The goblin made a triumphant sound, but Bram wasn't deterred. "Nothing is one hundred percent safe. I've been working my ass off to try different arrays and configurations for each design I have, and these are the safe ones."

"Even when they're all combined and in the house you live in?"

Bram's face reddened. "Yes! I'm the one gambling here. So trust me and let me deal with the risks."

"It's your funeral," said the goblin with a nasty grin. "If your house explodes with you in it, can I have the land? You know, if you're going to be gambling."

"Sorry," said Wil, "but I am pretty sure I have next dibs on this place. Me or Darlene."

The goblin sighed and backed off. "I'll get grab Mitts and start working on the stove and Freeze-it, then. Just saying that we have no way to guarantee how it's going to affect the water running through those weird pipes."

"Thank you," said Bram. He sighed as his worker went around to the front of the house. "What a headache. How're you doing, Wil?"

Wil chuckled, looking around at the chaos around them. There were almost enough of them to make him think of an anthill. With the scattered dirt everywhere, plateau, and arch of stone, it seemed a fair comparison. "I was actually going to ask you the same thing, and to see if there's anything I could do to help."

Bram nodded and took in his property. He had a satisfied smile Wil rarely saw. Most of the time, his friend fretted over the future and how to best meet it. Now, he looked at peace. Or at least, as much peace as the neurotic man ever got. "Honestly? Probably, but I . . . I don't think I need anyone's help. I've got it."

He sounded almost surprised, as if the words didn't feel right in his mouth. Wil was nearly as surprised, and part of him worried before he realized how silly it was. Bram wasn't his friend because he needed Wil's help.

"You do, don't you?" said Wil. "You've been doing so much and succeeding at everything. You should be proud of yourself."

"I . . . think I am," said Bram. "Huh. This is a weird feeling."

Wil burst out laughing. "You deserve it. You've been working your ass off, with and without me, for a year now. You don't need my help because you're capable in ways I'm not. Hell, I'm more likely to ask *you* for help these days. And I am so grateful for that. The last three months have been draining, but the most rewarding time of my life. And a huge part of that is seeing how far you've come along."

Bram looked like he was ready to cry. An entire childhood of failing to live up to an abusive father, hiding who he was from the world, and struggling to fit in with a community that didn't understand him . . . He needed more encouragement in his life.

"Um," he said with a conspicuous clear of the throat, "do you want to see what all I'm having done?"

"You're damned right I do," said Wil. "Show me what you got, and maybe I can still help after all. I'm feeling earth magic and plants today. How do you feel about topiary dragons?"

His eyes lit up. "How big are we talking?"

Wil took a few steps back and produced an illusion of a fifteen-foot dragon with a long neck that would be difficult, if not impossible, to grow naturally. As he went, he added more details, like glowing orbs for eyes and smoke coming out of the mouth. "Imagine a pair of these at the gates, guarding over the brewery."

Bram wrung his hands, eyes wide and a big grin on his face. "That would be incredible! I worry about it intimidating people, though. Hmm. C'mon." He went around to the front again, and Wil followed.

Now that the land was uneven and chaotic, there was no making it look clean and neat. Bram pointed to the arch, and Wil understood immediately. "You want the dragon to be on or in the arch? What about coiled around it?"

"Hanging from the top of it, looking down on its prey. You can do smoke and stuff. Could you make a plant breathe fire safely?"

Wil gave him a look that said "C'mon, now," and they laughed. He looked over at the building being constructed. "I really don't think that's going to be finished in two days, do you?"

"Never doubt the fae when it comes to hard work. Especially when it comes to creating something. We've got teams working night and day. It'll not only be ready for the party, but it's going to be twice the brewery we had before! More room to seat patrons, a place for an actual cook, and storage, cool but not cold all year round.

"More importantly, we're going to keep the barn mostly as is but improve on it. If I put a time bubble there, we could brew more beer in shorter amounts of time!" A familiar, manic glint in Bram's eyes told Wil that yes, he could and would get it all done. No more underestimating him.

"I can see why your one employee was worried about potential interference," said Wil. "That's a lot of things to tie together, but if we can make it work . . . Are you sure there's nothing I can do? Even just looking over your work for peace of mind?" He'd do that anyway, come to think of it.

Bram looked around the property one more time. He nodded with satisfaction at all the activity. "You can definitely help with the groundskeeping. I want this place to be green and lush when we open, a veritable paradise and a vision of what homes in the future could look like if we embrace the magical lifestyle. When we're done, Harper Valley will go from being considered a backward farm town to the envy of Calipan!"

There was more fire and strength in his voice than Wil had ever heard, even if the enthusiasm was a tiny bit disconcerting.

"Absolutely!" Wil held out his hand, and Bram took it. "Two days to the party, and nine more until Bullworth shows up and pardons me. Let's get going!"

CHAPTER 48

Liars, Cheaters, and Bastards

If there was one thing Wil was thankful for, it was that soon he'd no longer have to provide updates to Cloverton. Writing in the damned journal had seemed so interesting and cool when he first did it, but it had become tedious. All that remained was one update today and then another the night before the president and company were expected to arrive, for last-minute instructions.

He didn't drag his feet this time. Not too much, anyway. After doing some work orders and growing plants for Bram's land, he sat down in front of the journal and opened it. Like usual, Wil scanned the previous conversation as he collected his thoughts. Then he picked up the pen and began writing.

Hello, Cloverton! Master McKenzie for the last real report. How's it going on your end, Cloverton?

Like usual, he had to wait a minute or two before receiving a reply, but then the blue ink appeared beneath his greeting.

Master McKenzie, we have received disturbing reports regarding your research and attacking other researchers in Harper Valley.

Oh. Oh no. The writing continued and so did the sinking feeling in Wil's stomach.

In addition, we have a claim that your success is not your own, and an equal amount of credit belongs to Master Thomas Elliot, who is among those attacked. Please give your accounting of events.

That son of a . . .

One minute, Cloverton.

Wil took a deep breath and strangled the scream in his throat before it was big enough to carry to Darlene upstairs. The anger bowled him over like a rogue wave, and it was like losing control of himself. Thomas couldn't walk away and leave them alone. He had to pick a fight. Any sympathy or pity Wil had dried up in a flash.

Master Elliot turns out to have been giving our research to employees of Ferrovani, who used my work to create weapons and pass them out among the rural population irresponsibly. As for the attack, we had a bad disagreement that resulted in them breaking into my home and threatening my family.

I have no problem with rivals or other people doing the research. If you had alerted me of the other researchers, I might even have helped them.

That was a blatant lie, but Wil was past caring.

I'm going to be honest, Cloverton, I'm not happy right now. This other group has gotten in my way, harassed myself and my pregnant girlfriend, threatened us, and broke in, and now I hear that they're blaming me for it and trying to take credit? This is a load of crap, and I am not willing to tolerate their lies. Especially not after they broke the law and got themselves kicked out of town.

It wasn't as if Wil had anything he could do if Cloverton decided to just go along with it and cut him out of things. Nothing legal or healthy, at least, and he didn't like how his thoughts went to finding those bastards and really letting them have it. It scared him, how much he wanted to lash out and drive them away and out of his life permanently.

A few minutes passed as Wil fought to control his breathing and racing thoughts. Eventually, the blue ink returned, coming more slowly this time as the person on the other end took their time on their wording.

You must understand the difficulty we face, Master McKenzie. We have no way to corroborate either your claims or theirs. As of now, it is the word of several respectable employees of one of Calipan's greatest minds versus the word of someone under investigation for negligence and poor judgment. In addition, your reports have been inconsistent at best. It is enough to make some of us at the office inclined to trust this other report.

If you have any additional evidence or proof you can offer to help your case, we are listening. More than anything, our goal is the success of this research project, regardless of who provides it.

It figured that they only cared about results. Wil swallowed hard and wrote, slowly, trying his best to not lose his temper.

My team has kept an extensive journal of our research and attempts and prototypes. When President Bullworth and his associates arrive, I would be happy to turn a copy of that journal over for examination. While I haven't been the best at reporting in, the journal contains all the proof we need that this is our research. And while Thomas Elliot was a part of that research in the beginning, he no longer is a part of this team on account of being an admitted spy who gave our research away. When we prove ourselves, I expect our group to receive full distinction for purposes of credit.

The response took twice as long this time, long enough for Wil's anger and anxiety to throw a party in his head. When it finally came, Wil sighed. It could've been better, but it could've been a lot worse too.

Your terms are agreeable, Master McKenzie. Both groups will have a chance to offer proof and a demonstration of your inventions. From there we will clear up this misunderstanding, and those in the wrong will be punished for the trouble they caused. You have our word.

There was more, but it didn't matter. The gist of it was that he didn't have to update them. The presentation in a week would serve as that and determine his innocence. Thomas knew what was at stake for him, and apparently, he was willing to let him burn if it meant getting back at him.

Wil must have been wearing his mood on his face because the moment he left his office for the kitchen, Darlene asked, "Are you okay? What happened?"

"Thomas happened." Wil made himself some coffee, added a shot of whiskey, and told her what he'd just found out. When he was done, she shared in his fury.

"That two-faced, lying, rat bastard!" she shrieked as her face turned an awful shade of purple. "There's no way we're taking this lying down. Get in the car."

"Where?" asked Wil. "We don't know where they are now."

"Only one place they could be," said Darlene. "If they're not allowed in Harper Valley and they need to be close enough for the presentation, then they're in Gallard Springs. It's the only place close enough. You mapped out the leylines there, right?"

Wil nodded. "I did. And there are only a few places they could be now that you mention it. I think it's time Thomas and I had a little talk."

Darlene's eyes flared with shared, angry passion, but her sense hadn't left her. "Are you sure that's a good idea? We know they're out to get us and undermine us. If you confront them, and it leads to a real fight, it might look bad for us. I'd really rather you not get arrested when I'm not too long from giving birth."

"So what do you suggest I do, Darlene? I'm open to suggestions, but right now I want to go over there and punch Thomas in his stupid face."

"Talk. Tell him off. Warn him against further interference, and then leave. If you can promise me you will behave, you can talk to him about this." Darlene's expression turned sour. "Maybe he can be convinced to play nice or at least not try to screw you over like this."

Wil tried to picture that. He thought Thomas had been his friend, but more than ever, it felt like a lie. Part of him still wanted to give the jerk another chance to make things right. He nodded. "Fine. I won't fight Thomas, but if that McGinnis gets in my face again, I will not tolerate it."

Darlene sighed. "If that's all you can promise, then I guess it'll have to do. Go find him, and don't cause a scene if you can avoid it. Okay? No picking fights, but you can defend yourself if they attack. And for the love of the gods, don't destroy their stuff."

"I promise," said Wil. He finished his coffee and rose enough to kiss her forehead. "I love you, and I'll be safe. But they *will* understand how upset I am."

"Good enough. Now get going!"

Wil got on his Thunderhawk and headed east. He was fairly close to the border Harper Valley shared with Gallard Springs, but he still had to find where they were staying. It wouldn't take more than a couple hours to pull off, and he could push himself in the meantime.

The wind whipped through his hair, and he was glad he hadn't taken his staff with him this time. The anger had faded into a simple, dull throb in his head and heart that drove him on like the beating of a drum. It was still better than the raging river inside him from before. Wil knew he'd have to keep that dammed up if he was going to do this right. And he had to do it right.

Although he promised himself no violence, Wil did promise himself one thing: Thomas would regret everything.

CHAPTER 49

Bad Blood

It didn't take more than a couple hours to find Thomas and his people. They weren't exactly hiding, and Wil's ability to sense leylines had only gotten sharper over time. He started in the south and worked his way up until he sensed the rune off in the distance. Tucked up in the foothills to the northeast, they had set up out in the open.

The line between Harper Valley and Gallard Springs was blurry most of the time, but the houses and land in the higher elevations were where the rich of that city went. Wil supposed he wasn't surprised to see them there now that they no longer had to hide their efforts. He knew he was in the right place when he saw a crowd of people gathered around the edge of a house jutting over a cliff.

Wil parked his Thunderhawk at the base of the hill while people watched him with interest. He waved his hand over it, and it disappeared from view. A sharp, wizardly glare at those nearby made them remember they had elsewhere to be. Then he climbed the hill, the storm inside him building into a hurricane.

He'd considered every way he could yell or chew out Thomas for his petty lies, when suddenly an explosion from above shook him from his senses. Wil flinched and looked up, but the sounds of cheering and laughter came next. They were showing off weapons again.

He concentrated and covered himself in an illusion of an old, white-haired man, then continued walking up the slope leading to the top of the hill, putting a bit of a limp into his walk, though he doubted people were watching him closely. Even those who saw him apply the illusion would likely not say anything to his targets before he was ready.

Another explosion came as Wil's head peeked out over the lip of the hill. McGinnis stood at an altered cannon with a local, cheering as a big humanoid target one hundred yards away was encased in ice.

"Alright, nice shot! Who wants to see the ice shatter?" McGinnis called out. The screams of joyous assent made Wil want to flinch.

They had an entire setup there in the land surrounding one of Gallard Spring's more expensive homes on the side of the mountain. Aside from a row of cannons aiming toward targets at the foot of the mountain, there were several other stations where they showed off the fruits of their stolen labor.

More targets were set up in another area on the other side of a shimmering blue light. People took turns firing rifles at the targets, only for the bullets to hit the shield of light and clatter to the ground harmlessly. The old wizard Mark stood there, looking smug at their success.

Gayle was at another station, where a wide swathe of earth was disturbed. A young man held a metal rod with a faricite battery on one end and a rounded metal head on the other. As he ran it along the earth, dirt parted as easily as water at the beach. Wil kicked himself for not thinking of that one.

Thomas was at the final place, in front of the garishly large house. The car he took with him had been further altered over the last week and now had armor covering it and weapons strapped to its sides. Wil paused and watched his former friend converse enthusiastically with a boisterous-looking man.

Wil's blood boiled at it all. He, Bram, and Darlene had conducted a lot of their experiments in the open, but they still kept a healthy distance between them and the public until they were ready. Thomas and his crew did the opposite, and it made sense. How else could he succeed at discrediting Wil and the others if not by making himself more visible.

The cannon roared, and a second later, the frozen target shattered into a million tiny pieces as the teenage boy who fired it screamed and punched the air. McGinnis laughed and took the boy's money, and then it was the next person's turn.

Everyone here looked to be having the time of their lives, and they would no doubt talk about their experiences and spread the word. Back in Harper Valley they had people doing the same, but they were more whispers and rumors about their work rather than hands-on experience like this. It was brilliant, and infuriating.

Wil wandered closer to Thomas and the war machine he'd made. Thomas had just finished speaking to someone, when he met Wil's eye. The disguised wizard froze, but Thomas didn't recognize him. Instead, he smiled and motioned him closer.

"How are you enjoying our demonstration?" Thomas asked with a sly smile. "It must be exciting to see this kind of advancement out here."

Wil wasn't a particularly good liar, but he *was* a good illusionist and performer. It took only a second for him to magically throw his voice and slump as if the weight of the world and several decades pressed down on him.

"It's obscene," Wil growled in a low, gravelly voice. "Back in my day, we didn't have any of this magic crap to hide behind. We fought in wars without much magical help. We'd have to get up real close and make eye contact with those we killed."

Thomas didn't miss a beat. "And now we don't have to. All of these are to keep our men and women safe as they fight for Calipan and our right to grow. With this technology I've invented, we'll be at the forefront of a new way of fighting. And it starts with this, my War Chariot." He slapped the side of the car.

Wil swallowed hard, fighting the urge to throw off the illusions and chew him out. He couldn't restrain himself from saying, "You invented this, huh?"

He bowed his head. "I did. No one knows cars like I do, and with this new source of power, even nonmagical people will be able to operate magical devices. This is the future of warfare; this is the future of Calipan."

He could've maybe kept up the act, but a surge of anger made Wil stand up tall and dismiss the illusions. "You're a real piece of work, Tom. You didn't invent a godsdamned thing, and I can't believe you're lying to people like this."

The surprise on his face gratified Wil, but not as much as the look of rage. "I invented it just as much as you, Wilbur. All you did was blunder your way into things. You couldn't have done any of it on your own."

"Neither could you," Wil countered. Heat flooded all his senses. He wasn't ready to start throwing magic, but he did want to punch the other wizard. "You had to latch on to me like a parasite to try to make a name for yourself. Without me, you'd still be Ferrovani's stooge."

Thomas's face twisted into pure hate, and Wil immediately felt bad for going there. He thought of apologizing, but his rival acted first. "I at least had to work to get there. What have you done, other than being the magical equivalent of a day laborer? Without your friend Bram to come up with ideas, you'd be nothing. Without Darlene to pull your shit together, you'd get nowhere. And without my guidance, nothing would've been polished or worked properly."

"Yeah," said Wil. "That's what it means to be part of a team. Wasn't that what you were raving about, that night your 'friends' broke into my house? I can't believe we were so hyped up on our successes that we bought what you were selling. You must've been laughing your ass off at us."

Nearby, people drifted away as the wizards' conversation got more and more heated. Neither he nor Thomas cared about it. The Cloverton wizard flushed and shook his head sharply. "That wasn't me. I was going to call it all off and dismiss them before the dumbasses did that."

"And yet here you are, working with them and telling Cloverton that you came up with everything. I told you that you'd get all the same credit, but no, you're being petty just because you're facing consequences for your actions and trying to get me locked up." Wil spit on the ground. "You really think that's an appropriate retaliation?"

He was gratified when Thomas paused in surprise. "That would be Ferrovani. I had nothing to do with that, I—"

"Sure you didn't," Wil sneered. "You just passed it along, and it's someone else's fault, while you get to benefit. It's never you, right?"

"Screw you, McKenzie," Thomas hissed. He sounded equal parts enraged and shaken. "What else was I supposed to do here? You kicked me out and told me to go back to them. All I wanted was to keep working and make a name for myself, and you kicked me out. I didn't want any of this. I was going to walk away, but nooo, it was too late. Should I have just gone home and sat on my hands while waiting for you to deliver on your promise? What should I have done, Wil?"

It was a question he'd had plenty of time to think about. "You should've told me from the start Ferrovani was on your ass," he said. "I would've tried to help you out, and we could've thought of a way to work together without the baggage. That's what pisses me off the most about this. At every step of the way, you could've done the right thing, and it would've been fine. But you didn't. There's always an excuse why you let things continue.

"That's the problem, Thomas. You're a coward."

Thomas reacted as if he'd been slapped. He took a step back, leaning against the car. "You have no idea what you're talking about," he whispered as his face flooded with color.

Wil grinned fiercely at his discomfort and took a step forward before something collided with him and sent him sprawling to the ground. It hurt, sudden and sharp, but he didn't feel damaged or in danger. He looked up to find McGinnis standing over him, hands glowing with barely restrained power.

"You shouldn't have come here, McKenzie," McGinnis said. "Four of us versus you, we could send you home to Mom in a box."

For a second, Wil regretted not bringing Isom, but he didn't need for this to turn into a bloodbath no matter how angry he was. Wil got up slowly, making it clear he wasn't attacking. He opened his mouth to speak, but Thomas beat him to it.

"We're not going to do anything of the sort, McGinnis. McKenzie's here because he's filled with impotent rage. He's here because he's angry that we've surpassed him." Thomas smiled coldly. "By the time we're done, it'll be a fifty-fifty shot whether he gets in trouble or not. But I'm willing to bet the odds are greater that with our *weapons*, Cloverton will favor us. And there's nothing he can do about it. Is there, McKenzie?"

Gayle and Mark came closer, staying out of it but close enough to make it a four-on-one if Wil did lose his temper again. Their inventions were easily more along the lines of what Cloverton wanted, even if Wil and his friends' creations were more likely to improve the lives of the country at large. He wanted so badly to continue the fight, to stomp his feet and roar and lash out.

It wouldn't do any good. Thomas knew it, he knew it, and the other three were just waiting for him to make a move. Wil forced himself to relax and smile. "Your attempts to cheat and take credit for my work disgust me, but they won't work. We have extensive journals and eyewitnesses. Our work is better, even if you are pandering to the military.

"The fact is, I am on good terms with the president, and so is my friend Sylano. I'm not going to do anything here and now because I don't have to. My work will speak for itself, and when all is said and done, we're going to not only win but also embarrass you." Wil turned to McGinnis. "You have one week to apologize and back down. If you don't before the presentation, I will do everything in my power, call in every favor I have, to bury you."

McGinnis's eyes blazed, and the magic glowing a harsh red in his hands deepened. For a second, Wil thought that he'd get that fight after all, but Thomas stepped between them. "Get out of here, McKenzie. Before I let McGinnis tear you apart." The mage didn't look happy at the insinuation that people *let* him do anything, but he was eager enough.

Wil sighed. "Fine," he said. "Hope you're enjoying your nightmares, McGinnis." The mage let out a garbled yell and tried to jump him, but Thomas held him back. Wil turned around and walked away to the edge of the clifftop. He jumped off and magically slowed his fall. He landed next to his hidden Thunderhawk and dismissed the illusion.

Things hadn't gone the way he had hoped, but maybe it was the way he needed. They were threatening him, and Wil had an increasingly low tolerance for threats and movements against him. If they thought he could be scared off, they were wrong. Today strengthened his resolve.

With one last breath, Wil flew home. He had just a week to find one last discovery to blow them out of the water. He, Bram, and Darlene—they were a team. Together, they'd win.

CHAPTER 50

Too Far

In the early morning of the night before Bram's party, everything went wrong. Wil and Darlene were woken by a sky-shattering screech. In a flash, Wil jumped from his bed, reaching out with his senses. Nothing stood out, but the screech continued.

"What the hell is that?" Darlene asked as she clamped her hands over her ears.

Wil waved his hand, and the sound around them lessened, now encased in a bubble. "I don't know, but it sounds like my responsibility. Are you prepared to test out our messaging theory?"

Darlene nodded. "I'll get dressed and be ready to go to the embassy at a moment's notice, which I will do if that piece of yourself you left in me tells me to go. That's not weird or confusing at all."

Wil kissed her and threw his clothes on. With his staff in hand, he ran outside and saw the source of the trouble. A massive red and black dragon flew circles over Harper Valley. It screeched and belched flames that lit up the night before fading to a spark. His gut clenched as he realized that twice in a year he'd have to take on a dragon.

He got on his Thunderhawk and flew toward it. With any luck, maybe he could reason with it and drive it off with a bribe if things went well. Maybe a threat if things didn't go so well. The more he thought about it, the more confident he was that he could if he needed to, but the question begged, Why attack Harper Valley?

Twin lights came from the front of his vehicle and illuminated his path. At first, no one else had been out, but after the dragon screeched its challenge, some neighbors came out of their houses. Most of them ran right back inside, either to hide or to get their families and start running. Wil couldn't blame them. As he got closer and the dragon grew larger in his view, fear gnawed at him from the inside out.

Fear didn't matter. He had a job to do, and he flew straight toward the danger, pouring more power into the altered bike to climb higher. It could only reasonably get to about fifty feet in the air, but that would be enough to get a shot in and maybe lure the dragon away. It currently flew above the area around city hall, but it was heading in Wil's direction.

He flew past a car driving slowly in the direction he had come from. It didn't bear thinking too much about it. There were about to be many cars and carts flee-ing. Wil pushed the Thunderhawk to go as fast as it could, until he was under the dragon, which . . . Huh.

As soon as Wil was beneath the dragon and ready to try to communicate, it changed direction and headed west, letting out another roar that oddly wasn't any louder despite it being so much closer. Frowning, Wil gave chase.

"Noble dragon, why do you attack my home?" Wil's voice boomed as he followed.

But the dragon said nothing; it just flew in circles, occasionally roaring and making westward progress. Closer to Wil's house. His eyes widened, and he real-ized exactly where it was going.

Wil slowed to a stop, parking along a dark patch of road. Even with the stars out, he could barely see a foot past his face. It didn't matter, he didn't need vision to reach inward. He did his best to clear his thoughts and fall into himself on a deeper level than meditation allowed.

Naturally he had his sense of self, but it wasn't as simple as that. Most of him was right there, but there were two pieces of him off in the distance, one each left in Isom and Darlene. Isom's had already been there from when Wil had helped heal his tattered mind after his enslavement, but Darlene's was only a couple days old.

If she hadn't been the one to come up with it, he might've resisted delving in and connecting with her that deeply, but now he was grateful. Wil reached out to those pieces and focused with all his being on sending a message. "Run."

When he came back to himself, only a minute or so had passed. Enough time for the dragon to get closer to his home. Wil fired up the Thunderhawk again and pushed it to its limits. He caught up to the dragon again, which still circled endlessly.

"Dragon, stop this now! Do not make me strike you down. Turn back now or face my wrath!"

Wil was fully prepared for the dragon to take offense at being threatened, but it still kept flying in circles. "And when I kill you, I'll take your hoard of treasure as my own!"

Nothing.

"Godsdammit, it's not real." Wil continued after it, but the only thing out there other than him was the same car from before, slowly meandering toward his house.

All the pieces clicked into place. He tore away from the dragon and went lower, flying side by side with the car. In the driver's seat was Mark Marfolk with Gayle beside him in the passenger seat with a big, rune-carved box and a battery that had lost some of its luster. When Mark saw Wil, his eyes widened in terror.

Wil jerked his thumb to the side. Mark pulled over. A second later, the dragon disappeared. Mark rolled the window down, trembling.

"What in the hell are you doing?" Wil asked, though he feared he knew the answer.

"Uh, distracting you," Mark said with a nervous chuckle. "Please don't hurt us."

"Was this McGinnis's idea?" Wil asked.

Gayle nodded solemnly.

Wil nodded. "Give me one good reason to not feed you to my cat."

"Um."

Wil smiled. "Nope, too late. If you're not out of the Le Guin Basin by dawn, I'm going to send him after you. Get the hell out of here."

"Yes, Master McKenzie, thank you," Mark squeaked. With a squeal, the car took off down the dark road, taking with it the only other source of light. Wil let them go. They were small fry.

He flew to Bram's farm, occasionally shouting out a magically enhanced message that the dragon was defeated. Later, he'd set everyone straight. Maybe it would've been smarter to demand Mark and Gayle turn themselves in, but he would settle for their absence. If it was only Thomas and McGinnis, he could deal with them both without much of a problem.

He'd made it about halfway to the farm, when another sound broke up the silent tension. An explosion with a bright flash of fire appeared in the distance. Wil's heart jumped up into his throat.

The distance melted in a blur as Wil's thoughts fled him save for one: Bram had better be okay. The thought cried in his mind, louder and louder, as he spotted his friend's house in the distance.

Or what was left of it.

The roof and back half of the house was gone or on fire. The flames raged on as he got closer and saw with great relief that Bram was outside and okay. Physically, at least. By the time Wil pulled up beside him, Bram fell to his knees, sobbing. His face was covered in scratches and soot, but nothing serious. One of the lenses of his glasses had fallen out. Wil supposed he was lucky it hadn't shattered in his eye.

"Why?" Bram whispered. "*Why?* Oh gods, the flowers. Mom!" He pointed at the disturbed flowerbed, and the flames edged closer by the second.

"I've got this," said Wil, almost too quiet to be heard. He retrieved the staff from its compartment and spun it in loose circles, tightening as they sped up. There was no need to formalize a spell for so simple a working. Wil summoned the wind and dipped it in the lake. He directed the small waterspout toward the house, letting it crash against the fire.

It hissed as water and wind smothered the flames. There was no saving the house, but at the very least, the fire wouldn't spread. The flowerbed where Addie Stevenson rested was saved. Wil put his hand on Bram's shoulder and watched the last remnants of the fire fade to nothing.

Bram continued to cry, and Wil let him. He had tears of his own streaming down his cheeks, but it wasn't *his* home. The home they worked hard together to save and renovate. The home Bram had spent days and weeks working on to upgrade and alter for their experiments.

"When the dragon came, I ran out," Bram finally said, voice raw. "I ran out and then wondered how the hell I could deal with it."

"It wasn't real," said Wil. "It was an illusion by those assholes from Cloverton. They were distracting me."

Bram inhaled sharply. He stood, a storm brewing on his face. "Them? They distracted you . . . for this?"

Wil swallowed hard and looked at the ruined house. Only the front wall remained standing, and even that was a stretch in places. "It looks like it. This is my fault, Bram."

"No." Bram shook his head.

"It was. I went and picked a fight. I threatened them. And then they came after us. After you." Wil focused on regulating his breathing, but it was like a massive hand grabbed him by the chest and squeezed until his soul hurt.

"Let's . . . I need to see." Bram walked around the side of the house, and Wil followed.

Whatever had happened, and Wil was going to find out specifically, it had completely blown half the house to pieces, all the way down to the cellar. Their new garage was also in a million tiny pieces, with broken faricite scattered around the ground. Wil groaned.

"The faricite," he whispered. "How much of it was in the cellar?"

"Half." Bram wiped at his eyes again. His breath came faster. "You think that's what happened?"

"I'd stake my life on it," said Wil. "Thomas's friend McGinnis came here to intimidate us and maybe destroy our work, and he hit the faricite. The faricite went, and so did . . ."

Bram swallowed hard. He was close to hyperventilating at this point. "I'm going to kill him. I'm going to kill him!"

Wil didn't ask which one he meant. It didn't matter; he felt the same way. "We need to be smart about this," he said. "They went too far. We'll talk to my dad, and we'll go after them. I promise."

"Wil . . ." Bram wiped his eyes and looked at him in horror. "Our projects. Almost all of them were down there."

As one, they peered into the smoking crater where the cellar had been.

"I think that ship's sailed," said Wil. "We don't have anything to show Cloverton."

Too Late for Regrets

Thomas woke to the sound of someone pounding on his door. He started, then got out of bed and staggered to the door. He opened it to find a panicked, wild-eyed McGinnis. The man's reddish hair was singed and full of soot, and he looked bruised and burned.

"We made a mistake," McGinnis said before Thomas could ask. "It wasn't supposed to happen like that!"

Cursing under his breath, Thomas got out of the way so McGinnis could come inside. The mage limped in and collapsed on the couch in the living room. It hadn't taken much to rent a house for himself while the other three still shared a place. He'd meant for them to never be allowed in, but apparently that wasn't happening.

"What the hell did you idiots do?" Thomas went to the kitchen and got himself a glass of water. He drank it down, dreading whatever answer was coming his way.

"We lured McKenzie away so we could destroy their work at the brewery."

Thomas took a long, slow breath. He flung the empty glass at McGinnis, who only barely raised a shield of malevolent red light. It shattered against it harmlessly and scattered across the wood floor. "I told you bastards that we weren't doing that anymore!"

"Yeah, but Ferrovani . . ." McGinnis trailed off as he saw the other man's murderous expression.

Thomas pinched the bridge of his nose. "Ferrovani told you to do it anyway, and you're a rabid dog who *wants* to bite people. What happened at the Stevenson farm?"

It was a testament to McGinnis's understanding of the trouble he was in that he didn't complain or try to pick a fight with him. "While Mark and Gayle lured Wil away, I brought in one of our weapons. When I fired at the garage with the car in it, it went up way bigger! And then something in the cellar went, and the entire place broke!"

"So now Ferrovani's pathological need to be petty, cruel, and in control has doomed you. You just destroyed not only the work we all did, but the home of the best friend of the most powerful man in town. The mayor treats Bram like a third son, you know. There is no way you walk away from this unscathed."

"Ferrovani said he'd protect me," said McGinnis. "What're these backwater pissants going to do against him and his influence?"

Thomas thought about cursing him right then. He wasn't the strongest wizard out there, nor was he any good at combat, but McGinnis was battered and tired. Instead, he smiled at the man. "Think he'll be able to protect you from me? Or Wil's wrath? How've you been sleeping lately, McGinnis? Whatever McKenzie does to you for this, you'll have deserved it."

The mage opened his mouth to speak, but Thomas walked away. He came back a couple minutes later fully dressed. If they were going to survive this, it was on him to deal with it. "I'd consider skipping town if I were you. I will not protect you from the consequences of your stupidity. Not anymore."

He drove from Gallard Springs to Harper Valley. Thomas knew he wasn't likely to get a warm welcome, but he had to make sure Bram was unhurt and that they knew he had nothing to do with this. Past that, an inner voice that had been getting louder by the day crowed that this was his fault.

At any point over the last three months, he could have called it off and made things better. From the first time McGinnis proved to be a loose cannon, he could've ended it. The thought rattled around his head the entire hour-long drive.

He arrived as the sun began to peek over the mountains in the east. The ruins of the house weren't smoking anymore. The property was crawling with people, from the sheriff and his deputies to some of Bram's fae employees. Wil and Bram themselves stood in the center of it all, watching with the kind of stubborn vigor of the overexerted.

No one stopped him from driving up. Wil and Bram turned around as he got out. Thomas couldn't read the expression on Wil's face, but his friend was easy. Murder shone in his eyes. Thomas had just enough time to realize he should defend himself before Bram crossed the distance and slammed a fist like a sledge-hammer into his face.

The world went to a white void as Thomas's body hit the floor, his mind and feelings snapping back a second later. Only then did the pain explode in his jaw. He worked his mouth, wincing from the ache. At least it wasn't broken. "It wasn't me," he said stiffly.

"What was that, you duplicitous bastard?" Bram's fists remained clenched, and if it wasn't for Wil jumping in front of him, Thomas suspected he might've been in genuine danger.

"Hold on, Bram," Wil said. To Thomas, he scowled and said, "Explain yourself, then."

Thomas awkwardly stood. No one offered to help him up, and he couldn't blame them. He cradled his jaw and said, "I had nothing to do with this. Ferrovani snapped his fingers, and the others jumped. I would have never done this to you, Bram, I promise."

Bram snarled like a wild animal and made a move. Thomas flinched, but Wil held him back. Mostly. Bram advanced a couple of feet and dragged Wil with him. It was enough for Sheriff Harrington to disengage with Bob and walk up to them.

"Is everything alright here?" he asked, eyes flitting between the three of them. "We gonna have to separate you all?"

"No, sir," said Thomas. He eyed Bram, who looked ready to murder him.

"No, Sheriff," Bram eventually said, dropping his gaze to the ground.

Harrington looked around, then nodded. "I'm gonna wanna have words with you, Master Elliot. Get your statement on the whole thing."

"I understand, and I will give it," Thomas said. Sheriff Harrington grunted and then went back to talk to Bob.

When they were alone again, Wil motioned for Thomas to speak.

"Ferrovani is a cruel, petty tyrant," said Thomas. "He ordered sabotage, and the others knew I wouldn't go along with it, so they did it without me. I swear on my life, I would never have done this, and if I had known about it, I would've stopped it."

Wil laughed bitterly. "You could've stopped it months ago and you didn't. You picked your side, and now that they've blown up *our* friend Bram's house, you regret it? You may not have chosen this, but you chose your friends. And what a choice it was, Tom. Great going."

Bram shook his head slowly. Some of the murder had gone from his eyes, so now he looked more depressed than angry. "You were one of us, Thomas. I thought you were our friend."

"I was," said Thomas. "And I still am, no matter what you may think of me. I will cooperate and hand over McGinnis and provide a statement. I will personally pay for the reconstruction of your house, Bram. You might not be my friend anymore, but I'm still yours. I will do everything I can to make this right."

Wil stared him down. "And the presentation? Will you back out of that and defend our lack of evidence?"

"I will defend your lack of evidence and credit you with the work," he promised.

"And will you destroy the weapons you created?"

Thomas opened his mouth but faltered.

Wil chuckled. "That's what I thought."

"I . . ." Thomas looked between them, his heart racing. "I'll do everything I can to rid us all of those men and make it clear that you were successful and the victim of a crime. But my work, I can't . . ."

"Yep. C'mon, Bram. Let's leave Master Elliot to make his statement with Sheriff Harrington while we see if there's anything we can salvage from your house. But you should take him up on his offer to have it rebuilt."

Bram looked away from Thomas. He grunted, and then they walked off, leaving the Cloverton wizard on his own. His stomach churned and throat tightened. He wanted to spit or puke, anything to get that terrible feeling out of him.

But he did as they asked. Thomas spoke to the sheriff and the mayor. The rest of his morning was spent answering questions and abandoning himself to duty. It wasn't until nearly sunset that he managed to tear himself away and go back to his temporary home in Gallard Springs. He stopped for a meal he barely tasted and then walked through the doors. Collapsing into a bed for the night was the only thing he wanted.

But he wasn't alone. McGinnis had been arrested earlier that day, and they'd picked up Mark and Gayle, but there was one face Thomas wasn't surprised to see. A half-transparent image of Ferrovani waited in his living room for him.

"There he is, the wayward, foolish student. Are you really ready to throw away everything we've worked on because of qualms of conscience?"

Thomas ignored him at first and walked to the kitchen, where he put away the remnants of the meal into the icebox. A Freeze-it would have been so much better. His heart thudded as painfully as his jaw. He had a terrible bruise and speaking hurt.

"I'm already working to have McGinnis and the others freed. I have friends in high places, and they owe me favors. You still have a chance to make this your victory, Thomas. You don't have to be a failure."

Thomas sighed and addressed the projection of his master. "I'm not a failure. I'm doing quite nicely, thank you. Despite all this crap you've dumped on me. My name in history is secure, and I have a whole host of prototypes I no longer have to share. You may have friends, but they don't compare to the stubbornness and tight-knit nature of the community here. It's honestly fascinating, and some time out here could do you good."

Ferrovani's image became still. Thomas knew from experience he was holding back a great deal of anger and a desire to scream. Even the old monster could behave when he put his mind to it.

"As charming as I'm sure that would be, I don't think I need it. Your progress pleases me, and your discovery's worthwhile. When the others get released, you'll—"

"Not allow them back. This is my project now," said Thomas. He smiled, though it hurt, and he didn't feel it. "I'm not going to let you do anything else to McKenzie and his friends. This was bad enough."

"So some farmer lost his house." Ferrovani waved off. "So what? We can pay for that. The important thing is your *name*. Your legacy, Thomas! You need to take your place and edge the McKenzie boy out of it so that he doesn't eclipse your own."

Thomas thought about it. "No, I think the stage is big enough for both me and him. He discovered how to do it, and I made it better. That's how it's always been in my life, and I think it's time to embrace that."

"You're a fool." Ferrovani's limited patience evaporated. "I should've known that you wouldn't have the drive to do what's necessary to make it to the top."

"It's not necessary," said Thomas. "Wil and friends are already broken and beaten. I lose nothing by giving them their due credit. They have nothing left thanks to McGinnis. I have things I can show to the president and others that will still elevate my name above theirs."

He didn't like that fact, but it was true. Thomas could do everything in his power to try to make it up to those he still considered his friends, but it wouldn't change things. They had a week to put together something concrete for their presentation, and their workspace was destroyed. Wil had his house and could probably come up with some re-creations of their work, but the contest was over. Thomas would win by default.

"That might be so," said Ferrovani, "but I have still decided—"

"I don't give a damn what you've decided," Thomas snapped. "You're no longer a part of this. I've got this from here. You can butt out, and if you behave, I'll wax poetically about how I couldn't have done it without your mentorship. Now get the hell out of here. I badly need some sleep."

Ferrovani's image glowered at him, then disappeared. Thomas would pay for his insolence, but that was a problem for the future. As of now . . . everything hurt, and his friends hated his guts, but he had his work. One week until the presentation. Until his victory.

Maybe by then it would stop tasting like ash.

CHAPTER 51

A Friend in Need

When Hugo had briefly taken control of Harper Valley, it had been awful but was concluded quickly. Over the matter of a few hours, Wil had defeated him with Isom's help, and it was over. There was an aftermath to deal with, but it had been relatively easy, all things considered.

Nothing about losing Bram's house was easy. Even if it weren't secondhand loss, Wil grieved for the hours spent at the kitchen table or in the cellar, drinking and working with friends. After all this time, Bram's house had felt like another home to Wil. Now it and their summer of work was little more than smoldering slag.

There was nothing to be done for the house, nothing that could be saved. The faricite had damaged the foundation when McGinnis's explosive cannonball had hit. The entire thing would need to be leveled and rebuilt from the ground up. The only things that hadn't been damaged were the brewery itself and the majority of the land. Of course, they had torn it up long before the explosion. The leyline was out of shape, and Wil saw no reason to twist it back into a rune. There was nothing to power anymore.

The three of them sat at Wil's kitchen table the day after Bram's party was supposed to have happened. They had spent the last day getting Bram some temporary clothes and toiletries and moving him into Wil's wizard tower, as he liked to consider his home. Normally the thought would bring Wil amusement if not comfort, but he nursed his beer without any enthusiasm or excitement.

To his side, Bram did the same. He'd been drinking most of the day, and with his size, he was finally starting to get drunk. Wil knew because more tears filled his eyes but didn't yet spill. Bram didn't make a sound. He stared off into space until someone got his attention, and then he would go back to his emptiness afterward.

"We need a plan," said Darlene after the silence stretched on for too long. She'd missed almost all the excitement, but things were far enough along now that she didn't complain. Even trying to keep her head up and look forward was a great strain.

"What's the point?" Bram raised the bottle to his lips and drained it. He didn't slam the bottle down so much as let his hand drop to the table.

"They've won," Wil agreed. "I don't like saying it, but we have less than a week now. We could probably wrangle a few rough things in time for the presentation, but it won't be anything impressive. It won't be shields of light, or Thomas's War Chariot."

"There's Mack's Shack," Darlene said. She looked between the two of them for any cracks in their depression. "And we still have a couple cars. Including the one that can be powered by a leyline, right?"

Wil grunted in the affirmative. "Wouldn't be too hard to show it off on Mack's land. Not great for driving, but it could work. It would prevent us from being completely embarrassed."

Bram said nothing, but he reached for another beer. Darlene pulled it away from him.

"Dammit, stop acting like we've lost!" she snapped. "This is the worst we've ever gotten hit, but this isn't the end."

"My house blew up." Bram reached over and snatched the beer out of Darlene's hands. "I think I deserve to wallow a bit."

"I'm with him," said Wil. "Doesn't feel good to wallow, but I don't see myself doing anything else for at least another couple of hours. Solution later, pain now."

Wordlessly, Darlene stood up and waddled off, cursing under her breath. Will and Bram exchanged looks. A few seconds later, they heard the front door open and slam shut.

"Think I should go after her?" asked Wil.

Bram shrugged and popped the beer open. "Probably. I don't know how to handle relationship problems. Maybe I should've gone after Gallath instead of sticking around here. Maybe then I'd still have a home."

"Would it matter if that house was still standing if you were in Faerie permanently?" Wil asked, before realizing that he was being pedantic. "I mean, of course it matters. Sorry. You're free to stay here as long as you like. And read all my books."

"I've already read all your books," said Bram. "Half of them blew up with my house."

He supposed it made sense that nothing would or could get through to Bram. Wil couldn't imagine that kind of loss and what he would do if it happened to him. He didn't like thinking about it. They sat in silence for a good half hour.

Something had to give. Despite Wil's words, he didn't want to just sit there and give up. Not when they had been so close to an overwhelming success. Not with his name and freedom on the line. With Thomas's contributions, it might be enough to save his ass. If Thomas did as he said he would and spoke in Wil's favor.

He didn't much trust Thomas anymore, even when he believed him about not taking part in destroying Bram's house. His assessment held up. The man was a coward, trying to play every side and come out on top.

Thoughts of him made Wil go to the fridge for another beer. They were getting low, and Bram hadn't been brewing as consistently since they'd started their projects. Who knew how long it would take for him to get back to it now.

"I fully meant it when I said you can wallow as long as you like," said Wil. "It seems like a reasonable thing to do at the moment. But I don't want to see you give up either. Not when you've put in more time and work than anyone else." He popped open the beer and took a sip.

Bram grunted his acknowledgment but remained hunched over the table like a man only alive because he had to be. "It's all gone. Our notes too. There's only so much we can do by memory. Only so much we can do without tools and equipment."

There was a friendly rhythm knocked into the front door. Wil set his drink down and answered it. Anthony Bahks stood there, a big toolbox in his arms. "Hey there, Mr. Wizard. I heard about what happened, and everything you've lost. I brought some spare tools over, if they would help."

"I . . . uh, yeah, they might," said a dumbfounded Wil. "That's exactly what we need. I can give them back when we're done."

"Sure, whenever. I'm not in a hurry." Anthony handed the toolbox over to Wil. He gave a jaunty salute. "Good luck with the presentation."

And then he left, leaving Wil standing on his front porch, unsure of what happened. He went back inside and set the tools down outside the kitchen. "That was weird," he said to Bram. "Anthony Bahks just came by with tools."

Bram shrugged. "That's great, I guess. We're going to need a lot more than tools."

Another knock on the door made Wil look over his shoulder. Through the window on the door, the silhouettes of two people waited for him. He opened the door.

"Hi!" Mr. and Mrs. Higgins looked happy to see them, or as happy as circumstances allowed. "We know you and your friend Bram are going through it, and we wanted to open our farm up to you if you need it for your experiments. We're doing pretty well this year and can take a hit. Although if you could speed up the growth of crops . . ."

After they left, Wil was touched and confused. He didn't have much time to ponder it because the doorbell rang. This time Bram showed up, looking bleary and unsteady. Of all people, it was Jonjon.

"Hey, sorry to bother," he said with uncharacteristic caution. "But I heard about what happened, and if you need some faricite, I can let some go at cost."

"What's going on?" Bram asked when Jonjon left. "Is this Darlene?"

Another knock at the door.

"I think it might be," said Wil.

After Jonjon, the Pattersons came by with their daughter, Pearl, along with a platter of sandwiches. They wished them well, and Pearl ran inside to give Bram a big hug around the waist. That had been the first thing to pierce his fog all day, and Bram had gently patted her back as thanks.

After the Pattersons, Mr. Carrey came by to deliver backhanded, passive-aggressive comments about what it was like to lose a house, but he offered to help pay for Bram to get a new wardrobe made from the fibers of his beanstalks. It wasn't the worst thing he'd ever heard the old man say.

Things became a blur after that, and seemingly the entire town showed up to pay their respects and offer their help if needed. Eventually, Bram took over answering the door, and his unshed tears fell. He seemed okay with it, and slowly he came back to life with each new brief conversation. When the final people came, he had to call for Wil to join them.

Mack and Candy were there, along with a line of other people behind them. Darlene had finally come back, and she stood with Wil's parents and Sarah at the end of the line.

"Hey," said Mack. "We wanted to thank you for all the work you've done. Business has never been better, and you were right. I'm saving more money than ever, and the stove burns cleaner than Betsy ever did. Darlene told us about your presentation and how hard up you are. If you want to tinker with the Shack more, we'll do whatever we can to make it work and help you out."

"And if the president eats at the Shack, that's not so bad, right?" Candy added, looking excited at the prospect.

"Syl will definitely drag President Bullworth to the Shack," Wil confirmed.

Lonnie MacDougal offered his basement for brewing and was politely thanked for the spirit of his offer. Sam Brown gave some money, and Dante Boswell offered to personally design Bram a new house, and that more than anything brought him back to life. It was one of the bigger offers they took up.

On and on they went until it was impossible to stay in their funk. Eventually, it was Bob, Sharon, Sarah, and Darlene at the door, and they came inside. "A lot of support showing your way," said Bob. "I was gonna do something like this, but Darlene beat us to it."

Wil beamed at them all. "We really appreciate it. And to think, all of this was her mad at us for giving up."

"Well, obviously," said Darlene as she took her spot at the kitchen table. She looked and sounded exhausted from going all over town. Wil felt equal parts gratitude and guilt for the necessity of it. "We're not giving up. And no one in town will let you."

"It's true," said Sharon. "We want our wizard to stay in town and not get locked up, so whatever you three need, we'll do it. You gotta have some ideas on how to get out of this."

Bram had been mostly quiet, but at this, he nodded. "If there's a way forward, we'll find it. And we'll wipe the smirks off those bastards who blew up my house. By the time we're done, we'll have more than enough money to replace it, right? No need to take that traitor's money to do it."

Wil agreed. With all his family save for Jeb crammed into his kitchen, things felt different. It was one thing to know he had support and another to be able to see and feel it for himself. He reached over to take Darlene's hand in his and gave it a grateful squeeze.

"I love you," he whispered. "Where would we be without you?"

"Still wallowing," replied Darlene. "Like a bunch of babies. We're adults, dammit. We'll work hard, win, and then enjoy our well-deserved victory."

It sounded like the start of a plan.

CHAPTER 52

Marlowe's Mystery

With only a few days remaining until the president arrived, things still seemed impossible. They had decided to focus their re-creations on a few key inventions, like their altered car, the Freeze-it and new stove, and the Time-Stretcher, with the last being their biggest focus since the rest were already done and safe.

The actual construction of the Time-Stretcher wasn't hard with people from the town helping them. It had seemed like such an impractical thing at first, accepting help. How could a bunch of people without real knowledge of what they were doing lend a hand? With Darlene's direction, pretty easily, as it turned out.

With a few extra hands to work and people to run and get supplies as needed, it didn't take that much time to get everything needed for another Time-Stretcher. Bram put all his time in it, while Wil and some contractors built a small workshop on the edge of Mack's land. The cook and restauranteur welcomed the extra business that came from people watching and helping with the work.

It was almost funny to be locally famous again, but this time for something others did. Wil liked to think that he was accepted and appreciated, but nothing made him feel it more than the Cloverton wizards blowing up Bram's house and the outpouring of support because of it. It was the best bit of town gossip in half a year, so maybe it wasn't entirely altruistic. He'd take it anyway.

They had their Freeze-it, Time-Stretcher, stove, and car. It wasn't enough.

"I disagree," said Darlene. "We've proved you can change leylines and harness them, and then you have a selection of inventions that will change the world. Who cares if you're not outdoing the traitor? We're revolutionizing public transportation and medical care alone. We've got the proof we need."

They were on his porch in the midafternoon with a stack of plans and papers underneath books to keep the wind from blowing them away. Wil rocked back and forth anxiously. Not even the staggerleaf helped.

"I need to beat him," said Wil. "He can't have credit with us and then on his own and show us up. Not after everything he's put us through. Not after using me and lying to us all."

The anger lingered, but it was cooler than he'd ever admit. He was more hurt than angry, and the idea of Thomas successfully getting his way after betraying him like that . . . Well, it sickened him.

Darlene sighed. It wasn't the first, second, or even third time they'd talked about it. They'd gone around all the same points, and she had been a saint up until now. "I'm not any happier with him than you are, but what else can we really do? He's going to pay for Bram's house, he's going to testify against Ferrovani's men, and he did help us see it through.

"Think of it this way, Wil. Will you let it go or let it consume you? The best thing we can do is finish up and let Thomas go on his way and never speak to him again. If you'll excuse me, I need to pee for the fiftieth time today." She stood with a groan.

"As always, my apologies for the necessity. But we're getting close to seeing our kid, right?" Wil grinned, and a pang went through his heart. "You're right, by the way. I should just let it go. I *am* having trouble. If you think about it, the more success we have, the better we can provide for the baby."

She shot him a look. "That's a low blow, and you know it. We'll be fine either way." Darlene went inside.

They would be. She was right, and he wasn't about to deny it. Wil still wanted to do something big. Something that would belong to the three of them. Every time he stopped to think about it, he wanted to laugh.

Wil felt so greedy lately, and he was hungry for more. Where had that simple civil servant gone? He'd never chased fame or recognition before. Once upon a time, Wil had been proud of that. The sham tribunal had trampled all over his confidence and patience, and now he had bounced back and gone further.

He didn't care about impressing Cloverton. The government didn't care; they just wanted to get what they could from him. The rest was superfluous. Impressing them wasn't right. Wil realized then what he wanted above all else: to be taken seriously.

To be understood as a powerful, capable wizard and not the mage class wash-out who volunteered for a simple farming town. For people to know that he may have chosen something close to his heart, but that didn't mean he wouldn't excel at it. When he was done, Harper Valley would be *the* place where everyone, magical or not, fae or human, chose to live by blending together and providing for their collective benefit.

To be focused on helping one another and making it possible for everyone to thrive and live their best lives, by making their lives easier. That was why he had to win. Wil, Bram, and Darlene had led the way, here and in Faerie, for what the world could be if they tried to make it better.

Winning wasn't about beating Thomas or showing anyone up. It was about screaming their names for all the world to hear, shouting "Life should be enjoyed. Join us!"

Wil took a deep breath. He'd had his epiphany, now what the hell was he supposed to do about it?

The answer came ten minutes later in the form of Bram driving in with their

Time-Stretcher strapped to a small cart hitched to the car. He parked and got out. It was clear he was still unhappy, but his mood had lightened up from miserable. Now, there was even a spark in his eye behind his scratched glasses.

"I come bearing two pieces of good news!" He slapped the solid metal box that absolutely looked like a coffin. "I think I've gotten the Time-Stretcher working. We need a potential test subject who won't mind being in a box with weird temporal and spatial spells interwoven. Any takers?"

"Pass," said Darlene.

"Naturally," said Wil. "I'll handle it. It's just going to be a minute in there, right?"

"If my calculations are correct," said Bram. His lips twitched. "If I'm wrong, you could be stuck in there for a thousand years with only your thoughts to keep you company."

Wil nodded thoughtfully. "Good thing I can make illusions. I'll do a puppet show to keep me company if I am stuck in a temporal bubble gone wrong."

Darlene rolled her eyes. "The misery's getting old! But there's no risk, right?"

After reassuring her that the risk was minimal, they gathered around the Time-Stretcher. Bram opened it up and said, "I added one more thing to the design, which shouldn't tax the batteries too much. Remember how we said that sticking someone with life-threatening wounds alone in a box for even a minute or two might be a bit jarring?"

"Yeah," said Darlene. "The idea of bleeding out and being shoved into a box is a little terrifying. Did you make room for a second person?"

Bram beamed. "I did! That way a doctor or medic can be alongside them, administering care the entire time." He ran his finger over the metallic edges covered in runes. "It should be good for not jostling those inside much, but that's untested too. This is a simple box array that should balance all our needs, and—"

"Okay, we get it," Wil chuckled. "Let me in!"

Bram opened it up. Wil climbed up on the cart and stepped inside it. There wasn't enough room to stand up, but two people Bram's size could crouch in here, along with potential supplies kept inside. It was padded, so he could lie down and be relatively comfortable. "You know, if you keep me in here for about five days or so, it'll only be over two hours for me. I could have a nap and skip the presentation entirely."

"Long-term testing comes later," said Bram. "Can't get ahead of ourselves yet."

"Let's hurry it up," Darlene said. "I'm getting cranky."

"Getting?" Wil winked and closed the door.

It was dark, so he created a ball of light and stuck it to the top of the Time-Stretcher. Then he kicked back and waited. A second later, the entire box vibrated with a tension that made Wil's stomach churn. When the entire box listed left and right like it was rocking quickly, he became very glad he was lying down, but all in all, it wasn't too bad.

It was, he reasoned, likely Bram moving him around. Time moved slowly in here, so each bump must've been a jostle or turn taken too quickly. Now that he'd had about half a minute to get used to it, he—

The door opened. Wil blinked and looked up. Bram's face peeked in at him. "We drove to your parents' for dinner. Took us about twenty minutes all things considered. How long was it for you?"

Wil grinned. "An eternity due to your crazy driving! Each bump was super exaggerated. We might need to refine the design a bit to avoid people getting seasick. Otherwise? Less than a minute. How're the batteries?"

"About half dead. We'll need to put in slots for more so we can guarantee at least one or two hours of use. At a hospital with a leyline, it could be indefinite." Bram pulled him out of the box and helped him down from the cart.

Wil looked at his parents' house. It was tiny compared to the rest of the embassy, but it was the final unchanged part of the land. Twenty-four years ago he'd been born there, and here he was, stepping out of a coffin with a temporal distortion in it, ready to change the world. Maybe he didn't need anything else.

"You bring our notes?" Wil asked.

"And your books and leylines map," said Darlene, coming around the other way.

"Thanks," said Wil.

"You know your mom won't let you read at the table, right?" Bram said with a chuckle. He opened the cab and pulled out a book, the cover charred. "This is the other piece of good news, in case you forgot. I managed to save a couple books from the house."

Will took it and opened it. It was *Mysteries of Marlowe Manor*, still borderline readable. If you could count the confusing gibberish inside readable. "Thanks, Bram. Not sure I can crack this in three days, but I can always give it a try."

"I had a thought about that, actually . . ."

Darlene sighed. "I'll see you boys inside, then, whenever you're done and ready to eat." Slowly, she made her way in the house, groaning from a dozen aches and pains.

Wil winced, but he couldn't resist. "Go on."

Bram steepled his fingers. "You said that Marlowe Manor was in the confluence of a lot of leylines, right?"

Wil thought about it. It wasn't hard to remember, given how many times his senses had brushed up against them during his time spent there. "Not *a lot* of leylines, come to think of it. Sometimes it felt like one . . . big . . ." Wil handed the book over and dug through the cab for his map.

He unrolled it on the hood of the car. A sea of X's and notes greeted him, overlaid over an image of the entire basin. Wil trailed a finger in a circle along the edges, then over to his house near the center. He'd never had access to any of a leyline's power there in the center . . . but Marlowe Manor did.

Wil played over his time at the manor in his head, every time he walked along the boundaries of the property with Isom at his side. It had felt like one big leyline, not more powerful or potent but stretching on forever. At the center, magic came a little easier. It was where the most powerful wizards practiced and did their experiments and where all spells tied into the property lingered. The only thing they had were anchor spells in key locations, where they were able to control . . .

"What is it, Wil?" Bram looked over his shoulder.

Wil circled the map again. "What if this was all one big leyline, ringing around the valley?"

Bram blinked. "I've read that book and others, and I am still not sure what you're suggesting. What would that do?"

"I don't know," said Wil, excitement creeping into his voice. "But imagine if we linked them all, made them extend around and form a perimeter of combined leylines. And at key places"—he tapped the largest X in each of the four corners—"I twist the leyline into runes while still keeping the chain going. What do you get?"

"Gods," Bram breathed out. He shuffled from foot to foot, hands wringing the air. "You think we could turn the entire basin into an array?!"

"What if we could?" Wil buzzed with renewed vigor. "Take what we did on your property with the car, but extend that across the entire basin . . ."

Bram laughed in delight. Wil joined him, and soon they had tears in their eyes, and they laughed some more and screamed and shook each other. Darlene poked her head out along with Sharon.

"What're you boys doing?" Sharon demanded. "What's so funny?"

Wil thrust a finger to the sky. "We're going to beat Thomas and prove ourselves once and for all! We're going to shape the world."

"Great," said Darlene. "But first, dinner with family. You may tell us your plan after dessert."

"But," Bram protested.

"Nope." Sharon shook her head.

"Then let's eat." Wil rolled up his map and went inside. Plans tonight, work tomorrow. Victory was in sight.

CHAPTER 53

Shape the World

I t wasn't easy, but I managed to make it happen," said Bob.

They were in his office at city hall with only two days left before the president and others arrived. It would take Wil at least that much time to do the legwork. It might not be enough.

"Thanks, Dad," said Wil as he buried his inner critic deep within his psyche. "I know how much of a risk this is, and I couldn't do it without the help of the community. If this works . . ."

Bob laughed. "I've heard that one before. You don't have to convince me, son. You've got this. But if you don't, I might be one of the very few one-term mayors in Harper Valley. I'd be the third, I think."

"But if it does work," said Wil with a growing smile.

"Then clearly it's due to the McKenzie family leadership, and we will form a dynasty that will last for centuries," said Bob in his usual laid back drawl. They laughed together, and Wil's anxiety eased. "If it does work, then I'm pretty sure we could get away with anything. The amount of community trust we'll have will be second to none."

"We'll need to redo the roads if you want me to replicate Manifee City's trolleys but better," said Wil. He stole a piece of candy out of Bob's jar and popped it into his mouth. "I'll be happy to do it once it works and all the hoopla dies down. I'm pretty sure that we'll get a bigger budget for it."

Bob waved him off. "If it works, slow the hell down and enjoy it. You don't have to always be moving all the time. If you keep it up like this, life will pass you by. You're about to be a father. You should be fighting for less work to be able to spend time at home, not promising yourself to the next big project."

Wil's face heated up. "You're right," he said with an awkward chuckle. "I'm looking forward to that, but . . ."

"It *is* a lot of waiting and just looking at a little critter that cries, eats, sleeps, and craps all day," said Bob. "There'll be plenty of time for work but take your time and enjoy things. You'll appreciate slow and quiet soon enough. Especially if you and Darlene have more after this. You want busy, boy? Try having three kids before you're thirty."

"You know," said Wil, "I think I'll pass on that. But don't tell Mom; she wants as many grandkids as possible."

Bob laughed. "She does at that. Is there anything else I can help you with? I know you must be eager to get to it."

"One question," said Wil. "Did you manage to get the mayor of Gallard Springs to get me a permit to move things around?"

He knew right away by the pained expression on his father's face that something had gone wrong. "About that. Turns out Mayor Pam is not too happy with us for extraditing McGinnis and the others for their crimes. I'm guessing she was given plenty of incentives to protect them from us, but Sheriff Harrington was persuasive. So, you might run into trouble there."

Wil frowned but nodded. "I'm pretty sure I can handle anything they throw at me. I might have to bend a few personal rules, but I'm getting this done, and no one will be hurt."

"I'm glad for that," said Bob. "If you do, I'm the one who's going to have to deal with it. Keep your head on straight, son, and get it done."

Wil went downstairs, mind full of tasks for the next two days. His mother knelt on the floor, rubbing Isom's tummy while he rumbled his pleasure and his six paws kneaded the air. "Am I interrupting anything?"

Isom scrambled back to his feet. His ears flattened against his head, which Wil took to be the wampus cat's version of a blush. "Your mother understands respect," he said imperiously.

"Oh hush," said Sharon as she continued to scratch the back of his neck. He couldn't resist the purr that came tumbling out. "You got what you need, then? Good. We're almost done with prep, and the president's security detail should be here tomorrow. Is there anything you want me to tell them if they ask after you?"

"Yeah," said Wil. "I'll be available tomorrow night for any discussions they need, but I'll be much too busy before then. C'mon, Isom. We got a lot of work ahead of us."

It took Isom all his willpower to pull himself away from Sharon, but the big cat followed Wil, and soon they were off to the south center of the basement, where the road led south to Appleton and beyond.

This was where it got tricky. The leyline ran north to south, and he needed it to go east to west. It took a full hour of digging his feet in and twisting the land to change the flow of power. Where there had been flat land and road, there was now a spiral of rock jutting from the earth, and the roads were all but destroyed as Wil moved them farther south to give more space for the leyline.

"Your plan is foolish," said Isom as Wil finished up and had to take a break. Sweat ran down the wizard's face as he rested and fought for air. "If it takes this much effort each time, it will take you a month."

Wil shook his head. "It's not going to be this hard every time. I knew going in some would be hard, but others, they'll basically be flybys if the Faerie leyline is any indication." Of course, he didn't want to rip any more open. That would end his plans, and he was fortunate enough to not need the one still mending.

True enough, the next three leylines were a lot easier. It had been an ordinary effort to go from one to another, tearing up just enough of the land to pull and stretch on each leyline and snap them together. It wasn't a perfectly straight line, as Wil occasionally had to zig or zag to keep the chain unbroken. After three hours, he made it to the southwest corner of the map, right where the river ended, flowing off into a chasm between mountains where the lake he'd made nearly a year ago waited.

"You *are* destructive, aren't you?" Isom goaded him. After a few hours of sticking nearby and keeping an eye and ear out for bystanders, he'd grown bored and cranky. "And you reminisce loudly. I can see it all as you remember it."

"Yeah," said Wil. He took a sip of lukewarm water from his canteen before he magically chilled it and took a longer drink. "Can't help but think about everything that happened. Just think, my destructiveness brought you to me, and now you have all the beef you can eat."

Isom said nothing and looked away, but his tail lashed behind him. Wil knew cats well enough to know that Isom was never going to admit how much happier he was now. He didn't have to.

"Break's over," said Wil. "Time for the first rune in our simple array."

Simple it may have been, but this sort of thing had never been tried with leylines. Enchanters used it for their work, as did some alchemists and ritualists. Runes in the land made perfect sense for a one-time ritual, but at large? Well, Wil would either go big and win, or fail. No point in worrying about it.

Wil tapped into the leyline and observed it. From its odd, tangled shape, he reached out into the world and moved rock, dirt, trees, and animals and twisted them around. It wasn't about forcing his will into the world so much as using the leyline to make a proclamation that the land would hear and respond to. It was a promise to care for the land as well as for its people.

The leyline untangled and then wrapped up around itself again. The shape wasn't right, and it wouldn't be right for another forty-five minutes of steadily altering the land until the ends of the leyline not only stretched east to the previous leyline but also north along the river in the path Wil would go next.

Then came the rune itself, picked by Bram. At this point, Wil trusted his friend's judgment on arrays and configurations better than his own. It was a simple, boxlike shape, with two tendrils stretching out and a few nubs. It didn't look like much, and when he finished it, it didn't feel like much either. The *awaken* rune would do nothing until they were all linked.

Wil allowed himself enough of a break to lay out a blanket he'd brought for a short nap, while Isom hunted and kept an eye out for anything dangerous. After an hour, he realized he didn't want to get up, but he forced himself to move on, dreading the fact that he'd only done about a quarter of the work and it was nearly six in the evening. Oh well, the work continued.

Luckily, the river made his work easy. By providing a natural split in the land and a direction life went, most of the leylines went north to south, and it wasn't too bad spending the next two hours working his way up along the forest and farmlands. By the time he made it to the next spot for a rune, he barely had anything left in him.

It took all his remaining strength to shape the rocks and trees and a well-known cave into the next leyline rune: *unite*.

And then he went home and passed out.

"You're not going to kill yourself doing this, are you?" Darlene asked at breakfast the following morning. She wasn't much of a cook, and she didn't like standing for too long anymore, but she'd still made them passable eggs.

Wil devoured them. "Probably not," he said through a mouthful of food. "But there's always that possibility. I'll leave you the house and the Thunderhawk."

"Oh, please," said Darlene. "The only way I'm going to be able to ride that without you is if both you and Bram succeed. And if you die, chances are that's not happening."

"Fine," he said. "Bram gets my Thunderhawk."

The next day wasn't much better. It was like working out too hard and being hardly able to move the next day. Too much leyline exposure could be dangerous or addictive, but Wil was long past that point, he felt. If there were going to be any issues, it was too late to worry. Not when he still had a job to do.

He flew to the northwest corner and started the line east. In theory, this would be the easiest part of his mission but also the longest. By noon, he'd made it halfway across the basin along the north border, which meant he was half done with stage one. Occasionally people watched or talked to him on his breaks, but most of Harper Valley had gotten used to his shenanigans by now.

The trouble came, predictably, when he crossed the border into Gallard Springs. His father hadn't managed to get cooperation from the government there, which meant that by the time he was close to the foothills in the northeast, Isom had sent him a mental warning. Local law enforcement had come for him.

"What do you think you're doing now?" A man with a gold star on his chest came forward. He had a trimmed, dark mustache and salt-and-pepper hair. He was lanky, and even taller than Wil.

"A big magic experiment," said Wil. He hoped he could talk his way out of it, but if he couldn't . . . well, he had other methods. "I'm not causing any problems, am I?"

"I dunno," said the sheriff. "Are you?" His two deputies fanned out around him, not explicitly threatening Wil so much as inspecting his work and getting closer, just in case.

"Not at all, sir. Just twisting the earth a bit and getting . . . I suppose you can call them samples, but in a few days, everyone here in Gallard Springs will benefit." Wil gave his best trustworthy smile.

"That's private property, son. You're damaging peoples' land, and they're not happy about it." The sheriff put his hands on his hips. His fingers brushed over a gun, but his tone remained even and calm. Wil wasn't fooled.

"I actually have a permit for the work," he lied. "Let me get it out for you, if I may."

"Slowly."

Wil held his hands up. They were empty but not for long. A ball of light appeared in his hand, bright enough to be painful to see during the day. And then it started blinking. Slow, fast, in between, it flashed in sharp bursts of light and dark.

The sheriff's hand left his gun. He leaned over farther, and his deputies swayed in place. Wil kept it up until their wills turned to jelly, then he spoke. "Everything is fine. No laws are being broken. You met a kind young man who gave you a reasonable explanation, and then you took the day off and visited family. Maybe you should have a nice meal out. Doesn't that sound nice?"

None of them answered, though the sheriff nodded blankly. Wil kept the lights up and his tone soothing. "Good, good. Just remember, everything is fine. Today's a lazy day. In fact, I bet you want to go home and nap right now. So . . . walk home, see family, take a nap."

A working like this wouldn't last too terribly long, and it could be broken through by almost anyone. Wil didn't need to violate their psyches in order to buy some time. As far as mind magic went, this was as simple, unobtrusive, and safe as it got. It still came too close to controlling other people for Wil's taste.

You are not like the other one. Isom had kept out of sight and only reappeared when they had wandered off. Wil was pleased with his increasingly good behavior and grateful for his words.

"I'm going to make sure I never am," he said. "C'mon. We've got a time limit now, and I'm exhausted. We have to finish our work soon."

But there was still half a day's work remaining. He rushed along, linking more leylines until he got to one high above the others, on a hill he had to use magic to scale. It was all earth here, tons and tons of it, but when Wil extended his senses, he felt the complex cave system below and the life in there.

He had to be very careful to not collapse the hill itself. It still took an hour and a half to get the rune just right, and the land required the fewest obvious changes. The rune *embrace* flowed above the mountains on the northeast side of the basin.

That took about everything out of Wil. When he continued linking to the south, again aided by the land's natural borders, he found his strength faltering and his nerves on edge. He made it halfway to the southeast corner before discomfort turned to pain.

It was like a sunburn on the inside, and tapping into the leyline filled his veins with molten lava. He had to release it and take a break. He sat on a boulder and ate a snack. That's when the sheriff found him again.

"Get down off the rock and get on the ground. Hands behind your head!" The sheriff yelled from a couple dozen yards away. His deputies stayed back this time.

"Nice job, Isom," Wil muttered, but the wampus cat was just outside easy contact range. He still projected his need for help. To the sheriff, he took one of the last couple of bites of his apple and said, "Did you enjoy your nap?"

The sheriff was not amused. "Whatever you did to me terrified my wife and kids. They couldn't wake me for hours!"

"Sounds like a good nap, then. Sorry I had to do that, Sheriff, but I fear it might've been for nothing." Wil finished his apple and threw the core behind him. "If I can't finish up tomorrow, I'm screwed. But for now? I'm all tapped out."

"I told you to get on the ground. I'm not going to tell you another time, Wizard." He pointed his gun at Wil, and so did the other men.

"You ready to murder a man because you were mildly embarrassed?" Wil did as he was told, more or less. He slid off the boulder and landed next to his Thunderhawk. "I'm going home. I suggest you put your guns away, or else he might eat you."

"Who?"

Isom made himself known by sneaking up behind the three police officers and giving his best wildcat howl. They jumped and whirled around, firing their guns at the spot Isom had been before he teleported away.

Wil hopped onto his Thunderhawk and powered it on. It took twice as long as usual, and the pain flared back up. This wasn't a good sign. "Farewell, Sheriff! Next time, I'll come back with a permit."

He flew off as fast as he could, serpentining just in case they decided to shoot at him after all. Isom caught up with him a minute later as they dashed through the center of Gallard Springs. They went over and past surprised townspeople as they put as much distance between themselves and the police as possible.

CHAPTER 54

Last Resorts

It wasn't only Darlene waiting for Wil at home. Bob was there, as was Sheriff Harrington, and an unfamiliar bald man who looked permanently grim and ready for trouble. Darlene was happy to see him, but she was the only one.

"What in the hell did you think you were doing?" Bob asked as soon as Wil stepped inside his dim living room. He'd made it back as the sun was setting, and had walked in, ready to collapse. It wasn't the best way to be greeted after failing.

"You're going to have to be more specific," said Wil. He eyed the third man but didn't say anything about him yet. "Was it the tearing up land in Gallard Springs, or . . . ?"

Bob covered his face with his hand. "You know damned well it's about Sheriff Boone."

Sheriff Harrington spoke up. "He called me not long ago to complain about you. You're getting a bit of a reputation of lawlessness."

"Yes, I have some concerns." The bald man's voice was a low rumble. "Between the violence this winter, the bickering among wizards, a house exploding, and this, you people don't make a very good impression. We will not tolerate any shenanigans while President Bullworth is visiting."

Darlene sighed loud enough to be heard. "Welcome home, Wil. These gentlemen are here to see you."

Wil chuckled. "Thanks, babe." He continued past them and collapsed into his favorite cushy armchair. "I'll address these concerns in order if you don't mind. No? Good.

"Sheriff Boone, was it? He tried to stop me and threatened me, and so I sent him away harmlessly. He threatened me again, and I ran because I don't feel like being shot by someone who yells demands and threats first. We're supposed to be innocent until proven guilty, right?

"Which leads me to point two. My reputation as lawless comes from people in power who throw that power around recklessly. It's not my fault they start fights they can't win. I'm not going to surrender to some bully yelling orders just because they think they can point a gun at me and I'll do what they say."

Once upon a time, he would've done that, Wil mused. A lot had happened in the last year. Something his father had said to him came to mind. As he went through life and faced trials, Wil became a more refined version of himself. Sometimes that meant becoming more of himself, and sometimes it meant changing drastically.

"And the third point?" said the security man.

"Right. While these problems happen around me, I'm not the one causing them. I'm the one fixing them. The three men who invaded my home and blew up my best friend's house are no longer in town, and I'm sure you and your men are good at what you do. I will not cause any problems, and I didn't mean to cause them today. I was just trying to get my project finished."

"And did you?" Darlene asked.

Wil let himself sink farther into the chair. "No, I overextended and hurt myself. The sheriff caught up to me as I was resting, and I had to run. Thomas is going to win."

"I'm sorry, son," said Bob. "You tried. Is there any way to fix things?"

"Like maybe getting the help of your local sheriff in talking to neighboring towns to get favors," Sheriff Harrington suggested.

Wil laughed, holding his hands up in surrender. "You're right. Next time I will. But . . . I need time to recover, and I don't think we have it. It's okay. We've got enough to give President Bullworth a good showing, but not enough to blow everyone's minds."

"Aside from the fact that what we did is already going to blow their minds and be applied all across the country," said Darlene.

"I guess."

The bald man cleared his throat. "You clearly have things to talk about. I'm here as a formality. The president is not worried about you. The worry is my own. If you are sure that the people you've been feuding with aren't a danger and there are notable people of interest in town to worry about, then I'll leave this." He held up a folder full of files, slapped it down on a footstool, and left the house.

Bob waited until the man left and then turned to Wil. "Mayor Pam wants to lodge a formal complaint against you. This makes multiple times now you've come to Gallard Springs and caused trouble. She wants to ban you from entering."

Wil's stomach dropped. "Well, that's not good. What can I do to smooth things over?"

"Now you're talking sense," said Sheriff Harrington. "You can apologize to the sheriff, maybe spend a night in jail as a token show of contrition. Paying for or undoing the damage you did would go a long way in making sure you're not arrested on sight."

"Now hold on a minute," said Darlene. She tried to sit up but collapsed back into her seat. Getting around was hard for her now, but none of her fire had cooled. "That's not damage. That's a highly complex working of runes and ley-lines, one that's going to change their lives for the better."

"They didn't ask for it or want it," said Bob, although he made a face. "And

Pam is pissed at me specifically for letting you go ahead and do it anyway. It's not good for neighboring towns to feud needlessly like this."

Wil sighed and nodded. "After the presentation and the president's visit, I'll repair the damage and spend a night in jail and apologize."

"I appreciate that, son," said Harrington. "You don't have to be at odds with the law. We could be allies if you're willing to work with me."

Soon after, both of them left. Darlene waited ten seconds after the front door closed to ask, "You're not serious, right?"

"No, I was lying through my teeth," Wil laughed. "I'm going to use the president to smooth this over. I think I've got one chance to complete this, and it's not going to be easy or pleasant. In fact, I'm pretty sure you're not going to like my plan."

Darlene eyed him warily. "If I'm not going to like it, get me a drink and the footbath first."

Wil happily did as he was told. Most of his exhaustion was magical in nature, and although he wanted to curl up and fall asleep, he still had a little life in him to spare. Making a big pitcher of iced tea and heating the water for the footbath the old fashioned way gave him time to think of how he was going to pitch his plan.

"That's better," said Darlene as she rested with her feet in scalding water and a cold drink in hand. Her eyelids fluttered shut, and she groaned as she made herself comfortable. "Alright, hit me with the stuff I won't like."

He popped off the top of his beer and took a drink. The cold and bitterness soothed him after two days of working himself to the bone. "Well, I can tell you right now that there's no way I could possibly move any more leylines around. I'm done for the next few days and should probably avoid magic in general for now."

Darlene grimaced and set her drink down. "That's not what I was hoping to hear, but you sound awfully cheerful about it. If not you, then how are we going to do it?"

This was the part that he knew was likely to set her off, if anything did.

"Thomas is going to do it for me," said Wil. "He's not great at earth magic, and he doesn't have the knack for changing the leylines like I do, but he could finish it for us."

His wonderful, patient, darling girlfriend nodded patiently and took a slow, deep breath. "And how on earth do you plan on getting the traitor to do that? I don't exactly see him cooperating with us for any reason. Let alone one that might upstage him. Please tell me you've got a plan beyond asking nicely."

Wil smiled.

"Godsdammit, Wil," Darlene groaned and covered her face with her hands. She drew her hands down, stretching out her face comically before she sighed and said, "You can't be serious."

"I am, actually."

He didn't expect her or anyone else to understand. Hell, if he suggested it to

Bram, his friend might've gone on the angry tirade Darlene avoided. It wasn't because he had any special plan or idea that would help him convince his former friend. Wil didn't need one. Obviously, Darlene disagreed with that.

"Why? Why would he help?"

"He might not," Wil admitted. He took another long drink of beer, and his head swam and flashed out. He was more tired than he thought. "But every step of the way, he's talked about how much he regretted hurting us and being sneaky. If he's serious about it, he's going to get the chance to make things right."

Darlene waved him off. "I guess we really are down to our last resort. I don't think it'll work. I think it's a bad plan, actually. But I can tell by that stupid smile that you're convinced it will work and there's nothing I can possibly do to persuade you otherwise."

Wil smiled wider.

"I hate you sometimes," said Darlene.

"I know," said Wil. And then an idea hit him. "Wanna put a wager on it?"

"You want to place a wager on whether the man who betrayed us will have a change in heart and help us beat him in front of everyone and thus deny him his greatest desire? You want to bet on whether we'll win with the longest odds imaginable? Fine. What do you get if you win?"

Wil answered immediately. "You marry me."

Darlene blinked. "What?"

"You've said no to me so far," Wil said, "because you don't want to feel pressured into it because of the baby. Well, I want to marry you, and I am confident this will work."

"You're serious?"

Wil finished off his beer and set it on a side table. "Completely. I don't want to just squeak by, Darlene. I want the biggest win imaginable. And that includes having you by my side."

She turned red, and tears filled her eyes. "Stupid pregnancy hormones," she said, voice raw. "I was going to stick by your side regardless, idiot."

"Yeah," said Wil, "but this way you're stuck with me forever."

"And what if I win?" Darlene asked.

"I marry you. *And* you get to design the wedding that I'll pay for." He grinned as Darlene rolled her eyes.

"I'm designing it either way," she said. "But you better get me a good ring. Not an expensive one, a *good* one."

Wil stood up from his chair, then knelt by Darlene's side. He took her hands in his and said, "You have my word. I want it all, Darlene, and I want it with you."

She had no more objections.

CHAPTER 55

Hail to the Chief

Although there were still many details outside his control, Wil slept like a baby. He'd always been a worrier, but now he understood what it meant to shrug off things you couldn't affect. It made the start of the day less stressful than it had to be, although there were plenty of reasons to be anxious.

From sunup, recently arrived bodyguards and security experts scoured the train station and positioned themselves along the path the president and company would take throughout the tour of Harper Valley. Some of the people getting things together complained, and soon Sharon had her hands full soothing bruised egos and reassuring government agents that things were as safe as they looked.

Wil, Bram, and Darlene arrived an hour early, though they didn't need to worry about finding positions. The train station was beyond crowded as people found spots to wait for the president's arrival and speech. As far as Wil knew, no president had ever stopped in Harper Valley for more than a few minutes. The three of them had front row seats near some of the more colorful flower arrangements.

"Are you okay?" Wil asked for the tenth time that day. It was hot, even before noon, and sticky. She had more and more trouble with the heat as her pregnancy went on.

Darlene grunted, cradling her stomach. "She's kicking a lot, my stomach and back hurts, and I need to pee every five minutes." She'd answered similarly each time he'd asked. "I'm fine, really. But I think I might stay here for most of the day. I don't see a reason to get excited. Not after what you've told us about him."

"He's fine." Wil waved a hand. "Don't think it's likely any politicians are much better, and I'm getting a solid chance. If we all kiss his ass a bunch, maybe he'll give us that extension and we can make this work."

"What if he doesn't like us?" Bram asked as he continued pacing. Out of all of them in the front row, he was the only one standing. He hadn't stopped moving for about twenty minutes, muttering under his breath all the while. "What if we do something to offend him?"

"Then he'll probably have us killed," said Wil in his most serious tone.

Bram squeaked, and Darlene hit Wil in the arm. "Don't do that, we're all nervous. Except for you, apparently. Mr. Peace and Serenity, right— Oof!" Darlene doubled over, groaning. "Ex-excuse me a second."

Wil helped her up and to the nearby bathroom on site. She was right. Wil was calm, collected, and confident now that the time had come. Maybe he should try to spread it around and make sure Bram didn't have a panic attack.

"If it helps, Bullworth seems like a bit of a blockhead. Flatter him and laugh at his jokes, and you'll be his new best friend for five minutes." Bram visibly relaxed, and the mischievous side of Wil couldn't help himself. "You do have to worry about impressing the grandmasters coming with him."

Bram stopped pacing. His face turned as white as a ghost.

"I'm sorry, I'm joking," said Wil. "Well, mostly. You do have to impress them, but I don't think it'll take much and . . ." Wil followed Bram's gaze to the west.

The delegation from Faerie arrived with half an hour to spare before the train rolled in. Security, both theirs and Calipan's, escorted them over a platform of wood over the train tracks, so none of them would accidentally touch iron. It was a small group, no more than a dozen guards plus Jeb, escorting Arabella and Gallath. No wonder Bram froze up.

"Hey, strangers," Wil called out. "Welcome back!"

The fae came up to them, while their guards hung back for privacy. Jeb and Gallath politely waved at some cheers and greetings from people in the sea of assembled chairs, but their focus was on Wil and company. Jeb looked Wil up and down and whistled sharply.

"Damn, Wil, you clean up pretty nice. Did you rob someone with fashion sense?" he asked, as if his own golden armor wasn't ostentatious and garish.

"Yeah, the government," said Wil. "They gave it to me during my time in Marlowe Manor for my tribunal appearance. Pleasure to see you again, Princess. And Gallath . . . Um. What title does the leader of the Ogre Federation have?"

"General," Gallath said in his usual quiet, subdued voice. His eyes were locked on Bram. "I'm General Gallath now, though no one needs to call me that. I've never stood on ceremony and definitely not with friends."

"Are we still friends?" Bram asked in a tiny voice.

Gallath's face split into a crooked smile. It was more than he usually showed, so he must've been pleased. "Always, Bram."

Arabella sighed. "You two are so pathetic. Go somewhere to talk, get a room together, whatever you need to stop mooning at each other like children. Hello, Wil, good to see you again. Did you get what you needed for your presentation?"

"Sort of," said Wil. "All the faricite blew up, along with Bram's house, and we're left with only a few working machines and prototypes."

"What?!" Gallath's eyes widened.

Bram winced but nodded. "Yeah . . . maybe we should talk."

Arabella rolled her eyes as the two broke away to the side, then ducked out of sight behind the bathrooms. "Imagine crossing species lines and falling in love with a human. Pathetic."

Jeb snorted. "Yeah, imagine."

Darlene came out of the bathroom, looking flushed and sweating profusely. Wil rushed to her side in an instant. "You—"

"Yes, I'm fine," she said through short, sharp breaths. Every so often her face warped in pain, but she pressed on back to her seat. Wil helped her sit and joined her. She nodded in gratitude and then addressed Arabella. "Nice to see you again, Princess. I think."

Arabella's lips curled into a predatory smile. "Why Darlene, is that you? I didn't recognize you at first. There's a lot more of you than there used to be. And you're sweating and heaving a lot more. Is everything alright?"

Luckily, at this point their barbs were friendly, though Wil didn't miss the split second of homicidal rage in Darlene's eyes. He chalked it up to the pregnancy. A second later, Darlene smiled and said, "Princess Arabella! I'm surprised to see you still with Jeb at your side. I thought you had a new pet every week."

Jeb's eye twitched, but Arabella laughed and hugged his arm. "I do. I can have more than one pet. Sometimes, Jeb even—"

"Fantastic," said Wil. "How about a change in topic?"

Bram and Gallath remained gone as the minutes melted away and every available seat found an occupant. Bob came up and waited patiently, chatting with Sharon for the next twenty minutes, until a familiar whistle pierced the air. The train rolled into the station, slowing to a stop over the course of hundreds of feet.

Wil stood and checked himself. Arabella moved to her position as foreign dignitary. Darlene remained sitting, huffing occasionally with a sharp grimace. No one would begrudge her for remaining seated, and if they did, Wil would have some choice words for them. Some of his nervousness returned, but mostly he was excited. It was the moment they had worked up to.

Four bodyguards, two men with guns, and two wizards cleared the way and took positions on either side of the train doors. A second later, President Bullworth stepped out. He favored everyone with a broad smile and waved. "Afternoon, Harper Valley!"

Cheers met him, and Bullworth reacted with false modesty, waving them off. Wil resisted rolling his eyes. He found Darlene's hand and squeezed it before he moved into place to greet the president while keeping his distance from the bodyguards. The president all but charged Wil, grabbing him by the shoulder and shaking his hand hard enough to hurt.

"Master McKenzie, fantastic to see you again. My aides have been keeping me appraised of your progress. I can't wait to see what you've got in store for me!"

"I've got plenty, sir. I look forward to showing what we've got."

Behind them, Syl stepped off the train as well, dressed in mismatching clothes and a garish amount of jewelry, including a pocket watch tied around one of his horns. He sauntered over to them and grabbed Wil's other hand and shook it. "What a trip this has been, Wil! I'm glad to finally be back in Harper Valley, among my favorite humans in the world!"

The assembled crowd cheered even louder at that. The president visiting was special, but most people in Harper Valley had grown to know Syl.

"Hello, Harper Valley!" Syl shouted. A sharp whistle and loud "WOO" made Wil flinch. "It's so good to be back! President Bullworth and I are here for the next week to tour the basin and Faerie. It's going to be such a pleasure to show him around the town that welcomed me and my kind so warmly. Mostly."

There was nervous, scattered laughter. Bullworth released Wil's hand and threw his arm around the much taller faun's waist. "Hey, this is supposed to be my talk. Ahem. We're here on a tour of your fine towns and a trip into our neighboring country of Faerie. I'm pleased to announce a pact of friendship between us and the Woodlands. A friendship I'd love to extend to the others here, in time.

Arabella curtsied, bowing low. Wil rolled his eyes as Bullworth's dropped with all the subtlety of a teenage boy. "It's our pleasure to meet you, Mr. President. I am Princess Arabella. The Fair Folk are open to the idea of friendship. I am also empowered by the Wee Folk to speak on their behalf, as their representative is running the embassy."

"And the Ogre Federation?" Bullworth asked.

Arabella raised up, clearing her throat. She whistled a sharp, haunting tune that made Wil take an instinctive step forward before he caught himself. A few seconds later, Gallath and Bram returned from around the side of the station, looking disheveled.

Gallath took his place next to Arabella and inclined his head respectfully. "General Gallath of the Ogre Federation. I hope that our dealings may be fair, honorable, and prosperous for all."

Bram started back to join Wil and Darlene, but the president called out to him. "Hey there, you're a large lad, aren't you?" Bram froze, looking between the dignitaries and the people watching.

"Oh, yes," Syl chimed in with a wicked grin. "Bram here is not only brilliant and a good friend, but he's also the only human who can go toe-to-toe with an ogre in a wrestling match."

"Is that so?" Bullworth said, looking impressed. "Did you two wrestle? Who won?"

Gallath cleared his throat. "Both of us. Often."

Bram's face turned bright red. He shuffled awkwardly over to Wil and Darlene, as if going slow meant that people would have a tougher time noticing him. It had the opposite effect.

President Bullworth moved down the line, grabbing Bob's hand and shaking it vigorously. Bob shook back just as hard. "And a pleasure to meet you, Mayor Bob. I can't believe all you and your son have done for your town. What's the McKenzie family secret?"

Bob laughed as he took his hand back. "Honesty, hard work and knowing that no man is an island. We all live together, we might as well take care of each other."

"Damn, Bob, give it a few years, and you might have *my* job!" Bullworth guffawed, and people joined him. And quick as a flash, he moved on to the next subject. Wil was impressed at the man's ability to keep things moving. "I didn't come alone. Along with me are some of Calipan's brightest wizards, here to witness this historic discovery!"

From out of the train came a line of grandmasters, almost all of whom Wil recognized from his time at Marlowe Manor. Jim Rance was there, as was Rand Sandoval, Niobe Jameson, and in the rear, Ferrovani walked with the aid of a posh cane. All of them fanned out behind the president, eyes locked directly on Wil.

If anything could make him feel small, unimportant, and under scrutiny, it was people he feared and respected judging his every move. He swallowed hard and nodded respectfully to them. Rance and Sandoval smiled, but Ferrovani scowled at him.

"Chief among them is the legend himself, Enrico Ferrovani, along with his lead apprentice, Master Thomas Elliot, and crew."

Wil's stomach twisted in disgust. He looked down the aisle as Thomas strode up and stood by Ferrovani. He nodded at Wil, who returned it. And then, just to throw Thomas off, Wil smiled at him and waved. Thomas blinked, and half-heartedly returned the wave.

Bullworth cleared his throat and finished up. "Tomorrow will be the big presentation, but for today? Mayor Bob promised me lunch at the finest diner in town. I'll be seeing you!"

He gathered them all to pose for a picture. Wil's eyes darted to Bram, who was left out, and Darlene, who looked to be in a lot of pain. She doubled over, and her breathing grew labored. The light flashed as the picture took. As soon as it was over, Wil dashed to her side.

"Are you—"

"Yes and no," Darlene snapped. "I think it's time."

"It's time?" Wil asked. Then he realized. "It's time!? Are you sure?"

"Pretty sure," Darlene said. "Either that, or I just peed myself a lot. We need to get to the clinic, and fast!"

CHAPTER 56

It's a Girl!

Luckily for them, Doc Hawkins happened to be in the crowd. They picked him up and drove to his clinic, where he put Darlene in a bed, checked her vitals, and declared that she was, indeed, going into labor. And with that discovered, Wil was promptly kicked out and left in the waiting room, while Sharon and Darlene's mother, Angelica, were inside with her.

Wil discovered something, sitting in the lobby for hours: waiting was a special form of torture. At first it was almost a relief, not having to be in the room. It was tradition, after all, for the fathers to wait outside. Early on, it had been a time to socialize as friends and family came in and out of the clinic with their well wishes.

"Does it drive you crazy to have to sit out here and do nothing while your girlfriend does all the hard work?" Sarah asked him during one relatively quiet lull.

"Yes," said Wil. "Although it's worse with you asking that question, so thanks for that."

"Of course," said Sarah. She smirked at him and then looked around the clinic. At the moment they were the only ones there. Bob and the fae were showing Bullworth around town, and Bram had to represent their team while Darlene gave birth and Wil, as his sister so kindly pointed out, sat around being useless.

"Since they're only letting women in, do you want me to go in and draw a picture of the scene for you? Since you're missing out and all." When in doubt, tormenting one's siblings was always a great way to pass the time.

"I could peek in at any time I wanted," said Wil. He grinned wickedly at her and continued, "just like I could ever since I was a teenager. Scrying isn't too hard. I saw you steal money from Dad before I left. What did you spend it on?"

Sarah looked away, her lips pursed. Wil didn't know if she was holding back laughter or embarrassment, but he guessed the former. Either way, it bought him a little bit of peace and quiet. At least until he heard Darlene scream, and he stood straight up, staring at the door to the back.

"There it is," said Sarah. "Must be starting for real. Only took, what, five hours?"

The hairs on the back of Wil's neck stood up. He was tempted to send a spying eye in there to make sure she was okay, but he was told to wait outside for a reason. They didn't need his help, no matter how much he wanted to give it. There wasn't much he could do, medically.

"Sit down, it's going to be a while still. Probably." Sarah motioned with her hand for him to get down. Wil did and sighed.

That first scream wasn't the last, although Wil took some small comfort in knowing it sounded like pain but not fear. It was a very small comfort, and it wore out within minutes. Just as he'd been ready to charge in there and at least hold Darlene's hand, the door to the clinic opened. Inside walked the first and last person Wil wanted to see.

"Um. Hi," said Thomas as he stood in the doorway. "I can . . . I can leave if you'd prefer. I wanted to stop by and pay my respects. And my well wishes."

Silence.

"Well, this is awkward," said Sarah as she stood. "I'm going to let you two have fun. But if you hurt my older brother again, I'll persuade my dad to convince the president to let me break your knees."

"That's reasonable," said Thomas. He stepped out of the way to let her leave and then paused, the question obvious.

"Come in," said Wil. "I needed to talk to you anyway."

Thomas took Sarah's seat. Both were right next to the door leading to the back. Another cry of pain made Thomas twitch. "Wow. It's happening. Are you doing okay?"

Wil chuckled. "I think I'm doing a lot better than Darlene right now. I'm just nervous for her. I hate feeling helpless. You know, like when finding out that promises mean nothing to certain people."

"As much as I deserve that and whatever barbs you can send my way, you're not the type to be petty or cruel." Thomas smiled crookedly and leaned forward, hands clasped between his knees. "What did you need to talk to me about?"

There were a million different ways Wil could've approached it. He considered taking his time, letting a bit of silence simmer while he picked the right words. Instead, he went for the one that meant the most to him. "Were you serious about being sorry and willing to make up for what you did?"

"I was. I am." Thomas undid his bow tie and left it hanging around his neck. "Just so long as that doesn't involve backing down and not claiming credit for my work and the work of the bastards I tied myself to. I'm not throwing that away."

"Believe it or not, I'm not asking you to anymore," Wil chuckled. "You deserve credit for your hard work, and if you help me out, I'll sing your praises louder than I'll complain about your follies."

Thomas smiled. "Well, then I feel like I have to. What would you have me do, Wil?"

Again, he laid the cards directly on the table. "Finish my final project for the presentation. I got about ninety percent done, and then I pushed myself too hard right before I finished. If I'm able to finish, then your weapons will be nothing in comparison."

He whistled sharply. "As an apology, you want me to make it so you win our little pissing match?"

"If you like." Wil laughed. "I'm not concerned with beating you so much as wanting to go all the way. The fact that it will one hundred percent beat your weaponized car is a bonus, though."

A loud, guttural cry of pain rising to a high keen grabbed Wil's heart and crushed it. He stood before he realized it, breathing heavily. He wanted to run in. Maybe he couldn't do anything medically, but he could perhaps take the pain away. A simple deadening illusion and maybe . . .

"We could do this later," Thomas said quietly. "You have a lot on your mind right now, and I can see that it's maybe not the best time."

"No, no," said Wil. He sat back down, his hands gripping his knees so tight they hurt. "We don't have much time, I think. So, you willing to help me, or not? I honestly won't judge you either way. Well, maybe a little."

"What do you need me to do?" Thomas asked. "What is it you're trying to do for your last project?"

"Honestly, it's doing more of what I first showed you how to do," said Wil. "Moving earth around and changing leylines. I handled and changed a few dozen leylines in just two days, and I burnt out a little. There should only be about six or seven left, and once they're changed, it should prove Marlowe's research right."

At first, Thomas just nodded along as he listened. When Wil's words registered, he lit up. "You can't be serious," he said with a laugh of disbelief. "Did you seriously stumble into that too? I can't believe you, McKenzie."

Wil shrugged. "I don't know if it will work, but I want to try. Are you willing to help me out even if it screws you over?"

"Well, I kind of have to, don't I?" Thomas laughed. "A year ago, I would've shrugged it all off and moved on, but there's something about your irritatingly saccharine naivete that makes me want to live up to it. But that's not the number one reason to help."

"It isn't?"

Thomas stood. "It's a close second. The number one reason is that it'll piss off Ferrovani. That's good enough for me." Another pained cry made him wince. "If you don't mind, I'm going to be elsewhere. I hate that sound, and you've got more important things to worry about. When you need me, I'll be there."

And then Wil was alone again, except for the cries, coming faster and faster. Wil white-knuckled his grip on his knees and waited. It went on for another twenty minutes, and right as it became too much to bear, there was one last cry and then a higher pitched squalling. His heart skipped a beat, and he was on his feet.

Sharon pushed through the door, dressed in protective medical gear. "She's here! You've got a daughter!"

Wil let out a wordless cry of excitement and hugged his mother, who squeezed him back. "Can I come in yet?"

"That's why I'm here," said Sharon. She pulled away with a big smile on her face. "Let's get you dressed for it and back there."

He didn't need to get scrubbed up the same as everyone else, but Wil did need to wash his hands and put on an outer coat. When he went through the door, Angelica had her arm around a flushed, sweaty, and exhausted-looking Darlene. Bundled up in a blanket and mostly cleaned off was his daughter. His throat closed.

"I'm not too happy with you right now," said Darlene in a creaky, beat-up voice. "But I think I can forgive you."

Doc Hawkins chuckled. "You've got a healthy, strong daughter, Mr. Wizard. How about we all get out and give you three some privacy?"

Wil was grateful as people filed past him and headed to the waiting room. Each step to Darlene was a thousand miles, toward that adorably wrinkly pink thing in her arms. He sat down in the chair next to the bed numbly, eyes locked on to his daughter.

"I . . . Wow, I . . ." He swallowed hard, tears rising to his eyes. He didn't know how he felt, just that it was a lot. "You were right. It's a girl. I guess that means you get to name her, as per our agreement."

"Yes," said Darlene in tired triumph. "And I've had a name waiting for months. Wilhelmina McKenzie. Mina for short."

Wil's entire face screwed up. "You can't name her that! Everyone's going to think we named her after me."

"Yep," said Darlene with a twinkle in her eyes. "And no one will ever believe you when you say she wasn't. It's a strong name, and I like Mina."

"Fine," said Wil. "I get to name the next one, and I at least won't be cruel to the poor kid."

"Next one?" Darlene said. "Next one, *you* can have." She smiled and then gently raised Mina up. The baby squirmed and gurgled, seemingly just as tired. Wil couldn't imagine much being more exhausting than being born.

Silently, Wil took his daughter and cradled her against his shoulder. She may have been light in his arms, but with her, the weight of the world settled on him once more but with more joy than responsibility usually brought. "She's so little," he said.

"Didn't feel little a few minutes ago," Darlene complained good-naturedly. "I promise, I only halfway mean my jokes. I'm . . . I'm pretty happy," she admitted.

"Me too," said Wil. He gently bounced Mina against his shoulder. Silent laughter racked his body. "Wow, I talked to Thomas, and he agreed to help, but I really don't care too much anymore."

Darlene laughed and weakly reached for a cup of water that she drained in seconds. "I do. We have our daughter, and she's perfect. Now you and he better go out and earn our happy ending."

Wil continued to bounce his daughter, buzzing from inside as the strange euphoria colored the world differently. "Gladly."

CHAPTER 57

Make This Right

Between his newborn daughter and magical exhaustion, Wil collapsed in bed that night and had to force his eyes open the next morning. Six o'clock was a terrible time to be awake if you didn't have to be, but with their presentations starting at noon, Wil and Thomas had to get going as early as possible.

Once he made sure Darlene and Mina would be okay for the day, Wil slipped out and took the car to Gallard Springs. He hated leaving his Thunderhawk behind because it was faster and more fun to ride, but it was as unique as it was fast and would give him away. If he could avoid the attention of Sheriff Boone, all the better. Then there was the other reason, which Bram was already awake and doing.

By the time he got to the cottage Thomas had inherited from the other three, he felt rested. It might've been possible to do the rest of the work himself, but not without ending up just as exhausted as he was before. Besides, it was a good opportunity for the Cloverton wizard to make good on his promise to make things right.

"Do you want coffee first, or should we get moving?" Thomas looked groggy.

"I wouldn't say no to some coffee," said Wil. "But we can't linger more than half an hour. You're not as good at changing leylines as me, so I want to make sure we have enough time to get it right."

Thomas raised an eyebrow. "That didn't feel pointed, but it still felt like you took the opportunity for the diss."

Wil shrugged. "Maybe I'm being honest about the differences in our abilities. If it happened to get in a dig at you, is that something to be avoided?"

His friend and rival chuckled and welcomed him in. As the coffee brewed, Wil filled him in on exactly what he wanted to do, in what order, and what he hoped the effects would be. After two cups of coffee each, Thomas wasn't just ready, but he was flat-out excited for the final experiment. Even if he did linger on what it would mean for his presentation.

"I'm happy to do all of this," said Thomas, "but I won't say I'm not a little tempted to hold off and hog the spotlight for once in my life. I'm not going to do that, but if helping you is doing the right thing, it's not easy."

"Yep. Which is why I appreciate you at least making an effort. If we happen to fail because your ability to rearrange the earth isn't good enough, I won't hold it against you." Wil smiled and finished the last mouthful of his coffee.

They hit the road a couple minutes later and went straight east, where Wil had paused when Sheriff Boone chased him off. As he got to the area where the earth was disturbed, some of it had been cleaned up. His blood ran cold as he wondered about the rest of the leylines. It had only been a couple of days, and his father swore he'd do his best to run interference, but what if they had undone more of his work?

"You okay?" Thomas asked as they pulled to a stop.

"Yeah," Wil lied. "I was thinking about possible complications. We're fine. Probably."

"Uh-huh," said Thomas, eyeing him. "If you say so. This is where you and your awful cat ran away?"

"It sure is," said Wil. He pointed at the tall rock he'd been sitting on. "I think that's a safe place to work while you rearrange stuff."

Thomas nodded, and they both got out. They climbed the rock, and Wil sat on the edge while the other man worked. It took a lot longer for Thomas to grab hold of things, and even longer to change them. They had half a dozen leylines to go through, and this one took Thomas a good fifteen minutes to contort the river of power southward on one end, and another ten to connect it to the one flowing from the north.

"How many times did you do this when you were setting up?" Thomas asked after he finished. He collapsed to the rock, covered in sweat and panting.

"I lost count after thirty," said Wil. "I'm good at this, though. It's easier for me. According to the map, we only have another six to do if you think you can. If not, I won't hold it against you."

"Screw that," said Thomas. "I owe you a debt, and I intend on paying it. I need a drink, and then I'm good to go."

As Wil expected, having Thomas along helped deflect a lot of questions. Just as he was well known in Harper Valley, the last couple of weeks of displaying their experiments had elevated Thomas and the others to a semi-favored status. It made things more exciting, and, Thomas added, Ferrovani had provided plenty of bribe money to oil any squeaky wheels. It seemed only fitting to use the old man's resources against him.

The next two leylines went as smoothly as they could, all things considered. It took a lot out of Thomas each time, and the timing ended up being roughly forty-five minutes for each leyline, plus travel time and rest, bringing it up to about an hour for each. This was going to be close.

Trouble came when they reached the southeastern corner of the basin, where the fourth and final anchor rune of their massive array was to be placed. The best place for it, with the biggest and most vibrant leyline, was in the heart of Gallard Springs' biggest hot spring.

"Let me do the talking," Thomas said as they came in.

"Gladly," Wil muttered, suddenly wishing he'd brought Isom with him, even knowing he'd be recognized immediately with the wampus cat's ugly mug with him.

When Wil was young, he expected summer to be the least likely time for the hot springs to be busy, but that wasn't the case. People came from hundreds of miles away to bathe in the rejuvenating mineral water naturally heated from below or in one of the surrounding cool, crystalline pools. On a sweltering summer day or frigid winter night, there was always someone at the hot springs.

Thomas led them through. An hour before noon, there were several dozen people there, though it was a far cry from the hundreds that visited daily. To Wil's relief, no one paid them much attention as they went to the office to the side of where the springs began. Thomas knocked, then entered anyway.

"Sorry to bother you," said Thomas to the middle-aged woman sitting behind a desk, "but it's time. We're going to go ahead and close down the springs in light of the president's visit."

Wait, what?

The woman blanched. "That was you on the phone, then. Are you sure there's no other way? We can offer the president one of the more exclusive springs for his use. Wouldn't that be enough?"

Thomas shook his head sadly. "I'm afraid President Bullworth was very clear on his needs. Within the next month, you'll be compensated for your day of lost profits."

"I guess there's nothing to be done about it," she said with a sigh. "How long do we have?"

"If you let me take care of it, it'll be done in fifteen minutes. If you're willing to send a few runners to check and make sure no one's coming by. We have to do one last security check before the president's arrival."

The woman, Norma, the sign at her desk proclaimed, stood. "You got it. Might as well do it as soon as possible. You'd think they'd give us more advance warning, but nooo . . ." She continued to grumble as she pushed past Thomas and Wil and went out.

"What was that?" Wil asked incredulously.

"Clearing the way without causing a panic or getting shot at," said Thomas. "This is going to be hard enough without permanently damaging the hot springs. If we're even able to do so."

"It's smart," said Wil. "When did you set this up?"

"Yesterday after leaving the clinic. You told me what our big target was, and I figured you'd probably just try to wing it instead of, you know, *thinking things through*."

"Yeah, well . . ." Wil came up blank.

Twenty minutes later, the springs were mostly cleared. There was no getting rid of the manager or her employees, but they didn't need to. They had a bit of time to work with, which left only one remaining task.

"I'm not sure I know where to begin," Thomas admitted as they stood in the center of the springs, seeing through their wizardsenses. The leyline was one of the biggest in the basin and already coiled in a spiral. Wil thought that would make it easier, but Thomas didn't have his experience.

"Try feeling for the edges of the leyline and work the earth from there," said Wil. "It's not a one-to-one translation, so you have to be ready to listen to the earth and feel the changes as they're forming. Do that, and it will come pretty easy."

Thomas shot him a withering look. "Do you have any advice that works for those who had to actually try in school?"

Eventually, the elder wizard went for it. At first nothing happened, but then the water in one of the pools bubbled and shot into the air. Thomas exhaled and nearly collapsed before Wil caught him.

"I don't know if this one's going to be possible," said Thomas with a grimace. "I'm sorry, I want to help, but this is . . . Wow."

Wil shook his head vehemently and reached for the leyline. It felt like pouring hot water on a fresh burn, but he could handle it for a little while. He felt where Thomas tried to push rock and stone up and out. Actually doing it himself would be beyond him, but maybe . . .

"Do you trust me?" Wil asked. When Thomas nodded, he then said, "Then look me in the eyes and don't fight me."

His friend, rival, enemy, savior, whatever Thomas was, did as he said. Wil let himself fall forward halfway but didn't go inside Thomas's mind. He stayed there, as a bridge, and did something difficult, even for him. He shared his senses to a partially closed connection and took some from Thomas.

Through his eyes and otherworldly sense, Wil felt how Thomas perceived the leyline and the rock and stone beneath it. Immutable, heavy objects that were anchors for magic and life. Even after all this time, he still had trouble seeing them as changeable. Wil shared his impression of every spec of dirt and rock, the water carrying rich minerals and heat, and how it shaped this little corner of the world.

"Try changing it now," said Wil. "Slowly."

Thomas reached out, and through feelings and flashes of thought, Wil guided his hand. He couldn't lend his raw strength, whatever was left of that, but he could share his intuition and senses. It took a few minutes of prodding around and following the rush of water underground, but then they found a weak spot, and Thomas pushed with all his strength.

Rocks cracked, loud enough to feel like the world was being torn asunder. All around them, in the four main pools in an upward spiral leading up to this rocky overlook, cracks grew and spread. Water erupted skyward in blasts of steam and pressure. And little by little, the leyline changed.

As the hot springs warped and shifted into something new, Wil and Thomas worked together to shape the leyline into something old and familiar. One final rune in their array, to bring the others together. Something they knew would work, and hopefully unite the rest. In the other corners, Wil had set the runes for *awaken*, *unite*, *embrace*, and now Thomas set the final one: *feed*.

Thomas did collapse at the end, and Wil joined him for a casual sit on the ground. Both were pouring sweat from the effort and the already relentless sun. "There's no way you did three of these and the rest of the filler in just two days," Thomas protested.

"I'm going to earn that victory," Wil said, wishing they had a couple of cold drinks with them.

"If it works," said Thomas. "Which, I hope it will. If not, I'm content stealing your thunder and letting you share partial credit for my weapons and War Chariot."

"Very magnanimous of you," said Wil. He was about to give Thomas some good-natured crap back, when he pointed off in the distance.

Sometime during their efforts, Norma and the others had run off. Wil could hardly blame them for it, with all the earth-rupturing noise and spewing water. But she had returned with, who else, Sheriff Boone. And even though Wil hadn't done direct work, he was too tired to run or fight.

"Let me handle this too," said Thomas. "I'm not sure we'll have time to finish the other three leylines. Not when my part of the presentation is in an hour. Do you think you could finish the other three?"

Wil grimaced. "If I do, I'm not going to be happy, but Bram's already going to cover the last-minute things at the house. What if, instead . . ."

He explained his plan to Thomas, who laughed and nodded. "You and your melodrama," he said. "I'm up for it. Let's do this."

Master Stevenson

Even though Bram completed his part of the plan flawlessly, if he did say so himself, he wanted to scream until all the stress left his body. So much of the day hinged on him not only doing his part mechanically, but also hosting things. If there was one thing that meeting all the grandmasters from Cloverton taught Bram, it was that he didn't like being scrutinized.

"And you say you have no magical abilities at all?" Rand Sandoval asked Bram for the second time. The excitable grandmaster had latched on to Bram from their first meeting. "Not even latent?"

Bram and the other representatives were in the northeast corner of Gallard Springs, where Thomas and the others had demonstrated their projects to the town. Now, they waited on the two master wizards to make an appearance for their presentations. There were drinks and snacks everywhere, but the grandmasters hovered around Bram, the only representative from both groups.

"Uh, no, sorry," said Bram. His face heated up, but he'd been steadily flushed and ready to puke for about an hour at that point. "Pure mundane human. I just read a lot, and I like to think of the what-ifs, you know?"

Rand's eyes lit up. "'What-if' is the best question of all!"

"Disagree," said Ferrovani, swirling his glass of wine. The silver-haired Ramenian had kept suspicious eyes on Bram for the entire time he waited with the grandmasters. "'How' is the best question. Like 'How does a simple farm boy think he knows what he's talking about?'" He threw his head back and laughed. Some of the other grandmasters laughed with him.

"Oh, knock it off," Rand said, though he didn't lose any of his good cheer. "We've got to welcome and encourage any bright minds we find, regardless of where they come from. And even then, Harper Valley's given us two shining stars in a short period of time. Tell us again about the Time-Stretcher."

Bram opened his mouth to speak, when he saw Gallath following the president. All rational thought left him. Their brief conversation the day before had been . . . Well, it was nice to have hope, even if it was distracting to see his boyfriend mingling with others. It wasn't fair that they had to deal with all of this instead of disappearing and—

"... and I think that time distortion is something dangerous, but potentially useful. You said the fae taught you?" Rand kept on.

Bram blinked and brought himself back to the moment. "Y-yeah, the fae taught us how they more efficiently twist time. It's not something I'd do lightly, though, and making it go by faster is a *lot* harder than slowing it down. I'm not quite sure why, but I have some theories."

"I suppose theories and a pair of hands to get work done means you'll always be a little useful." Ferrovani sipped his wine. "My apprentice has talked about your handiness. He said you made things much easier for *his* discovery."

A grumble went through the assembled grandmasters. Jim Rance groaned and said, "Give it a rest, Enrico. No one's going to buy that Thomas Elliot masterminded this discovery. He's good, but he's not that good."

"And you think the McKenzie boy and his nu— normal friend are?" Ferrovani barked out laughter.

Throughout the years, Bram had flip-flopped his anger. As a child, it had consumed him and led him to getting into all sorts of fights and problems he hadn't been equipped to deal with. As an adult, he went the opposite direction, afraid of a lot of people and situations, but reverting to how he'd been when he most hated himself.

Sometimes, the anger was welcome.

"Kind of questioning your status as a grandmaster," said Bram with his best scowl. "Thomas and the others only kept up by taking our work. On your orders, if I recall. I really wouldn't be bragging or trying to make others look bad when you have that little faith in your apprentice."

Rand smiled, but Jim laughed at the way Ferrovani smoldered. "You disrespectful, impertinent..."

"Null?" Bram supplied. "Watch it. Here in Harper Valley, we ain't shy about finishing fights others start. And you started when you had my house blown up." The old man's eyes flickered down to Bram's clenched fists. Each one was about the size of Ferrovani's skull.

The president came up with the fae delegation close behind. Gallath winked solemnly at Bram, but Syl waved enthusiastically. "Where are Masters Elliot and McKenzie?" the president demanded. "It's enough that I'm clinging to my legs, if you know what I mean."

Ferrovani turned away from Bram and bowed. "My deepest apologies, Mr. President. I know my apprentice has better manners than this. Do you think, perhaps, Master McKenzie has done something to him?"

"Wil would never," Bram started, right as others spoke up as well.

".... never happen," Syl said firmly, shaking his head.

"Preposterous."

President Bullworth looked around before snorting and saying, "All I know is that if we don't have a show or presentation of some kind in the next ten minutes, I'm going to cancel this entire thing and everyone's going to be facing trouble."

"That won't be necessary, Mr. President," Thomas said as he ran up. He panted for breath and looked wiped and sweaty already, so Bram chose to have hope.

"Where's McKenzie?" The president asked.

Thomas waved the question off. "He's going to catch up with us in Harper Valley for your demonstration. We greatly appreciate your patience and willingness to indulge in our showmanship, sir."

That soothed Bullworth well enough. He laughed and shrugged with faux modesty. "Any good politician knows the value of showmanship. Besides, you two have led me to believe that no matter what, I'm going to come out of this looking better than ever."

Bram knew Thomas well enough at that point to recognize when he held back his glee and kept it to a gentle smile. "Sir, after today your administration will be looked at as the greatest since we first broke away from Albetosia. And after today, you'll never need to fear a southern incursion from Ilianto again."

"Tall promises, but I love them! Let's get a move on then, shall we? How soon until you can present?" Bullworth motioned, and an aide produced a drink for him.

"Ten minutes, sir," said Thomas. "Just have to do one last look through what we've got, to be sure. Would you care to help me out, Master Stevenson?"

Bram's heart skipped a beat, and he wasn't the only one to notice the honorific. "Master?"

"Master?" Ferrovani echoed in disgust.

Thomas looked around the group of high-end wizards and smiled. "Yes, Master. He might not be able to do magic himself, but he's kept up and exceeded what Master McKenzie and I have been able to come up with. As far as I'm concerned, he's worthy of the title."

"It isn't for you to decide," Ferrovani scoffed.

"It was a pleasure speaking with you, Master Stevenson," Rand Sandoval said. He looked perfectly content with the title, if not extra pleased by the sour expression on his colleague's face.

"We look forward to your presentation, Master Stevenson," Jim Rance said.

Bram promised himself he wasn't going to cry. At least, not while everyone watched. He nodded, swallowing the spiky lump in his throat and joining Thomas. The anger wasn't completely gone. It would be there until he had a replacement house, but appreciation outshone it. "Thank you," he whispered. "And sorry for punching you. Mostly."

Thomas nodded respectfully to all involved and led them up to the house where they'd stored their inventions. "I could explain to you how these work, but it'd be faster for you to just take a look."

He did so, and even though he hated that all this work existed only because of terrible circumstances, Bram found himself ecstatic at getting to fiddle with

Thomas's work and see where he took their research. Ten minutes quickly passed by, and then another ten as they set up. The president was almost out of patience when they were finally ready.

The presentation started with a brief lesson on leylines and what they knew about them. It passed by in a blink as Bram worked in the background to help someone who had screwed them over, but it looked like bygones were well and truly gone. They went through a handful of Thomas and company's inventions, though McGinnis and the others weren't mentioned once.

The crowd loved the cannons, except for the fae, who weren't fond of human weapons in general. When the target at the far end became encased in ice that then shattered, someone screamed in delight. The next shot went up against one of Thomas's other inventions, the shield projector, and did no damage. Neither did the next two shots there. It was less flashy, but still received a healthy amount of applause.

The earthen rod was Bram's favorite of their inventions, and that could've been because it was something anyone could use, not just the military. He'd been proud to demonstrate the way it made the land part through its high-frequency vibrations, though as it worked, several dogs howled in the distance.

Thomas drove the War Chariot around. From the outside, it was an ugly mishmash of a car, but it was covered in weapons both magical and mundane, and well defended. Bram itched to take it apart and figure out how Thomas had layered the enchantments, but that could come later.

All in all, they spent about twenty minutes on the four big inventions. There were others, but the summer sun suffocated them all, evaporating enthusiasm by the second. Thomas had to drain a bottle of water before finishing up.

"Thank you so much for your attention. This is a handful of stuff I and a small team worked on over the past few months. None of this would be possible without the aid of Masters Stevenson and McKenzie nor our quartermaster, Darlene Johnson. All this pales in comparison to the next presentation, now headed up by my friend Master Stevenson here."

All eyes turned to Bram, and his will turned to jelly. He swallowed and smiled awkwardly, raising a hand. It had been so much easier when he was just the assistant, even if the only change was in his head. "H-hello! I hate to be a bother but . . ."

Ferrovani shook his head in disgust. Irritation strengthened Bram's resolve. "I'm going to need everyone to accompany me. Master Elliot was correct in keeping these experiments in a specific place for safety and responsibility. Wiseman Enchantment and Brewing has already been providing our new technology to the masses! And it's there that we'll demonstrate everything."

Silence met him, minus a few whispers and grumbles. Syl broke it by clapping enthusiastically and whistling sharp enough to hurt. Arabella and Gallath joined in with just as much fervor, and that broke the spell around the group. Bram jerked his thumb in the direction of Harper Valley.

"So let's get a move on, and I'll show you the next revolution in Calipan!"

Still no Wil, but they knew there was a chance he wouldn't show until late. That didn't matter. Everything would work without him. With Darlene down for the next few weeks, it was Bram's time to save the day. If his calculations were correct, and if he could keep the attention of a bunch of wizards with mixed feelings about him.

"Our first stop," said Bram, "is the best diner in the basin, now powered entirely by magic!"

Whispers started up again. Thomas flashed Bram a thumbs-up, and together they climbed down the hill to where their cars waited.

CHAPTER 58

Land of the Leylines

For a while during the last three months, Wil had wondered if he had some special immunity or resistance to leyline burnout. As much as he worked with them day to day, it seemed a rational question. Well, after reaching his limits and crossing them twice in a week, he believed that while he may have been resistant, he was very much not immune.

As the second to last leyline fused with the one before it, Wil felt a flash of heat. The next thing he knew, his extended senses crashed back into him with all the force of a runaway train. He woke up a few minutes or hours later with the weight of the world crushing him.

"Well, damn," Wil groaned. He forced himself up on rubbery legs. For a second, he was tempted to reach out to the leyline and double-check his work. The thought of it caused a stabbing pain to shoot through his skull, so he threw the idea out as soon as he had it.

He was tired, shaky, and worst of all, unfinished with his job. He and Thomas had already accounted for that as a possibility, and it wouldn't ruin everything. Not on its own. Wil made his way to the car and guzzled the last of the water he'd brought. He took a few minutes, then started the car up, grateful to the faricite batteries for keeping the strain off him.

The drive home gave Wil many things to think about. The presentation succeeding was high on his list, but it paled in comparison to the twin thoughts of getting a nap and holding his daughter again. The exhaustion blurred out the rest of the world until only the most important things remained. He still had a ways to go, but soon it would be time to rest and enjoy the fruits of his labors.

He supposed he shouldn't have been surprised to find that the president and his entourage were already at his house when he arrived. Including his friends from Faerie, there were about twenty people there to inspect their work and lend their expertise, and they listened attentively as Bram explained something in the front of the house. Their most polished Time-Stretcher lay open and waiting for a volunteer.

Wil got out of the car and trudged over to Bram's side. As soon as he came up, all eyes shifted to him, but he ignored them and motioned for Bram to keep speaking. Thomas caught his eye, and Wil held up one finger and pointed toward where he came from. The Cloverton wizard nodded and discreetly slipped away to the car.

". . . and as you can see, we have applied more of our rechargeable faricite batteries to this one so it can be used anywhere regardless of how many leylines are or aren't around. Once we have our test patient and medical technician inside the box, we close it up and it completes the runic circuit, arresting time inside. No more will people die on their way to receiving critical treatment."

Despite his usual nervousness, Bram spoke loud and clear, with an energy Wil usually only saw after a few drinks. The fact that he was a full head taller than the next tallest person there lent him some added authority and presence, but more than anything, he knew their products well and had a passion for them Wil could never match.

"How do we know it works?" Bullworth called out over the smattering of applause. "That time reversal or slowdown or whatever, it sounds great. How do we know it's safe?"

Wil cleared his throat. "We've tested it on me. What felt like forty-five seconds to me was almost an hour on the outside. If we've got any brave volunteers who don't mind missing out the rest of the presentation, we can send them in with a pocket watch and compare times. Grandmaster Ferrovani, might we have your help?"

The surly old man scoffed.

Syl raised his hand. "I'd be glad to volunteer! I've got full confidence in my dear friend Master McKenzie. Even if it somehow goes wrong, I'll probably be fine and not explode or anything."

"As always, thanks for the backup, Syl," said Wil. He motioned to the Time-Stretcher. "Get inside and watch your head."

The faun climbed in carefully, ducking in a box that should've been too small to hold him. Bob pulled out his pocket watch and held it up. "It says two twelve," he announced before dangling it down for Syl to take.

Syl waved one last time before Wil closed the box and locked it, activating the enchantment. It would only have about an hour and fifteen minutes of time to it unless Wil was right. He motioned for Bram to continue, but Bram waved at him. Now that he was here, it was his turn.

Wil looked out over all the people now intently watching him, talking among themselves. Several of the grandmaster's aides had journals out, furiously scribbling notes the entire day. Now that it was his turn to talk, his throat dried up and the need for a nap flared.

"Well, Syl's going to be in there for an hour, and I'm sure everyone's had a very long day so far. I love Harper Valley, but the summers here are rough, right?" He chuckled, but he was one of the only people to do so. His father gave him a supportive nod. "So why don't we take a moment to adjourn for drinks before we show our grand finale?"

Bullworth didn't look happy, but he masked it with a casual laugh. "Well, why not? We've got some good stuff coming in. It's a shame you weren't there for most of it, Wilbur. Did you have something more pressing?"

Oh gods. Wil smiled and nodded. "I did! My side of the presentation required a little more time and work, and it's almost ready. I just need a quick drink."

The president waved him off, and Wil disappeared into his house, Bram hot on his heels.

"What happened? Are we not ready?" Bram asked.

"Thomas is taking care of it now," Wil said. From the kitchen he grabbed a pitcher of lemonade and a glittering blue potion. Grimacing, he pulled the stopper of the potion out and guzzled it. Then he drank straight from the pitcher, guzzling lemonade to get the foul taste of his pick-me-up out.

It worked almost immediately, cooling some of the edges of the perpetual burn. He still wouldn't trust himself handling leylines directly for at least another week to be safe, but this would let Wil work some easier spells without feeling like he wanted to collapse.

"Classy," said Bram. "What if I wanted some lemonade too?"

Wil put it away. "If you're this high-strung, get yourself a beer. We're almost out of this, I promise. And it's going to be grand. How did the presentation go so far?"

Bram blew a breath out. "Hard to say. Thomas's side of things looked great. He has consistency we don't, and direct appeal. I think the president and others were irritated that we had to go to so many places to demonstrate what we've made."

"They can thank Ferrovani and his cronies for that," Wil grumbled. "It'll all be worth it. We're buying Thomas some time to finish up. You going to be alright for your part? I know you don't like heights. Or moving fast. Or—"

"I get it," said Bram. "I'll be fine. I don't even have to do anything exciting, just show that it works. I've got this. And . . ." He squirmed a little. "Thomas called me Master Stevenson, and then some of the grandmasters did too!"

"They did?" Wil lit up, and more of the lingering fatigue vanished. He clapped his hands on Bram's arms. "You deserve it and more. I'm feeling better, and it shouldn't take Thomas too long to get there. Shall we, Master Stevenson?"

"After you, Master McKenzie."

Once more Wil was grateful for Darlene and her foresight. Even in the last days of her pregnancy and with plans changing every five minutes, she managed to organize things for the day of the presentation. She and Sharon together had made sure there was water and lemonade, but also places to sit outside the house. No one was happy about having to wait, but it was more pleasant than it could've been.

Wil went up to the president, pausing for the bodyguards to give him a once-over. "If I may be so bold, Mr. President . . ."

Bullworth laughed and motioned for him to continue. "Be bold, by all means. You've caught me in a good mood."

"And it's only going to get better," said Wil. "But I have had a very long day, and there's a chance this final thing won't work. Have we given enough to get me out of trouble?"

"Oh, yeah, of course," said Bullworth with a wave of his hand. "I see no reason to keep harassing you after this. Wouldn't have had to if you'd cooperated in the first place."

It was long past worth being angry, but Wil still felt the momentary urge to give the bodyguards a reason to vaporize him. "I would've cooperated if I hadn't been threatened. But who wants to try to find the start of a circle, right? The important thing is that we're all happy with my progress."

"You've given us a lot to work with, Master McKenzie," said Jim Rance. He stepped away from the group of wizards he'd been chatting with and inserted himself between Wil and the president. "Happy is an understatement. You're going to be a very rich man."

Wil shrugged. "That's nice, but I'll be happier if people leave me to my own devices and give me the benefit of the doubt in my actions."

Rance laughed. "Fat chance. The rest of your life, you'll be under surveillance and pressure. Welcome to the club; there's no getting out of it."

"Great," said Wil. And then a second later, he meant it as a great plume of black smoke wafted into the sky. It meant Thomas was in place.

Magic was a bit harder now, but Wil made his voice carry for a quarter mile. "Attention, everyone! Our presentation will now be concluded. If you'll follow me . . ."

Wil led them around to the back of the house where his backyard had been torn up beyond belief. A strange, boxy shape had been carved around the edges with a faricite battery in each of the four corners. He ushered people around the area but kept them out of the box.

"Our final discovery is something people have been after for a century. First of all, will all wizards feel for the leyline here?" Wil waited patiently as they humored him.

"There's nothing here, McKenzie," Rand Sandoval called up. "Unless you've learned to hide them!" He got a couple polite laughs, but it was just as Wil planned.

"Exactly right! There are no leylines here in the center of the Le Guin Basin, but there are a ridiculous number along the edges. Not only did I learn how to change leylines, but I also learned to fuse them and bend them to my will. And now you will see the culmination of not only my research, but that of Master Morgan Marlowe's!"

Wil gathered his power and sent up a cloud of black as well. He hurried it into the air. Even after he saw it, Thomas would have to quickly move earth and finish things up.

"What are you talking about?" Ferrovani shouted. "Marlowe was a crackpot."

"Maybe, but he was also brilliant. When I stayed at Marlowe Manor as a guest of the president, I noticed something." His heart pounded with excitement. A traitorous part of him whispered that it would be funny if he failed and embarrassed himself in front of everyone, but he refused.

"The property was ringed by not just a cluster of leylines, but a cluster connected to one large ring, stabilizing the power and directing it. Before today, Marlowe Manor was the single most valuable place to study magic in the world. After today, Harper Valley will be the magical capital of Calipan."

Silence, then more derisive laughter from Ferrovani. "This place has a lot of leylines, McKenzie. I'll give you that. But what does that have to do with anything? What did you do?"

Wil couldn't have timed it more perfectly if he'd tried. The four faricite batteries in the corners came to life with a glow. He stepped into the center of his backyard and pushed himself. Not a lot, only enough to carve the final rune into the center of the basin. In the corners were *awaken, unite, embrace,* and *feed,* and now in the very center was the key to them all: *vision.*

The faricite batteries glowed even brighter until they were hard to look directly at. The earth rumbled, and the box carved into the ground warped. Some places were raised, others dipped and filled with water. Grass and little bushes grew rapidly. Faster and faster it all came together until in Wil's backyard: a map of the basin.

"I linked the entire Le Guin Basin into an array, providing power for everything inside its borders," Wil said, spreading his arms. "As of now, *all* our gadgets will work in Harper Valley without needing to be tied to a specific leyline. Which includes . . . Bram, you want to take it away?"

A muffled cry of terror answered him. A second later, Bram flew around the side of the house on the Thunderhawk, newly adjusted to work on leyline power. He shook in the air, swaying from side to side about eight feet off the ground. The nearest people ducked away from him.

"That right there is a man with all brains and no magic, flying a device I made for wizards! As of today, the gap between those with magic and those without shrinks to mere inches. We are now the first place in the world with this power, and I intend on making sure everyone, no matter how big or small, has access to it."

There was so much more to say, but Wil's words failed him. The looks on everyone's faces as they tracked Bram in the sky or looked at the thirty-by-twenty-foot topographical map of Harper Valley said that he had them. So all he had to do was wrap it up.

"This is only the beginning," said Wil. "But together with the help of Quartermaster Darlene Johnson, Master Bram Stevenson, and Master Thomas Elliot, we're ready to lead Calipan to a better future."

He caught President Bullworth's eye. The man nodded thoughtfully, then brought his hands together. Others joined him, soon whistling and screaming as their excitement caught up. "A better future," he echoed.

CHAPTER 59

Victory Lap

As soon as Wil had a chance to escape the handshakes, accolades, and celebrations, he checked on his map of Harper Valley to discover two things. The first was that if the map was correct, one of the runes in the array wasn't working. The second was that no one else noticed. The northeast corner rune of *embrace* was inactive, but the combination of *feed* and *unite* linked together worked as they'd suggested.

Rather than brilliant, Wil felt incredibly lucky. In the winter, it felt like everything that could go wrong did, but spring into summer had been smooth sailing. Minus Bram's house being blown up, the worst they'd faced were tiny hiccups and inconveniences. Maybe it had less to do with how hard they had it and more to do with the good company and doing something they cared about.

A season's labor later, and everything changed. Wil was a father, an inventor, a pillar of his community, and a friend to a good group of people. Harper Valley was not only no longer in danger, but it was poised to be the most important place in the country. Calipan and Faerie were friends now, with a treaty in place and good relations between the president and the fae leadership.

And Wil was no longer in trouble and didn't have anything waiting for him other than friends and family. After the most intense year of his life, it was time to enjoy himself and relax. Bob and Sharon were already way ahead of him on that mark.

There had been no guarantee that Wil's big project would work, but Bob was a betting man, and Sharon good at organizing. After the presentation was over, everyone went to the fairgrounds, which had been set up for celebration. It wasn't the same sprawling event it was during festivals, but it had food, drink, and music along with some of their prototypes tweaked for the event.

Smaller, imperfect versions of the Freeze-it were scattered around. Now with the entire valley powered, it was nothing for people to generate ice for their drinks, or for some of the fae to blow frost around and cool the hot day off.

Half the town showed up, many invited personally. The top shop owners and innkeepers, cooks and farmers alike were invited to come take a look at their inventions, now usable without having to destroy the land around them. Clean power would keep people warm in the winter. It would help farmers preserve their crops without spoiling. There'd be less need to burn coal and wood, and their waste would be more easily disposed of. New levels of security and protection, the likes of which the world had never seen, would keep homes safe and protected from the worst of the elements.

Wil let himself be directed around the fairgrounds. Faces both foreign and familiar came in and out of his focus.

"I knew you were going places," said Jonjon, vigorously pumping his hand. "Everyone said you were a risky gamble, but I was behind you the entire time!"

Mack didn't bother shaking Wil's hand. He pulled him into a hug full of back-slaps and a couple of sharp squeezes. "Like I said, you eat free forever, Mr. Wizard. Don't forget us just because you're famous."

Again and again, they came until Wil faced the last person in town he wanted to see. Mr. Carrey seized his hand in a vicelike grip. "I guess if you're gonna make a new kind of omelet, you end up breaking some eggs. And houses. But now you'll definitely have enough to pay me back, I think."

A low, blistering snarl made the old man let Wil's hand go and take a step back. Isom came up beside Wil and rubbed his head against his hand. "I know what you're thinking, old man," he purred. "You should try it."

Mr. Carrey looked between them, wetting his lips nervously. He nodded and shuffled off. Now that Wil had the wampus cat at his side, they gave him a little more breathing room.

"Thank you," said Wil. "You shouldn't scare old men. Even crotchety bastards like Mr. Carrey. Also, didn't I tell you to stay home?"

Isom thrust himself against Wil's leg until he got scratches behind the ears. "You did. All of Harper Valley is my home now, is it not? Wouldn't you define that as home? Besides, you need me. Three of the wizards want to kill you."

Wil sighed. "Only three? Is one of them Ferrovani?"

Isom growled in the positive. "And even more want to hurt the beefy one. His skill embarrasses them."

Bram was in a group with Rance and Sandoval and a couple of their people. Sandoval looked pleased to speak to him, but Niobe Jameson wasn't amused. Wil got closer to listen in as his friend spoke about their discovery.

"As far as I know, Marlowe Manor is in a circle, right? But Harper Valley, well, the whole basin, it isn't a perfect shape. But I figured it didn't need to be because the lines at that scale are probably close enough. I figured a simple array would work if we could successfully connect the leylines into one smooth loop, perpetually repeating it."

Bram paused, clearly proud of himself. He took off his glasses and cleaned them with a handkerchief. "The trick was finding a series of runes you could fit in as corners that could be drawn in one smooth motion, to help stimulate the direction of the leyline."

"Son of a bitch," Rand Sandoval whispered. "Are you serious? You applied Zoola's Principle to the leylines themselves? How did you figure that out?"

"A lot of luck," said Wil, stepping forward. With Isom at his side, people got out of the way. He clapped Bram's shoulder. "Writing those runes into the earth did not happen in one direction or with specific timing, but Bram had an idea."

"Yeah!" His friend lit up. "Ink magic. Where every stroke and movement matter in powering the runes that way. Wil always describes them as rivers of power, so I thought that maybe they would follow the metaphysical weight and direction of the runes the same way. So, honestly, just lucky that guess was right!"

Jim Rance raised his drink. "Real humbling to learn something from someone doing this for only a year. What are your plans for the future, Master Stevenson?"

Every time someone used Bram's unofficial title, he squirmed. "I am not entirely sure yet. The most important thing right now is rebuilding my home, which was lost in an unfortunate accident involving Ferrovani's minions blowing it up."

"Ahh." Rance nodded with understanding. "That sounds like Enrico. Before we leave, I'm going to set up a meeting, us and your company. See how we might help each other as you find your place in the sun."

The betrayer is being punished. Isom stared off into the distance.

"Hey," said Wil, tugging on Bram's arm. "Let's go check in on Thomas."

"Ahh," Sandoval said knowingly. "He's upset about being upstaged."

"Something like that."

They made their way around the edge of the crowd, creeping closer to Thomas. They arrived at a bad time.

"How can you stand there and be unaffected by this humiliation? Do you have any idea what you've done to me?"

Bram started forward, but Wil held him back. Thomas saw them over Ferrovani's shoulder and shook his head, smiling. "It's funny, I'm fine with everything, but this is somehow embarrassing to you. You truly have a gift."

Ferrovani jabbed a finger in Thomas's face and shook it. "You represented all my years of teaching and innovating, and you pissed it all away. Why did you help him?"

"Because he's my friend, obviously," said Thomas. His smile grew. "And because it was the right thing to do. But mostly? Because I knew it would hurt you. I've got all the credit I want or need, and I'll be rich beyond my wildest dreams. And if anyone remembers anything about you today, it'll be you throwing a temper tantrum every ten minutes. Poor old Ferrovani needs a diaper change."

The old man raised his cane. Before Wil could do anything, Bram reached over and ripped it out of his hands. It was an elegant, expensive, enchanted thing with jewels embedded in the wood. Ferrovani whirled around, head full of steam. He stopped when he saw the giant's grim rictus of a smile.

"You going to apologize for destroying my house?" asked Bram. When Ferrovani said nothing, he nodded and snapped the cane in half over his knee. The pieces fell to the ground.

Ferrovani took a step back, clutching his chest. "You . . . you . . . you all saw that! This big bastard attacked me!"

The president stepped forward with his bodyguards. "Oh hush, Enrico. You're lucky that boy didn't break it over your head. If you make a scene here, you'll be removed. Master McKenzie, may I borrow you for a second?"

Wil nodded and turned to Isom. "Go to the clinic and tell Darlene we'll be coming by soon, and then guard her and Mina. Understand?"

The wampus cat ran off without a word.

Bullworth brought him over to the bandstand, where a mixed human and fae group was between sets. As always, his bodyguards flanked them and kept an eye out.

"How can I help you, Mr. President?" Wil asked.

Bullworth set his beer down on the stage. "I've got a bit of advice for you, and a request. The advice is to know your worth, and how to leverage it."

"I'm starting to understand that one, I think," said Wil, thinking of the rules he'd broken that had been forgiven due to the results. Perhaps not the best lesson to learn, but that was how the world worked.

"No," Bullworth chuckled. "Not even a little bit. You've just made yourself one of the most valuable people in the country. People will improve on what you've done, but you'll get a piece of all of it. You need to understand that you're not a simple country wizard. Did you know that Rance is suggesting you be made into a grandmaster for this?"

"That's . . . Wow." Wil took a deep breath. "Okay, your meaning is setting in. I'll think about your advice. What about your request, sir?"

Bullworth grinned. "I want you to work for me. For the military, specifically. With this advancement, we have a chance to turn the war on the southern front. We can finally establish our claim and drive Ilianto away and—"

"I'm sorry, sir, but the answer's no," said Wil. "I have no interest in military work."

The president sighed. "You really going to say no to me again after your time stuck in Marlowe Manor? Did you learn nothing, boy?"

"Sure," said Wil with a smile. "I learned to understand my worth and how to leverage it. You can't afford to punish me right now. And more than that, you don't have to. I won't do it, but Thomas will. Talk to him about it, and he'll sign up. He wants continued employment, and I want a chance to spend time with my family."

That earned him a thoughtful nod. "Alright, fine. Fine. But that doesn't really answer the question of your future, does it? You're too important to be stationed in Harper Valley forever."

"On the contrary, sir. I need to guide the growth and make sure it happens smoothly, safely, and with proper education and care. More than that, this is my turf. I am going to make what I do for Harper Valley the gold standard for all resident wizards. Give me another ten years of this and my stats will embarrass everyone. I anticipate a golden age."

The words poured out of him, and his concern for word choice and propriety dropped the longer he went. The exhilaration of victory and exhaustion of the last week of work ruined his ability to care. Everything was a pleasant, dreamlike experience, and he had every intention of riding the high.

"I'd be happy to talk with you more about ways I can serve our country that don't involve the military, but maybe give me a year or three to adjust first, sir."

Bullworth laughed and retrieved his drink. "I suppose you are entitled to something of a break. Enjoy that time with your kid while you can. Powerful men, we don't get the chance as often as we'd like."

Wil took that blessing and went back to his friends. "The president's going to offer you a job in the military. I figured you'll probably take it, won't you?"

Thomas shrugged and nodded. "I'm not the type to stay in one place too terribly long, and I've been here for three excellent months. Obviously, I'll come back often now that I have reason to. What about . . . What are you looking at?"

Bram smiled at Gallath, who was with Syl. Someone finally remembered to pull him out of the Time-Stretcher, which could now theoretically have kept him indefinitely. Wil patted his friend on the side. "Why don't you take some personal time and see what happens?"

"Yeah . . . maybe." Bram drifted in that direction as if pulled along by magic.

Thomas looked back in the direction Wil had come. "Think the president would be willing to talk to me about it today?"

Wil shook his head with a laugh. "Go for it. And remember that this discovery makes defense easier than offense."

"Noted."

Although it took a good amount of his available magic power, Wil layered himself with an illusion and a compulsion. People wouldn't notice him, but they would be aware enough to not bump into him. He slid through the crowd, taking in the sights one last time.

Bob and Sharon stood on a platform apart from the crowd, and people came in and out to pay their respects and chat. Even during a celebration, they stayed working. Well, not Wil. He smiled as he passed by.

Down the path toward town, Arabella stood with her arms crossed over her chest. She rolled her eyes as Jeb took a knee and presented a ring. Sarah stood nearby with a clipboard and a pencil. She laughed openly as the elf princess walked off. Poor Jeb.

Syl and Candy danced, and even Mack looked on with approval. Not that Syl was ever likely to settle down, but Candy deserved something nice for a bit.

Bram and Gallath had found a copse of trees to hide behind. Wil didn't bother them on his way out. He just headed for his house to pick up the car and then drove north to the clinic.

Doc Hawkins had stayed behind while most of the town had their celebrations. Someone had to keep Darlene company. The older, white-haired man stood with a creaky groan. "There you are. They're doing great, Mr. Wizard. Mina's healthy, and Darlene is recovering well."

"Can I see them?"

The doctor motioned with his head for Wil to go back.

Mina was asleep, but Darlene looked up as soon as he came in. She held a finger to her lips as she gently rocked their daughter, who was wrapped up like a wrinkly, pink parcel. Wil sat by the bed, reaching out with a finger to touch Mina's tiny hand.

"I take it that things went well?" she whispered.

Wil grinned. "Now you have no more excuses. You have to marry me."

"Guess I gotta lock that down now that you're one of the hottest wizards around. I knew I picked well." Darlene kissed the top of Mina's covered head.

Wil laughed. "There has never been a gold digger as cunning or as sharp as you."

"And don't you forget it." Darlene gently lifted Mina up and offered her to Wil, who gladly took her and supported her neck with his shoulder. She gurgled a little but was out like a light.

"So, now what?" Darlene asked. "How many job offers have you gotten?"

"Nothing that I'm going to accept," said Wil. "I plan on taking a few years to enjoy things with you and Mina. I'll do work orders like normal, and we'll keep the business going once Bram rebuilds, but other than that? It's the family life for me."

"Huh," said Darlene. She sank into the bed and closed her eyes. "I give it one month before you're stir-crazy."

"You're on," said Wil. He may have always had to be on the move, but now he wanted to stop and smell the flowers. Someone else could deal with the big things. Now, the only thing that mattered was home, whether that meant friends, family, or Harper Valley. It was on him to guide them all into a world they created together. That was more than enough.

CHAPTER 60

Four Years Later

Wil couldn't remember ever being a problem as a child. He was quiet, read a lot, and only lost his temper every so often. Wilhelmina Ryland McKenzie, on the other hand, was his greatest treasure and worst nightmare. The four-year-old ran through their house like she did every day. Her mad giggles echoed down the hallway as he gave chase.

It wasn't that she was faster than him so much as more maneuverable. She turned corners better, and she knew it. Isom had been teaching her how to chase and be chased. Wil vowed to cut off his supply of beef for a month if Mina broke anything.

She turned the corner to the stairs as Wil slid to a stop against one of the bedroom walls. Mina giggled again, but by the time Wil got to the stairs, she was gone, and it was suspiciously silent. He crept down, keeping his senses open, but the only ones there were Darlene and their two-year-old son, Oliver, in the bathroom.

"Did you see her go down?" Wil asked.

"Did you lose her? Again?" Darlene didn't sound angry so much as amused. She continued changing Oliver's diaper as he fought her. He had her dark hair but Wil's green eyes.

"She's slippery! C'mon, you gotta help me. We've got places to go, things to do—"

"Awards to receive?" Darlene interjected. "Another one."

"Another one," Wil sighed. "I never thought I'd be annoyed by them, but here we are. It doesn't matter, I need to find her before she gets into something and destroys half the house!"

Tired of playing nice, Wil cast a spell to detect life. He looked around and froze when he felt a sign of her. She was either in the kitchen, or back upstairs. But there was no way she could've gotten by him to go back upstairs. He saw her go down, didn't he? Wil tiptoed into the kitchen.

There was no sign of Mina, but there was a stray kitten on top of the fridge. It was black and white, like it was wearing a little tuxedo. It nuzzled up against the cookie jar. Wil relaxed. "How'd you get in here? What are you doing?"

The kitten wasn't much more than the length of Wil's hands, but it threw itself at the cookies. Again and again. Wil sighed and caught the jar as it fell. He wasn't prepared for the kitten to run down his arms and back, clawing him all the way down.

"Ay, dammit, I thought Isom kept other animals away!" Wil set the jar down on the table and turned to the cat. Mina sat on the ground, looking at him with the pure, innocent joy of a child who didn't understand it wasn't time to play. Wil looked around, but there was no ignoring what his gut told him.

"Mina? Are you a kitty?"

"Uh-huh," said Mina, nodding her head. "Wanna see?" She jumped into the air, and as she did, her frame twisted and a little kitten landed in his arms. Mina nuzzled his cheek sweetly before jumping and landing hard on the dinner table as a human again. Rather than be hurt, she laughed with delight.

"Did you have to show so young?" Wil groaned. Being able to shape-shift at all was rare, let alone at that age. "Anything else you can turn into?"

"Uh-huh! I can be a bird, Daddy!" Mina flapped her arms, which quickly became black wings as she shrank to the ground. Her new crow form cawed enthusiastically and flapped wildly, but she couldn't obtain flight. Not yet.

"Oh gods." Wil buried his face in his hand. "Darlene?"

"Yeah?" his wife called back.

"Cancel the next two weeks of events. We're staying home and spending time with the kids."

"Why?"

A wicked idea crossed him. "Hey, Mina. Can you turn into a mouse?"

His daughter nodded her bird head and went straight from a crow to a mouse. Wil scooped her up and headed for the bathroom. He'd get in trouble, and teaching his daughter to prank people might have been a poor decision, but he couldn't resist. A few seconds later, Darlene screamed while Wil howled with laughter.

They had a lot of training to go, but his daughter was going to have the best education, the best advantages she could. By the time she was old enough to go to Saint Balthazar's, she'd be at least as strong as he was. He just had to make sure she was wiser, and, of course, had a good heart. At the end of the day, it was the best thing he could give her.

Acknowledgments

Look, Ma, I finished my first series! It was one of the best learning experiences I've ever had, and I can't wait to use what I've gained from writing Friendly Neighborhood Wizard on future series. Finishing is bittersweet, honestly, and I can't help but look back on everything I've done over the last three books and suddenly understand how I could've fixed things or made them just a little bit better. It's always how it happens.

That said, I am proud of what I've created and couldn't have done it without the love and support of my partners, Max and Kittra, as well as, of course, the team at Podium helping polish my work. Through their edits, suggestions, and guidance, I think I might have a shot at this for real. Just gotta keep on writing. The best book I'm ever going to write will always be the next one. So, I hope to see you for my future books, and thank you for reading.

About the Author

SmilingSatyr is a millennial bookworm and the author of the Friendly Neighborhood Wizard series, originally released on Royal Road. He writes stories because he's not really equipped to do anything else—them's the breaks!